SPECIAL MESSAGE TO READERS

THE ULVERSCROFT FOUNDATION
(registered UK charity number 264873)
was established in 1972 to provide funds for
research, diagnosis and treatment of eye diseases.
Examples of major projects funded by
the Ulverscroft Foundation are:-

- The Children's Eye Unit at Moorfields Eye Hospital, London
- The Ulverscroft Children's Eye Unit at Great Ormond Street Hospital for Sick Children
- Funding research into eye diseases and treatment at the Department of Ophthalmology, University of Leicester
- The Ulverscroft Vision Research Group, Institute of Child Health
- Twin operating theatres at the Western Ophthalmic Hospital, London
- The Chair of Ophthalmology at the Royal Australian College of Ophthalmologists

You can help further the work of the Foundation
by making a donation or leaving a legacy.
Every contribution is gratefully received. If you
would like to help support the Foundation or
require further information, please contact:

THE ULVERSCROFT FOUNDATION
The Green, Bradgate Road, Anstey
Leicester LE7 7FU, England
Tel: (0116) 236 4325

website: www.ulverscroft-foundation.org.uk

CHRISTMAS FOR
THE DISTRICT NURSES

The East End of London has been devastated by the Blitz and the people are struggling to come to terms with their ravaged city. Rationing bites ever deeper and everything that makes life better is in short supply. For the district nurses, the challenges are tougher than ever. Gladys loves her work in the Civil Nursing Reserve, but just when she needs to rely on her sister to help out at home, she turns into a handful of trouble. Edith is learning to cope with her boyfriend's injuries after Dunkirk but will she have to choose between her love for him and her career? With no end in sight, the war reaches its darkest moment . . . Can the nurses — and the families and patients that rely on them — find the strength to carry on?

ANNIE GROVES

CHRISTMAS FOR THE DISTRICT NURSES

Complete and Unabridged

MAGNA
Leicester

First published in Great Britain in 2019 by
HarperCollins*Publishers* Ltd
London

First Ulverscroft Edition
published 2020
by arrangement with
HarperCollins*Publishers* Ltd
London

A catalogue record for this book is available
from the British Library.

ISBN 978–0–7505–4816–8

Published by
Ulverscroft Limited
Anstey, Leicestershire
Set by Words & Graphics Ltd.
Anstey, Leicestershire
Printed and bound in Great Britain by
TJ Books Limited, Padstow, Cornwall

This book is printed on acid-free paper

Heartfelt thanks to Teresa Chris,
Kate Bradley and Pen Issac, without
whom the stories of the district nurses
would never have been told.

1

December 1941

'I don't see why I have to do it. Why can't you?'

Gladys shut her eyes and took a deep breath. She knew that there would be no point in getting angry with her younger sister. That never achieved anything. 'Because I'm on duty this evening,' she said calmly.

Evelyn threw up her hands, groaning theatrically. 'Of course you are. You're always on bleeding duty. Proper saint, you are. How did they ever manage without you?'

Gladys took the two steps necessary to cross their tiny kitchen and reached for her gabardine coat that hung on the back door. She still hadn't grown out of the thrill of putting it on, of having her own uniform. She'd waited long enough to be able to join the Civil Nursing Reserve. She was damned if she was going to let her sister make a drama out of nothing, yet again. 'What's so important that you can't make a bit of stew?' she asked.

Evelyn scowled. 'I was going to do my hair.'

Gladys laughed. 'Do what to it? Didn't you just do it?'

'I wouldn't expect you to understand,' Evelyn snapped meanly. 'It's not as if you ever took any trouble with yours. Look at it, just hanging down straight, all flat and horrible.'

Gladys shrugged, pulling on her heavy coat. She knew her mousy-brown hair was lank but she was far too busy to spend hours curling it in papers or hunting down bleach or whatever smelly substance it was that Evelyn used to lighten her carefully coiffured locks. 'Not much point when it's mostly hidden by my cap,' she pointed out.

'Exactly.' Evelyn pouted. 'You're always down that blasted first-aid post, when you aren't running round after those district nurses in their precious home. You never have no time for us no more. I have to do everything and it's not fair.'

'Not fair?' Gladys couldn't bite back her instinctive response. 'I tell you what's not fair. Having to miss nearly all my schooling cos Ma couldn't cope with all seven of us. Working my fingers to the bone for you lot when I was only a kid myself. Only learning to read when I started work at the nurses' home. Even that was just good luck in that two of them made time to teach me. Now, when I finally get a chance to do nursing like what I've always wanted, you still expect me to cook for you first, so you don't have to give up an evening doing your hair.'

Evelyn wasn't impressed. 'Oh, not that again. Poor old Gladys. You'd have hated school anyway — I know I did. So count yourself lucky.'

'Pity you didn't make the most of what chances you had,' Gladys said, taking out a pair of navy gloves from her coat pocket.

'I don't need school learning for what I'm going to do.' Evelyn's eyes flashed boldly.

Gladys paused. This was new. 'What do you mean?'

Evelyn folded her arms in defiance. 'I'm going to go on the stage.'

Gladys stood still and stared. 'You're going to what?'

'Go on stage.' Evelyn sounded more defensive now. 'Don't look at me like that, Glad. I've got a good voice, I have, and I'm going to be famous like those film stars. I could be the next Vivien Leigh.'

'Your hair's the wrong colour,' Gladys pointed out. Typical, she thought. She herself had a good voice, and it wasn't being boastful to think so, because one of the district nurses who was really musical had told her so. But she wasn't daft enough to imagine she could go on stage with it. A few carols around the home's piano were enough for her. 'Anyway, I've got to go. There's a bit of lamb on the cool shelf in the larder and potatoes under the sink. Make sure they all wash their hands before they eat. Oh, and by the way,' she halted briefly before stepping out into the cold of the December evening, 'you might have to wait before you start your stage career. The government's just brought out a law saying that every woman who's not married between twenty and thirty has to sign up for war work. I don't think they count singing.'

Evelyn snorted. 'You're just jealous. I'm not twenty yet, anyhow.'

'Not far off, though,' Gladys shot back. 'You've got, what, about eighteen months to become a star, then you'll have to sign up for the

Land Army or whatever.'

'Never! I'll break my nails.' Evelyn looked aghast. 'But I tell you what, I shan't ever do what you do. I think it's disgusting, all that blood and all. You don't know who half those people are or anything.'

Gladys smiled, unmoved by her sister's final comment. She carried on smiling as she made her way along the back lane and headed towards the first-aid post, which was in the nearby church hall. She didn't care what anybody else thought. She had believed that nursing was beyond her wildest dreams and yet here she was, about to start a shift in a job she loved. It didn't matter that she'd already done a day's work, cleaning and cooking at the nurses' home. She truly could not think of a better way to spend her evening.

★   ★   ★

'You awake, Billy?' Kathleen turned over on the narrow mattress and shook the shoulder of the man lying next to her. 'It's nearly time for your shift.'

Billy groaned. 'Just two minutes' more kip, Kath.' He stretched, his feet pressing against the cold wall of the small room. He'd often wished he was taller, but now he realised his average height was a blessing. He wouldn't have fitted into Kathleen's bed otherwise. Strictly speaking he shouldn't have been there at all.

'It's no good, Billy. I can't hold back the clock. Shall I make us a cup of tea while you get ready?'

Kathleen was half out of the bed but he pulled her down to him again and stopped her.

'Let's wait a bit. Let's have a cuddle, warm me up before I have to go out.' He smiled up at her, scarcely able to credit his good fortune. Here they were, together at last. It wasn't exactly as he had imagined it, squeezed into a tiny bedsit instead of their own home, but he didn't care. As long as he had Kath with him, he could move mountains.

She sighed. 'Not long now and we'll have a proper big bed.'

'That day can't come soon enough,' Billy agreed, moving his feet so they didn't touch the freezing wall. 'We'll deserve it an' all. Lord knows we're due a bit of comfort, you and me.'

Kathleen hugged him, pressing her face into his dark hair, cut short but still with a bit of curl to it. She still had to pinch herself sometimes. Despite the disappointment of having to postpone their wedding, she counted herself lucky to be in his arms. She didn't care about the poky room. She had never known much better, and soon they would have their own home, a real house with a separate bedroom for her little boy, and their own yard out the back which they wouldn't have to share with anyone.

She shifted slightly, careful not to make too much noise. Her landlady lived downstairs and didn't approve of Billy coming to visit, although she generally turned a blind eye. Sometimes Kathleen felt guilty that they had pre-empted their wedding vows. But after the horror of what had happened, she couldn't bear the thought of

5

never having had Billy in her arms, not knowing his love. Life could be snuffed out at any moment.

For years she had lived in a small downstairs flat on a side street in Dalston. She had moved in when she'd married her first husband, Ray, full of hope for the future. That had soon vanished when she realised what sort of man he was — mean, unreliable, violent. She'd been blinded by his good looks, although everyone had warned her. She hadn't listened. The only good thing to come out of the marriage was her boy, Brian, who would be three in the new year. Now Ray was dead, killed down at the docks where he'd been trying to cash in on the black market.

Kathleen had tried to show some respect for him; he was her son's father and she wanted to do the right thing. However, she had been harbouring her secret love for Billy ever since the scales had fallen from her eyes about Ray. They had been at school together and, once Ray had disappeared, supposedly to find work, she would never have managed if it hadn't been for Billy helping her out, along with their good friends around the corner, the Banham family.

She had been overjoyed when Billy had proposed. He'd announced it at a Banham family christening and it had brought tears to her eyes when she saw how happy her closest friends were for them. Finally it looked as if their life together could begin.

Billy had always lived with his mother, who had been thrilled to hear that her son had at last become engaged to the love of his life. However,

6

she felt she was too old to cope with a toddler around the house. Billy had understood. He had planned to move in with Kathleen after they married, even though her place was really just one big room with a back kitchen and a shared privy in the yard. He was out most of the time anyway, working down at the docks in Limehouse, or on ARP duty in the evenings.

They'd fixed the date even while the Blitz had rained down on the streets around, causing havoc, destroying houses, roads, entire families. They had been under no illusions about the danger, but one day in the summer their plans fell apart.

Kathleen had been at home with Brian when she heard the familiar wail of the air-raid siren, which had sounded practically every night for months on end. 'Off we go, then,' she'd said to her little boy, hurriedly bundling him into his siren suit and snatching up the bag she kept in readiness by the front door. Together they had hurried to the local church hall, set up for those who had no Anderson shelters in their gardens. At the last minute she had decided it would be quicker to push him in his old pram, and that meant she could load the shelf underneath it with his teddy bear and wooden bricks, extra food, and a few of her own essentials.

Never had she been so thankful to have acted quickly. When the all clear came the next morning, they had returned to a scene of devastation. Jeeves Place had taken a direct hit, and Kathleen's home was nothing but a pile of smouldering bricks. She could see straight through to the yard and the houses that had backed on to it. Neighbouring properties had lost all their windows, some of their roofs and brickwork. The smell was indescribable.

'This your place?' a kindly policeman had said. 'Afraid you can't come any closer — it's not safe.'

'But . . . my things,' she had gasped. 'All my clothes, all my boy's clothes, they're in there.' Even as she said it, she recognised that they had very little left behind worth saving.

'You can come back later when we've made it secure,' the policeman had suggested. 'Do you have anywhere you can go in the meantime?'

Kathleen had gulped, taking in the changes to her old street. Its narrow pavements were shrouded in dust and rubble, a few residents grey-faced with shock standing at the far end beyond the cordon. 'Y-yes, I think so.' She hoped the Banham household was still standing. She didn't think her shaking legs would take her any further.

She had the desperate urge to get Brian away from all of this before he could realise what was going on, that the only home he had ever known was now in ruins. 'We'll go to my friends,' she had said, and swung the pram around as fast as she could.

It was a matter of minutes before she arrived at the Banhams' front door, which was still mercifully in place. Jeeves Street had taken a pounding earlier in the summer and there were gaps in its once-solid terraces, but the house she sought was intact. True, the air stank of fires and brick dust and, worse, an underlying stench of decay and rust. But the Banham home, for years her sanctuary, stood firm.

Mattie, her best friend, had cried with relief and hugged her hard before pulling her into the heart of the house, the big kitchen, with its view over the awkward wedge shape of not-quite-garden. Flo, Mattie's mother, had immediately set about making tea and pouring precious orange juice for Brian, as Mattie still got extra for nursing her younger child. Kathleen had collapsed onto a chair, relieved beyond measure that she was safe and so were her closest friends and their children. Mattie's father, Stan, was an ARP warden in the same section as Billy, and Flo promised to inform him at once that they were in one piece. 'We thought you would be,' she said. 'We knew you went to the church shelter whenever the siren went, no matter what time of day or night. We all squashed up into our own shelter, packed in like sardines we was.'

Kathleen had stared around, taking in Mattie, her face tear-streaked, with her daughter Gillian pulling at her sleeve, and younger child Alan grizzling from his cot in the corner — the one that Gillian and Brian used to share when they were smaller. Flo looked worried but resolute, as usual. Only then, once Kathleen had her cup of tea and could see that Brian was chatting away happily to his teddy, did it occur to her that everything would have to be changed.

So the wedding was postponed until Kathleen and Billy could find somewhere to set up home together. That was easier said than done. Both wanted to stay in the area; as well as Billy's mother, his work was relatively close by. Kathleen had family down in Haggerston but wasn't close to them. They had all but washed their hands of her when she had married Ray against their advice, and although she sometimes visited her mother, it was more out of duty than anything else.

She and Mattie had often talked about taking Brian, Gillian and Alan out of Hackney to somewhere safer in the countryside; as mothers of such small children they would be eligible to be evacuated with them. Yet it was hard to leave Mattie's parents. Both of Mattie's brothers had joined up when war had broken out, Joe in the navy and Harry in the army. Harry had vanished at Dunkirk and for many bleak months everyone believed he was dead, but he had survived . . . just. He was still recovering in hospital, and was in no position to help his parents should they need it. Mattie's husband Lennie had been taken prisoner at the same time and nobody could say when he would be home, though they all talked determinedly of 'when' and not 'if'.

Mattie and Kathleen had worked together to keep the household running smoothly, while everyone kept their ears to the ground in case word of a house or flat came up. Even so it was many months before Stan got wind of anything likely.

Then, in November, he'd been on duty one night when there had been an accident with a gas main and he had helped to evacuate a nearby block of flats. A grateful elderly resident had confided in him as he slowly walked her towards a WVS mobile canteen so that she could have a warm drink on the chilly evening.

She was worried that her sister's house would be broken into by looters. The sister had left it to go to her daughter's, and wouldn't be coming back as she was too frail. How could she find reliable tenants? She didn't know what to do for the best. Stan had offered to put her in touch with the ideal young couple.

Now Kathleen turned in Billy's arms, thoughts of the new house filling her mind. It was between her old flat and Butterfield Green, an open space which would be good for Brian to play in come the better weather. It had two bedrooms upstairs, a large one at the front big enough for a proper double bed, and a smaller one at the back. Downstairs was a front parlour, a kitchen that was more like a scullery, and, an unexpected luxury, a lean-to bathroom at the back, with a copper for hot water and no need to step outside on a cold night. It was more than they could have hoped for.

Once again she briefly wondered if she and Billy should have waited until the wedding before sleeping together but, after the postponement, they had decided that enough was enough. They had waited for years, always acting properly despite their strong attraction and ample opportunity. Who knew what awaited them. So Kathleen had found a temporary billet with Brian, and Billy had taken to visiting between his days down at the docks and his evening shifts. It wasn't much but they savoured

11

every second they had together. After all, they would be together officially soon, with a new date for the wedding set just before Christmas.

'Come on, sleepyhead,' she said, reluctant to leave the comfort of his arms. She had never felt safer in her life, secure in the knowledge that this was where she belonged. 'Nearly time to go.'

He smiled easily as he turned onto his back and looked at her, the waves of brown hair falling around her beloved face, brushing his own shoulders. 'Got a few minutes yet, haven't we?' His eyes grew bright.

She took in his look and smiled back. 'I thought you were tired, Billy Reilly?'

His smile grew broader as he drew her closer to him. 'Never too tired for you, Kath,' he breathed, before kissing her deeply and drawing the covers over them once more.

2

'This is what comes of taking up the tram tracks to use the metal for the war effort,' groaned Edith as she set down her Gladstone bag in the common room of the nurses' home. 'Or not having any spare metal for new bikes. Kids try to ride ones built for adults. Then they fall off. I've had two broken arms to look at in one afternoon. It puts me off riding my own bike, I can tell you.'

Alice had got in from her rounds ten minutes earlier and had made a pot of tea. 'Here, have some of this. It'll put you in a better temper.'

Edith collapsed into a comfy chair with well-worn cushions and looked up at her tall friend. 'Thanks. I will. Brrr, I'm freezing, there's a bitter wind out there.'

Gladys was passing by and caught her words. 'Shall I build up the fire a bit? Gwen said we can have an extra bag of coal to boost our morale.'

Edith nodded enthusiastically, mindful that this was a big concession from their deputy superintendent. 'That would be lovely. Sure you don't mind? I'd offer to help but my fingers are numb.' She wrapped her red hands around the cup of tea, feeling its warmth as her fingers began to tingle. 'That's more like it. Thanks, Al.'

Pushing back her dark blonde hair behind her ears, Alice took a seat beside Edith. 'That's what

13

should be top of your Christmas list, then. New gloves.'

Edith nodded. 'I think Flo's knitting me some. That's why I haven't tried to replace these old ones, which are full of holes.' She pulled out a bundle of navy wool from her pocket and held it up. Her hands were scarcely bigger than a child's, appropriate to her birdlike frame. 'Call that a glove? It's more like a fishing net now. Mind you, I've had these since we qualified. So that's, what . . . ?'

'Two and a half years,' said Alice at once. 'We began as district nurses back in the summer of 1939.'

'Before the war.' Edith raised her eyebrows. 'Hard to imagine there was such a time, isn't it?'

Alice nodded, sipping on her own tea. 'No shortages. No air raids. A proper night's sleep. Remember those?'

'Only just.' Edith took another gulp of tea. 'I know the raids seem to have stopped now but I still feel as if I'm making up lost time for all those hours of sleep we missed. Sometimes I wake up and imagine I can hear the siren going, out of sheer habit. Does that mean I'm going crazy?'

'Probably.' Alice set down her saucer. 'I know what you mean though. You get used to going to bed expecting to be woken up and having to run down to the refuge room. If you'd told me a few years ago that I'd be able to sleep sitting up on a hard chair, I'd have thought it was impossible, but now we know better.'

'Still prefer my own bed though.' Edith loved

14

her little attic room, which had few extra comforts but all the essentials. Before coming to the Victory Walk home she'd never had her own room. It was her haven, and she resented every air raid that took her from it. 'I'm tempted to go up and have forty winks now before the evening meal, but it won't be as warm. Gladys, that fire's lovely — come on, Al, let's sit right beside it now it's blazing.'

Gladys beamed in triumph. 'Me ma always said I was good at getting a fire going. When we had any coal to burn, that was. Sometimes me little brothers would come back with wood they'd found and we'd use that.' She brushed her hands across her apron. 'I'd best be going, I'm on duty at the first-aid post tonight.'

'How's it going?' asked Alice.

'Very well. I love it,' said Gladys honestly. 'The most difficult thing is to get me sister to help out at home. That's why I want to be off now, so I can leave again in good time for my shift. Our Evelyn, that's the one who's only a couple of years younger than me, needs to get into the habit of being the cook around the place and I ain't giving her any chance to make excuses.'

'Quite right.' Edith frowned. 'You've done more than enough for them, Gladys. You're needed elsewhere now.'

'That's what I says to them,' Gladys replied with determination. 'Give that fire a good top-up before you eat and it'll keep going all evening. See you tomorrow, then.' She hurried out.

Alice shook her head. 'Doesn't sound as if that sister is making life easy.'

15

'Don't you go worrying about it, Al, you can't make no difference. We did the best we could, teaching Gladys to read. She's got to sort out things at home. High time her sister stepped up, but it's not our business.'

'I know.' Alice sighed and stretched back in the wooden carver chair she'd pulled as close as she dared to the roaring fire. She rolled her shoulders back a few times, easing out the tensions of the day, made worse by cycling around in the cold. Then she brightened. 'I forgot, I had a letter today.' She dug around in the pocket of her Aran cardigan, a present from her mother on her last visit home to Liverpool.

'Is it from Joe?' Edith asked eagerly, her dark eyes gleaming. She knew Alice received regular letters from Joe Banham, and plenty of the nurses speculated that this meant there was romance in the offing, although Alice m~~~~ it was no such thing.

'No.' Alice's face grew solemn. 'I haven't heard from him for a while. Not that it means anything,' she added hastily as Edith's expression grew anxious, 'there might be problems with the post.' With Joe in the navy, they were never sure where he actually was at any given time.

'Of course.' Edith was equally determined not to jump to the worst conclusion. Joe would be all right. He had to be. His parents had been through enough when they believed his brother Harry was dead — as had they all, her more than anyone. Harry was the love of her life and she had felt as if part of her had died too; now he was slowly recovering, there was not a day that went past when she didn't count her blessings. 'So who is it from, then?'

Alice drew out the envelope and showed her friend the handwriting on the front: bold, forward-slanting lettering. 'Dermot,' she said.

'Oooooh, Dermot.' Mary had arrived, her face breaking into a broad smile at the mention of the doctor who had temporarily worked at a local surgery when the regular doctor had been unwell. 'How is the divine Dermot? Still breaking hearts all along the south coast?'

'You're late back,' Edith said, watching as Mary found another carver chair with a faded cushion and pulled it across to join them. 'Was there a problem?'

'No, not really. Mr Emmerson was feeling a bit lonely, that's all, so I stayed for a chat,' Mary explained, warming her hands in front of the flames. 'He misses his sons, poor old devil. But then one of his daughters-in-law popped round so I left them to it.' Mary's elderly patients loved her as she had the knack of getting them talking. She often said that it wasn't simply their aches and pains that needed attention, it was that since the war broke out more and more of them were on their own. 'So what has the lovely Dermot to say for himself?'

'Anyone would think you had a soft spot for him,' teased Edith. 'Better not let Charles hear you saying that.'

'Chance would be a fine thing. Charles has been too busy recently to hear me say anything. I hardly see him.' Mary's face fell and her chestnut curls drooped a little. Her boyfriend was a

17

captain in the army and, even though he had been based in London for much of the war, he found it difficult to spare time away from his duties at headquarters. 'So, cheer us up, Alice. What's the news?'

Alice scanned the sheets of paper, covered in vivid navy ink. 'All right . . . good . . . he's well, he sends his best. Reading between the lines, they're working flat out, there's no let-up even though the raids over the airfields have died down. Lots of his colleagues have gone to serve abroad so there's twice as much to do for those left on the home front.'

'Sounds familiar,' said Edith.

'No budding love interest, then?' Mary was always keen to hear about other people's romances as hers had gone into the doldrums.

'If there is, he isn't saying.' Alice looked up from the letter and folded the top sheet. 'He might not tell me, of course.' She counted herself immune to Dermot's considerable charms as he'd trained as a doctor at the same time as she had studied for her first nursing qualification, back in Liverpool. Their relationship had always been that of colleagues, whereas his arrival in Dalston had caused uproar among the single nurses, and even those not so single.

'That's too bad. Well, I live in hope.' Mary's good mood had bounced back.

'He's wondering what it will be like treating American troops, now they've joined the war,' Alice went on, skimming the second page. 'He's going to be working alongside a couple of surgeons from New York, by the sounds of it.'

Belinda rushed in, her dark, tightly curled hair a tangled mess. 'Budge up, I'm frozen solid,' she said, bringing across yet another chair to the fireside. 'I thought I was going to be late for the meal, the ambulance took so long. Woman in labour with a breech birth,' she explained hastily. 'Did somebody say 'American troops'? Go on, Alice, tell me about my favourite subject.'

Alice pulled a face. 'Nothing specific, sorry. Were you hoping for news of a battalion of them to be stationed up the road?'

'We should be so lucky.' Belinda made a face as well. 'Look, I know Pearl Harbor was terrible but we have to look on the bright side. All those handsome young men coming across the ocean just to rescue us.' She rolled her eyes.

'Bringing gifts of nylon tights and choco-late . . . ' Mary sat up straighter. 'I know, I know, better not let Charles hear me say that. Still, you can't deny that things might start to get interesting.'

'Exactly.' Belinda beamed in anticipation.

'The only good thing is, it might mean that the war is over faster,' Alice said seriously.

'True. No, you're right, I realise that,' Belinda said hastily. 'It's just that you're not looking for a boyfriend, are you, Alice, but some of us like to keep on the alert just in case. There's a bit of a shortage of eligible men around here if you hadn't noticed. So if there are thousands of them about to board ship for Europe, then I for one intend to be ready. What are you looking at me like that for? I'm just saying.'

Edith got to her feet. 'Looks as if the meal's

ready. Stew again, by the smell of it.' She reached for her bag as she rose. 'I'll take this back to my room and see you down here in a mo.'

Alice stood as well. 'I hadn't really thought about it like that,' she admitted.

'Well, some of us have,' said Belinda with spirit, unfolding her tall, slim frame from the warmth of the chair. 'Who knows, Alice, we might get you out dancing yet.' She ran after Edith, her thick nurse's cloak over one arm, her Gladstone bag swinging from the other.

Alice watched them go, reflecting on Dermot's letter, less concerned by what he had said than what he hadn't. There had been no mention of Mark, Dermot's best friend, who had also trained at the big Liverpool hospital when they were there. Mark had broken her heart. She had believed that they were destined to be together and that he felt the same as she did. However, the lure of the Spanish Civil War had been stronger and Alice found herself deserted, not for another woman but for a rival against which she could not hope to win: a cause. Gradually she had hardened her heart and poured everything into her work instead.

Yet it was only human to wonder if he was all right. She knew he had returned from Spain and enlisted as a doctor, and was — to the best of her knowledge — somewhere on the south coast, treating the Forces and also any enemy airmen who had been shot down this past year. She told herself it was enough to know that he was alive, doing the work that he loved and was so supremely good at. There could be nothing further between them. But it did mean that, however enthusiastic her colleagues were, the very last thing she ever wanted to do was to go dancing.

3

'I thought these new girls were meant to help us out but this has been the slowest day I can remember in all the time we've worked here,' Peggy Cannon complained, pulling off the dusty headscarf that she wore while working in the gas-mask factory. 'I know they've got to register for some kind of war work, but why didn't they sign up for something they're good at?' She rolled up the fraying piece of cotton and shoved it into her bulging handbag.

Clarrie was more forgiving. 'You forget what we were like at first. We were all fingers and thumbs. Give them a few days and they'll catch up.' She shook free her own hair, which was a striking red, all the more noticeable in the dull changing room of the factory.

'They'll have to,' Peggy grumbled. 'We're going to be making more than gas masks and boxes now, aren't we? I heard we were going to do stuff for weapons, rubber seals and that.'

Clarrie glanced around. 'Don't go saying that outside these walls.'

Peggy snorted. 'What do you take me for? Do they seriously think we won't notice that everything we're working on is a different shape?' She buttoned her coat, with its worn patches from several years' use. 'Don't mind me, I'm just in a bad mood.'

Clarrie shrugged, used to her friend's

impatience. 'Well, my sister's gone and put her name down for the Land Army,' she said. 'Can you credit it? She can just about peel a carrot; she's never grown a thing in her life. Pity the poor farmer who ends up with her.'

Peggy grinned at the idea. 'Maybe she'll be good with animals. Used to take that dog you had when you were little out for walks, didn't she?'

'Yes, but she didn't have to kill it and eat it,' Clarrie pointed out. 'No, she's in for the shock of her life. And she'll most likely be out in the middle of nowhere, no dancing or nothing.'

One of their fellow workers passed by, half hearing their conversation. 'Oh, are you going dancing?' she asked casually. 'Well, good for you, Peggy, cos you're over him by now, aren't you? Let's face it, he's been dead much longer than you was wed. Best to get back out on the dance floor!' and she was off in a trail of cheap perfume, leaving Peggy with her jaw dropping at the insensitivity of the comment.

Clarrie tucked her arm through her friend's. 'Pay her no notice. She don't know what she's talking about.'

Peggy swallowed hard. 'I know. She's nothing but hot air, that one. She don't know the half of it and that's a fact. Come on, let's get out of here.' She found it was suddenly hard to breathe. She'd go for ages convincing herself that she was all right, but all it took was one callous remark and she was back down in the deep well of grief, mourning Pete, who'd been her husband for less than a year when he'd been killed at Dunkirk. As if a bit of dancing could put right the unfairness of that.

Not that she hadn't tried. Where Edith had stayed in, craving silence and stillness to remember her Harry, Peggy had thrown herself into escaping, drinking, dancing, staying out, and generally carrying on as if there were no tomorrow. Sometimes it helped her to forget, more often it just brought it home to her how wonderful Pete had been and how nobody else came close. She'd had one particular dreadful incident, when she was attacked by a Canadian airman whose dark good looks hid his violent heart. She had even bounced back from that, as far as the few people who knew about it could tell. Only Peggy knew that her love for Pete was so deeply buried that nothing could touch it, and she couldn't see how she would ever get over his loss.

Clarrie glanced at her watch. 'Tell you what, shall we have a quick one down the Duke's Arms? It's Friday, there might be some of the old gang from school there.'

Peggy perked up. That was one place it wouldn't matter if two young women came in for a drink on their own. They had plenty of friends who often went there and most of them had known Pete.

'Yes, let's. Pete's mum won't be waiting for me, it's her WVS day.' Peggy continued to live with her mother-in-law and, although the two women had their occasional differences, there was comfort to be had in the knowledge that they had both loved Pete.

24

The cheerful old pub was not far from the factory and already the main bar was buzzing with conversation. There was nothing fancy about it, and from the outside it was impossible to tell, in the blackout, that it was full of old metal lamps inside and well-polished woodwork, with a welcoming atmosphere that drew the regulars back time after time. Clarrie waved at a few people as she pushed her way in, Peggy — who was shorter — following behind. Clarrie was like a beacon with her bright hair, and Peggy sometimes felt in her friend's shadow.

'Hello, girls, what can I get you?' A familiar figure was standing at the bar.

'Billy! What you doing here? Shouldn't you be at home getting ready for the big day?' Peggy came to an abrupt halt at the sight of the young man grinning sheepishly over the top of his pint.

'Dutch courage,' he admitted, setting down his glass. 'Come on, what'll it be? You might as well take advantage of my last night as a free man.'

Clarrie laughed. 'Surely you of all people aren't having second thoughts, Billy?'

Billy gave her an incredulous look. 'Me? Of course not. It's just, well, you know, I've got to stand up in front of everyone and say my vows. What if I mess it up? I'm getting all nervous just thinking about it.' He grinned to make a joke of it but they could see his hand was shaking a little.

Peggy faced him seriously. 'You won't, Billy. And, even if you do, who's going to care? Kath won't, she'll be glad that you finally made it to the altar at last. She won't want you smelling like

25

a brewery though, I can tell you that for a fact.'

Billy shook his head firmly. 'I only just got here. I won't be staying. Only wanted to settle me nerves a bit then I'll get back to Ma's, make sure she's all set for tomorrow. What can I get you?'

'Half a shandy,' said Clarrie at once.

Peggy was tempted to say port and lemon, but that drink had been her downfall once too often. 'I'll have the same,' she said, and caught Clarrie's brief glance of approval.

'Then I'll have a half meself as a top-up and that's it, no more till after the . . . the wedding.' Billy suddenly went bright red. 'I still can't believe it. I'm really marrying Kath tomorrow. How about that?' His eyes shone as he passed them their shandies.

'Cheers, Billy,' said Clarrie. 'If anyone deserves to be happy, it's you and Kath. We'll be there in our glad rags to wish you well. Half eleven, isn't it?'

'I got to be early,' Billy grinned. 'I'll be in no end of trouble otherwise. I'm not even on duty this evening.'

'I should hope not! Not on the eve of your wedding, Billy. Let the ARP cope without you for once.' Peggy took a sip of her drink.

'Anyway Stan's working tonight so we're all in the best hands possible.' Billy carefully poured his half of bitter into his pint glass, wishing he didn't feel so shaky.

'I'd have thought he'd be wanted back home,' Clarrie said. 'Aren't we all going back there tomorrow after the service?'

Billy nodded. 'Yes, Ma couldn't cope with having a crowd of people, Kath's bedsit is smaller than that table over there, and we don't have no spare cash to hire a hall. Besides, she feels as if Jeeves Street is her second home, so it's the best thing all round. I'm ever so grateful.'

'It's only what you deserve, Billy,' Peggy repeated with sincerity, even as a little voice whispered that she too had known that thrill of anticipation and sheer happiness, and would never find it again.

★　★　★

The atmosphere in the church was calm, with a faint smell of dust, flowers and beeswax. There was a moment of silence which felt to Billy as if it lasted a lifetime. Then Kath looked up at him, blinked hard and said, very clearly so that everyone could hear: 'I do.'

Billy thought his heart would burst with happiness and pride. He looked down at her and met her eyes, which were the most beautiful in the world.

'You may kiss the bride,' said the vicar, and Billy didn't need to be told twice. Even as he did so he could sense the rush of approval from their guests, ranged along the front pews.

Kathleen had not wanted to wear white. She had done so for her first wedding, and that had brought her precious little joy. Now that clothing was growing harder to come by, it was a waste of time, effort and material to have a dress that could be worn only once. She had gone for the more practical choice of a neat suit in soft grey featuring a nipped-in waist, with a deep rose blouse that she had made herself. It flattered her delicate colouring. Mattie had done her hair first thing in the morning, persuading it to fall in waves, sweeping it up at the sides so it wouldn't get in her eyes.

Billy knew this was not a repeat of her previous disastrous marriage. They would start out differently, and do everything differently. He would be a proper husband to her. After today, they would move into their new house and start their life. He would show her what a happy partnership could be like. He remembered how it was when his own father had been alive — how contented his parents had been, comfortable to accommodate each other. He would build on that. She deserved nothing but the best.

The organ began to play and the vicar gently gestured to the newlyweds that they should turn and make their way back down the aisle. Billy grinned and Kath smiled back up at him. 'Off we go, then,' she breathed, tucking her hand through the crook of his arm.'

'Off we go,' he repeated. 'You and me, Kath. Together from now on.'

* * *

The Banhams' kitchen was full to bursting, and so was their front parlour. If the weather had been warmer, the guests would have spilled outside into the back yard, but the bitter chill had put a stop to that. Everyone crowded inside, enjoying the spread that Flo had conjured up from pooled ration cards, friends' and family's generosity and sheer ingenuity. At the centre of it all stood the happy couple, both of them still grinning from ear to ear.

Billy was in his only good suit, with a new white shirt and borrowed smart striped tie. He'd loosened the knot and undone his top button as soon as he'd reached Jeeves Street, not being used to such formal restriction. Now he laughed with relief. He hadn't made a mess of his vows after all, but had stood at the altar and spoken with complete conviction. Kath could now set aside the hated surname of Berry and become Kathleen Reilly. They would change Brian's name too. Billy loved the little boy as if he was his own son, and in truth had already been a far better father to him than Ray had ever been.

Brian himself wore a new pair of smart tweed shorts and had started the day in a new pale green shirt that now had food down it. Nobody minded. Flo privately vowed to clean it later, and he could borrow one of Gillian's jumpers. Gillian was proudly copying Brian and smearing her own blouse with pickle. Flo was tempted to intervene but it would have meant dashing through a group of people and creating a scene; today was not the day for it.

Attracting nearly as much attention as Kathleen and Billy was Harry Banham, back on a rare visit home. He sat in an armchair, carefully propped on cushions. Even though he had suffered his injuries eighteen months ago, he was still receiving treatment for them, and had recently undergone yet another operation. His old spirit had returned, though, and he encircled Edith's waist with his good arm. She was perched on one arm of the chair, happy to be snuggled next to Harry, conscious of the warmth of him through the material of her best frock.

'Us next,' he murmured, his eyes glinting.

Edith giggled. 'Can't wait, Harry.' She turned to face him. 'We'll get you patched up a bit more first though.'

Harry pretended to be offended. 'What, you mean you miss my ravishing good looks?'

'You'll always be the most handsome man in the room to me, Harry.' Edith's voice grew serious. 'But you know as well as I do that there will be more operations to come. We don't want to ruin the chance of them succeeding. I really, really don't want to wait but it's for the best. For the time being, at any rate.'

Harry pulled her closer still. 'I'd marry you tomorrow if I could. You mean the world to me, Edie.'

She tipped back her head and laughed. 'I know,' she said happily. She wanted to be Harry's wife more than anything, but realised that any delay in his treatment might mean it was less likely to be fully effective. There were all sorts of new developments in the treatment of facial burns, as so many airmen had suffered them during the Battle of Britain. Harry didn't need the kind of reconstruction that some of them did, but he'd had a skin graft on one side of his face to repair the worst of the damage there. Fortunately his hair had begun to grow back and he could wear it a little longer than the standard army crew cut, to mask the upper scars.

Edith couldn't decide if it made it better or worse that she was a nurse. Sometimes she could take a step back and recognise how wonderful it was, that the surgeons had such skill and could help mend what would have been permanent terrible disfigurement only a few years ago. Next she would remember all the risks that came with any surgery and her heart would fill with dread that Harry would react badly to the anaesthetic or go down with a dangerous infection. Then she would give herself a talking-to. After all, she had thought she had lost him for good. She would take him back into her willing arms whatever shape he was in; if he could be given some semblance of his former appearance, then so much the better.

Clarrie came over, balancing a plate of Spam sandwiches in one hand. 'They let you come home, then?' she asked. 'We didn't know if you'd be allowed out yet.'

Harry smiled up at his old school friend. 'Didn't want to miss this,' he said. 'I felt bad that I couldn't say for certain that I'd be here. Billy wanted me to be his best man but there was a chance the last operation would be put back a week and I knew I couldn't say no to that.'

'Course not.' Clarrie put her plate down on a side table before its contents fell off. 'There, help yourselves. Anyway, his mate Ron did a grand job. He scrubs up well, don't he? I've never seen him in a suit before. And it was lovely that your dad gave Kath away.'

31

'Yes, well, she's almost family so it was only right,' Harry said, accepting the sandwich that Edith passed him. 'Her own dad passed away years ago and she don't get on with her brothers. Their loss, I say.'

Edith nodded vigorously. She knew what that felt like; she had very little to do with her own brothers, who had thought she'd got ideas above herself when she'd taken up nursing.

'Joe didn't get leave, then?' Clarrie asked, smoothing down her turquoise cardigan, which she'd teamed with a blue and green scarf, knowing those colours set off her red hair.

'No, he hasn't made it,' said Harry, his expression fading. 'Haven't seen him for ages, have we, Edie?'

'No, more's the pity. We don't even know where he is these days.' Edith automatically cast a glance across the room in Alice's direction, to where her friend was talking to Mary. If Alice didn't know where Joe was, then nobody did. As their friendship was partly based on a common love of books, he would write to her and tell her about what he was currently reading. Then Alice would work out where the author of the book was from, or where it was set. That would be where Joe was at the time of his writing the letter. But there had been no letters for a while. Edith had the feeling that Alice was more concerned than she let on.

Clarrie picked up the empty plate. 'I'll get you some more, shall I?' she asked, and moved off before either of them could answer. Edith appreciated it; she just wanted to stay cuddled

32

up tight to Harry, and the less he moved around the better.

'I don't suppose Kath and Billy are going on honeymoon,' Harry said.

'No, it's too hard to travel and they don't have much money to spare,' Edith said. 'They're going to their new house and Brian's staying here, so they can have a bit of time on their own.'

Harry gave her a squeeze. 'Lucky them.'

'Yes,' Edith sighed. 'Oh Harry, how I wish it was us.'

He squeezed her again. 'Me too. But our day will come, Edie.' His voice was quiet but full of conviction. 'Our day will come.'

4

Mary stood in the doorway between the service room and the common room and clapped her hands loudly. 'Excuse me!' she shouted over the general hubbub of the nurses enjoying their Saturday morning leisure. Very few had had to work and they were making the most of a few hours with nothing more pressing to do than listen to the wireless or read the paper. 'Gladys here has something to say.' She turned to the smaller young woman behind her.

'Er, yes.' Gladys cleared her throat. Although she wasn't as shy as when she'd first started working at Victory Walk, she hated speaking in public. She was grateful to Mary, who had no such qualms, for getting everyone's attention. Mary didn't flaunt her upbringing but her family's money and connections meant that she had never lacked confidence. 'The thing is, I need volunteers. For the victory garden. What with us having a few frosty nights, the parsnips are going to be ready, and I can't get them all in on me own. So I'd be glad of a helping hand.' She blushed furiously but held her nerve to the end of her sentence.

'Any takers?' Mary demanded brightly. 'I'd do it myself but I've promised to sort out donations of clothes down at the church hall. Come on now, don't be backward about coming forward. A lovely fresh morning like this, who'd want to be cooped up inside?'

One look at the faces turned towards her gave the answer — they all did.

'Cos you're getting parsnip soup this evening,' Gladys explained, 'only there won't be no soup if there's no parsnips.'

Belinda sighed dramatically. 'Stands to reason. All right, I'll do it. I'm not going on my own though.' She looked meaningfully at the rest of them.

Bridget put down her newspaper, wrinkling her freckled nose, the crossword only half completed. 'They've made that extra difficult this week,' she said, pointing at it. 'I'll join you. Can't deprive you brave girls of your soup, can I?' After over a year in London, her Irish accent was as strong as ever.

This made Edith feel guilty. She wasn't particularly fond of parsnip soup but it would be filling. 'I'll join you,' she said. 'And Alice will come too, won't you, Al?' Alice was absorbed in a long article in *The Times* and had barely registered what was going on.

'Right, yes, of course,' she said, hurriedly refolding it. 'Why did you say that?' she hissed at Edith as they made their way up to their attic rooms to change into their oldest clothes.

'Because you always spend the weekend with your head in the paper or a book and exercise is good for you,' Edith replied instantly. 'Are you going to wear that green wool scarf, Al? Can I borrow it if not? I've gone and left mine at Dr

Patcham's surgery. I remember taking it off when I popped in yesterday and then I forgot it.'

'We could go and collect it later,' offered Alice. 'I've got my blue one, I'll wear that.'

'Thanks.' Edith disappeared into her small room.

Alice opened her own door and crossed to the small desk on the opposite side, under the dormer window that looked out over the Dalston rooftops. Gaps were visible in many of the terraces where houses had taken direct hits in the air raids, but Alice's eyes were drawn to a creased and battered Christmas card which stood on her desk. The print of the robin was somewhat the worse for wear, but she didn't mind in the least. It was nearly a month late, and must have taken a very indirect route, but finally she had confirmation that Joe was still alive — or at least he had been when he wrote the card.

She picked it up and read it again, smoothing the card as she did so. As well as the standard good wishes for Christmas and the coming year, he'd added, 'I'm looking forward to rereading *Lorna Doone*.' That had made her smile. She couldn't imagine him reading it even once as it was so romantic, let alone twice. So he'd included that to tell her where he was. She knew the book was set on Exmoor, and thought it unlikely any naval ships would be based there — but, of course, it wasn't far from Plymouth. That would be it.

Setting it down once more, she gave a deep sigh. First Scapa Flow, then Plymouth. Opposite ends of Britain and both cruelly far from

Dalston. She knew it could have been much worse: naval vessels were now in North Africa, or India or the Far East. Yet Plymouth felt impossibly far away. 'Stop it,' she murmured. 'You can write to him. He's alive and well, that's the main thing.' She could not quite admit even to herself just how much she missed him, how worried she had been when Christmas came and went without a word.

'Al, you in there? You ready yet?' called Edith from the corridor. Hastily Alice grabbed her oldest jumper and began to change.

* ★ *

The victory garden had once been a pair of terraced houses two streets along from the nurses' home, but they had been totally destroyed in a direct hit in a raid last spring. Rather than let the land go to waste, it had been turned into a plot for growing vegetables. All over London, green spaces were being dedicated to producing food for a nation under siege. Those who were lucky enough to have front or back gardens planted them up. Even the grounds of Buckingham Palace were being put to good use. Closer to home, vegetable plots were to be found in Victoria Park, and allotments were in demand all around the borough.

The hardest thing had been the digging down to find uncontaminated soil. The first few feet were likely to be toxic after the bombing, and so the nurses had set to with determined energy. Stan and Billy had been recruited to help. Harry had come to watch, on one of his few visits home, and had been amazed to find that Edith, with her tiny frame, had been able to wield a spade as well as the rest of them.

'Hah, you think that just because I'm small that I'm delicate,' she had laughed. 'I tell you, riding around on that old boneshaker of a bike, you have to have muscles of steel. That, and lifting patients of all shapes and sizes. Don't you forget it.'

Now Edith plunged ahead, climbing the slight mound that marked the boundary of the plot. Gladys was already there, a large trug at her feet. She had pitched up the sleeves of her shabby coat, and her hands were muddy. Bridget and Belinda had also arrived before them, and they were taking out trowels from a canvas bag. 'Here, we saved a couple for you,' Bridget called.

Alice didn't mind digging out the vegetables. Her father had been proud of the vegetable plot in the back garden of her childhood home in Liverpool, and her mother would encourage the young Alice to help her pick blackcurrants, which she would then turn into delicious tarts, crumbles and jam. Her parents had written to tell her that they had got rid of the flower beds and planted vegetables and fruit there as well. They'd even started keeping chickens. Alice sighed as she thought of the luxury of fresh eggs for breakfast every day.

'Something wrong?' asked Edith.

Alice shook her head and laughed. 'Just trying to imagine my parents and their chickens. They won't like it if they make a mess of anything.'

38

'I don't think you can tell that to a chicken,' Edith replied, pulling out her first parsnip. 'Look at that, a real beauty. I do miss scrambled eggs though. Do you think we could build a henhouse in the yard, next to the bike rack?'

Bridget laughed. 'They'd have to be miniature birds, wouldn't they? I like a boiled egg for breakfast as much as the next person, but you'll be hard pressed to get away with that.'

Edith frowned. 'What about over at Jeeves Street? What do you reckon, Al?'

Alice shrugged. 'I know it's got a big yard, or small garden, whichever way you want to look at it, but lots of it is taken up with the Anderson shelter. Mattie's already growing greens on the top of that, and potatoes in old dustbins. She even got radishes to grow on the windowsills last summer. Not sure where she'd fit the chickens.'

'Ah well, just a thought.' There was something in Edith's tone that told them that she hadn't given up on the idea just yet.

'Nearly spring and then we can start sowing all sorts of things,' Gladys said with enthusiasm. 'I want to try carrots. Maybe some peas and beans too.' She brushed the worst of the mud from another parsnip. 'How are you getting along, Belinda?'

The tallest nurse straightened up, dashing her tight black curls from her eyes. 'There are a few good ones over here. I'm trying not to get too filthy though. Got to look my best this evening.' She gave them a bright smile.

'Why, where are you going?' Gladys always liked to hear about the nurses' evenings out, as she never had any of her own, caught between the demands of her first-aid duties and the need to look after her siblings as Evelyn was still being difficult.

'Dancing,' said Belinda, turning on the spot in a twirl. 'Peggy and Clarrie asked me to go with them. Any of you fancy coming along? The more the merrier.'

Alice and Edith automatically shook their heads, but Bridget looked interested. 'I might do that,' she said. 'I'll see what Ellen is doing.' Ellen had come over from the same big Dublin teaching hospital, and they shared the two-room annexe to the nurses' home. The home had been full but the superintendent, Fiona, had been eager to recruit more trained staff to her team. They had joined them when the war was already well underway. 'Where were you thinking of?'

'West End,' said Belinda grandly. 'We can get the bus. We'll be there in no time at all. After the parsnip soup, of course, we wouldn't want to miss that.'

'Not after all this hard work.' Bridget stood up and stretched. 'Do you think we have enough yet, Gladys?'

Gladys looked around critically at the now-filled trug and the other bags the nurses had brought along. 'Yes, that should do. Thank you, it would have taken me hours on my own.'

'Hours you don't have,' Edith said under her breath. She had never known Gladys to have any time to herself and wondered if that would ever change.

'We can go back and get cleaned up, then pop

over to Dr Patcham's,' she said to Alice, who was shaking the worst of the earth from her hands. 'Then I might write to Harry this afternoon.'

Alice nodded. 'And I might write to Joe,' she said quietly, unable to keep the delight from her voice.

'Joe?' Edith stopped in her tracks. 'Joe? Have you finally heard from him?' She was all but hopping on the spot.

'Yes, at last.' Alice gave a huge smile, allowing the strength of her feelings to shine through. 'He's safe; he's probably based in Plymouth. He's alive. I got a card this morning. He's safe, Edie.'

5

Peggy smiled as she caught sight of Belinda being swirled around the dance floor. Her partner was in a Canadian uniform and the top of his head reached as far as the tall nurse's ear, but he was full of enthusiasm and she seemed to be having a good time. At least he was keeping to the right beat. It was too bad when you were asked for a dance and the man turned out to have two left feet.

The place was crowded and the air felt hot, despite the coolness of the winter evening outside. Peggy took a moment to compose herself. She had had three different dance partners so far, all of whom had been perfectly polite, friendly even, but she did not feel inclined to seek out any of them again. She didn't want to give them false hope. She was interested only in dancing, nothing more. She patted her light brown hair into something like its intended shape.

Clarrie whirled by, the skirt of her bias-cut frock flaring out just as it was meant to, emphasising the shape of her calves. In this light, and moving at that speed, nobody would notice that the hem was frayed and the seams much mended. It had lasted for several dance seasons, and would have to last for many more unless the war ended soon. They all knew how unlikely that was.

Peggy grinned and shook her head as Clarrie raised her eyebrows at her and cocked her head a little to one side. She knew it was shorthand for 'Are you going to dance with any of them again?' Clarrie could be very protective, which Peggy appreciated, but she still didn't want to accept a second dance with any of the young men.

She was in no hurry to get back on to the dance floor. Sometimes it was more fun to watch, guessing who was going to dance with whom, or trying to recognise anybody she had met here before. The music was lively and she tapped her feet along with the rhythm, almost without realising it. She knew most of the tunes from hearing them on the wireless, which was on full blast throughout her shifts at the factory.

'You look as if you like the music.'

A voice sounded from just behind her, and she turned to meet the eyes of a man who was clearly a GI from his uniform. The Americans had begun to arrive now their country had entered the war good and proper and already some people resented their presence, but Peggy had nothing against them. He was taller than her, perhaps by a head. He was slimly built but she could tell he was fit from the curves of his muscles beneath his olive shirt. Something about the way he held himself made her think that he would be a good dancer.

'Want to have a spin?' He smiled, and his expression was bright, almost teasing. She thought his accent might be from New York — or as far as she could tell from watching *Broadway Melody* more than once at the local

43

Odeon. His skin was a warm brown colour, a couple of shades lighter than his eyes, which sparkled as they fixed on her.

Suddenly the idea of standing at the edge and watching the entertainment was not as compelling. 'Yes, all right,' she said after a moment. It didn't do to seem too keen.

His smile broadened as if he knew exactly why she'd made him wait, then he opened his arms and she stepped into them. She fitted exactly. As he began to move to the first notes of the new song, she knew she'd made the right choice. He was an excellent dancer — not flashy, but naturally assured. He made her seem as if she was far more accomplished than she'd ever been before.

'Do I pass the test?' he asked lightly, never missing a beat.

This time she didn't pause. 'You do,' she said, tipping her head back and laughing in surprised delight.

★   ★   ★

'Oh, I don't want to go home yet.' Peggy's voice was full of regret. 'Go on, Clarrie, stay for another song. Just one more.' She gazed soulfully at the entrance to the dance hall as they lingered by the chilly cloakroom.

Clarrie shrugged into her big winter coat with the astrakhan collar. 'No can do, Peggy. It's my sister's last day at home tomorrow and it's all hands on deck to make her a Sunday roast to remember and give her a proper family send-off.

She'll have my guts for garters if I oversleep and ruin it.'

Belinda shivered theatrically as she pulled on her own big coat. 'I'll be too late for curfew but I can get in through the back fence and the common room window. Mary's going to make sure it's unlocked. I don't want to push it too far, though, or they'll think I'm taking the mickey.' She buttoned up her cardigan all the way to the neck. 'Good evening, wasn't it? I think you've made a conquest, Peggy.' She nodded to the group of American soldiers to one side of the entrance.

Peggy raised her eyebrows. She knew she should deny it and play along, but life was too short — she of all people should know that. 'He was a lovely dancer,' she said, keeping her voice as neutral as she could. 'We only had a couple of turns though.'

'Six or seven, more like,' Clarrie said at once.

'Ooh, who's counting?' Peggy didn't know whether to be flattered or annoyed that her best friend had noted exactly how much of the evening she'd spent in the soldier's arms. 'Anyway they'll all be off soon, so nothing will come of it. They're just passing through.' More's the pity, she thought.

She fiddled with her clip-on earring; it had become tangled in her hair, which she had worn loose for once. It wasn't a valuable earring, just paste, but she liked it — it was one of a pair Pete had given her for a birthday years before. She didn't want to lose it. God knew she had little enough to remember him by.

'Peggy?'

She was shaken from her memories by the voice at her side. It was the soldier.

'You want me to walk you home?' His voice was warm. 'I'd be happy to do so.' He gave a small grin.

'No . . . no, you don't need to bother. I'm with my friends.' She nodded across to where Clarrie and Belinda were tying on their scarves.

'It's no bother.' His smile grew and she had a sharp feeling of certainty that he meant it. Her knees weakened at that voice and those melting eyes. But he was just passing through.

'Thanks, though.' She wanted to prolong the moment a little longer.

'Peggy, come on, we have to get the late bus,' Clarrie called. People were milling all around them, all keen to catch the transport while they had the chance. The building was noisy, its once-smart gold paint now cracked and shabby in the dull light.

The soldier nodded. 'You got good friends. I'm glad, cos I wouldn't want no harm to come to you.' He reached into his uniform pocket and brought out a small notebook and pencil. 'Can I write to you, Peggy? Will you write to me? I'll put down my address here, so you don't forget me. The name's James, in case that's slipped your mind already.'

'I don't . . . ' Peggy was going to protest that there was no point, they'd had a fun evening and that was that, but then she asked herself what harm could it do? Maybe he would come through London again. He might be one of the

46

lucky ones. 'Yes, all right,' she said. 'Here, give me that, I'll write it down.' She hastily scribbled down the address of the house in which she lived with Pete's mother, wondering if it was a betrayal of her late husband.

'I'll be sure to take good care of it,' James assured her, tucking the notebook back into his pocket. 'You do the same, now.' His eyes flashed with good humour.

'Peggy, come on!' Clarrie was losing patience.

'I'd better go.' Peggy felt rooted to the spot. The noise of the crowds seemed like miles away; even the irritated sound of her best friend couldn't pierce the shell around the pair of them.

'Be seeing you,' said James lightly, but in such a way that she knew he meant it. 'I hope so anyway. So long now.'

'So long.' Peggy took a step away, raising her hand in a silly wave. She watched him turn and rejoin his friends, then was conscious of Clarrie tugging on her arm, and the spell was broken. 'Yes, yes, coming, don't fuss.'

The three young women hurried from the dance hall, along with scores of others, many in uniform, all buzzing from their night out. The bus stop was only a short distance away and, judging from the number of people there already, one must be due any moment.

'Thank God for that, I hate waiting around in the cold after going dancing,' grumbled Clarrie.

'I know what you mean,' Peggy muttered absently, her thoughts elsewhere.

'Yes, you got quite overheated there,' Clarrie said, raising her eyebrows.

47

'Stop it. I was only having a bit of fun. You were dancing with plenty of men yourself — in fact the pair of you were.' Peggy felt around for the small page from the notebook in her pocket.

Belinda chuckled. 'Well, that's why we came out, isn't it? There were a few decent dancers there. Most of them a bit short for me, though. I don't think I'll ever find a man tall enough.'

'What's that game they play over there? Basketball, isn't it? You need a basketball player,' Clarrie said with certainty. 'Look, isn't that our bus? Quick, head for the top deck.'

Swiftly they climbed onto the bus and up the stairs, finding three seats together at the back.

'What was that last song you were dancing to?' Clarrie demanded, her eyes sharp as she observed Peggy's response.

Peggy looked down at her hands. ''Whispering Grass',' she said slowly.

'That's by the Ink Spots, isn't it? Your favourites.'

'That's right.' Peggy's mouth curved in a slight smile. They were her favourite singers and that was their best song. She'd never had the chance to dance to it with Pete but had often imagined doing so. She stared out of the window at the dim shapes just visible in the blackout and hummed the tune to herself, oblivious to Belinda and Clarrie's teasing. They could say what they liked. This had been an evening to remember.

6

'I should have guessed this is where you'd be if you weren't at the home.'

Alice pushed back the sleeves of her old jumper with muddy hands and squinted into the springtime sunshine, unable to properly make out the figure who called to her from the cracked pavement. But she knew that voice, despite not having heard it for far too long.

'Joe! You're back! You're here! Why didn't you say you had leave?' She rushed across the vegetable beds of the victory garden and up the little slope that marked the boundary. Then she stopped short. 'But . . . you're injured.' She took a breath. 'What happened? Should you be here — haven't they told you to rest?' Anxiety creased her forehead as she reached to touch his arm, but then dropped her hand as she realised it was covered in earth. All the same her instinct was to stretch out and make contact, to convince herself that he really was there, and not a figment of her imagination. He was rarely far from her mind, even if there was nothing she could do to ensure his safety.

'I'm on the mend, don't worry.' Joe automatically glanced down at the cast around his left leg, and gripped more tightly onto his walking stick. He hoped what he said was true and that he wouldn't make a fool of himself by stumbling. Then he looked up again and met Alice's concerned gaze and smiled broadly. 'Honestly, I'm all right. I'm much better. It's just a broken leg and they say it's going to be fine.'

Alice frowned. Trust Joe to make light of it. She didn't want to panic him but he must be in pain, and that cut her to the quick. 'Shouldn't you at least be on crutches? I'm not sure that a stick — '

'Alice, don't worry,' Joe said hastily. That was the trouble with nurses. They never stopped doing their job. 'I've been on crutches for weeks and I'm sick of them. They get in the way. People fall over them. I'd never have managed on a crowded train. Whereas with a stick, I can get around more easily and yet still get a seat. Works wonders, being a wounded sailor. You should try it.' His eyes danced with merriment.

'Maybe I will.' She grinned, more relieved to see him than she cared to admit, a little more reassured now that he didn't seem to be in agony. 'Do you need to sit down now? We have some wooden boxes somewhere . . .'

Joe looked at the slope and the uneven ground beyond and shook his head. 'No, and I can't stay long. I just wanted to see how you were and to find out if you have plans for tomorrow.'

Alice took in how his appearance had changed since she last saw him. He had lost a little weight, she thought, although he was still tall and muscular, but he'd acquired more lines on his face. She could guess that he had indeed been in considerable pain recently. 'Some of us

50

thought we'd go to the special Easter service at church in the morning. Then maybe a walk, if it stays fine.' She paused. She didn't want to dig up bad memories but she had to know. He was too important to her. 'Go on, tell me, put me out of my misery. How did it happen?'

Joe sighed. 'All right. We were part of a convoy across the Atlantic and we got hit by a U-boat. I was lucky, I got out with only a broken leg — well, and a few cuts and bruises. Some of my crewmates died.' She gasped in horror and he hastily continued. 'We weren't in the water for long, we got rescued by an American ship, it could have been far worse.' He looked away, unable to watch her face as she took it in. He didn't want to see her distress. 'Then we got brought back to port and I've been laid up ever since.'

'Joe . . . ' She rested her hand on his arm, regardless of the mud. She struggled to find words to encompass the terror of what he must have been through, and failed. 'We had no idea . . . '

'No. Well.' He cleared his throat. 'Didn't want to worry anyone, did I? And as you can see, I'm almost as good as new. This will mend in no time.' He smiled, to try to convince her. 'So will you come for dinner tomorrow? Ma's planning one of her specials, and she'll be mortally offended if you turn her down.'

Alice nodded immediately. 'I wouldn't dream of saying no. I can bring a contribution too — as you can see, we've been busy with the vegetables. We've got the last of the leeks, and I was just sowing the new lot when you got here.' At least there was something practical she could offer.

Joe nodded appreciatively. 'Ma would love that. As long as we aren't depriving you. Will you ask Edith as well?'

Alice looked over his shoulder. 'You can ask her yourself.'

Edith had come around the corner and was waving a brown paper bag at Alice. 'Found them! I'd put them in my drawer after that seed swap . . . Joe! Oh my goodness! Is that really you?' She ran towards him and then halted abruptly, realising he was leaning heavily on a walking stick. 'What happened?'

'Good to see you, Edith.' He grinned affectionately at the diminutive young woman who would one day be his sister-in-law. 'I'll let Alice explain my mishap, and then with luck we can talk properly tomorrow — you will come to dinner, won't you?'

'Just you try and stop me!' Edith beamed. 'Wait, you're not off already, are you? I've only now got here.'

Joe shrugged. 'Sorry, but I'm needed back at home.' He kept his smile steady, not wanting to reveal that the short walk from Jeeves Street had cost him more than he had thought. He would have to sit down very soon and not try to go so far next time. He'd half-planned to ask Alice to come to their old café with him, but now that was out of the question. How he hated being a semi-invalid. He didn't know how his brother Harry bore it. 'Sorry to leave so soon but it's good to see you, it really is.'

Edith nodded and Alice looked at him straight

in the eye, realising what the problem was. 'Yes, you'd better get back, you don't want to make your leg any worse than it is,' she said seriously. She could see how his face was becoming more drawn by the minute. 'Why don't I come with you and tell you everything you've missed these last few months. And of course we'll be there tomorrow, and we'll arrive early so we can help cook the leeks. Can't wait.'

'Yes, give your parents my love,' Edith said, her eyes growing darker as it dawned on her that the tall man in front of her was in increasing pain. 'You get home and have a good sit down, do you hear? Let Alice take your arm. That's my professional advice and you ignore it at your peril.'

'I wouldn't dare,' said Joe.

★　★　★

It was almost like old times around the big table in the Banham kitchen, except for the absence of Harry and Lennie. Flo was determined to make it special, and had invited Kathleen, Billy and Brian as well as the two nurses to join the family. She had managed to persuade one of the stallholders at Ridley Road market to get her a large chicken, which she had roasted, along with carrots and potatoes, now glistening and golden. Even better, as Alice got there early as promised with her big bundle of leeks, she had made soup for them to start with, and the savoury aroma had made everyone's stomachs rumble in anticipation.

Flo had reacted with horror when Alice offered to cook the soup. 'Never let it be said that a guest in my house had to make their own food with ingredients they brought themselves,' she scolded. 'As if you aren't on your feet every day of the week. You go and have a nice cup of tea and I'll see to that soup.' She had wiped her hands firmly on her old apron, worn to protect her Sunday best outfit. Alice recognised the maroon blouse with a pattern of daisies as the one Flo had worn for Kathleen's wedding.

So Alice had retreated to the parlour with her cup and saucer from Flo's best set, brought out in honour of the day, where she found Joe in an armchair by the window, facing the street.

'Don't get up,' she said hurriedly, but too late, Joe was already rising. He was leaning on his stick, but she could see less heavily than yesterday. He really shouldn't have tried to walk to the victory garden and back, she thought, but didn't say so. By the time they had reached his parents' house he had been all but silent, all his energy going into putting one foot in front of the other.

'Can't let my manners slip just because of a broken leg.' His usual grin was a little laboured. 'Sorry about yesterday. Tried to do too much too soon.'

'Doesn't matter,' Alice said, setting down her cup on a side table and pulling across another chair to join him. 'Shall I fetch you a cup of tea?'

'Good God, no. Ma's been bringing me tea ever since I set foot through the door. Not that I

54

don't appreciate it but you can have enough.' He sat down again, pulling a face. 'So, tell me your news, but properly this time. I didn't really take it in yesterday.'

She leaned back and smiled, taking in the welcome sight of him looking less haggard, better rested, bringing back the colour to his intelligent face. His dark hair had been freshly cropped into its regulation service style, but his deep brown eyes were relaxed, without the sharp edge she'd detected yesterday.

'Stop looking at me like I'm one of your patients.'

'I'm not.' She blushed a little and tucked a strand of hair behind her ear.

'You are. I can tell.'

'Oh, all right. I can't help it. I'm bound to be concerned — you've been away so long and then you turn up with a broken leg and horrific story about how it happened.' She shifted a little in her chair. 'Anyway, you've heard everything in my letters. We're just glad the raids seem to have stopped, for now at least. You'd better tell me the rest of your news though.'

Joe nodded and grew serious. 'As it's just us ... I don't want to make my parents more worried than they already are.' He paused and then went on. 'It seemed for a while as if we were getting better at working out where the U-boats were, and there were fewer attacks. But now we're suffering more of them and we aren't able to predict their movements like before.'

Alice wrinkled her nose in concentration. 'So what's changed?'

Joe looked a little uneasy. 'I can't really say . . .'

'But if I guessed that someone from the Allies had worked out how their signals were coded,' Alice said slowly, feeling her way carefully through her train of thought, 'and then the Germans realised their code had been broken and so altered it, would I be right?'

Joe smiled wryly. 'You haven't changed a bit, Alice.'

She exhaled deeply and then looked at him with a quizzical expression. 'So is that what you do, Joe?'

She knew Joe had exceeded what might have been expected of a boy growing up in the heart of Dalston, by winning a place at technical college and then training as an engineer with the Post Office, before deciding his talents would be best put to the nation's service by enlisting in the navy. Flo and Stan were extremely proud of their son's achievements and feared that his golden future might be curtailed by the risks he ran. Yet they would have it no other way; the country needed talent like Joe's.

Now he gazed out of the window before answering. 'Not quite. The real brainboxes stay on land, working behind desks. They'd never be able to think straight on board a ship like ours — well, what it used to be like. No, but someone's got to put their ideas into practice, and that's more or less what I do. There. Now you know. Not to be mentioned outside this room.'

Alice briefly shut her eyes to absorb this new

knowledge. Her admiration for the man grew even stronger. 'Of course not,' she breathed. She realised her pulse had quickened. What danger he must be in, for so much of the time. But she didn't want to give away that worry. He was home to recuperate, not be burdened with her concern. 'Well then, you'd better not ruin your chances of getting back to it by walking too far on that leg of yours.' Her eyes met his as he turned away from the window, and again she felt that jolt of connection that went beyond words.

'Yes, nurse,' he said mock-meekly, and they laughed, just as the door opened.

'Here they are!' Edith sang out, and Gillian rushed in, keen to see her uncle on his all-too-rare visit. 'Mind his leg, duck. And here's Alan.' Edith held the little boy, now eighteen months old, in her arms and beamed at him as he waved his hands. 'Can you say 'Joe'? Try it.'

'Ow-ow-ow,' said Alan obligingly, smart in his checked shirt and flannel shorts that Alice thought must be made from one of his mother's worn-out skirts. As Edith was distracted by the baby and showing him to his uncle, Alice noticed her friend's face. Delight was written all over it, in a way that she never showed when at work. Alice wondered with a start how long it would be before Edith could marry her Harry and have a child of her own.

Then there was no time to think further about it as the food was ready and they were all summoned into the kitchen, drawn by the irresistible smells of delicious soup, overlaid by roasting chicken. Alice quietly made sure that Joe

57

could sit at the end of the big table and rest his stick in one corner, while the others settled onto the mismatch of chairs as best they could. Gillian and Brian proudly perched on plump cushions placed on dining chairs and Alan was placed in the high chair.

'Don't give him more than one potato at a time,' his mother Mattie warned as she cleared away the soup bowls, 'or he's liable to throw them at you. He thinks it's a great game.' She frowned lovingly at him as she helped her own mother pass the platters laden with vegetables. 'Here, Billy, try some carrots.'

Billy heaped Kathleen's plate before his own, passing the platter to Alice. She caught the look that passed between them and wondered what it meant. They seemed to be full of suppressed excitement, beyond the thought of one of Flo's famous special dinners. She wondered what it could be. All in good time, she told herself, piling carrots onto Joe's plate.

'You don't have to do that — it's my leg that's broken, not my arm,' he protested, half putting out a hand to stop her.

'I've done it now,' she grinned, registering the warmth of his hand as it brushed against her own.

'Tuck in, everyone. Let's not stand on ceremony,' Stan urged them, and nobody needed to be told twice.

It wasn't until Mattie led the two toddlers into the back kitchen to have their hands and faces wiped at the end of the meal that Billy let slip the secret.

'There'll be another one to clear up after soon,' he laughed, and then clapped his hand over his mouth, realising what he'd said. Kathleen began to nod and then saw that everyone was staring at them.

'Really, Kath? Is that why you've been eating like a bird?' Edith demanded. 'I wondered what was up. Aren't you the dark horse?'

'Congratulations, that's wonderful news,' said Flo warmly. 'How lovely, a brother or sister for Brian. When is it due?'

'In the late summer,' said Kathleen, leaving the date deliberately vague. She knew that nobody around this table would judge her, but wanted to get into the habit of giving that answer. She was fairly sure that if anybody counted, they would know that this baby had been conceived before the December wedding. She hoped that if it was late then no one would bat an eyelid. Whenever it arrived, she knew it would be loved by everybody here.

'Well done, Billy.' Joe jokingly punched his friend's arm. 'Good job you had plenty of practice going without sleep in the raids. You won't get a full night's kip now.'

'Don't I know it,' said Billy, trying to look regretful and failing.

Once again Alice caught the look on Edith's face, similar to the one she'd noticed when her friend was carrying Alan earlier that afternoon. Sooner or later, Edith was going to want a family of her own. Alice didn't want to think about it; she had relied on Edith ever since they'd met on their first day of specialist training to become

59

district nurses. They had been inseparable ever since. Of course she had known that this could not continue for ever, especially when Edith became serious about Harry. But there had been so many changes in those few short years; this felt like one too many.

'Is something wrong?' Joe murmured, giving her a careful glance. He edged a little closer to her.

'No, nothing at all,' Alice assured him, keeping her voice low so that nobody else could hear it over the buzz of congratulations. 'Everything is lovely. Such a wonderful meal.' She could feel the warmth emanating from him.

'Good,' he said, watching her keenly.

For a moment she fervently wished that he could stay for longer than his brief leave, that she could share her cares and worries with him and he would tell her not to be so silly. He could always put things into perspective for her. Yet that was impossible. She must not even think about it. Gratefully she looked at him and absorbed his warmth while she still could.

7

Peggy was bored. Mrs Cannon had tried to persuade her to go to church on Easter Sunday morning but she hadn't attended. There seemed no point. It was at moments like these, when families traditionally gathered together, that she missed Pete most keenly. Mrs Cannon had been a little disappointed but hadn't pressed her. 'I've been invited to eat with my WVS friends afterwards,' she'd said. 'Would you like to come too?'

Peggy had only just avoided shuddering in front of her mother-in-law. To sit and talk about knitting for hours at a time was her idea of torture. Now she sat at the kitchen table with the wireless on in the background, the Halle orchestra blazing away, staring blankly out of the window into the small yard.

Perhaps she should copy Mattie's example and grow a few things. That would give her something to do and Mrs Cannon would appreciate it. It would be an excuse to get outdoors, now that the raids had stopped. Mattie had said she could have some seeds, and Edith could maybe get more from those seed swaps she went to. Peggy sighed. She'd never grown anything before and wasn't sure if she could start now.

She glanced down at her hands. Her skin was pale, and prone to freckles. Her nails were short, necessary for working in the factory. Nail polish was hard to come by and she hadn't bothered for ages. Just one more thing lost in the misery of the war. For two pins she could have burst into tears.

There was a knock at the door.

Peggy had no idea who it could be. Not Clarrie — her family always had a big meal on Easter Sunday, and she would be on kitchen duty. No one else came to call for her. Perhaps something had happened to Mrs Cannon. Hastily she ran her fingers through her hair to bring it to some semblance of tidiness and tugged at the collar of her frayed pink blouse. She hadn't expected to see anyone today and had dressed in any old thing, Easter or no Easter.

The front door had a glass panel towards the top, crisscrossed with brown tape against bomb blasts, and with one corner cracked since a raid last spring. She could pick out the silhouette of a figure, taller than her but not as tall as the Banham brothers. She was none the wiser.

Peggy could not have been more surprised at the man in unfamiliar uniform who stood there as she opened the door.

'Well, hello, Peggy. Remember me?' He smiled broadly and swept off his olive-coloured cap.

'James?' She could scarcely believe her eyes. She had heard nothing from the young soldier after their night in the dance hall, which at first had surprised her, but then she assumed anything could have happened. He could have been stringing her along — plenty did. He could have met another girl he liked better. He might have been killed in training or combat. You could drive yourself mad thinking about the what-ifs. It was better not to think at all.

'That's right. Ain't you going to invite me in?'

Peggy could see at least one set of net curtains was twitching in the houses across the narrow road. Well, this will give the old gossips something to talk about, she thought.

'Yes.' She smiled back at him, remembering what lovely eyes he had. 'Yes, of course. Come on through.'

'I'm sorry to turn up all of a sudden,' he said, as she took him into the small kitchen. The front parlour was too suffocating and formal. She didn't know how they did things in the States. 'You must have thought I forgot you, not writing to you like we said.'

'Well . . . ' Peggy felt caught out. After all, she hadn't written to him either. She had felt that would be too forward. She didn't need to go chasing after any old soldier on scant acquaintance; she had her pride, which God knew had been dented enough. If he wanted to contact her first, that would be a different matter.

'See, I mislaid your address,' he rushed in, hastening to make things right. 'I thought I had it tucked away safe and all, but when I came to look I couldn't find it. You got to believe me, Peggy, I was real keen to write to you.' He hesitated and she sensed he meant it. She relented a little.

'I'll put the kettle on, shall I?'

He looked at her blankly.

'To make tea. You do drink tea?'

He laughed. 'Sure I do. Yes please. Got to have a cup of tea in a proper British home.'

'That's right,' she said, wondering if this was what he thought a proper British home was like. 'Only we don't have much sugar. Will just milk be all right?'

'I don't have much of a taste for sugar,' he said, easing the collar of his olive shirt. 'What happened was, I must have slung my jacket down and the notebook fell out. I couldn't find it nowhere. I searched high and low, but it wasn't until I opened a pocket of my bag that I found it. Must have fallen in. Then they said we were coming through London at the end of our training and I thought a letter might not get here in time, so I'd take a chance and just show up.'

Peggy nodded, taking this in. Was it likely? Was he spinning her a tale? He sounded genuine, and he looked contrite.

'Did I do right?' he asked.

She decided to take a chance. 'Yes,' she said. She had the sensation that she had just crossed a line. Steadying her hands she made the tea, pouring a careful amount of fresh leaves into the warmed pot, taking the milk from the cold shelf in the back pantry, putting it into a little jug. The familiar ritual calmed her. 'Sorry, I haven't got any biscuits.'

'Don't need no biscuits.' He smiled up at her and she could see how good-looking he was, in his army uniform. She remembered how strong his arms had felt as they moved together on the dance floor. He sipped his tea with appreciation.

64

'Say, is this your place? Do you live here with your folks?'

It was the moment of truth. Of course everyone around here knew about Pete. Yet when she'd gone out dancing since his death, Peggy had never so much as mentioned him. That part of her life was closed to the servicemen she met at dances or in the pub, who thought she was looking for fun and a good time.

'Sort of,' she said, reaching a decision. 'Tell you what. Let's drink our tea and then go for a walk.' She couldn't talk about Pete in his own mother's house. That felt like a betrayal. But for the first time since the news from Dunkirk had come, she felt she could confide in a stranger. 'Then I'll explain. Does that sound all right?'

His eyes brightened, clearly relieved that she hadn't slung him out on his ear. 'Sure, Peggy. Whatever you say.'

★　★　★

'I'm so sorry to bother you,' said the young woman in smart uniform. 'I know you'll probably have other plans for Easter Sunday afternoon, but we're dreadfully short down at the ambulance station, so we thought we'd try the nurses' home for backup. There's been an accident; at least one child's been badly hurt.'

Belinda stepped back from the large front door, which was shiny as ever in a fresh coat of navy paint to show that — no matter what the neighbourhood had been through — the nurses' home was still in good shape. 'It's all right. You'd better come in and wait while I grab my bag — it's Geraldine, isn't it? We worked together before, with those people from the block of flats with smoke inhalation.'

The woman with the bright blue eyes nodded. 'Clever of you to remember. And you're . . . Belinda, aren't you? I do apologise for ruining your Easter.'

Belinda shrugged. 'I'm Jewish, actually, and I don't celebrate it. So I'm free to come along.' She ran up the stairs towards the upper-storey bedrooms and reappeared a minute later, now changed and with her Gladstone bag. 'Let's go. Where's it happened? Do you know what we're likely to find?'

Geraldine hurried out towards the ambulance parked at the end of Victory Walk. 'It's only the other side of the Downs; that's why we got the call, as our station's so close,' she explained. 'A wall collapsed, and apparently there were several kids playing on the pavement beneath. Perhaps they'd been trying to climb the wall, we don't know, but it didn't sound good.'

'Oh, poor things.' Belinda hopped into the passenger side as Geraldine swung herself into the driver's seat and instantly started the engine, her muscular arms turning the wheel in a well-practised move. Belinda remembered that the woman had been extremely competent in the smoke inhalation incident, and was relieved that — if they were to be the only two on the scene — she would be partnered by somebody who knew what she was doing.

The far side of Hackney Downs, the big green

open space a stone's throw from the nurses' home, was only a short distance away, and before the war it would have been an easy drive, but Geraldine had to navigate numerous potholes, keeping a fine balance between arriving at the accident as quickly as possible and yet not shaking her passenger and herself half to death on the bumps, cracks and craters in the road surface. Belinda had to grit her teeth as the vehicle shuddered along, thanking her lucky stars that the injured children weren't further away.

It was obvious where the trouble was as they drew closer. An old brick wall had clearly given way, and the back of a shop was visible through the gap. A couple of small boys were sitting on the pavement, and leaning over the pile of bricks was an ARP warden. Belinda screwed up her eyes to try to see who it was; it wouldn't be Stan or Billy, as they were going to be at Flo's big dinner. It must be Brendan, their colleague, who was a stallholder at Ridley Road market. She knew he was good with children, and exhaled in a sigh of relief.

'Ready?' Geraldine swung the ambulance close to the kerb, her hand already on the door handle.

'Ready,' Belinda confirmed, picking up her leather bag and jumping out. She ran towards the bricks and then stopped. Brendan was moving them one by one but at high speed, and from this close Belinda could see why. A small pair of feet stuck out from the edge of the pile.

'Brendan, what's happened?' she asked.

He turned. 'Ah, Nurse Adams. I'm glad to see you.' She could tell he was keeping his voice deliberately calm in order not to frighten the little boys, but his eyes were dark with urgency.

'Tell you what,' said Geraldine, pitching up her sleeves, 'I'll give you a hand there if you, nurse, wouldn't mind checking on these two. No sense in us all crowding round that poor little blighter.'

Belinda could see the sense in that and turned her attention to the two boys, one of whom had a huge cut on his head and was bleeding all over his ripped shirt. The other was pale and sweating, his eyes almost black with horror. She recognised the symptoms of shock and got to work straight away. 'Now you let me see what you've done to yourselves,' she said, keeping her tone light and friendly. 'My, that's a cut and a half, isn't it? Not to worry. They often look much worse than they are.'

'He's bleeding, miss,' said the white-faced boy. 'That there wall just came down and squashed us. We didn't stand a chance, we couldn't get away.' He sniffed and wiped his nose with the back of his grubby hand.

Belinda regarded the wounded boy gravely as she reached inside her bag, the contents of which she could by now identify without even looking at them. 'You're going to have to be very brave while I clean you up,' she said. 'I want you to look over there,' she pointed to beyond the ambulance, to distract him, 'and keep your head very still while I — '

'Ow, miss!' the boy cried. 'That bloody hurts, that does!'

Belinda smiled to herself. Perhaps he wasn't

hurt too badly after all. 'Yes, it will,' she said. 'Not much I can do about that right now, but the main thing is to get you clean. So I'm just going to bathe your cut again . . . '

'Miss!' But he kept his head steady, and she could work quickly to staunch the blood, disinfect the open wound and cover it with a sterile pad, held in place with a bandage. 'There, you're being an excellent patient. Almost finished. Just let me get out my biggest safety pin and fasten the end of this . . . ' she bit her lip in concentration, 'and there we are, all done. Right, now, as for your friend . . . '

She turned to the other boy who was even paler now and shivering. At once she took off her navy blue cloak and wrapped it around him. 'Are you feeling cold?' she asked gently. It was a warm day; this boy needed treatment, and fast. 'You'll feel better with that on, I know I always do.'

He nodded mutely, as behind them Brendan and Geraldine methodically cleared the bricks from the third child. Belinda knew she had to keep her charges from watching.

'What's your name?' she asked the boy with the head wound.

'George, miss.' He gulped. 'Will my head be all right? I didn't see it but it didn't half thump me, worse than me ma giving me the back of her hand.'

'Yes, I can see you must have taken quite a blow,' Belinda said, wondering how to get hold of his mother. 'What's your name?' she asked the other child.

69

'Benny, miss.' He sniffed again, but she could see he had grown no paler.

'Miss, can I ask you something?' George seemed to be recovering now. 'You're a nurse, aren't you?'

'Well, yes,' said Belinda. 'That's how I knew what to do to help your head get better.'

'And the warden called you nurse,' George continued. 'Do you come from that big house near the high road?'

'That's right.' Belinda cast another surreptitious glance at his little friend.

'We had a nurse from there come to our school,' George went on. 'She was nice to us. She showed us how to brush our teeth proper. Course it was a long time ago cos we all know that now we're older. I'll remember her name in a minute.'

Frowning, Belinda thought it rang a bell. Some of the others had mentioned it — there had been a local campaign of some kind, but before she had come to Victory Walk. It had come up in conversation but she couldn't recall who had been involved.

The boy wrinkled his nose as he thought long and hard. 'Something like water,' he said eventually.

Belinda grinned at him. 'Was it Nurse Lake?'

He grinned back. 'That's it, miss. Do you know her? She was ever so kind. Didn't shout at us or nothing, or give us the cane.'

'I should hope not,' Belinda said at once, remembering now that this must be how Alice met her teacher friend, Janet. It all made sense.

She also thought that Alice might be able to identify these boys if they couldn't give their addresses.

'Yes, Larry's sister used to like her too.'

'Who's Larry?'

'Him, miss, our friend.' George went to look behind him and Belinda was too late to stop him. 'Oh no, miss. He's only little, he's younger than us and we was meant to look after him . . .'

Turning around herself, she saw that most of the bricks had been cleared away and the small body could now be seen. It was lying completely still.

Geraldine caught her eye. 'Swap places,' she called. 'We need you here. I'll come to the other two.'

Belinda grabbed her bag and leapt across the jagged pile of rubble to where Larry lay.

Brendan crouched beside him. 'I did it as fast as I could,' he muttered. 'I couldn't pull the bricks off any-old-how, I didn't want to hurt him even more. What do you reckon, nurse — are we too late?'

Belinda lowered herself down to their level, her long legs awkward on the sharp stone. 'You'd better let me see.' It would not be the first time she'd seen a dead child but it never got any easier. This one was so young, too — maybe four or five, although the children from the nearby streets were often malnourished and appeared younger than they really were. 'Larry, can you hear me? I'm just going to reach for your wrist.' She took hold of the cold little hand, careful not to move the arm in case it was broken, but she had to ascertain if there was a pulse. It was no good. She moved around so that she could try to feel his throat instead. She noticed that the other arm was bent out of shape and the small woollen sleeve of his jumper was covered in a dark red stain.

Maybe she could detect the faintest throb. Leaning forward, the sharp pain in her knees almost forgotten in her concentration, she brought her ear as close as she could to his face and listened for a breath, waiting to see if she could feel it on her own cheek.

It seemed as if she was frozen in that position for hours, every nerve stretched to recognise any sign of life. She was oblivious to Geraldine's reassuring voice as she tried to command the boys' attention away from what was happening directly behind them, or Brendan's anxious shifting from foot to foot. She shut her eyes to block out everything but the slightest clue that little Larry might still have a chance.

Finally, just as she thought she would have to give up, she felt the tiniest puff of air. She blinked. Was it a stray breeze? No. There it was again. She felt once more for the pulse at his throat. Yes, faint and erratic, it was there, it was definitely there.

'Stretcher!' she called. 'Get me a stretcher right now!'

'Can't we lift him?' Brendan asked.

'No. Absolutely not. Look at that arm. And we don't know about his head or spine,' Belinda said firmly. 'Well get it as close to him as we can and ease him onto it, with as little disturbance as possible, supporting the injured arm as we do so.'

'Right you are,' Brendan said, sounding as if he was relieved not to have to make such a call. 'What about the others?'

'They need to come to hospital,' said Belinda decisively. 'At least one of them's in shock and I suspect the other has a risk of concussion.'

'Hope there's a bed free,' he muttered.

Belinda stood, her knees in tatters. 'There will be. They'll have to make room for these. We're a whisker away from losing this small boy.'

* * *

In the back of the ambulance, keeping the stretcher with its precious load as steady as possible, she barely had time to notice the young couple walking along the Downs. It was only after they had arrived at breakneck speed at the nearest hospital and ensured that all three boys were safely admitted that it occurred to her who she had seen. Belinda had done her best to extract addresses from the boys, with George able to explain that Larry lived around the corner but not what street or house number, and promised the harassed admissions clerk that she would telephone her with the full details. 'One of my colleagues has worked with the family,' she explained. Then she had sunk onto a chair near the clerk's desk as Geraldine offered to find a quick cup of tea to revive them before driving back.

Now that she had a moment to herself the

image came back to her. It had been Peggy — well, no surprise there, as she lived nearby and would sometimes go for a walk on the Downs, as they all did, strolling along what was left of the grass and avoiding the trenches and the new allotments. It was the young man with her who was so unexpected. He had been in American army uniform. He had dark skin. It was the soldier from the dance hall, all those months ago. They had looked to be very close indeed. Now what was all that about?

8

'You've got another one of those letters,' said Mrs Cannon as Peggy came downstairs in her light cotton dress and sandals. Now that summer was properly here, the temperature had risen, though the hallway of the small terraced house was still shady and cool. The older woman stood at the parlour door, half-hidden in the shadows, and held out an envelope to her daughter-in-law.

'Thanks.' Peggy took it and tucked it into her patch pocket. She had given up hiding the arrival of the letters, as it only made things worse. Besides, she didn't want to skulk about and pretend nothing had happened.

She had been seen, of course. Belinda had teased her, which she didn't mind; after all, Belinda had met James, if briefly, and had seen how genuine he was. It was the reaction of the neighbours that had caught her unawares.

It had been downright vicious. Mrs Bellings across the road had lost no time in making her feelings known. 'It's a disgrace,' she'd spat, catching Peggy as she came home from her shift not long after Easter. 'You flaunting yourself like that, with that man. A GI, of all things. Don't think I don't know what they're like. You should be ashamed of yourself.'

Peggy had found herself speechless for a

moment and then had recovered. 'I'll thank you to mind your own business,' she had retorted sharply, letting herself into the house and slamming the front door in her indignant neighbour's face. She had leant against the coolness of the hallway wall, catching her breath. Spiteful old woman, she thought. She's just jealous.

However it had not been a one-off incident. Plenty of people were beginning to object to the presence of the American servicemen. More and more were preparing to sail across the Atlantic, and the British were often at a loss as to what to make of them. 'Overpaid, oversexed and over here' was the general complaint. Women who associated with them ran the risk of being scorned, or being considered mercenary and just in it for the nylons, or worse. Peggy had compounded the problem because James was black.

To give her credit, Mrs Cannon had not been one of them. She had asked Peggy if it was true and Peggy had told her what had happened: she had met James and liked him but not really thought anything of it when she didn't hear from him; he'd called for her out of the blue; they'd gone for a walk and got along like a house on fire. Now he had been posted to another army camp, she wasn't sure where, but they had agreed to write. That was all there was to it.

What Peggy hadn't admitted to her mother-in-law was that she had been able to talk to James about Pete, and how understanding he had been. There had been no awkwardness. 'I won't say I know how you feel because I don't,' he had said. 'But I had a brother who died. It was an accident. Weren't nobody's fault — he was just in the wrong place at the wrong time. A truck came crashing onto the sidewalk and he was gone. We was close. For a while I didn't care what happened to me, nothing felt real.'

'That's exactly what it's like,' she'd said, dizzy with relief that he hadn't stepped away at the thought of her having being married, or been embarrassed at her sorrow, or thought she was an easy target because she was likely to be vulnerable. If anything he stepped even closer to her, and for a moment she sensed he would protect her and how much she had missed that feeling.

It had not been a long walk. He had had to get back to base and wasn't sure what time it would take. He had promised to write and not lose her address again. They had not so much as kissed when they'd said their goodbyes.

Yet Peggy had been sure that something important had taken place that afternoon. She had kissed quite a few men in her time and not one had meant anything, apart from Pete. She felt something shift, and the way she looked at the world seemed different somehow.

She could not explain that to Mrs Cannon. She played it down, not wanting to be disloyal to Pete or to offend his mother who had shown her nothing but kindness. The last thing she wanted was to cause trouble. However, it looked as if trouble might come her way anyhow. She had overstepped the mark. She had overheard one of

Mrs Bellings's cronies comment that if she absolutely had to walk out with a man, what was wrong with a good British one?

Peggy had been out at the market with Mrs Cannon when she heard that. Mrs Cannon had taken her aside. 'Don't mind her, duck. Never had no sense, that one. You had the best young British man there was, and that did you a fat lot of good in the end, didn't it? I don't begrudge you a bit of fun, dear; it's been nearly two years, after all.' Despite her cheery words the older woman had bitten her lip, still nowhere close to accepting the death of her only child.

Now Peggy picked up her cardigan, much mended at the elbows, and turned for the door. 'I'll go to the market after work and see what bargains I can find,' she promised, trying to brighten her mother-in-law's expression. She sensed that every letter from James was a nail in the older woman's heart, but Mrs Cannon would never rebuke her for receiving them.

'You do that, dear. I'll make us a nice potato pie for later. Now you go on, you don't want to be late.'

Peggy nodded and left, holding her head high as she strode along the dusty pavement. The rows of terraced houses were almost identical, all the worse for wear, all still with windows taped in case the raids started up again. Mrs Bellings could twitch her curtains all she liked. The more she objected, the more determined Peggy became.

★　★　★

78

Edith checked her watch. All nurses had to have one but for once she wasn't using it to check a patient's pulse. She wanted to catch her superintendent at the end of her working day but before she set off for one of her numerous committee meetings. It required careful timing.

Edith had returned to Victory Walk as swiftly as possible after her rounds. She hadn't exactly cut any visit short, tending to everyone as meticulously as ever, but she hadn't hung about to chat. She needed to see Fiona while her courage was strong. If Fiona denied her request then Edith would have to come to an important decision, and she already had a pretty good idea which way it would go.

She would restock her Gladstone bag later on. Leaving it in her attic room, she looked at her watch one more time, walked swiftly down the wooden stairs, which glowed in the late afternoon sunlight, and reached the superintendent's door. She knocked firmly.

'Come in . . . ah, hello, Edith.' Fiona rose from behind her desk, to her full height, though she was even shorter than Edith. 'What can I do for you? Your timing is excellent; Gwen and I have only now finished reviewing the training budgets.'

Edith saw that the deputy superintendent had also risen. Gwen towered over both of them, her severe face made even more so by her hair scraped rigidly back into a bun. 'Have you come to enquire about one of the bursaries?' she asked.

Edith had not counted on the outwardly

fearsome deputy being there as well, but in for a penny, in for a pound, she told herself. 'No, it's not that.'

'Well, sit ye down.' Fiona subsided onto her chair and immediately stacked her folders out of the way. 'Enough of those figures, I simply cannot bear to look at them for one second longer.' She smiled brightly, her auburn hair now showing streaks of grey. Edith stared at them, for a moment taken by surprise. Fiona was so energetic that she forgot that the woman was older than most of them, and to be reminded of this almost threw her. Then it strengthened her resolve. The years would catch her soon enough; she must make the most of them in the meantime.

'No, it's not that,' she said again, sitting on a narrow wooden chair to one side of the desk, as Gwen took a position to Fiona's right. Edith took a deep breath. 'The thing is, I would like . . . that is, Harry and I would like to get married. Quite soon.' There. She'd said it.

Fiona nodded, raising an eyebrow. 'Well, Edith, there's no real surprise in that. You have been engaged, what? Over two years now, isn't it?'

'That's right.' Edith was always impressed that Fiona kept track of all her charges' personal lives as well as their professional ones. 'Yes, we agreed it before he was posted to France, but then there was Dunkirk . . . '

'And we are all extremely thankful that he made a recovery after such a terrible time for you all,' said Gwen, leaning forward to

80

emphasise her point.

'Yes indeed.' Fiona regarded Edith. 'So I imagine you've come here to talk about more than your wedding plans?'

This was the moment of truth. Edith took another deep breath and plunged ahead. 'Yes, that's why I wanted to see you before deciding on a date or anything like that. It's because I want to keep on nursing. Please.' There, she had said it. Now her fate was out of her hands.

Gwen nodded slowly. 'I see. You are aware that strictly speaking you would be expected to resign your post upon marriage? Of course you are.'

Edith twisted her hands but refused to buckle under the scrutiny. 'I know.'

Fiona tapped her pen against the edge of the solid old desk. 'More than one of your colleagues has left for that very reason.'

'I know. I'm not saying I should be a special case,' Edith rushed on, 'but Harry and I probably won't be able to live together anyway. He still has to have more operations even though they aren't as serious now. A couple more to try to hide the burns on his face and to improve the movement of his damaged arm. Then he'll be able to perform desk duties even if he can't go back to his unit and fight any more. That could be anywhere.'

'But if he's going to be well enough for desk duties, he'll be well enough to be married,' said Fiona. 'Is that your thinking?'

'Sort of.' Edith twisted her hands still tighter. 'It's also, I came so close to losing him — it's made us want to waste no more time. We'd like

81

to be together when we can, depending on where he's posted, but also I don't want to stop nursing, not when we're all needed so badly. I won't use it as an excuse to take extra leave or anything. I wouldn't let you down. I wouldn't,' she added, not sure what the two senior figures were thinking. Gwen's serious face gave no clue. Then Fiona beamed at her.

'I can't imagine you would,' she said. 'I realise that the standard procedure is — Gwen, hear me out,' she went on, as her deputy looked as if she would interrupt. 'Those rules were made before the war began. Circumstances have altered completely. We've changed the design of our uniform to accommodate the shortages — why not extend that to the scarcity of experienced nurses? I don't want to lose you, Edith. You are a highly valuable member of our team here.'

'Thank you.' Edith could not quite believe she was out of the woods yet.

'It is highly irregular,' Gwen stated, her back ramrod straight. Then she relented. 'Yet as Fiona says, we can ill afford to send you packing. It takes time, money and effort to recruit staff, and you have shown yourself to be extremely competent. Furthermore you know the area now and your patients and the doctors all speak well of you.' Her face softened, a rare sight. 'Besides, I can remember what it was like to meet somebody you are certain you wish to spend your life with. Nobody knows how long they will have together. Who are we to deny you that?' The usually stony-faced deputy looked away, as Fiona caught her eye in sympathy.

Edith was one of the very few younger nurses who knew that beneath Gwen's fierce carapace lay a tale of sadness and heartbreak. Her fiancé had been killed in the Great War and, to add to the sorrow, her two brothers had also died in the fighting. A generation of young men had been lost and the women left behind had been permanently marked. Edith appreciated what must be going through her mind now.

Fiona stepped into the gap, after a respectful pause. 'Exactly. We wish you every happiness, Edith. The Banhams are a fine family altogether and they will be lucky to have you. We will count ourselves lucky to keep you. It cannot have been an easy decision to ask us and we appreciate your directness.'

Edith nodded mutely.

'May I ask, what about children?' Gwen said. 'As we are being direct. Don't glare at me, Fiona, we might as well raise the subject.'

Edith tipped her head in acknowledgement. The angle of the sun had changed and she moved a little to avoid being blinded by it. It lit occasional dust motes as they floated by the big bookcase of medical reference works.

'We'll take our chances and see,' she said honestly. 'We would both like to have children, of course. We were worried that Harry's injuries and then all his treatment might have affected our chances but he's asked his doctors and they say not. I know he's had lots of new drugs and nobody can say for sure, but we're going to hope for the best.'

'Very well.' Fiona put her pen down. 'You'll

have to see how you go. I defy even you, Edith, to cycle around on one of those old bikes while heavily pregnant. I would have to advise against that.' Her eyes twinkled. 'Meanwhile, accept our congratulations and start planning your nuptials.'

Edith smiled in relief. 'We won't have a big do. But that's all to be decided anyway.'

Fiona rose. 'Now I hate to rush you but I have a meeting to attend. Gwen, a word with you about those blasted budgets; I've now realised that one of our assumptions is wrong.'

Edith knew she was being dismissed and saw herself out of the office, the nerve centre of the whole building. She was delighted with the result of the meeting and could not wait to tell Harry. She loved nursing with all her being but, if it had come to making a choice, the truth was that she loved Harry more. She had been prepared to give up everything to marry him. She was heartily glad that she would not have to.

9

'Everything all right, Gladys?' Alice thought that the younger woman was looking worried.

'Oh, you gave me a fright. I didn't know you was there.' Gladys swung around from where she'd been cleaning the counter in the service room. 'Do you want a cold drink? It's warm out there today, isn't it?'

Alice could see that Gladys was avoiding her question and decided to bide her time. 'That's a good idea,' she said, although she wasn't really thirsty. 'I'll get myself a glass of water, don't stop what you're doing on my account.'

'I got some lime cordial around here somewhere,' said Gladys. 'How about a splash of that? Bet you haven't had any for ages.'

'Yes please. Wherever did you get it?'

Gladys scrabbled around in the far reaches of the end cupboard. 'Here you are.' Then her face fell. 'To be honest, I couldn't rightly say where it came from. My sister Evelyn gave it to me, sort of as a peace offering. We had another row. She said she would look after the little ones but then she scarpered off to the pub again.'

Alice drew cold water from the tap and carefully added a small drop of the precious green cordial. 'The pub? Isn't she a bit young for that?'

Gladys sighed and pushed a strand of straight dull brown hair out of her eyes. 'Yes, you're

85

right. I try to stop her but she don't listen. They let her do a bit of singing and she thinks she's going to be a star. I'm just an old killjoy who's out to spoil her fun. She don't see how she's being taken advantage of. All those men from the docks who go there . . . I worry about her, but the more I say, the more she sneaks out.'

Alice's face creased in sympathy. 'I bet you do.'

'Think I'll have some of that meself.' Gladys reached for the glass bottle. 'I try not to have it too often so it'll last, but now and again I give in.'

'You deserve it. You work so hard,' Alice said. 'Doesn't it smell lovely? All fresh.'

Gladys took a sip, closed her eyes and nodded. 'I feel better already.' But Alice could see she was putting on a good front, and the worry had not left her eyes.

'Are you on first-aid duty tonight?' she asked.

Gladys shook her head. 'No, not until tomorrow. Thought I'd go down to the victory garden and fetch some more potatoes.' She sighed again. 'That's the other thing, all the shortages. I know I shouldn't say it but it gets me down sometimes. Always wondering how we'll manage. You nurses out on the district all day long, you need to be well fed, but I dread not finding enough food for you all.' She looked around in case anyone else had heard her confession.

Alice realised that Gladys felt the weight of the world on her slender shoulders. She had grown up with such heavy responsibilities and there had been no let-up since. The war did that to everyone; despite trying to maintain a cheerful outlook or — failing that — a stoic one, it was only natural to feel despondent sometimes. The campaigns in the East and in North Africa were in trouble, the U-boats were preventing supplies from crossing the Atlantic, and rationing was biting ever harder. No wonder Gladys was slumping against the counter.

On top of that, just when she might have expected some help at home from her sister, the opposite had happened and Evelyn was refusing to pull her weight. Not only that, she was actually a cause of extra worry. It was not fair.

'Shall I come with you later?' she offered, feeling it was a barely adequate response.

'Oh no, you don't have to do that,' Gladys said at once. 'You done enough hard work for one day, you don't want to be out grubbing about for potatoes.'

'I don't mind, I like it,' Alice said. She took another sip of cordial. 'Reminds me of helping out my parents when I was little. At least, I thought I was helping.'

Gladys brightened. 'If you'd like to, then I won't say no.'

Alice finished her drink and gave a satisfied smile. 'It's made such a difference, having that garden,' she said. 'You have worked miracles with it.'

'Ain't just me, you all help out,' Gladys said immediately.

'You do the brunt of it,' Alice pointed out. 'You're too modest, Gladys. You think about what we need, work out when and where to plant it, and then pick it when it's ready. We really just do what you tell us.'

At last Gladys gave a quick grin. 'I like it too, really. It helps me to think, straightens out my head when I don't know what to do with myself.' She drained her glass. 'Thanks, Alice. I'd better finish here and go to help Cook with the evening meal, but I'll see you later.' She picked up her cleaning rag again.

'Right you are.' Alice made her way back through the common room and into the hall, wondering how Edith's interview with Fiona had gone. With luck she was up in her room right now, writing to tell Harry the good news. That's what we all need, Alice thought to herself. Some good news. It seems like a long time since we had much of that.

★   ★   ★

'What are you doing on Saturday evening?' Mary asked a few weeks later. They were in the common room after a particularly tiring day. Alice couldn't have said why; it was still hot, although no more than it had been for much of the summer; her patients were demanding, but only as much as they usually were. It was that background sense of constant unease, the drip-drip-drip of depressing news on all fronts. She hadn't been able to shake it off properly.

'Let me guess,' Mary went on, settling herself in a comfy chair. 'Sitting in your room reading a boring book. Or sitting down here reading a boring newspaper.'

'They're not boring,' Alice began in protest but Mary took no notice.

'Doing the crossword and then listening to more news on the wireless. Same as you do every day. Well, how about a change?'

Alice looked warily at her friend. 'What sort of a change?'

Mary beamed. 'Charles can get us tickets for the last night of the Proms. How about that? Wouldn't you like to come?'

'Really?' Alice perked up. 'Edie, did you hear that? Do you fancy a night out at the Albert Hall?'

Edith came across to join them, her expression slightly dubious. 'I'm not sure. I don't know much about that sort of music. I might not like it as much as some of the others.'

'Nonsense,' said Mary briskly. 'It'll be Beethoven, everyone likes that. It's fun, Edith, it won't be stuffy, I promise.'

Edith shrugged. She had been thinking of Harry's latest letter with news about his forthcoming operations. If they went well then he would be recuperating through the autumn, and perhaps they could set a definite date for their wedding after that. A Christmas wedding — that would be perfect.

'I don't know . . . '

'Oh, go on, Edie,' said Alice, almost laughing as she realised it was usually the other way around, Edith begging her to go out for once in her life. 'You might enjoy it. I'd love to go, Mary. It's very kind of Charles. Are you certain we won't be in the way — don't you want him to yourself for an evening?'

Mary generously shook her head. 'This is too good an opportunity to waste. Edith, you're coming along and that's that. It's so exciting. I used to go all the time before the war — of course that was when it was in the Queen's Hall, but that got bombed. I was afraid they'd cancel the whole thing but it started up again and better than ever, because the Albert Hall is so big. It's good for boosting morale. Look at it like that, if you're worried you won't like the music.'

'It's all right for you, you grew up playing the piano and having singing lessons,' Edith retorted. 'We didn't have so much as a harmonica in our house. If anyone sang too loud, my father clipped them round the ear. It puts you right off.'

Mary would not be dissuaded. 'All the more reason to start now, then,' she said smartly, standing up once more. 'I'll write to Charles straight away, before you change your mind.'

★ ★ ★

The staff car cautiously weaved along the damaged roads, past Hyde Park and through the centre of London, headlamps shaded because of the blackout, but as far as Alice was concerned it was as good as being in a sports car. It had been ages since she'd been in any kind of private vehicle. Even though she was crammed in the back with Edith, it felt like a decadent luxury.

The skies were lit by anti-aircraft spotlights, a far cry from the pre-war bright lights of the West

End, and yet there were revellers out on the streets, making the most of a raid-free Saturday night on the town. Men and women in uniform alternated with those in civvies, some linking arms and wandering along singing.

In the front passenger seat, Mary was singing as well. She'd picked up the stirring melody of the sea shanties in the second half of the programme and was improvising her own version, tapping out the rhythm on the dashboard. From anyone else this would have been annoying, but Mary had a fine voice and it was all part of the evening's fun.

Alice caught a glimpse of Charles's face as he looked quickly across at Mary, before turning his attention back to the road. She knew that her colleague often despaired of him, as they saw each other far less often than she would like, and she doubted if their romance would ever come to anything. Yet Alice could tell from that brief glance that he thought the world of Mary. From the moment they had all met up earlier, he had been extra attentive to her, smiling even when she couldn't see he was doing so, gently helping her with her jacket or making sure she had the best seat.

It wasn't Charles's fault their love could not progress; it was the war's. He was an army captain and put his duty before everything, although this evening had made Alice realise how much that cost him. In any other situation he would have put Mary first.

Alice looked sideways at Edith, catching her animated face as a spotlight beam swept the sky above them. Far from hating the concert, Edith had loved it, swept along by the stirring music and the sense of occasion. It had been a night to remember. She began to hum along to Mary's spirited rendition of the 'Sailor's Hornpipe'.

'Sounds as if you don't mind that sort of music after all,' she said when her friends had finished.

Edith laughed. 'I don't know if I'd want to go to it all the time but that was just what we needed. I can't get the tunes out of my head.'

Mary turned around to face them, and in the intermittent light Alice caught her broad smile. 'See, I said you'd like it. We could go to other concerts if you want, when our days off coincide. There's usually something on at the National Gallery at lunchtime. Myra Hess, you know.'

Edith made a non-committal noise.

'Charles used to take me before he grew so busy,' Mary went on, laying a hand on his arm. 'Didn't you? We used to meet there for some music and a quick bite to eat. Remember when they had really strange food? I suppose it was all they could get, and they always like to provide something.'

Charles chuckled and again turned briefly towards her. 'Honey and raisin sandwiches, as I recall. Absolutely delicious, if you like that sort of thing.'

'I don't remember having much choice,' Mary said archly. 'But it was wonderful all the same.'

Alice thought that she might give it a try, if there was ever a spare moment. Not so much for the peculiar sandwiches but for that sensation of being part of something beyond herself, one of a big audience all enjoying the same thing. It lifted you, took you out of your day-to-day worries. 'I'll go with you, Mary,' she said.

Mary turned again and beamed before catching Charles's eye as she faced the windscreen once more. Alice caught their look and again sensed that Mary's concerns had no foundation. If all went well, their day would come.

Edith sat back against the dark leather of the car's back seat and Alice thought how she too deserved her chance of happiness. With luck what would be Harry's final major operation had been booked in for September. In a matter of weeks he would be recuperating and so Edith's longed-for Christmas wedding was on the cards. Even if such a future was not the one she herself could expect, Alice knew that this was the path Edith dearly wanted, and it looked as if she could continue nursing as well. She felt a little guilty at the relief that news had given her. She relied on Edith's presence far more than her friend realised.

For a moment Alice wondered what it would be like: to be able to carry on nursing and yet have the comfort and thrill of a husband. She gave herself a little shake. She must not even let that thought enter her head. No good would come of it. Memories of her heartbreak were still all too vivid and she had absolutely no intention of ever risking such a thing again.

She shivered and drew her light cotton jacket more tightly across her best summer blouse. All around the crowds were singing, shouting, in high spirits, as the spotlights continued to rake the sky.

★ ★ ★

Charles drove them all the way to the end of Victory Walk, which Alice suspected was stretching the petrol regulations, but she was glad as they'd only just made the curfew. He'd slowed the car right down to navigate the last couple of streets, so as not to wake any of the neighbours. The tall, narrow houses rose up from the warm, cracked pavements, their bay windows catching what light there was on their angled glass panes. She and Edith mounted the steps of the nurses' home, leaving Mary a few discreet moments to say her own goodbyes. They were expecting the home to be winding down for the night but instead a buzz of chatter greeted them.

'Quick, shut the door so the light doesn't shine out,' said Edith, surprised that the main hallway lamp was still on. 'We don't want to end the night with a telling-off from the ARP warden.'

'Well, it won't be Billy, that's for sure.' Bridget appeared at the foot of the stairs.

Alice carefully left the door open a crack so that Mary could get in, and turned to face her colleague. 'Why, what's happened to Billy? Is he all right?'

Bridget nodded emphatically. 'Oh yes. He's more than all right. He'll just be a bit busy.'

'Busy? What do you mean?' Alice was becoming concerned. She half-shrugged off her

94

jacket and then stopped, wondering if she would need to pull it on again.

Bridget relented. 'We just got the call. We're getting ready to go round . . . Ellen and me.'

'Go round? Go where? Why?' Edith demanded.

'To Jeeves Street. That's where the patient is. Can't you guess? Kathleen's gone into labour.'

Edith gasped, then stood stock still. 'Already? Typical, the one night we go out . . . '

Bridget nodded. 'It's true. She must be about a month early. So, apparently she had an inkling the baby was on its way and went around to take Brian to Mattie. Then, while she was there, she felt the first proper labour pains. Flo and Mattie told her to stay put rather than try to get back to her house. Stan went out to use the ARP phone to call for a nurse. It all sounds straightforward, even if it's come on a bit fast.'

'Well, you and Ellen had the specialist midwifery training and so it makes sense that you go.' Alice flashed a look at Edith, who nodded in acknowledgement.

'Yes, but you and Alice delivered a baby in the Anderson shelter in a raid,' Bridget pointed out. 'After that, anything else must be a doddle.'

Edith raised her eyebrows but said nothing. Delivering Mattie's son in such circumstances wasn't something she'd care to repeat, although at the time there had been little choice; they'd simply had to get on with it.

'Wouldn't she rather you two went?' Bridget asked. 'I know you've just come in, but you're her friends. I mean, we're almost ready to leave, but if you wanted . . . '

Edith had been all for going upstairs to her attic room but now she had a surge of renewed energy. 'What do you think, Al? Shall we? It is Kath, after all.'

Alice too had been looking forward to a proper night's sleep but this news changed all that. She nodded vigorously. 'I think we should.'

Edith smiled in anticipation. 'Just think, Kath and Billy's baby! I can't wait to meet him, or her. Come on, Al, let's get our bags and go over there as fast as we can.'

★ ★ ★

In the end it made little difference who turned up from the nurses' home. By the time Alice and Edith arrived, an exhausted but ecstatic Kathleen was sitting propped up in Flo and Stan's comfortable old double bed, a tiny scrap with jet-black hair in her arms. A small pink face was just about discernable, surrounded by clean white sheets and a crotcheted baby blanket that Edith recognised from when Alan was a newborn.

The new mother was not too tired to grin broadly at the nurses. 'Here she is,' she whispered. 'My little girl.'

Edith dropped to her knees. 'A girl! Oh how lovely. Brian has a baby sister. What a little beauty.' She rocked back on her heels. 'We've brought our bags — is everything all right, Kath? We should check you over, the pair of you, now we're here.'

Flo laughed from the doorway. 'Yes, we'll

make the most of you. But I can tell you everything is how it should be. After all, I should know.' She gazed affectionately at the young woman who lay in her own bed. 'Gave birth to three of my own and been there for my first granddaughter's arrival, don't forget. I might not have the medical words for what just happened but I'd call it a textbook birth. Couldn't wait to come into the world, this little one.'

Kath gave a short laugh. 'I wouldn't say it was easy, but compared to when I had Brian, or even worse, what Mattie went through with Alan — well, I'm lucky.' She returned her gaze to her daughter. 'Very lucky. Just look at her. She has her daddy's hair.' She looked up again. 'Where's Billy gone? He went downstairs just before you two arrived.'

Flo folded her arms across her apron. 'Well now, Stan thought it only right to wet the baby's head, so he's opened some of that beer he was given at Christmas. He's pleased as Punch of course. I'll let you two do what you have to do and then you must come down and join us.'

★　★　★

Alice and Edith left again shortly after, knowing they were surplus to requirements. They pushed their bikes along, too tired by now to ride them the short distance to Victory Walk.

'Oh, she's a healthy little creature. Seven pounds ten,' Edith said and Alice nodded. 'They haven't decided what to call her yet, have they? There's talk of maybe Billy's mother's name, but

97

I didn't catch what it was.'

'Probably won't be named after Kath's mother,' Alice commented, knowing that relations between the two were strained, to put it mildly. 'Still, time enough for that. Are you going to mass tomorrow morning, Edith?'

'I might well do that.' The Irish nurses were much more frequent attendees than Edith was, but perhaps she could go and give thanks that Kath and Billy had their daughter safe and sound.

Alice trundled the bike across the high road, feeling a pleasant sense of weariness overtake her. There were no cars, vans or buses to be seen, and the night all around them grew quiet. 'I might go to church myself,' she said. Then, catching the expression on Edith's face, she paused. 'What is it?'

Edith gave a small grin as she rebalanced the creaking old bike, bumping it up over the white-painted kerb. 'That's quite an impressive weight for a baby that's come a month early, don't you think?'

Alice navigated the kerb beside her. 'Seven ten — I suppose so . . . why, Edith, what are you getting at? Oh. I see. Yes, you could be right.'

Edith shrugged. 'Not that I mind, but I'll bet you anything that's no premature birth. No, odds are that she's a full-term baby. I shan't say so to anyone else but that's what came into my mind as soon as I saw the weight.'

Alice rolled her eyes. 'Doesn't matter, does it? As long as she's well, and Kath's all right, and Billy's happy.'

'Doesn't matter one bit.' Edith swung the bike neatly around a pothole. 'Tell you what, after mass and church, we could maybe make something for them — see what ingredients we can get together. They'll be too busy to cook.' She blinked in sudden tiredness and stifled a yawn. She for one would not judge Kathleen if she had indeed pre-empted her marriage vows. She was in no position to do that. Not that she'd confided — even in Alice — just how she and Harry had said their farewells before his last trip to France. She was the last person to begrudge a loving couple whatever comfort they could find, before who-knew-what perilous future might overtake them.

10

Clarrie waved to Peggy across the production line and mouthed something, but the combined noise of the machinery and the closing moments of *Workers' Playtime* on the wireless meant that whatever she was saying was completely inaudible. Peggy frowned at her friend. 'Good luck, all workers!' said the man on the wireless, as he did at the end of every show, and Peggy sighed with relief. That meant she and Clarrie could go for their late-meal break. The factory no longer stopped for lunch; half the workforce had to carry on through the usual hour, and then they were released to the canteen when the first half had finished eating. By that time, Peggy's stomach was usually rumbling.

'I'll need more than good luck, thank you very much,' she muttered to herself as she pitched up the sleeves of her overall. It was too warm for long sleeves but they had to wear them for their own protection. Dust rose as she did so, making her sneeze. Crossly she kicked aside a fragment of cardboard box.

'Here, watch what you're doing, I could have tripped on that,' Clarrie complained, though it didn't sound as if she really meant it. 'So what do you think of my idea?'

Peggy looked puzzled. 'What idea? No, don't stop to tell me, let's get to the canteen. I could eat a horse.'

'Fat chance of that,' said Clarrie, hurrying to keep up with her hungry friend. They fell into line with the rest of their shift, eyeing the watery stew that was on offer. At least there was a good dollop of mashed potatoes to go along with it. They took their trays and found the end of a table where there was room to sit down.

'So, my idea. You still haven't said.'

Peggy shook her head. 'Is that what you were trying to tell me before we stopped? I couldn't hear you. I could see you were saying something but couldn't work out what it was.'

Clarrie took a mouthful of stew and made a face. 'Not much meat in that, horse or otherwise,' she said flatly. Then she brightened. 'All right, what I said was, we should save some of the scraps from the floor before they're swept up.'

Peggy's expression was dubious. 'What, like the bits of cardboard?'

Clarrie put down her fork. 'No, more like the plastic or rubber.'

'Whatever for?' Peggy tried the stew and grimaced. 'Ugh, I see what you mean.'

Clarrie explained. 'I'm fed up of not being able to buy nice things, not being able to dress up, so I thought we could make our own.'

'How do you mean? What, like clothes? I can't see how that would work.' Peggy shovelled more stew and potato into her mouth, too hungry to care what it tasted like.

Clarrie shook her head and loose strands of her red hair gleamed in the late summer sunlight pouring through one of the high windows, with its panes still crisscrossed with tape in case of bomb blasts. 'No, not clothes. Jewellery. I've tried mending my necklaces when they break, of course, and I'm always catching them in this.' She patted her hair, still tied up in its old scarf. 'But I'm tired of them, same old things every time. I reckon we can use the bits that get thrown away, make brooches maybe.'

Peggy cocked her head. 'Really? Could we?'

'I'm sure my pa would let us use his tools.' Clarrie was warming to her theme. 'If we cut shapes with his hacksaw, we could then file the edges . . . all right, I can see you don't believe me but I haven't come up with the details yet. Give me time, then you'll see. We could make ourselves glamorous, Peg. Knock 'em dead on the dance floor and all that.'

Peggy nodded, considering. 'Been a while since I went near a dance floor. I wouldn't mind a few new things, and that's a fact.' She looked down sadly. They couldn't wear jewellery while on a shift, for fear it would catch in the machinery, but she had precious little to start with. Her wedding ring was on a chain around her neck these days, and a bracelet Pete had given her after they got engaged sat safely in her bedside drawer. In money terms it wasn't valuable but it was priceless to her. Other than those, she had a few bits and pieces of costume jewellery but not much else. 'Do you want to try to make a start later on, then?'

Clarrie scraped the last of the potato from her plate. 'I can't, I'm on fire-watching duty.' Even though the raids had died out, a group of factory workers had formed a roster to ensure no damage befell the building overnight. Clarrie had recently been recruited, and trained to deal with the effects of incendiary bombs. 'But you could start looking out for any odds and ends. We should make a start collecting them and then pool what we've managed to gather at the weekend.'

'Fair enough.' Peggy glanced at the big clock above the serving counter and stood up. 'Come on, time to go back. There's never long enough to chat properly, is there?'

Stretching with a groan, Clarrie also got to her feet, then followed the shorter young woman through to the factory floor, tucking her stray locks back into their faded strip of fabric. 'There, that's the sort of thing I mean.' As they approached their work stations her eyes were caught by a small fragment of clear plastic, not much bigger than a penny. 'Not much on its own, I admit, but a few of those together with a bit of decoration, well, who knows?'

Peggy nodded, but if Clarrie said anything further it was lost in the rising hubbub of noise as the production lines pounded away and someone turned up the wireless once more.

* * *

With no Clarrie to talk to after the shift finished, Peggy decided to pay her first visit to Kathleen and Billy's new daughter. The baby was now two weeks old but there hadn't been a convenient moment to go around to the little house before, and Peggy suspected that the new arrival would not have been short of visitors for the first fortnight of her life. She found Kathleen smiling and happy in her living room, which was such an improvement on the poky flat she'd lived in before. There the main room had been lounge and bedroom to both Kathleen and Brian — and to her ex-husband Ray on the very rare occasions he had been there. Trouble had always followed him on such occasions and Kathleen was far better off without him. Now she finally had a household that she could be proud of.

Brian solemnly led Peggy to the cot in the corner, where his sister lay sleeping. Peggy breathed in, absorbing the little face crowned with an impressive amount of thick dark hair, just like her father's. 'She's beautiful,' she said. 'Does she sleep like this all the time, Kath?'

'No,' said Brian before his mother could answer. 'She cries a lot and wakes me up in the night.'

Kathleen came across to him and ruffled his hair. 'But we don't mind, do we? It's only because she's hungry. She soon stops when she's had a feed.' Brian nodded and then retreated to the opposite corner, where he had been building a mighty fortress of coloured wooden bricks. Peggy stood up straight again, afraid of waking the tiny creature.

'I brought you something.' She reached into her battered handbag and drew out a paper-wrapped bundle. Kathleen took it and undid it to reveal a pair of small white woollen bootees, edged in pale yellow ribbon.

'Peggy, you shouldn't have.'

Peggy grinned. 'I didn't make them, in case you're wondering. Pete's mum got the wool from one of her WVS friends and knitted these the moment she heard the news.'

'Well, you must thank her from me,' said Kathleen, her eyes shining, in full knowledge that knitting was not one of Peggy's strengths. 'You can never have too many when they're this age. Even when it's warm weather, it's a struggle to keep everything washed and clean.'

Peggy looked around; the room was spotless, and as tidy as it could reasonably be expected to be, given that it contained a young baby and a very active toddler. 'Do you want a hand with anything?'

Kathleen laughed and sat on the settee, new to her at least, even though it was second-hand. 'No, Flo was round earlier and insisted on doing everything. I'm barely allowed to lift a finger really. I told her, I've got to do something or I'll never shift my baby weight.'

'What baby weight?' Peggy looked at her friend's trim figure in her bright printed dirndl and matching blouse. 'You're scarcely different to how you were this time last year.'

Kathleen shrugged. 'Maybe. Can I get you anything? Would you like to eat with us? Brian's had his tea but I was waiting for Billy to get home.'

'No, no,' Peggy said hastily, knowing that — even with extra rations for nursing mothers — there would not be much food to spare. 'I'm on late lunch breaks this week.' She sought to change the subject. 'Now, don't keep me in suspense. You must have chosen a name by now?'

Kathleen rose to put the kettle on in the small back kitchen. 'We have,' she called though the interconnecting door. Peggy smiled to see her. Her friend's old kitchen had been dark and grim, even though it was always scrubbed and polished, but here the sunlight came through the back door to the little yard, as well as piercing the small window above the big ceramic sink. 'We liked what Mattie said when Alan was born — give him his own name first of all and then have a family name in the middle. So she'll be Barbara for herself and then Frances for Billy's mother.'

'Barbara Frances Reilly.' Peggy tried the name out aloud. 'I like it. Goes well with Brian too.'

Kathleen reached for cups from the row of hooks beneath the wall cupboard. 'And Brian is now officially Brian Reilly,' she said with a mixture of delight and relief. 'We wanted to have that sorted out before he's old enough to start writing his name. Billy's so proud, you can't imagine.' She carefully measured tea leaves into the slightly chipped brown pot she had inherited from their landlady.

'Oh, I can,' said Peggy, turning so that she had a good view of the little boy demonstrating his building skills. Billy had always been extremely fond of Brian, far more than his biological father had ever been. 'He's good at that, isn't he? Perhaps he'll be an engineer like Joe.'

Kathleen brought the tea through. 'Sorry there

aren't any biscuits. Mattie made some but we finished them yesterday.'

'I'm really not hungry,' Peggy insisted, even though she was. They were never still for one moment at the factory, and used up plenty of energy, meaning they were usually ravenous by the end of the day. Gratefully she accepted her cup.

'Would you like to hold her?' Kathleen offered.

Peggy hid her expression by taking a swift sip. 'Oh, no, it would be a shame to wake her,' she said. 'Of course I'd love to but let her sleep — I'll give her a cuddle next time I'm round.' She couldn't offend her friend outright, but she definitely did not want to hold the child. She had told very few people, even her closest friends, about the miscarriage she had suffered not long before the news of Dunkirk had reached them. Even though it had happened eighteen months ago, the memories of losing what would have been Pete's child were still painful, and every sight of a newborn brought it all flooding back. She hoped Mattie had never noticed when Alan was tiny, and she would have to revive all the excuses she'd made at the time now that Kathleen also had a small baby.

Quickly finishing her tea, she made her apologies for the visit being so brief and rushed back outside, into the side street not far from Butterfield Green. If she had stayed longer, she knew Kathleen would have pressed her to join them for their evening meal, shortages or no shortages, and Peggy couldn't allow that. Also, she was thrilled to see her friend so happy, in her new house with its cheerful aspect and homely proportions, obviously content in her marriage and delighted with her children. Yet Peggy was devastated as well, as that was what she should be enjoying herself: in another life, with no war, Pete would be with her and their child would have lived.

She had had to get out.

★ ★ ★

Peggy arrived back home just as Mrs Cannon was preparing to go out. 'Oh, Peggy love. I have to leave you on your own this evening. We just got word, there's an unexploded bomb down towards Liverpool Street and we need to provide a mobile canteen for those brave UXB boys.'

Peggy hung her old handbag over the newel post at the bottom of the stairs. 'Goodness, you mean you'll be right there if it goes off? Please be careful!' It struck her that she would be lost if anything were to happen to Pete's mother. Annoying as she could sometimes be, she had shown no lack of bravery since joining the WVS.

'Don't give it another thought. I'm sure they'll make sure we're somewhere safe,' said Mrs Cannon, fastening her light jacket with its cheerful ric-rac edging. 'Now, did I pack my apron? I don't want to get splashes of milk on my good frock.' She turned around to check her own bag. 'Yes, of course I did. What am I like, I'd forget my own head if it wasn't screwed on.' She tutted as Peggy smiled.

'Nonsense, you're the most organised person I

108

know. Oh, Kathleen says thank you for the bootees. She loved them.'

Mrs Cannon broke into a wide smile. 'And did you see the new arrival?'

'I did. She's gorgeous, looks just like her dad.' Peggy made a supreme effort to keep her tone light; if Mrs Cannon noticed it falter, she had the decency not to say. 'Hair as black as ink.'

'How lovely.' Mrs Cannon had one hand on the front door and then she stopped. 'Goodness gracious, I've gone and forgotten that other thing. Mrs Bellings from over the road brought a letter for you that went to her by mistake. It's the new postman, he's still getting used to who's where. Did you know that nice Mr Chandler has signed up for the army?'

'Really? I thought he was my dad's age.' Peggy gasped in surprise.

'Maybe not quite, but he didn't have to go. Still, he said he wanted to do his bit. Very good of him, but the new fellow is a bit slow at learning the ropes. He's not exactly in the first flush of youth, shall we say. Ah yes, here we are. From that American gentleman unless I'm much mistaken.' Mrs Cannon's eyes gleamed. 'Must be off, Peggy dear. There's a cold pie in the larder.' She hurried off, leaving Peggy in the shady hall, holding the letter.

Peggy bit her lip as she felt a giggle rise inside her. She would have loved to have been a fly on the wall as Mrs Bellings handed over the letter. Perhaps she'd worn gloves so she wouldn't have to sully herself by touching the same envelope as the soldier of whom she so deeply disapproved.

Peggy's spirits perked up as she went through to the kitchen, which faintly smelt of the pie that had been baked earlier. She reached into the cutlery drawer for a knife.

Gently she slit open the envelope and put it carefully to one side; paper was becoming too short to waste. Then she savoured the moment before reading the letter itself.

Damn that interfering neighbour. How long had she had this before handing it over? Then Peggy stopped that line of thought, deciding that the mean-spirited woman wouldn't have wanted it in her house for any longer than was strictly necessary. The main thing was that James was in London for a brief period of leave. He was staying in the centre of town, at a Red Cross dormitory. Would she like to come to meet him, show him the best spots to go dancing?

Would I ever, breathed Peggy. Even if I haven't got any new jewellery to brighten myself up, I don't reckon he'll care. She checked the date and worked it out on her fingers. She could go on Friday — in two days' time. Suddenly the world didn't seem so bad after all.

11

Friday night was often busy at the first-aid post in the church hall, even if there wasn't a raid. Gladys busied herself tidying the bandages, which the previous shift had left in a mess, humming as she did so. People got careless on Fridays. Even though the working week was hardly over, what with all the extra shifts, and then everyone pulling together to fire-watch or perform other home-front duties, the idea still remained: welcome in the weekend with a trip to the pub or night out at the cinema with chips after.

Then a fight might break out, or an accident happen, as well as the regular injuries from damaged buildings, ruined roads or pavements. You never knew who would walk through the door on a Friday, or in what state. That was why she liked to have all her equipment in order, the bandages rolled and arranged in order of size and shape. That could save precious seconds.

'Aren't you good, Gladys. You're never still for a minute,' said Mrs Freeman, who was the other nurse on duty. She had installed herself in an armchair in one corner of the draughty hall, and was drinking a cup of tea. She peered at Gladys over her glasses, which made her look rather like an owl.

'I like things to be ready so we're not caught out,' said Gladys mildly. She quite liked Mrs

Freeman, who was at least twice her age, and had once been a proper nurse in a hospital and so was very experienced. Of course, when she married she had had to give up working, and Gladys knew she had three children, all teenagers now. Yet Gladys wasn't entirely sure that the older woman always said or did the right thing. She wasn't very up-to-date with new methods, which Gladys followed assiduously in the *Queen's Nurses Magazine*, and from listening intently to everyone in the Victory Walk home. It had also become apparent that Mrs Freeman was more than happy to sit down and supervise while Gladys ran around doing most of the work. Still, she wasn't bad company, and didn't go to pieces in a crisis.

Gladys looked up as a woman rushed in, all of a fluster, pulling her coat closed with one hand as she swept her pale hair off her forehead. 'Oh, nurse. I do hope you can help me.'

Gladys immediately set aside the bandages. 'Yes, what's wrong? Please sit down, and take a deep breath. There, that's better.'

The woman perched uneasily on the edge of the old wooden chair, looking as if she might spring up again at any moment. 'I need advice,' she said. 'I don't know what to do for the best.'

Gladys nodded. 'Are you injured?' She couldn't see any signs but it was as well to check.

'Oh no. It's not for me.' The woman's expression was confused, as if she hadn't expected the question.

'I see,' said Gladys, although she didn't, or not yet. 'So, what is the trouble?' She hoped the

112

woman wasn't making things up just to get attention. Sometimes that happened and Gladys was never sure how best to make the person go away.

'It's Ma.' The woman clasped and reclasped her hands. 'She went and got diabetes, you see. It's ever so hard. I try to keep an eye on her but I got to work all funny hours now my kids went off to their other gran in the country. She don't take her medicine right.'

Gladys looked across to Mrs Freeman, who must surely know this condition better than she herself did, but her colleague was taking no notice of what was happening on the other side of the hall. She was studying an old copy of the *Radio Times*.

Gladys exhaled slowly. This was something she knew a little about. She had read articles in the magazine and spoken to some of the other nurses. 'That must be difficult,' she said kindly. 'Does she have to take insulin?'

The woman smiled hesitantly. 'Yes, that's it. I never remember the word, but that's what it's called.'

Gladys nodded. 'And she's under the care of a doctor?'

The woman nodded, more confident now. 'Yes, but her usual one went off to the army and she don't like the new feller. Reckons he don't know what he's talking about.'

Gladys frowned. 'That's not very likely, really. They have to train for years, you know.' She knew how hard the local doctors worked, but supposed it must be hard if you didn't want to take the medicine — it was easier to blame someone else.

'Well, she won't talk to him no more. Then she goes all funny, loses her balance and whatnot. I can't make her see sense.' The woman stopped and gave a small sniff, wiping her eye hurriedly with the back of her hand. 'I can't stay home and mind her, I just can't. I got to do my job, we need the money as well as everything else.'

Gladys nodded in sympathy. She knew exactly how that felt. Then inspiration struck. 'Would she talk to a district nurse?' she asked. 'There's one in particular who has treated a lot of diabetic patients. She might be able to help her and then that would put your mind at rest.'

The woman brightened. 'Do you think she would agree?' she asked. 'Ma doesn't mind the nurses. She says they're more sensible than the doctor.'

Gladys smiled. 'This one's very sensible. You want to speak to Bridget, that's Nurse O'Doyle, at the Victory Walk Nurses' Home. Do you know where that is? Your doctor can refer you.' She knew that Bridget had once had a deep fear of needles, which she'd managed to hide even from her best friend Ellen for years. Bridget had persuaded Gladys to help her practise, and Gladys had borrowed one of her youngest sister's squashy rubber balls so that they could try injecting it. She herself wasn't qualified to give injections, but she'd watched Bridget, and knew that the Irish nurse now sometimes helped out at Dr Patcham's special diabetic clinic.

The woman stood up again, far happier now

114

that she'd got the worry off her chest. 'Thank you, I'll do that first thing Monday. I can watch her myself over the weekend, but knowing there's someone to turn to, that's such a help. Thank you,' she repeated, as she stood and turned to go.

Well, thought Gladys, watching her leave, if that's the sort of thing we have to deal with this evening, then it'll be a doddle.

Just then, there came a loud crash. Mrs Freeman jumped up and dropped the *Radio Times*. 'Good heavens, whatever is that?'

The blackout curtain blocking the front door billowed and two figures fell into the hall. It was dimly lit at the far end, and Gladys had to squint to make out what looked like a middle-aged man, his face hidden by the brim of his battered trilby, and a young woman on the verge of collapse. She swayed and reached out one hand to the distempered wall.

'Right,' grunted the man, 'they'll see to yer,' and he hurried out again before his companion could protest. The woman — surely scarcely more than a girl — slumped to the floor. Gladys rushed across, realising that Mrs Freeman wouldn't be able to see much with the combination of low light and her thick glasses.

'My God.' Gladys looked at the woman before her with a sick feeling of dread in her stomach. That bright blue coat was familiar. So was the hair and the once-glamorous clutch bag, its beads now hanging loose. So were the groans emanating from the figure's throat.

'Evelyn, what on earth has happened to you?'

115

She crouched and caught the unmistakable whiff of sour alcohol. 'Evelyn, are you drunk? Oh God. Here, let me help you up. Come, sit over here. Are you all right? Did you get hurt, or what?'

Evelyn was a dead weight and floppy as a rag doll as she half-steered, half-dragged her over to the nursing station and deposited her on the wooden chair. Evelyn slumped forward and Gladys caught her before she fell onto the splintered floorboards. 'Put your head down on my desk if it'll help,' she hissed, hoping against hope that Mrs Freeman hadn't realised exactly what was going on. 'Listen to me, Evelyn, don't go to sleep. Are you hurt? This is a first-aid post, you know. It's for people who have had accidents, not gone out and drunk too much.'

Evelyn raised her head a little and glared at her sister. 'Why're you here?' she mumbled.

Gladys was instantly relieved that at least her sister could speak and had recognised her, and then furious that she was in such a state. 'Because I work here,' she said with barely concealed anger. 'I'm a Civil Reserve nurse, remember. You've ended up at my post. So what are you doing? Did you fall over or something? Can you feel anything?'

Evelyn hiccupped and rubbed her eyes, smearing the boot polish that was a poor substitute for the hard-to-come-by mascara. 'Ankle,' she said after a pause. 'Fell and hurt my ankle.'

'Let me see.' Gladys bent to look, noticing her sister was wearing high-heeled patent sandals that she hadn't seen before. She herself could not have walked in them even when sober; no wonder Evelyn had lost her balance after goodness knows how many drinks.

Sure enough, one ankle was swollen and tender to the touch. 'Argh, what are you doing?' Evelyn protested as her big sister carefully felt around the joint. 'Put it down, put it down.'

'It's for your own good,' Gladys said brutally. 'You came in here wanting help, well, that's what I'm giving you. You've twisted your ankle, most likely sprained it. I'll strap it up enough to get you home and then you'll have to keep it raised up. We'll soak a towel in cold water and wrap it round it. Did you hear me, Evelyn? Don't drop off. You'll need to rest it for days, if not longer, I should think.'

That made the younger woman sit up, alert now. 'No, no, I can't do that,' she said, eyes frantic.

'You'll have to.' Gladys reached for the right bandage, just where she'd left it earlier in the evening. 'Sit still now while I take your shoe off.'

'You don't understand,' Evelyn wailed. 'If I'm not there they'll choose somebody else and that'll be it, I'll have missed my chance.'

'I understand ankles,' said Gladys firmly. 'You aren't going anywhere until yours is better.'

Evelyn began to sob. 'You don't care, you've never cared, this is my big chance and you're trying to stop me.'

Gladys finished bandaging the badly swollen ankle and fastened the end with a safety pin. 'Keep your leg still or it'll scratch you,' she said as she completed the task, before coming to sit at the same level as her sister. 'Now what do you mean? What can be so important that you won't take the time to rest your injury?'

Evelyn sobbed again and would not meet her eyes. 'They've got visitors coming to the pub tomorrow,' she said between sniffing and wiping her nose with a ragged lacy handkerchief. 'Proper important ones. Maybe one from America, even. They want me to sing for them. This is my big break, I know it.'

'Broken ankle more like,' said Gladys crossly. 'Don't be daft, Evelyn, you aren't going to be able to walk on this by tomorrow evening. You'll just have to sing for them another time.'

Evelyn twisted the handkerchief tightly around her fingers. 'It's no good. That Patty Walker, she's always been jealous of me, and she wanted to do it. Now they'll let her and she'll end up on stage when it should have been me.'

Gladys sighed deeply. This was not the time to talk sense into her sister. She would probably have forgotten it all in the morning anyway, and wake up wondering what had happened to her ankle. Surreptitiously she checked her watch. Her shift was nearly over.

'Come on, fasten your coat. I'll help you home,' she said, thankful it was not far to go. 'Put your arm around my shoulder and hop on your good foot.'

Evelyn pulled a face. 'Oh why would I even expect you to understand,' she said, her expression turning vicious, 'you're just a bleeding nurse. A skivvy in the daytime and in the evening just a bleeding nurse.' Her voice rose in frustrated fury, alerting Mrs Freeman at the far end of the hall, who rose and made her way over.

'Everything all right?' she said, her words kind but her tone steely. Now her thick glasses made her look stern.

'All under control,' said Gladys with a cheerfulness she did not feel. 'It's time I was going. I'll take this patient with me — we are heading the same way.' The last thing she wanted was for her colleague to realise Evelyn was a relative.

Mrs Freeman drew herself up to her full height. 'If you're sure, then maybe that's for the best.' Her face showed that she had caught the potent fumes of stale alcohol. 'I'll shut up everything after you, then.'

Gladys nodded in gratitude. 'Thank you,' she said, hauling Evelyn to her feet, grabbing her own bag and her sister's gaudy but ragged one. She knew she would be in for a grilling the next time they were rostered together, but at that moment she didn't care. She just wanted to get Evelyn home without any further mishaps. 'Off we go, then.'

Evelyn glared at her but, having little choice, went along, hopping unsteadily on her one high sandal. Gladys shuffled around until she got the best angle to help her sister, through the creaking big door and out into the street, lit by little other than the antiaircraft beams crisscrossing the night sky.

'He'll kill me,' Evelyn muttered, now more sad than angry.

'Who?' asked Gladys.

Evelyn didn't answer.

'Was it the man who just dumped you here?' Gladys persisted. She'd been too caught up in her sister's predicament to wonder about the circumstances of her arrival, but now she thought about it, she was filled with anger towards the man who had simply disappeared. 'Who's he when he's at home, anyway?'

Evelyn sniffed again. 'That's Max,' she said. 'His brother runs the pub. Max does the entertainment side.'

Gladys raised her eyes to the heavens. 'Does that include getting his singers drunk?' she asked.

'Don't be like that, he was only being kind. He's very kind to me, he is, he's kind a lot.' Evelyn was rambling, and Gladys knew she would get little sense from her. But she was filled with disgust at someone who pretended to be on the girl's side and then left her at the church hall door, without so much as checking if she was all right. Anything could have happened to Evelyn, she realised. Somehow she would have to try to persuade her never to go near this Max again.

12

Peggy dismounted from the bus, pleased to be away from the press of people which had meant she had had to stand the whole way from Dalston to the West End. She was glad that she had thought to put her best dancing shoes in her bag and wear her old flat work shoes, or she'd have started the evening with sore feet before the fun had even begun. Still, it was hard not to get caught up in the general air of excitement that pulsed through the crowds on the busy streets. Dusk was turning to nightfall but the pavement was heaving.

Quickly she found a shop doorway with a broad windowsill. Brushing it clean as best she could, she sat down, opened her bag and drew out her shiny shoes with their delicate diamanté buckles, changing into them.

'Look at those legs,' said a young man in a naval uniform, nudging his army friend. 'Coming dancing with me, are yer?'

Peggy could tell there was no menace behind the comment, just a sailor trying his luck.

'Fat chance,' she said cheerfully, fastening her bag again. She wondered whether to add a pointed barb about him being barely old enough to shave, then decided against it. He was probably off risking his life for his country most of the time, and this was his one chance to have a bit of relaxation and fun.

She threaded her way between her fellow revellers until she was approaching Leicester Square tube station. She had been relieved that James had suggested meeting there, as she wasn't sure she would like to meet the other GIs at the dormitory. That would make her feel as if she was part of a couple and she didn't know if that was what she wanted. She scarcely knew him. He came from a foreign country. He was hardly ever in London and when he was away would be facing who-knew-what dangers. The list of why she should not take any of this seriously went on and on.

Then she caught sight of him and all her misgivings fell away.

His eyes lit up at the sight of her and Peggy found herself almost running the last few steps, only to come to a halt just in front of him, unsure about whether to shake his hand, give him a peck on the cheek, or what. She didn't know what he would expect. What did people do in America?

'You came,' he said, and reached out to hug her. She fell into his warmth, not giving a fig what anyone around them thought. His uniform jacket was scratchy but she didn't care. For a moment she felt safer than she could remember, as if she had come home. Then he released her and held her off at arm's length, drinking her in.

'Of course I did,' she said, slightly breathless. 'Couldn't pass up the chance of a dance, now could I?'

'Even with an old crock of a Yank?' he said, raising one eyebrow, but laughing as he did so.

'Not so old, I think.' She fell into step with him, tucking her arm through his. The breeze was colder now, a sure sign summer was ending and autumn on its way. She stopped herself thinking about time passing by and tried to concentrate on every precious minute.

'So, where are you taking me?' he asked. 'My friends are all jealous that I've got me a local guide.'

Peggy smiled. 'The ballroom near here. They'll have a dance band — they're very good. You won't be disappointed.'

'No,' he said, turning to face her and melting her heart with his warm gaze. 'No, I dare say I won't.'

For a second it was as if they were the only people on the street. Time stood still. Then the hubbub returned and they had to move along or get swept away with the momentum of the crowds; all the hundreds of people determined to defy the war and celebrate the weekend as best they could.

'Come on then. It's this way.' Peggy ushered him around the corner, glad of his arm to lean on as groups coming the other way pushed against her, threatening to topple her from her high heels. There was a queue forming but not so long that they wouldn't get in. They took their place among young people in every sort of uniform, and many in civvies too, all animated at the prospect of dancing the night away.

James looked up at the impressive building with its tall columns and grand air. 'What is this place?' he wondered.

Peggy giggled. 'Believe it or not, it used to be the opera house. They stopped all that when the war began and now it's a ballroom. You can go dancing every day of the week, if you've got the stamina.' She looked up at him with a cheeky grin. 'We used to go to the Café de Paris but that got bombed. So now this is the place to see the latest dance steps.'

They moved forward, nearing the front of the queue. 'Can you jitterbug?' he asked, reaching for his wallet.

Peggy hesitated. 'Well, no.' She unhooked her scarf from around her neck, expertly rolled it up and stuffed it in her coat pocket.

He smiled down at her. 'You mean, 'not yet'.'

★ ★ ★

Two hours later, and Peggy could honestly say that she could now do the jitterbug. Her leg muscles ached and her hair had come loose from its slides, but without a shadow of a doubt she knew the steps and could keep up with the best of them.

'You look as if you could do with a drink,' James commented, giving her his arm again and leading her up to the balcony where the refreshments were being served. 'You seriously didn't know that dance before? I wouldn't have guessed. You sure picked it up quick.'

Peggy sank onto a chair with a padded velvet seat and rested her tired feet on a railing. 'Oh boy. I've never known anything like it.' She closed her eyes for a second. 'Helps to have a

124

good teacher of course.'

'Of course.' His eyes danced with merriment. 'What can I get you — a shandy?'

Peggy shook her head and her hair swung away from her face. 'No, just a lemonade. I'm so thirsty.'

He ducked into the crowd clamouring for drinks and she leant back in the chair, exhausted but happier than she could remember. Was it wrong to feel like this, with Pete only eighteen months dead? But she couldn't waste her life. She didn't know when moments like these would come again. She smoothed her skirt, in a silky eau-de-nil fabric, which she hadn't worn since . . . she gave a little start as she realised it would have been when Pete had been home on what turned out to be his final leave and they had gone to a party with some of his friends. She wouldn't feel guilty. Those had been happy days, and maybe her luck was now finally on the turn.

Here came James balancing two glasses of lemonade, his face open and smiling. She felt a small somersault in her stomach.

★ ★ ★

'Here, let me help you with your coat.' It was late and the ballroom was emptying after the final dance of the evening. Peggy had danced every one with James, apart from those when she'd had to insist on sitting it out to catch her breath. She was too hot to want her coat, but knew it would be chilly once they left the building. She appreciated his gentlemanly gesture as he held it for her, its shiny lining catching the lights as he swung it around her shoulders. She fished out her scarf and wrapped it around her neck.

'Let me.' He took it and carefully tied it around her neck, his fingers brushing against her throat. She shivered at the touch.

'Too cold?' he asked, with concern but also with humour.

'Not at all.' He knew exactly what he was doing, Peggy thought. She wasn't going to stop him.

The streets around Covent Garden were still busy, with those who had stayed until the bitter end of the dance and others who were simply wandering. The crowds were relishing an evening out with no sirens warning of incoming planes, while as ever the antiaircraft beams lit the sky above the city.

Peggy hugged James's arm as they strolled along, putting off the moment when she would have to find her way home. She pointed out the landmarks, the market, the actors' church, the old pubs. He took it all in, laughing, saying he'd heard about some of the places but had never imagined when he was growing up that one day he would be walking those very streets.

'With my own special guide,' he added, squeezing her hand. She took her other hand from her pocket and squeezed his back, confident now with him from their night of dancing, holding each other close, marvelling at how well they fitted together.

'It's only fair,' she said lightly. 'You teach me to jitterbug, I show you the sights. There, that's the Lamb and Flag — it's been there for ever. We could go there when you next have leave, if you like.' She knew that some would have told her she was being forward with a remark like that, but she found she didn't care.

'Yes, I'd like that,' he grinned. 'It will be good for my education. A history lesson, you could say. Where I'm from, we don't have much real old stuff like this.'

'Where is that, then? I thought you came from New York. You sound like they do in the films.'

'You're close,' he said. 'We ain't so far from there. You could live in our little town and go to work in the city if you've a mind to. Some folks do. My pop tried it but he said he couldn't keep an eye on us kids all the time — that's me, my brother that I told you about, and our little sister. So he got a job in a garage closer to home. Mom prefers it that way too. We ain't got anything historic there though. So I'd be mighty grateful if you showed me what you got here.'

She laughed, enjoying his rich voice with its intriguing accent. 'It's a deal, then.'

They heard a sudden scuffling noise and the shadowy narrow alley behind the pub disgorged a couple, both obviously the worse for drink, the woman hastily rearranging her skirt and tugging her coat into place, the man finishing buttoning his trousers, both with hair awry, giggling and staggering as they came out onto the broader pavement. There was little doubt about what they had been doing.

Peggy looked askance at James. She wasn't one to judge, especially given some of the scrapes she had got into since Pete had died, with drink being to blame for the worst of them. She didn't know how her new friend would react, though. Some people said GIs had loose morals and would try to get away with anything; others claimed the Americans were very strict and looked down on British women who were free with their favours. She hadn't seen a trace of either extreme in James, but you never knew.

He slowed down, putting pressure on her arm so that she came to a halt, allowing the couple to stagger along and out of sight. He sighed. 'I would never do that to you, Peggy. I hope you know that.'

She turned towards him and he put his arms around her, but looked her steadily in the eye. She could just make out his intense expression in the silver light.

'I know we haven't had a chance to spend much time together,' he went on, 'but I got to tell you, this isn't just a bit of fun. Well, not for me anyway.' He paused to take a breath. 'Sure, we have fun, and I love that. But . . . I respect you, Peggy. That's important to me. I wouldn't take advantage, just so that you know.'

Peggy gulped. This was suddenly turning serious, catching her unawares. But she couldn't pretend he hadn't spoken. 'No . . . I didn't think you would. I . . . I trust you, James.' She realised this was true as she said it and what a big thing it was to admit. Many men had indeed taken advantage of her, knowing she was vulnerable, or simply not caring. She understood deep down that this one was different.

'Good.' He bent down and tipped her chin up a little with his warm finger. Then he brought his lips to hers and kissed her, gently, then with more insistence.

Peggy felt her knees begin to melt. This was no drunken smooching after a dance or fumble after closing time at the pub. This meant something. She wasn't entirely sure what. She kissed him back.

She had no idea how long had passed before they stopped.

He pulled her head onto his shoulder and hugged her close, and even if the jacket was still scratchy, she didn't mind in the slightest. She held him tight, tighter than when they had been dancing, for the full wonder of being close to him, to feel his heart beating through his staid uniform.

'Some of my comrades have been sneaking girls in after dark, but I ain't going to do that, Peggy,' he said. 'We ain't got much time together, but I wouldn't ask that of you.'

'Then we'll just do this.' Peggy sighed into the stiff wool. She didn't fancy sneaking into a dormitory, no matter how well she fitted into his arms.

'We've got all the time in the world, I just know it,' he said confidently.

Peggy said nothing, hugging him even tighter, hoping against hope that it was true.

13

Edith waited until the biggest table in the dining area was free and then commandeered it, spreading out her papers. There was a big map of the south of England, a more detailed map of south London showing railway and tram stops, a set of various timetables and a notebook. Finally she took out a pencil from her cardigan pocket and set to work.

'What are you doing?' Belinda came across from the service area to see, pushing back the sleeves on her red and white gingham shirt.

Edith looked up. 'Oooh, is that new?'

Belinda laughed and gave a shrug. 'Sort of. It's made from a tablecloth. Miriam, you know, Gwen's friend, was having a clear-out and I thought I could make something of this.'

Edith nodded, impressed. 'I didn't know you were so handy with a needle and thread.'

Belinda frowned. 'I wasn't really. It's important to try, though, isn't it? I've been having a few lessons from Miriam, as she knows what she's on about.'

'I didn't realise you knew her so well.' Edith put her pencil down.

'She sort of knows my parents from ages ago. We got talking one time when she came round to see Gwen and she asked if I was their daughter

— one of those coincidences. Anyway, they'd just started putting up those 'Mrs Sew-and-Sew' posters to encourage us to make do and mend, and she offered to teach me, so I said yes. And here's the result!' She spread her arms out and performed a twirl. Edith dutifully clapped. 'I took the buttons from an old summer frock that was falling apart, it had been washed so often.' The little mother-of-pearl buttons twinkled softly in the remains of the autumn sunlight. 'I suppose I could have saved my coupons for one of those new Utility blouses but they're still so expensive. I just fancied something that at least looked new, to cheer myself up. To think you can't even buy a bar of soap on impulse now that it's rationed — I always loved to do that, but it will have to wait. Anyway, you didn't answer my question.' She stood over Edith, her hands on her hips, clearly not moving until she had an answer.

'Well.' Edith pushed her dark curls from her forehead and leant back. 'I want to go to see Harry, now he's recovering from his last big operation. He's in a hospital in the middle of nowhere. I can take a day's leave, so I'm trying to work out the best way of getting there and back. If everything runs on time I reckon I can do it.'

Belinda pulled out a chair and sat opposite her friend, aware that she towered over her while she stood. 'That's a big 'if', isn't it?'

'Not much I can do about it.' Edith sighed. 'I've got to see him. I won't know how he really is until I do. He always says he's doing well, but that's what he's like — he wouldn't want to worry me if he wasn't recovering properly.' She tried hard not to let her worry show in her expression, but Belinda wasn't fooled for a moment.

'Not easy, is it?' she said. Then, knowing Edith would not want to dwell on what she couldn't change, she peered at the map. 'Show me where the hospital is.'

Edith pointed to a small town near the border between Sussex and Surrey. 'It's around there. Look at that, all that lovely fresh country air he'll be having.' She shivered.

Belinda laughed. 'Not a fan of the country-side, then?'

Edith shook her head. 'Give me the city any day. That's all I know, really. It was bad enough doing that training year in Richmond. No, it wouldn't suit me at all. Nothing to do but watch the sheep.'

Belinda smiled but her mind was clearly racing. 'There's something familiar about those names . . . that village. No, hang on,' she raised a hand to interrupt her colleague before she could speak, 'it'll come to me . . . I know. It's where Geraldine used to live. She's still got family there.'

'Geraldine?' Edith frowned.

'Yes, you remember, one of the ambulance drivers from Hackney Downs. You're bound to have come across her. Short sandy hair, bright blue eyes.'

Edith scratched her head and then the penny dropped. 'The one who slams into first gear like

132

she is trying to wake the dead?'

Belinda grinned. 'That'll be her. I'm going to the cinema with her later, as it happens. I can ask her for advice.'

'All right.' Edith smiled back. 'That's kind of you. What are you seeing?'

Belinda pulled a face. 'She wants to go to *In Which We Serve* but I fancy something a bit lighter to cheer us up. That Gert and Daisy film, something like that. I've had enough of serious stuff.'

Edith caught her undertone. 'How's your brother? Have you heard from him lately?'

'He's all right, or at least he was, the last letter I had.' Belinda's face showed that she didn't want to talk about David the pilot any more. She worried enough about him as it was. 'So I had better be off. But your maps have given me an idea.'

Edith looked quizzically at her. 'What?'

Belinda shook her head and tapped her nose. 'Never mind. It may come to nothing. I'll let you know.'

* * *

One week later, early in the chilly morning, Edith stood outside the nurses' home in her siren suit and shivered. She wasn't sure if it was in the cold or with nerves. 'I must be mad,' she muttered.

Belinda stood beside her, wrapped in a warm coat, woolly scarf almost covering the lower part of her face. 'Don't be silly. You'll be all right. It's easier than taking five trains and six buses, isn't it?'

'It wasn't five,' said Edith petulantly.

Belinda shrugged and drew her coat more tightly around her.

Edith cast her a jealous look. She herself wore a short jacket, which Belinda had said would be best, and so her legs were cold. She checked that her leather gloves were properly fastened. Why had she allowed herself to be talked into this? Nervously she patted the big satchel slung across her front.

'What have you got in there?' Belinda asked, her breath puffing a little in the chilly air.

'Proper clothes,' said Edith. 'So's I can get changed when I get there.'

'Harry wouldn't care if you were wearing a sack, as long as you're there,' Belinda pointed out.

'Yes, but I care,' Edith retorted, her teeth chattering.

The sound of an exhaust firing split the air and there was movement at the end of Victory Walk. The pair of them hurriedly made their way to where Geraldine was pulling up on her motorbike, taking off her helmet and shaking her short hair.

'Morning!' she called brightly. 'You all set, Edith?'

Edith's face said that she would sooner walk across hot coals, but she lifted her chin resolutely. 'Yes, thanks.' She looked nervously at the machine. 'What do I do?'

Geraldine handed her a spare helmet. 'You put

that on and climb up behind me.'

Edith took it and fumbled with the strap. 'It'll squash my hair,' she groaned. 'And how do I get up there? It's all right for you, Belinda, you've got long legs.'

'Look, you rest your feet on these little bars here. If you can get up on the windowsill to climb in after curfew, then this'll be a piece of cake. Here, I'll help you.'

Belinda boosted Edith up onto the pillion seat, and Geraldine obligingly shifted forward. Edith cautiously balanced her satchel behind her. 'Are you sure this is all right?' she asked. 'What about petrol restrictions?'

Geraldine shook her head and looked backwards over her shoulder at her first-time passenger. 'You let me worry about that,' she said. 'Just hang on tight and you won't have a thing to worry about.' Before Edith could object, she started the engine once more, causing a few curtains to twitch in annoyance in the neighbouring terrace of houses.

Edith could only do as she was told as the bike wheeled around in a neat circle and took off.

★ ★ ★

Edith forgot all about the journey as soon as she saw Harry. He was sitting in the grand entrance vestibule of the hospital, in his army uniform trousers but with a hospital gown on top, his uniform jacket draped around his shoulders. She had persuaded Geraldine to drop her off at the edge of the grounds, before the big sweep of a driveway, so that she could find somewhere to change. Feeling very daring, she had pushed her way into an overgrown copse and swiftly stepped out of the siren suit, which had at least kept her fairly warm, and pulled on the pretty skirt she had bundled into her satchel. It had a bright geometric print that she thought he would appreciate — that, and it nipped in at her waist, making the most of what curves she had. She rolled up the siren suit and shoved it into the satchel, ready for the return trip.

Now all worries left her as she saw him stand and come towards her. 'Harry!' She broke into a run for the final few paces, hugging him tightly on one side, careful not to jog his bad arm. His good arm came around her and squeezed her close to him. She did not quite come to his shoulder.

'Let's go out into the sunshine,' he said. 'It was all misty earlier — I wasn't sure that you'd make it.' He kissed the top of her head, breathing in the unique scent that was hers.

'Oh, it was no trouble,' she said, dismissing the terrors of the ride. Towards the end, if truth be told, she had begun to relax and almost enjoy herself. Standing back a little she took in the sight of him. Was he thinner or was that her imagination? Her eyes went to his face. The side where his burns had been was noticeably tighter and shinier, now he'd had the skin graft. 'How did it go really, Harry? Your face . . . it's still a bit pink.'

Harry strode out of the glass-paned front doors and then waited for her. The air had warmed up and it was pleasant, with fallen leaves blowing and crunching underfoot on the wide drive. 'I told you, everything went according to plan.'

'Yes, I know.' Edith watched him carefully. 'Does it still hurt? Just a bit?'

Harry raised his good arm and touched his face where the new skin had taken. 'Honest, Edie, it's all right. I know it's still not quite right but you should have seen it when they first did it.'

'Yes I should!' she cried, then bit her lip. Getting upset wouldn't help. 'Sorry. I just worry about you, you know that. Having a general anaesthetic is never without risk.'

Harry grinned, somewhat lopsidedly but a grin nevertheless. 'Stop being a nurse, Edie. It will keep on getting better. I've got all sorts of salve to put on it so it doesn't go all stiff. Don't look like that, I'm not showing you the stuff or you'll only go looking it up when you get back. The doctors are happy with me, that's the main thing.'

Edith nodded, and allowed him to put his good arm across her shoulder as they walked along, the trees showing their autumn colours and smoke from a bonfire rising almost vertically in the distance. She put her arm around his waist, making sure not to jog the arm on the far side. 'And how did the other operation go?' she asked quietly.

'They reckon it will give me much more movement,' he said. 'I'll never have the biceps and triceps like they were before, but they're confident. It's just got to heal and I can start getting back to normal.'

She flashed a look back up at him. 'That's good to hear.'

He chuckled. 'Let's go down this way, there's a bit of a valley where it'll be even warmer.' He guided her across the broad swathe of grass and into a dip, which shielded them from sight of the big hospital building with its many windows.

Edith tilted back her head and let the sun warm her face, banishing the remnants of her concerns. She had been deeply fearful of what he would be like, knowing how he always gave a rosy picture even when he was in considerable pain. Yes, his face still looked more damaged than she would have wanted, but he was right, she hadn't seen it immediately following the skin graft and so had no idea how much better he was now.

Anyway, it didn't matter. She wanted him to look as normal as possible because she knew that would make him happier and his life easier. But for herself she didn't mind. He was still her Harry. That was all that was important.

After a few minutes they came to a big branch which must have broken off in the first of the autumn storms. 'Shall we sit down?' he suggested.

Edith carefully sank onto the wood, testing it for balance. It would never do to have successfully survived her first ride on a motorbike without falling off, only to go head over heels from a tree branch. 'It seems all right,' she said, moving along so that he could join her.

With a contented sigh she snuggled against him. To think that she had believed she would never do this again. She should count her blessings. Somehow, against all the odds, he was returned to her. A few scars here and there were nothing when set against that.

'Penny for 'em,' he said teasingly.

'All right.' She looked up at him again. 'If you're feeling well enough to talk about getting back to normal, then ... then I reckon we should start planning the wedding. Do you feel ready for that?'

'Ready to make plans?' he said, still teasing. 'You'll be in charge of them, Edie, I know that for a fact. I wouldn't dare interfere.'

She dug him gently with her elbow. 'So just how back to normal do you think you'll be by Christmas?'

He raised his eyebrows, catching her drift, and then looking away as if he couldn't quite give her an answer. 'Ah, if you're asking what I think you're asking ... ' he began, a little evasively. She gave a slight smile and then reached up to him, kissing him gently and then more passionately. His injured face made little difference to her, although at the back of her mind she registered it all felt slightly one-sided. Her arms came around him, pulling her to him, as hard as she dared, scarcely able to believe he was really and truly here with her once more. She broke away only when she was in desperate need of a breath.

'See? You've got nothing to worry about on that score,' she grinned, her eyes warm with longing. 'If only we had somewhere more private . . .'

'If only,' he echoed, although with a hint of hesitation, as if he couldn't quite believe she was here either.

She laughed and ran her hand across his chest, not perhaps as muscular as when they'd first met, but still a physique most would be proud of. How she had missed this, the shape of him, having him so near, her handsome Harry. For a moment she simply wanted to stay like this, not to break the spell. But time was short and she had questions to raise.

'Do you want to get married in church?' she asked hesitantly. 'As a Catholic I'm not even meant to go into your church, you know, though I did for Alan's christening. Should we do it in my church? You'd have to convert though. Or how about the register office?'

He shifted against her, exhaling slowly, and she felt his breath on her face.

'I don't mind,' he said. 'Would it be easier to have it at the register office? Or is it important to you that it should be in church?'

Edith thought for a second. 'No,' she said. 'It's much more important that we're married, and I don't care where. If it's easier, let's not worry about which church, as we're bound to offend somebody either way.'

Harry snorted. 'It's our day, not theirs. It's your day, most of all. So you have it where you like.'

Edith nodded, her forehead brushing against the warmth of his shirt. 'Good. We'll do that then. Shall we all go back to your parents' afterwards or how about hiring somewhere?'

At that he sat up straight. 'Now you know as well as I do that Ma will be very upset if we go anywhere else,' he said at once. 'She won't have that.'

Edith agreed immediately. 'I don't want to cause her extra bother but I can't think of anywhere I'd rather be.'

'Why don't you go and see her as soon as possible and tell her,' Harry suggested, and Edith cut him off before he could finish.

'I was going to anyway — she'll want to know how you are from the horse's mouth,' she assured him. 'I know you send her letters saying you're right as rain, but she believes them about as much as I do.'

Harry half-laughed, half-sighed as he settled his back against the curve of the branch. 'Sounds as if you have me all sorted out,' he said. 'You two just go ahead and make all the arrangements, tell me where I've got to be and when, and I'll turn up.'

Edith cocked her head to one side. 'As long as you realise that, then we're all right.' She paused. 'Who will be your best man?'

Harry made a wry face. 'That depends. I'd love to ask Joe of course, but he might not get leave. I can try. If he can't, then Billy.'

'Good.' Edith was very fond of both men, but knew how deep the bond was between the Banham brothers, even though they were chalk and cheese in many respects. She wasn't sure where Joe was at present; Alice hadn't mentioned him lately. She wondered how pleased her friend would be to see the oldest Banham son back home where he belonged.

14

Gladys sighed. Now that the nights were drawing in, it was becoming more and more difficult to go to the victory garden in between finishing work at the nurses' home and starting her first-aid shift. She didn't like to ask to leave early, or to take time in the middle of the day, but perhaps she would have to. After all, she was picking vegetables for the nurses to eat, but she'd always prided herself on managing to do that in her own time. It was good to have some help.

Mary wasn't the most experienced gardener but she could be trusted to cut chard leaves and soon she had filled her trug. 'Is this enough?' she called.

Gladys stood up, easing her aching spine by bending backwards. She knew that the big leaves cooked down to a fraction of their original size and that they would need as much as they could carry, but she didn't want to be discouraging. 'Nearly,' she called back.

'Better pass me that little wooden crate then, as I can't fit any more in this,' Mary replied. Gladys moved across the plot, as Mary stood up as well. Voices from the pavement drifted over to them and Mary turned her head in recognition.

'Hello — Billy, is that you?' She peered towards the figures in the gathering gloom. There was no doubt that one of them was the ARP warden, but still in his working clothes from the docks. The other two were also vaguely familiar, one with glasses and one taller, a little stooped. She couldn't remember their names but seemed to recall they had been in the Duke's Arms more than once. They too were in their docker's overalls, with donkey jackets and collars turned up against the late afternoon chill.

'Mary? That you? I see they got you working hard.' Billy grinned and stood on top of the mound of earth dividing the pavement from the vegetable plot. 'Can I give you a hand?'

Gladys stood up straighter at that. 'Oh, we couldn't possibly . . . ' she began.

Mary interrupted to do the introductions. 'Billy, have you met Gladys? I always assume you know everyone at the nurses' home but you might not have seen her — she works behind the scenes, when she's not saving lives at the first-aid post in the evenings.'

Gladys blushed furiously at this effusive praise and almost forgot to hold out her hand in her embarrassment. Hastily she wiped the earth from it and then shook hands with Billy.

'Don't think I've had the pleasure,' he said easily. 'You know my wife Kathleen, I expect? And these are my colleagues, Ronald and Kenny.' Gladys nodded, too shy to shake hands with the strangers as well.

'Oh yes, of course.' Mary beamed, relieved at not being caught out forgetting the men's names. 'Yes, we've met at the Duke's Arms a couple of times, I believe. Is that where you're going now?'

Billy shook his head. 'No, I'm off home to clean up and change before my evening shift.

144

These two are planning a night out elsewhere.'

Ronald shuffled a little. 'It ain't nowhere special, just a place where lots of the other dockers go when they want to get away from the pubs by the river. The Boatman's, down near the canal. You won't know it, it ain't like the Duke's Arms. A bit rough around the edges, you could say.'

'But it's cheap,' Kenny added, wiping his glasses.

Mary gave a shrug, as if to say she wouldn't be seen dead in such a place, but Gladys went rigid. 'Oh.'

Mary swung around to face her friend, curiosity plain on her face.

'I . . . er. No, I never been there,' Gladys said hurriedly, 'but I think it's where my sister goes.' Dismay flooded through her, knowing that Evelyn had started sneaking out again. To hear these men, who must be respectable if they were mates of Billy, call the place a bit rough . . . well, it only reinforced her fears for her sister. But she was powerless to stop her going there. As Evelyn had taunted her, what was she going to do? Lock her in her room? Follow her and cause a fuss? Nothing would work, because Evelyn was determined to keep going there until she had another chance to sing for the important Americans.

She caught the look that passed between Billy's colleagues.

'She sings there,' Gladys blurted out, wanting to make it clear that Evelyn wasn't there to pick up dockers or servicemen, but unsure whether she was making things worse.

Kenny put his glasses back on. 'Oh . . . right. Maybe we've seen her.' He came to an uncomfortable halt.

Ron rushed in to reassure her. 'It ain't all bad down there, you know. It has a bit of a name, I grant you, but you know, the likes of us go there . . . it ain't all bad.' He met her eyes, earnestly trying to backtrack from the impression they'd first given. 'She'll . . . she'll be all right,' he added.

'We best be going,' Billy said. 'Come on, lads, I got to see my Barbara before she has her feed.'

'Give our love to Kath and the children,' Mary said as the three men headed off into the dusk. She turned to her colleague. 'Are you all right, Gladys? You sounded a bit shaky there.'

Gladys took a deep breath. 'Yes, I'm all right. I worry about my sister sometimes but, like they say, it can't be so bad a place if they go there.' She thought about the look in Ronald's eyes as he had tried to make things better, and hoped that somehow there would be enough good men in the pub that her sister could come to no trouble. Yet, with the likes of Max around, it didn't bear thinking about. She rolled back her sleeves with resolution. 'Come on, let's fill that crate with chard and go back before it's dark.'

★ ★ ★

Alice warmed her hands around a welcome cup of cocoa, inhaling its chocolaty scent. She didn't mind that it wasn't as sweet as it used to be; they were all having to become accustomed to less and less sugar. Chocolate itself had been rationed since the summer. Even though she had worn her woollen gloves while riding her bike on her rounds, her fingers were practically numb. It had been a long day.

Her final call had been to a house she'd visited before but for a different member of the family. Perhaps Belinda should have taken this case, as she'd been there at the original incident, and it would have meant fewer complications, but that wasn't how the rota had worked out. So Alice had been left to check on Larry, the little boy who had been crushed by the collapsing wall back in the summer. He'd had to spend some weeks in hospital as he had been very poorly immediately after the accident, but was now back home. Even so, the nurses kept a special eye on him. He'd had an extremely lucky escape.

Larry's gran had been against Alice for years, ever since she'd politely suggested that the children should be evacuated. Larry's sister Pauline had predicted that wouldn't go down well and she had been right. The family had sat tight throughout the Blitz, and the worst thing until now that had befallen them was that the grandmother was suffering from ulcerated legs. Alice had drawn the short straw and nursed her through the worst of it, and the crotchety old woman had reluctantly conceded that she'd done a good job. The kids were staying put, though.

She had therefore been unsure of her welcome at the small terraced house, one of the most rundown she had ever encountered, but as it was the grandmother was out anyway. Pauline had let her in, delighted that her favourite nurse had turned up. 'Gran's ever so much better thanks to you,' she'd said, leading Alice into the filthy sitting room. 'She can walk down the pub on her own now, she don't need me to fetch her gin no more.'

Alice had nodded, unsure whether that was an improvement. 'So who's in charge here now, looking after Larry?'

'Me of course.' Pauline gave her a withering look, as if to say she was stating the obvious. 'Do you want a cuppa?'

Alice shook her head, knowing what state the crockery was in, and reflected that Pauline — who she reckoned must be ten by now — was very probably much more reliable than the grandmother. Even if she was young, she was at least sober. As for Pauline's mother, she seemed to be permanently absent, and there had never been any sign of the father.

Larry had always been small for his age and his accident had not helped, but Alice checked him over and he seemed none the worse for his brush with death. His broken ribs were healing well and he could breathe properly. 'Just make sure you let me or Nurse Adams know if he gets a bad cold or flu,' Alice had said as she repacked her bag. 'His lungs might not be as strong as before. We'll never be sure what he breathed in when he was stuck under those bricks. So don't worry that you're making a fuss over nothing — you make sure to tell us.'

'I will, miss.' Pauline had seen her out of the

house with an expression that made clear she had never worried about making a fuss.

Now Alice smiled to herself. She knew she shouldn't have favourites but Pauline had always been that little bit special — coming from such a background, it was a miracle the way she had survived and kept an eye on her baby brother, let alone done it so cheerfully.

★ ★ ★

'Oh, my poor feet!' Edith collapsed next to her on one of the few sofas in the common room. 'Shove up, Al, room for another. Let me put my poor pins up on that dining chair. Ah, that's better.'

Alice obligingly moved along, although Edith took up hardly any space. She was just letting off steam. 'What's wrong?'

Edith leant back into the lumpy cushions and rolled her eyes. 'Mrs Vallence, you know that new mother I saw last week, couldn't collect her own ration of extra orange juice so I said I'd do it. The shopkeeper knows me, it should have been easy, but no. There was a mix-up and her juice was waiting at another shop further away, then they kept me waiting because the coupons didn't add up — we got it sorted out at last but I could have done without it.'

Alice grunted in sympathy. 'That doesn't sound like much fun. You've got enough to do without fetching someone's orange juice. Still, I bet she was grateful.'

Edith nodded. 'She was. At least I think so.

She could barely keep awake, poor woman — that baby's not sleeping well at all.' She stretched her arms above her head and the loose sleeves of her old grey cardigan fell down to her elbows. 'I must have cycled halfway to Shoreditch and back.'

Alice reached into the pocket of her old tweed skirt. 'Here, this'll help. Have a toffee.'

'Where did you get that? They're like gold dust. Are you sure?'

Alice laughed. 'Course I am. I've had a couple already. My mother sent them. Makes me feel guilty for not going to see her more often.'

Edith turned against the arm of the sofa so that she could look properly at her friend. 'She knows you can't get away very often, Al. It comes with the job and she wouldn't expect it. And don't you even think of going home for Christmas. I shall need you here to help with everything.'

'Pfff, as if I would.' Alice raised her eyebrows. 'I'll be here when needed, you can rely upon it.'

'Good. Because I do.' Edith moved on hastily to the question that was plaguing her. 'Do you think I should tell my family about the wedding? I haven't heard a thing from any of them since Mick wrote to say he got the money I sent. That was ages ago.'

Alice paused before answering. This was a difficult one. Edith had had virtually no contact with any of her family for the entire time they had known one another. They had never approved of Edith becoming a nurse, telling her she was getting above herself. If she was set on going out to work then she should have stayed at home in south London and helped out with her younger brothers and sisters, rather than going off to train elsewhere. There had always been that underlying resentment. Edith had been close only to her older sister, who had died of diphtheria when Edith was about twelve. Some time ago her brother Frankie had tried to winkle money from his sister, claiming it was to get their younger brother Mick out of trouble. Edith had got around that by sending Mick some money direct, believing that Frankie would take a sizeable cut otherwise.

'I suppose it wouldn't hurt to let them know you are getting married,' Alice said slowly. 'After all, if they want to contact you in the future, they'll need to know your new name, won't they?'

Edith beamed at the idea. 'I'm going to be Edith Banham. Doesn't that sound good? No more comments about the name Gillespie being too Irish. You'd think people would have enough on their minds, but every now and again somebody still says it.'

'There's no accounting for such people. You just have to ignore them,' Alice said sombrely, hating the fact that her friend had had to put up with such insults for as long as she could remember.

'I know.' Edith clasped her hands in front of her. 'I think I'll write to tell them but do it just before the wedding so they won't have time to stir up trouble. Frankie is bound to be on active duty anyway. Mick will have had his call-up papers, I expect. He wanted to join up at sixteen so I bet he's raring to go.' She stopped, suddenly sad at the thought of the young man who wasn't as bad as the rest of them putting his life on the line. 'No, there's no chance any of them will want to be there. I mean, if they can't be bothered to send a Christmas card, then they're hardly likely to come all that way north of the river in the depths of winter. It's not as if they wish me well or anything like that.'

She pursed her lips in annoyance. Despite being used to the idea, her family's indifference still stung at times like this. How different it would be if it were Alice getting married: her parents adored her, even though the fact they were up in Liverpool meant they hardly ever saw her. Yet they were always sending her little gifts; nothing fancy as they weren't particularly well off, but tokens to show they thought of her. They were proud of her.

'Write to them,' Alice said decisively. 'Doesn't mean you have to invite them. After all, look at the family you're marrying into. You'll never be without a warm welcome there, that's for sure.'

Edith nodded and leant back again, understanding that what Alice said was absolutely true. The Banhams had fallen over themselves to make sure she felt like one of them, and Flo was like a mother to her. Of course she was ecstatic at the idea of marrying Harry and would have done so no matter what his background; but to have the added bonus of the whole Banham clan to turn to, no matter what, was deeply reassuring.

'I will. Just not yet, then.' She glanced wryly at Alice. 'Does that sound too sneaky?'

'No,' said Alice at once. 'It's being practical. Don't you worry, Edie, we'll be with you on your big day.'

'We certainly will!' cried Mary, coming up behind the sofa, dressed in what looked like a new frock in bright yellow taffeta, far more glamorous than any of the rest of them this grey November evening.

'Going out?' asked Edith. 'Or are you dressing up to brighten our gourmet meal of vegetable and barley stew?'

'Very funny. And how do you know that's what we're having?' Mary plonked herself down on the arm of the sofa, carefully tucking the folds of taffeta underneath her first.

'I can smell it. Is that new?' Despite herself, Edith sounded impressed. It had been a very long while since she had had a new dress, or anything new at all, apart from an updated uniform.

Mary nodded, smoothing the gorgeous fabric. 'A present from Charles. He had it made specially for me.' Then her smile slipped. 'It's because lots of my other frocks don't fit properly any more. I'm losing my curves.' For a moment she looked utterly despondent.

'We all are, even those of us who didn't have many to start with,' sighed Alice. It was true. Increased rationing set alongside such physically demanding work meant that they had all lost weight, despite Gladys's attempts to keep them well fed. If Mary — with her well-connected boyfriend taking her out for posh meals — couldn't keep her figure, what hope was there for the rest of them? Then she brightened. 'Still, chin up. There's been good news from North Africa, have you heard?'

Mary shook her head, clearly thinking that somewhere so remote was of less concern than her immediate worries about changing shape and looking less feminine.

'No, really,' Alice went on, 'it's only come through today, but Rommel's been beaten. It could mean the tide is turning at last. Don't you see, Mary? This is very important. General Montgomery's gained the upper hand.'

Mary brightened at the familiar name. 'Oh, Monty's terribly good. Charles always says so. I always knew he'd win.'

Alice nodded slowly, realising she should have expected that reaction — Mary was never very sharp when it came to current affairs. Still, it made no difference to the impact of the news. It really was something to celebrate.

'We should do something to mark the occasion,' Edith said, filled now with enthusiastic energy. 'How about the cinema later?'

'I can't, I'm afraid, I'm meeting Charles,' Mary said apologetically.

'I can see that,' Edith grinned. 'Al, how about it? We can ask the others. There's a Flanagan and Allen on down at Mare Street. We could go there.'

Alice stood up. 'Yes, why not? I haven't been out for ages. And in that case,' she cast a glance at Mary, 'I'm going to put on something a bit more glamorous than this old skirt. Even if I don't have a new party frock, I feel like dressing up for once.'

15

Peggy pulled her coat more tightly around her against the bitter weather. She hadn't intended staying out so late, but Clarrie's sister was home on leave from her Land Army posting and they'd all gathered at their family's house, enjoying her stories of learning to feed pigs and milk cows. 'It's the uniform that's the worst,' she had complained. 'It's so dull — green and fawn, like we're trying to hide ourselves away in a forest or something. It's enough to get you down.'

But the evening had been such good fun that Peggy didn't feel down at all. She'd given the young woman her first effort at brooch-making to cheer her up, which everyone had agreed was just the ticket. Clarrie's mother could play the banjo and they'd had a bit of a sing-song, before Clarrie had had to go back to the factory for fire-watching. Peggy had said her goodbyes, knowing she should return before Mrs Cannon got back from her own evening out with the WVS so as not to worry the older woman.

It was a cloudy night and the blackout made it feel even darker, so Peggy hesitated before taking the shortcut down the back alley between two rows of terraces. It would save five minutes, though, and in this cold it would be worth it. She grinned as she looked down at her coat, her new luminous buttons reflecting what little light there was. Mrs Cannon had heard about them through her WVS activities and managed to get some, for herself and for her daughter-in-law. 'They'll help keep you safe, dear,' she'd said, and had sewed them on Peggy's coat herself, carefully saving the old chipped ones in case they might come in useful.

Peggy carefully made her way along the alley, hoping to keep clear of whatever filth might have accumulated along the ground over the course of the day. She was concentrating so hard that at first she didn't hear the noise. It was coming from behind her. She stopped, unsure if she had imagined it. At first there was nothing but then it came again. Footsteps? Or was her mind playing tricks on her, making the dark alley seem more dangerous than it actually was? She started walking once more, cross with herself for being so easily spooked.

Before she reached the end of the alley she heard the noise again and now it really did sound like footsteps. They got louder and faster and, just as she was about to turn into the street, something grabbed her shoulder. She tried to scream but a hand came over her mouth and stopped her, pressing hard, a hand that wore a rough leather glove that smelt of engine oil.

'We know what your sort are like,' breathed a voice. 'You're filth, consorting with people like that. Don't think you haven't been seen.' Peggy was powerless to respond as the gruff voice continued. A man's voice, a little breathless, as if he had been running. A London accent. Not someone she recognised. 'You stick to proper men, British men. You stick to your own. You heard me? We'll be watching. Consider yourself warned.' Then he shoved her hard in the back so that she fell, scraping her face on the harsh brick wall of the alley as she did so. Her vision clouded over but she could hear the footsteps running away.

It took a minute or two for her to properly come round — longer than the incident had lasted. Cautiously she put one hand to her face. It came away wet. She smelled the liquid and knew it was blood. The first thought that came into her head was not to let it drip on her coat, which was looking so smart with its new buttons. Fat lot of good they'd been to keep her safe from an attack like this.

Slowly she got to her feet, and reached in her pockets until she found a handkerchief to press against her injured cheek. She tried to work out if she was hurt anywhere else. She didn't think so. For a second she wished she were out with Edith or Alice — they would have known what to do — but of course if she'd been with anyone else this wouldn't have happened anyway. Whoever had done it was a coward, waiting until she was on her own, where she wouldn't be seen and couldn't fight back. What a charmer.

Her best bet was to get home as quickly as possible and then clean herself up before Mrs Cannon saw anything. She would simply say she'd fallen, tripped on something in the blackout. It happened often enough and had some truth to it. She didn't want to frighten the older woman.

Wincing, she cautiously headed for the safety

of their little terraced house with its immaculate brasswork, polished regularly every week, on the front door. The letterbox glinted slightly in the minimal light as she shakily put her key in the lock. The house felt empty; Mrs Cannon had not yet returned. Good.

Peggy hurried to the back kitchen and lit the gas lamp. The tarnished mirror beside the back door revealed a large cut to her temple and a scratched cheek, grit sticking to the drying blood. Hastily she wetted her handkerchief under the cold tap and dabbed away the worst of it. Then she fished around under the sink for an old tea towel, which would at least be clean, wetted that and then took it upstairs to her bedroom to clean up the rest of the damage as best she could.

Only when she had done that and sunk onto the creaky bed, which she and Pete had shared with much laughter and attempts to silence the springs, did she think about the foul warning.

So some random stranger had decided she shouldn't see James again. Peggy gave herself a resolute shake. Well, if they imagined their cowardly attack would stop her, they had another think coming. James was a better man by far than whoever had done this. If anything it had made her even more determined. They'd picked on the wrong woman to try to scare with their underhand tactics. There was no way on this earth that such a thing would prevent her from seeing James again.

★　★　★

Flo busied herself making a big pot of tea, delighted to have her large, homely kitchen full of excited young women. There was little she liked more than planning a big occasion, and occasions didn't come much bigger than this. To add to the challenge, it would happen just before Christmas, so there would be food to find and decorations to put up. Lists would have to be made. She had brought out a big box of pencils, usually kept for Gillian's colouring, and found the end of a roll of wallpaper, so they could write on the back of that.

'Now don't let me hear you say you don't want any fuss,' scolded Mattie, picking up a pencil and twirling it between her fingers. 'We want to make a fuss of you, all right? It's your special day but it's a special day for all of us. So don't try to get out of it.'

Edith shrugged and then gave in and laughed. 'You win, Mattie. Go on, make a fuss of me.'

'Right.' Mattie drew a line on the back of the wallpaper. 'The wedding itself. Even if it's not in church, it has to be special.'

'I've already booked the register office,' Edith said. 'We reckoned lots of people in the services would apply for leave over Christmas and so it would be the most popular time. We made sure to get in there first. So it'll be at eleven thirty, on the twenty-third of December. That's a Wednesday.'

Flo put the teapot down in the centre of the big table, alongside the row of cups ready and waiting. 'Which means we'll have a bit of time to recover before celebrating Christmas itself,' she said happily. 'There you are, help yourselves. Here's the milk.' She reached for an earthenware jug and set it down.

Alice poured a cup for Edith, one for herself and then one for Flo. She knew how hard the older woman had worked already to make the forthcoming day a success, saving food coupons from the minute she'd been told, making two fruit cakes, one for Christmas and one for the wedding. Her own mother had sent a recipe for fake marzipan, using semolina and almond essence, and they just needed to find rice paper to use instead of icing.

'What are you going to wear, Edith?' asked Kathleen, casting an anxious glance towards the fire, beside which stood the big cot with Barbara safely asleep in it. The child had developed the ability to nod off regardless of how much noise was going on, which was a great relief to her parents.

'I can't decide,' Edith said. 'I know it should be something useful that I can wear again, but part of me wants something just for the day — I spend all my time in my sensible nurse's uniform or old clothes. Although I know I'm being silly.'

'Not at all.' Flo understood the younger woman's dilemma only too well. 'You want to look your best for Harry but you don't want to waste coupons or material. Let's have a think.'

Edith frowned. 'It's bound to be cold, for one thing. That rules out a lacy dress for starters.'

'Pity,' said Kathleen. 'You'd look good in one, with your dark hair.'

'What did you wear, Mattie?' Alice tried to

remember if she had seen a photograph.

Mattie put down her pencil. 'It was different then — it was before the war. I had Ma's dress and veil, but the bridesmaids had new frocks. We didn't have to worry as much. Lennie had already joined the army and he was in his uniform. It was in springtime and so I didn't need a coat.' Her expression grew nostalgic and for a moment Alice felt bad for reminding her that Lennie would not be at her brother's ceremony, trapped as he was in his prisoner-of-war camp.

'You looked beautiful,' Flo said proudly. 'I was so pleased you could wear my dress. Maybe one day Gillian will wear it too.' She tilted her head to one side, regarding Edith thoughtfully. 'I'd love to offer it to you, Edie, but I don't think it will fit, if I'm honest. Even if we took it up and took it in . . . '

'No, no, don't even think about it,' Edith said hurriedly. 'I'm so much shorter than either of you, and we were only saying recently how much weight we've all lost.'

'Not that you had any to lose to begin with,' Mattie chipped in. 'Lose any more and you'll get blown away in the next high wind.'

Flo was still thinking hard. 'But the veil, now, that's another story. That fits onto a hairband and could be adapted for anybody. Will you want to wear a veil, do you think?'

Edith drummed her fingers against the well-scrubbed wood of the old table. 'I hadn't thought to, no, because I really assumed I'd wear something practical like a two-piece suit and

162

then it wouldn't go.'

Flo set down her cup. 'Practical be damned. If you want to wear a veil, then so you shall. Let me get it down from the attic.'

Mattie leapt to her feet at once. 'Ma, you're not to. You were only saying yesterday how much your hands ached. Don't you go messing about with that heavy ladder. I'll do it.' She hurried from the room before her mother could object. Flo looked as if she was about to complain and then nodded in resignation. Perhaps her days of racing up ladders really were coming to an end.

'Let's say you did like the veil,' Kathleen said slowly. 'If you had a pale dress of some kind — it needn't be white, but cream, or light grey, or powder blue — maybe it would go. It wouldn't look heavy or strange. How about that?'

Edith's face brightened. 'That's clever, Kath. I like powder blue. I don't have much in that colour but it suits me, if I say so myself.'

Kathleen beamed at the praise. 'We could go down the market, see if they've got some nice material in that colour.'

Alice privately wondered if they might take advantage of Charles's connections to track down the right fabric, as he apparently found it so easy to treat Mary to new frocks, but she knew that Kathleen would love to take Edith shopping. It would be another way of paying back all the favours Edith had done for her, now she was finally in a position to do so.

'We could. I'd love that,' said Edith, and Alice was glad she'd kept her mouth shut.

Flo bustled over to the oven, checking her

watch. 'If I'm right, these should be just about ready.' She opened the heavy door, and a delicious spicy aroma emerged. It had traces of sweetness and richness, adding to the air of festivity.

'Oooh, what are they?' Edith asked as Flo carefully lifted her old metal tin out and placed it on the iron trivet.

'Cinnamon buns,' said Flo proudly. 'I'm adjusting the recipe now there's hardly any sugar to be had. You can use parsnips instead. I know it's a bit early to dig them up but I wanted to try, so we can have them just right for Christmas. Anybody want to taste?'

Nobody needed to be asked twice, and by the time Mattie returned from the attic, with a large ivory-coloured box in her hands and strands of cobwebs in her hair, Flo had brought out a pile of side plates and was gently easing the buns from the tin.

'Don't get crumbs or grease on the material,' she warned. 'Come and have one of these first and then we'll try the veil on Edith. I hope the moths haven't got it. I did pack it properly with lavender, but you never know.'

Edith was torn between wanting to try on the veil at once and savouring every mouthful of the little bun, moist and golden and round. 'It's the best thing I've tasted for ages,' she said honestly, licking her fingers after she had demolished the last bit. 'I'll wash my hands in the back kitchen and then let's see how it looks.' She ran the water from the tap, trying not to get her hopes up. This was such an unexpected offer. For one moment she thought she might cry at simply having the chance to try on the veil; her own mother had never hinted that her daughters could wear anything from her own wedding day. Come to think of it, Edith couldn't remember what her mother had worn. She couldn't recall ever having seen a picture; perhaps they hadn't been able to afford a photographer.

Mattie wiped her own hands carefully and then tackled the ivory box, which had been tied with a cream ribbon. With great concentration she lifted out the fine netting, looping it on one arm until she reached the headband, which sparkled with tiny seed pearls. 'Oh, it brings it back like it was yesterday,' she said, failing to disguise the wobble in her voice. Then she rallied. 'Right, you sit down on this wooden chair, Edie, and then I can stand behind you and fix this on. That's it. Now don't fidget. Keep very still while I let the material fall. No, a bit further forward . . . don't hunch your shoulders, I can't see if it's straight . . . back a bit . . . all right. That's it. Now stand and come to the mirror over the fireplace.'

Alice stood and moved out of the way, smiling as she did so, not only at the sight of Edie — transformed from the usual restless bundle of energy to a stunning bride — but at the fact that Mattie was beginning to sound more and more like her mother Flo.

Edith approached the mirror with trepidation, almost as if she was afraid of what she might see. She kept her eyes downwards until the last moment, and then raised her gaze. What she saw caught her breath. She nearly did not recognise herself. Instead of the regulation nurse's cap, her dark curls were now topped by beautiful foamy lace, which set off her dark eyes and pale skin; it looked gorgeously feminine and very definitely not in the least bit practical. 'I . . . I don't know what to say.' She stood stock still, unable to look away. 'It's . . . I'm . . . '

'You look beautiful,' said Flo with certainty. 'It could have been made for you. Do you like it?'

Mutely Edith nodded, too overcome to say more.

'That Harry's a very lucky boy,' said his mother. 'Of course we knew that the first time he came home and spoke about you. But to see you like this, Edie, I tell you straight, it makes me proud to have you as a daughter-in-law. That veil looks absolutely right on you.'

Mattie stood to one side and checked it again. 'It's not even too long. Good job you didn't have a full-length one, Ma. Do you know if you'll be wearing high heels, Edie?'

That brought her out of her trance. 'Heels? I don't expect so. I spend so long in my work shoes that I've forgotten how to balance in them. Anyway, now they've restricted crepe heels to two inches, there's not much point, even if I do manage to buy a new pair.'

Mattie giggled. 'What about wooden clogs? They're all the rage now.'

Flo protested at once. 'Wash your mouth out, young lady. I won't even hear of such a thing.'

Edith looked at the women gathered around her, all keen for her to look her best and to help out in any way they could, and knew that she was lucky — beyond lucky, indeed. Harry had come back from the dead. He loved her and she loved him to distraction. Soon she would marry him and then she would be a proper member of his wonderful family. She had the most enviable group of friends on top of that.

'I don't mind what shoes I wear,' she admitted. 'As long as you're all there with me on the day, that's what really matters.'

16

Billy was so tired he could barely put one foot in front of the other. It was the end of a demanding day at the docks, as they were several men short. A couple had gone down with flu, another had joined the army. That had left Billy, Ronald and Kenny with the brunt of the work.

It wouldn't have been as bad if he'd had a proper night's sleep, but Barbara had been keeping them awake for most of the week. That was on top of his ARP rounds for a large part of the evening. At least he had tonight off.

Kenny pulled on his battered cap and rubbed his hands. 'You're off tonight, aren't yer, Bill? Fancy coming down the Boatman's with me and Ron?'

Billy laughed ruefully. 'You got to be kidding. I can hardly stand up straight, I'm so knackered, and that's a fact. The pub's for you young, free and single types. I just want to get home to me bed.'

'At least you got a lovely warm welcome waiting for you,' said Kenny dolefully.

Ron pulled a face. 'Well, you ain't going to get anything like that down the Boatman's, Ken. I hope you ain't going there with that in mind. You want to stay away from any female company on offer down there, if you got any

168

sense. Which you ain't.'

Kenny punched his arm in mock-protest.

Ron's mind went back to the conversation in the nurses' victory garden. Mary's friend had obviously been worried about her sister, and Ron couldn't blame her. If he'd had a sister who was a regular down the Boatman's, he'd have been worried too. He wondered which one she was. There were two singers there: a woman in her late twenties with long sandy hair and a knowing eye for all the men in the crowd, and a much younger woman with bottle-blonde hair. He'd put good money on the blonde being the sister. The other one looked well capable of looking after herself.

He'd seen the young woman hanging around with the landlord's brother, a nasty piece of work if ever there was one. She'd looked besotted. More fool her. Anyone could see he was out for one thing only, and Ron had a nasty feeling he was having his way without having to try very hard. Should he warn the nurse? He had only met her the once. He could get in touch with Mary —

'Ron, you coming or what?'

Ron snapped out of his train of thought and shoved his hands in his pockets, following the other two down to the bus stop near the big junction at Limehouse. Perhaps the big sister knew about what went on. He wasn't exactly in a position to stop it. Yet he felt for her, remembering how protective he'd been when his only brother had been shot down in the Battle of Britain. Alfie had survived but it had been touch

169

and go for a while. He'd never be the same, having suffered terrible injuries, leaving him with poor eyesight — and you needed 20/20 vision to be a pilot. He was grounded for the duration of the war.

'Got plans for the weekend, Billy?' he asked now.

'Going to be baby-sitting,' Billy said, his delight clear from his expression. 'Kath's taking Edie out shopping for her wedding things. I don't want to get involved in all that. I'm better off leaving it up to them.'

'You're right there,' said Kenny. 'You upset not to be best man, then?'

Billy came to a halt at the end of the bus queue. A row of people were in front of them, all stamping their feet and huddling to keep warm in the early winter cold.

'No, it's only fair,' he said after a moment. 'Joe should have been Alan's godfather but they knew he couldn't get home. Now there's a chance he can manage some Christmas leave. If he doesn't make it back then I'll step in. Between us we'll get Harry to the altar in one piece.'

'Won't exactly need dragging, will he,' said Kenny.

'Ken, I do believe you're jealous. We got to find you a woman, and not one from the Boatman's,' Billy declared as the bus pulled up. They crowded on, although there were no seats. He didn't mind. He could doze off standing up, given the chance.

'All right, let's find someone for Kenny,' said Ron, joining in the joke, but suddenly wondering if he really wanted to spend his hard-earned cash at the Boatman's. The expression worn by the landlord's brother as he sweet-talked the young singer would not leave his mind. Despite himself, and the steamy warmth of the over-full bus, he shivered.

★ ★ ★

Kathleen was a past master at manoeuvring a pram around the bustling stalls of Ridley Road market. Barbara slept on oblivious as her mother turned on a sixpence, while Brian pulled on his knitted reins. He'd seen the big pile of glistening tangerines on Brendan's stall, and knew he usually got treats from the kindly tradesman. Kathleen noticed what he was looking at and halted in her tracks. 'Edie, stop! Look what Brendan's selling! However did you come by those?' she asked, knowing how scarce such fruit was these days.

Brendan tapped the side of his nose. 'Don't ask,' he said cheerily. 'It's all legit, Kath, don't you worry. Someone owed me a very big favour and this is what I got as a result. Like a miracle, eh? You'll want some for Christmas, I dare say?'

'Oh, yes please.' Kathleen could not believe her luck. 'Are they very dear? I'll take a handful anyway.' Time was that Brendan had had to help her out with an extra scoop of bare essentials, in the days when she hadn't had two pennies to rub together. Now things were better but she was hardly flush.

Brendan's eyes fixed on her companion. 'And

171

you're the happy bride-to-be, aren't you? Please accept a small gift for your big day, then.' He indicated to Edith that she should open her shopping bag, and he poured in a generous amount of fruit. 'You're going to be Stan Banham's daughter-in-law, aren't you? Can't have you going hungry.'

Edith's eyes were out on stalks. 'That's very kind,' she stammered. 'You shouldn't have.' Yet she knew how much these tangerines would be appreciated. There was enough to put out a bowl in the canteen, where their festive fragrance would fill the room, and still keep some for the wedding feast at Flo's. Their bright orange skins and shiny deep green leaves were reason to celebrate in themselves.

Brian watched in disbelief as the fruit disappeared into the bag and turned to Brendan, imploringly holding out his hand. 'Please,' he said in his politest voice.

'Brian!' Kathleen exclaimed. 'You can't just ask like that.'

Brendan leaned forwards and ruffled the boy's hair. 'Just this once, as it's coming up to Christmas,' he said, and picked one more tangerine off the pile and gave it to him.

Edith laughed as they pulled away from the stall, back to their original route towards the ones that sold fabrics and sewing materials. 'He's got the knack already,' she teased. 'He'll go far, that one.' Her expression grew more serious as she broached the question that had been worrying her. 'Kath, you aren't upset that I didn't ask you to be a matron of honour, are

172

you? If things had been different, I'd have loved to have you, and Mattie too, but it just all felt, well, a bit much.' It had been on her mind ever since she'd made the decision to have only one attendant: Alice.

Kathleen vehemently shook her head. 'Don't be daft, Edie. Of course I'm not offended. Neither is Mattie. What would I do if Joe couldn't get back and Billy ended up being best man? I'd have to manage these two on my own most of the day. I couldn't do that and be matron of honour. Flo would end up with them as well as Gillian and Alan — no, you're much better off with Alice on her own.'

Edith sighed in relief. 'Really? I felt awful, but it's so tricky. I mean, I could have asked Mary too, but then Belinda might get upset — once you start, there's no end to it. Besides, we don't know how many nurses can get time off on the same day. Some of my closest friends might not manage even to get over to Jeeves Street for a quick bite to eat. We'll have to see how busy the rounds are that day.'

Kathleen nodded. 'You're bound to be snowed under, what with Christmas being two days after. Still, it means you only need to think about one bridesmaid's dress.'

They reached the stalls and their faces fell. 'Maybe that's just as well,' said Edith, surveying the slim pickings. 'It doesn't look as if we're going to be spoilt for choice, does it.'

Kathleen glanced sharply at her friend, catching her disappointed tone. 'Maybe not here, but we'll find something, Edie. These aren't the only stalls selling fabric.' She ran her gaze along what was on offer, dull and sensible patterns in hard-wearing cotton and wool, just the sort of thing they had determined Edith should avoid.

Further back into the market, away from the main road, was another row of stalls that used to supply everything a dressmaker might need. Today they had a fraction of their former treasures on display, and again the choice of colour was very restricted — nothing that would suggest a blushing bride. Edith frowned. 'Maybe this is a sign that I shouldn't have a pretty dress after all. Look at that grey check — I could have a neat skirt and jacket and then it would do for all winter long.'

'No.' Kathleen didn't even need to think about it. 'You shall have your special dress, come hell or high water.' Swiftly she tried to work out where they might go — somewhere she could reasonably take Brian and Barbara in her pram. She hadn't packed a change of nappies or any spare clothes in case of accidents. Perhaps that had been a mistake.

All the same, she was determined to make something of this day for Edith. The nurse had been so good to her when she was down on her luck; she wanted to show how much she appreciated her friendship over the past few years. Friendships like this were what got you through the bad times.

She had never paid much attention to a stall on the corner to their left, as it had always stocked men's work boots and suchlike. Maybe she'd stopped there once or twice when Billy had needed kitting out. When the stallholder called over, it took her by surprise.

'Hello, ladies! What can I do for such lovely customers?' The man was older than Stan Banham but had a twinkle in his eye all the same. 'I know you, you're the wife of that young man what got Brendan to join the ARP.'

Kathleen looked a little abashed, not sure if this was a compliment or not. 'Yes, that's right,' she said, somewhat distracted as Barbara had started to grizzle. Brian began to pull on his reins again, obviously bored now there were no more treats to be had. Kathleen wasn't inclined to stop and chat.

'I bet I've got something you'd like to see,' the man went on, oblivious to Kathleen's doubting expression. 'I've been expanding my range — not easy to do in these hard times, but sometimes you got to take a risk in this game.'

Seeing that her friend had other immediate concerns, Edith stepped in. 'Oh, really?'

'Yes indeed,' the stallholder said, smiling to reveal he lacked two teeth down one side of his mouth. 'Shoes for the ladies. Not your second-hand ones neither. Proper new shoes, leather uppers an' all. Bet you wasn't expecting that.'

Edith glanced quickly at Kathleen, but she was bent over the pram, checking on her daughter. 'No, can't say we were,' she replied, playing along.

'Let me show you.' The man bustled to one side of his stall, briskly flicking some imagined dust from his brown overall, and fished out a set of boxes. 'Here we are. Red patent sandals for the summer . . . '

'Ah, I'm not sure that's what we're after,' said Edith tactfully, eyeing the sandals with horror. They were far too high for her, and rather spindly.

' . . . and elegant beige court shoes for that big occasion . . . '

They looked like something Kathleen's old neighbour and babysitter might have worn in her heyday, and Edith would not be seen dead in them. 'Nor those,' she said.

' . . . and we got these, very special . . . ' He took off the cardboard lid and revealed a small pair of pumps with a little heel, in a combination of cobalt blue and ivory. They had small bows in ivory cord at the toe and ivory piping around the sides and were possibly the loveliest shoes Edith had ever seen.

'Oh,' she gasped.

Kathleen looked up at the change in her friend's voice. 'What is it?'

Edith looked longingly at the blue shoes. 'These aren't bad, Kath. What do you reckon?'

Kathleen handed Edith the woollen reins and took a close look at them, picking them up and examining them. 'What size are they?' she demanded.

The man counted on his fingers. 'We got the larger sizes for the taller ladies, six and a half or seven. Then we got the more petite ones, a three and a three and a half. I regret to say we do not have the middle of the range.'

Edith turned away from a disgruntled Brian

and met Kathleen's gaze. 'I take a three,' she said. 'But I don't know, Kath. New shoes — it's a bit of a waste, isn't it? I could find some old ones and polish them up, and nobody would know.'

'But you would be hard pressed to borrow any if you wanted something different. None of us would have the right size.' Kathleen couldn't think of anyone else who wore a three.

The man could tell how interested she was and moved in for the kill. 'Perhaps you'd like to try them on?' He took both shoes from their box, and with his handkerchief he swiped the dust from a stack of crates. 'You sit down here nice and comfy and see how well they look on you.'

Edith was in an agony of indecision. If she spent clothing coupons on shoes she would have fewer for the dress, whenever they found something suitable. But if, just if, they did discover her dream in powder blue, these would be perfect. She had to make up her mind. Brian and Barbara were obviously ready to go home and she could sense that Kathleen was growing anxious about them.

Just then Brendan came over, waving a pound note. 'Norman, you got any change? Oh, Kath, you're still here. Now what have you got there?'

Edith had taken off her old black winter shoes and had put on the blue ones. Slowly she stood and flexed her feet in them. 'They fit,' she said. She dared not say more, in case her longing for them outweighed her common sense. She took a couple of paces forward and then back. They might have been made for her.

Brendan meanwhile picked up the box and looked at the price. He whistled. 'Norm, you got to be joking.'

Norman shook his head. 'I tell you, straight up, that's a good price. I'm almost ruining myself as it is.'

Brendan scoffed. 'Norman, you told me yesterday you got the lot for next to nothing because the warehouse was about to collapse from bomb damage. You're turning a pretty profit there. Don't tell me you've been giving these two your old soft soap. You know who they are, don't you? Billy's wife and this other one will soon be Stan Banham's daughter-in-law? You got to treat them right.'

Norman protested. 'Brendan, you'll bleed me dry.'

Edith cleared her throat. 'It's all right. I can pay. I don't want to be some kind of charity case.' She hoped that she wouldn't regret such rashness.

'Charity be damned, if you want them you should pay a fair price,' said Brendan, all businesslike now. 'Norman, how about you take that number and divide it by three. Then you'll still have a 50 per cent margin of profit.'

Norman's eyes bulged.

'See, you should never have told me how much you paid to begin with,' Brendan went on seamlessly. 'If you want to go around taking advantage of gullible customers, be my guest, but not with these two you won't. And you better decide quickly or young Brian here will be running off home and you won't have the chance to finish your deal.' He folded his arms, his piece said.

Kathleen could barely disguise her delight. It might not be what they'd set out to buy but she could see those shoes were the best thing in the entire market. If she hadn't been here, Brendan would not have intervened, and so Edith probably wouldn't have been able to afford them. Now there she was, settling up with a rather deflated Norman, and still with some cash in her pocket for dress material. They'd decide what to do about that later. For now she needed to get the children back home. But the look of stunned delight on Edith's face was a sight to treasure.

17

Harry shook his head, still finding it hard to take in the changes to Jeeves Street and the surrounding neighbourhood. He'd been back so rarely since Dunkirk, and even then he had travelled in the back of an ambulance. He'd barely been in a state to take in what the area was like. Although he hadn't said anything to his family or Edith, he had been on such strong pain medication that he wouldn't have noticed if there had been an elephant tied up to the nearest lamppost.

Now he had been given a generous chunk of leave, prior to his wedding and Christmas, and for the first time he had made his own way home to his parents' house. Even in the blackout he could just about see the destruction: houses missing roof tiles or windows, or simply missing altogether. The pavements and roads were pitted and cracked. He shuddered. Dunkirk had been hell on earth, of course, and his recollection of what followed was hazy. Yet he had been safe in his hospitals ever since. Here, they'd all been on the front line. He could not imagine what it had been like, night after night of taking refuge in the shelters, wondering if your house would still be there the next morning.

Now he was on his way to Billy and Kathleen's house for the first time, having enjoyed one of his mother's stews to fortify him for the evening.

For once Billy had agreed to go to the pub, in honour of Harry being home. Harry had said he'd drop round to pick him up. It wasn't far.

He was relieved to be walking the short distance under cover of darkness. This afternoon had unsettled him. In hospital, his changed appearance caused no reaction. Some of the pilots were virtually having their faces rebuilt. His own scarring and skin grafts were minor in comparison. He'd grown his hair a little longer to compensate and had almost got used to what he saw when he looked in the mirror.

On the train to London he had been one of many servicemen and most didn't bat an eyelid at his injuries. They would all have known somebody who had something similar, if not worse. He'd had to be careful not to knock his bad arm, but having bagged a corner seat he had felt safe enough.

No, it had been on the final leg of the journey that the problems had started. He had got off the bus, slinging his pack over his good shoulder, and walked slowly along the main road through Dalston, recognising the shops, noticing how bare their windows were. A few of the shopkeepers had waved and one or two had called out in welcome. Yes, he was back on his home patch. He had sighed in contentment.

But then a group of schoolchildren had come towards him and he'd felt their stares as he passed them. They hadn't said anything, but he could tell they were looking at him strangely. It wasn't aggressive exactly but it definitely wasn't friendly. He was sure that if he turned around they would be nudging each other and pointing.

Then a couple of older lads, just too young to have their call-up papers, had come around the corner. He vaguely recognised one of them — a younger brother of someone he used to box against. They had openly stared, and the brother had laughed. 'Oy, Banham,' he'd called. 'Bet you wouldn't beat our Reggie now, would yer?'

They had sauntered past, eyeing him curiously as they did so. 'Scar face,' the other one had said when he was just within hearing.

Harry had not broken his step, even though he was tempted to give them a piece of his mind. Didn't they realise why he was like this? It had taken a few minutes for it to sink in. Vaguely he recalled a doctor warning him that he should expect such reactions, but he had never encountered them until now and so he had not bothered to listen.

Harry had grown up taking admiration as his due. He was tall, handsome, sporty and popular. Not for him the anxieties of adolescence. Women had thrown themselves at him; he'd trained hard for boxing success but sure enough it had come his way. If he wanted something, he tended to get it. He wasn't conceited about it; it was just the way things were.

For the first time it hit him that the world would view him differently from now on. Kids who knew no better would think his scars were strange. Young men with chips on their shoulders would see him as weak, a potential victim, rather than someone they would instinctively know not to mess with. He had no idea how to cope with the prospect. He already had certain anxieties about whether he would live up to Edith's expectations. Now there was this to contend with as well.

Flo and Stan had given him a hero's welcome, of course, and even Mattie hadn't teased him as much as she once would have done. Sitting at the old kitchen table, he'd set his troubles to one side, relishing being back with his family again.

Now Billy ushered him into their new parlour and Harry knew this would be a home from home for him if he needed it. Although the window was covered by the obligatory blackout blind, Kathleen had made the room cosy, and Brian had been allowed to stay up to see the man he'd always called Uncle. Harry had scooped him up in one arm and Brian had hooted in glee. Then Barbara was presented to him, and Harry cooed at her tiny face, commenting that she was the spit of her father. It was good to see his old friends finally settled together and with their own family. Everything about it felt right: two good people reaping their just rewards.

Chatting to them distracted him from his worries, and it wasn't until they were in the Duke's Arms and Billy had gone to get the drinks in that the disturbing thoughts returned. The bar was full of mirrors and shiny brass, presenting Harry with his reflection from many angles. Self-consciously he swept his hair forward and down to cover some of the scarring. It could only ever be partially successful, though. He would have had to grow his hair as long as Mattie's to hide all the damage.

Billy returned with two pints and set them down on the polished table. 'Didn't even have to put me hand in me pocket. Remember old Clarence Witherspoon from down the baker's? He got us these, said it was a welcome home present for you.' He raised his glass to the old man propped at one end of the bar, who nodded back. 'You all right, Harry? What are you sitting like that for — is your arm giving you gyp?'

Harry made the effort to sit upright and took a long sip of beer, feeling its goodness warm him. 'Not in particular,' he said, although he was usually in discomfort if not actual pain from where the arm had yet to fully heal after the last operation. He didn't talk about it. There was no point, as it wouldn't change anything.

'Well, what, then?' Billy persisted. 'Not having second thoughts about marrying Edie, surely?'

'Oh, God, no. Nothing like that.' Harry snapped out of his misery at such a ridiculous idea.

'Good, cos she's the woman for you all right,' Billy said with total conviction. 'Everyone says you're meant to have wedding nerves and all that, but I reckon it's a load of rubbish. Best thing I ever did, marrying Kath.'

Harry smiled at the expression on his old friend's face. 'I reckon you're right. Anyone can see you're happy together. A proper advertisement for the wedded state, you are.' He sipped some more beer.

'You'll be like that with Edie,' Billy predicted. 'She won't stand for any of your nonsense for a start. Keep you on the straight and narrow, she will.' He set his glass down once more. 'Well, go on, tell me. You looked like you had the weight of the world on your shoulders for a minute there. Here you are, back in your old local, about to be married to the love of your life — why so glum, then?'

Harry took a deep breath, unsure whether to voice his thoughts. However, it didn't look as if Billy was going to let him off the hook. So he plunged in, describing what had happened that afternoon.

Billy listened and exclaimed at the end. 'Those useless brats. I know who those two lads are. I'll give them a talking-to next time I see them. Sooner they join up and have some sense knocked into them, the better.'

Harry shook his head. 'No, don't do that, Bill. They're just being stupid — they'll grow out of it soon enough. It's just . . . I wasn't expecting it. Wasn't ready for it. You've all been so kind about what happened, never made me feel bad — '

'I should hope not!' Billy interrupted forcefully.

' . . . but the fact remains I look different now. People who don't know me will point. I'll be like something from the circus. I feel . . . I don't know. Less of a man, I suppose.'

Billy looked quizzically at his old friend. 'Less of a man? You? Don't talk daft.' Then he paused to reflect what his old friend might mean. 'You talking about your wedding night, are you? Afraid it won't go right?'

Harry cleared his throat, unwilling to admit

even to Billy what he was worried about.

'Not exactly,' he said carefully. 'It's more like
. . . it's hard to put into words. But if I'm not
like I used to be, will she think less of me? I
know she says she won't. But if I'm honest I
know I'll be different — only one arm works
properly, my face moves differently either side,
and . . . I don't know what else will be affected
if you get my drift. Then the way those kids
behaved . . . I'm not the same as I was, no
getting away from it.'

Billy frowned. This was a new side to Harry. 'I
was worried when I got hurt in that car
accident,' he said. 'I know it doesn't compare,
but for a while I didn't know if I'd walk again or,
if I could, if I'd walk proper or not. Made me
feel very low, I don't mind telling you.' He bit his
lip. He hadn't admitted that to anyone, not his
mother, not Kath. He had had some very dark
thoughts for a time. Yet he had recovered and
scarcely recognised those feelings now. What
would he have been like if he had been left
permanently marked though?

Harry nodded. 'Thanks, Billy. Yes, it gets like
that sometimes. I don't like to complain, cos
really I'm one of the lucky ones. Just now and
then, I feel really miserable about it. There, now
I've told you. So cheers, bottoms up, it's good to
be back.'

'Cheers.' Billy watched his friend carefully.
'You should tell Edie, you know.'

Harry shrugged. 'Maybe. I'm meant to be the
strong one, protecting her from all that sort of
thing.'

186

'Perhaps. But all I know is, if I have any worries or anything, I talk to Kath and then they don't seem so bad. That's what marriage is for, really. I couldn't have imagined it a year ago, but it's one of the best bits. Sharing everything, good and bad.'

Harry nodded slowly. 'We'll see. I reckon not everyone is as well suited as you and Kath. She's special.'

'She is.' Billy's eyes glistened. 'No doubt about it. But so is Edie. You got a good one there, Harry Banham.'

'I know.' Harry sensed the mood shifting and went along with Billy's attempts to bolster his confidence. 'Anyway, I've got to get cracking on sorting out my uniform for the wedding. Can't turn up looking like something the cat dragged in. I dare say Edie will have words about that. Not that she'll tell me what she's wearing.'

Billy grinned easily. 'As it happens I know more about that than you do.' Kathleen had told him about the shoes, and then that Belinda had stepped in to help with the dress, by introducing Edith to Miriam's collection of fabric that she had amassed over many years. There, among the bolts of material, was one in the perfect shade of powder blue. Belinda was going to help sew the dress itself and all would be ready by the twenty-third.

'I'm better off not knowing,' Harry said. 'You can tell Kath that her secret is safe.' He drained his glass. 'How about another? Seeing as we haven't been for a drink together for so long.'

Billy nodded. 'Why not? But don't be

187

surprised if they don't let you pay. Cos no matter what some idiot boys might think, everyone else knows you're a hero.'

18

'Something old, something new, something borrowed, something blue. Reckon you've got the lot, Edith.' Kathleen angled her dressing-table mirror up so that Edith could see herself, dressed and ready for her ceremony. It had been her idea to invite Edith to dress at her house. It would have been pandemonium at the nurses' home. And of course she couldn't prepare at Jeeves Street, because it would be terribly bad luck if Harry saw her.

'Reckon I have,' said Edith, her dark eyes bright as she ran her fingers along the pearl necklace that Mary had insisted she wore. She had protested, saying the piece was far too valuable and what if one of the children broke it? Mary had insisted, asking what was the point of having such fine things if they only ever stayed in her bedside drawer?

Besides, the pearls were perfect with the head-band that kept the veil in place. They were the borrowed element; the veil was old, even though it didn't feel it; the shoes were new; the dress was the exact shade of blue she had dreamed of. It simply could not have been better.

Alice came in from where she had been changing into her own outfit in Brian's little bedroom, Brian having been left with Mattie. 'Oh, Edie.' She stopped in her tracks to admire her friend.

'Will I do?' Edith kept her voice casual but Alice could detect the shake of emotion in it.

'Yes, you'll do,' she said with a grin. 'Kath, you've done a grand job there.'

'Glad you think so,' said Kathleen happily. 'Helps to have such lovely clothes to dress the bride in, though. Belinda's done her proud.' For a second she let herself remember how jealous she had been last year when she had mistakenly believed Billy preferred Belinda to herself. That was now all water under the bridge, thank God.

Alice smoothed the sleeves of her pewter-grey jacket, teamed with a grey-blue frock which had been revamped from another of Miriam's finds. She felt she looked suitably elegant and toned with the bride's colours, without remotely threatening to overshadow her. Not that anybody could. Joy was radiating from Edith like beams of light from the sun.

'Are you sure you want to walk?' Alice asked now. 'It's cold out there. I know you've got that lovely cream wrap but all the same . . .'

Kathleen chuckled. 'We could get Brendan's van. He'd be happy to lend it. You might have to brush off the cabbage leaves though.'

'Or what about the back of Geraldine's motorbike?' Alice teased. 'Your veil would trail behind you in the wind — it would look spectacular.'

Edith fixed them both with a glare. 'No, thank you very much. I want to walk. It's not far. It's not as if my dress is long enough to drag along the ground. I love this part of London and I want to walk through it to my wedding, if you

190

please. It's my big day and so I'm allowed to choose.'

Alice nodded, having expected nothing else. 'Then let's go. Stan is waiting downstairs.'

Edith nodded, happy that Stan had agreed to give her away. She hadn't really expected anyone from her own family to turn up and perform that role. She wouldn't have trusted any of them to do it properly anyway. Stan had done it before; besides, he was more of a father to her than her own one had ever been.

'Yes,' she said, rising to her full diminutive height. 'Let's go.'

★　★　★

The entrance to the register office was sandbagged, as were the doors to all the municipal buildings. The windows were covered in tape. There were only a few artificial flowers and most of the guests were wearing clothes that had seen many winters already. Yet Edith could not have been happier had she and Harry been exchanging their vows in St Paul's Cathedral.

As she stood with him in front of the registrar, her heart was full of joy, pride and overwhelming relief that he had survived to see this day. So what if his smile was one-sided and one arm hung awkwardly in its army uniform jacket. He was the most handsome man in the world, and he was hers.

Alice held her cream wool wrap, and cast supportive glances as the pair of them turned to face their guests after pledging to stay together for better or worse. Edith knew that the worst had already happened. The despair she had felt when Harry had been reported to have been killed at Dunkirk was as low as anybody could ever sink. Everything now was a bonus. She looked up at him and she thought she would burst from the sheer wonder of the moment. Nobody and nothing could take that from her.

★ ★ ★

'Happy now, Mrs Banham?' Harry tenderly kissed his bride on the tip of her nose. They were safely back in the welcoming house on Jeeves Street, having got through the ceremony without fluffing any lines or other embarrassments, much to his relief.

Edith giggled. 'I can't believe I'm Mrs Banham. That's your ma's name. Doesn't seem right that it's me as well now.'

'Better get used to it,' he said, looking at her with amusement. 'It's got to last you a lifetime, after all.'

Edith nodded. 'Yes, no more Gillespie for me. I'm so pleased to be part of your family, Harry.'

Flo came up to where they were standing near the front door and caught the last words. 'Almost as pleased as we are to have you as one of us,' she said, giving Edith's arm a squeeze. 'Now don't hang around here in the draughts. I know we want to keep the door on the latch so that when your colleagues finish their shift they can come in and join us, but come through to where all the food and drink is. Let me hang up that

192

wrap — oh, it's very fine material. Where did you get it?'

Edith stroked the beautiful fabric as Flo moved to loop it onto a coat hook. 'Mary lent it to me, as well as the necklace. She's about the only one of us who has such gorgeous things. It's very warm, even though it's so light.'

'Merino wool I dare say.' Flo took a step back to admire Edith's frock. 'You look a proper picture. I do hope that photographer fellow got some good shots. It was so cold, I was afraid he'd shiver too much and all the photos would be shaky.'

Joe came up behind her and laughed. 'Ma, he's a professional, he'll know better than to shiver all the way through the pictures. I'll see to it that you get nothing but the best.'

'Thanks, Joe.' Edith smiled up at her new brother-in-law, conscious that this was his present to them: hiring a proper photographer, who had met them on the steps of the register office. She would have been quite happy with a few snaps from Billy's new Brownie, but it was extra special to have the real thing. Anyway, it meant Billy could be in the photos, holding his new daughter in his arms while Brian shyly held Kathleen's hand; he'd never had his picture taken before.

Joe smiled back, and she couldn't help but notice the dark rings under his eyes, despite his cheerful expression. She knew why. Harry had reported that he had arrived home late last night, just when they were all thinking Billy would have to step in as best man after all. He'd been

193

travelling since before first light, the long journey from Plymouth taking the entire day, with many delays and not many chances to sit down.

No wonder he looked tired — and yet he was clearly pleased to have made it back, delighted to have been best man. If there was ever anybody to entrust with the responsibility of guarding the ring, Joe was the one. She flashed a look downwards at the golden band on her finger. Not a flashy one — but another Banham family heirloom. It had once belonged to Flo's own mother, and had been altered to fit Edith's small hand.

'Why are you all out here in the hallway when we have a perfectly good parlour and kitchen, where it's warm?' Flo scolded. 'In you go, the lot of you.'

Edith grinned to herself. Flo's children might be fully grown and two out of the three of them married, but it didn't stop her fussing over them and telling them off.

* * *

The Christmas wedding feast was in full swing, with a big bowl of glossy tangerines in the centre of the groaning kitchen table, an extra present from Brendan. Around it Flo and Mattie had arranged more treats: the cake with rice paper for icing, parsnip and carrot buns, meat paste sandwiches, a platter of corned beef with Mattie's carefully preserved home-grown vegetables as accompaniments.

All around were boughs of holly, on the top of

the pictures, along the edges of shelves, hanging from the window and doorframes. Candles burned brightly, some in metal lanterns and some in old jam jars, which Mattie had made more festive by tying coloured ribbons around them. She had made sure to place them where Gillian and Brian couldn't reach.

Edith and Harry were surrounded by well-wishers, not only the immediate family and friends who'd come to the ceremony itself, but more and more who had finished their shifts or, in the case of some of the nurses, got off early for once. Peggy and Clarrie had just arrived, having taken the early morning rota in order to leave the factory mid-afternoon. Even so, the dusk had fallen by the time they made it as far as Jeeves Street.

'No fire-watching tonight then?' Harry teased his old school friend. 'I heard you were up on the roof every night now.'

Clarrie tutted. 'What, and miss this? I had to make sure you were actually married good and proper. About time someone made an honest man out of you.' Her red hair caught the light of the many bright candle flames. 'Never thought I'd see the day that you settled down, Harry Banham.'

Edith recalled how when she'd first met Clarrie, she had felt immediately on her guard, assuming her chatter was flirting, before realising that she and Harry went back so far that it was almost like a reflex action, with nothing behind it. Now Clarrie tucked her arm through Edith's. 'You keep him on a short lead,' she advised.

'Dreadful man that he is.'

'He'll toe the line from now on,' Edith assured her. 'What will you have to drink, Clarrie? I think Joe's managed to get hold of some port, if you'd like some of that.'

'Maybe I will.' Clarrie brightened up. 'Beats being stuck on the roof of the factory with a lukewarm thermos of tea. Peggy will have one too — she says she's gone off it but she really hasn't.'

Edith broke free to fetch their drinks, only to be told off by Mattie who said she shouldn't have to wait on her guests at her own wedding. She was only too happy to organise the refreshments, while Edith stood centre stage, beaming from ear to ear.

Alice helped herself to a small slice of the wedding cake, quietly relieved that they had been able to provide one at all. She knew how much it meant to Flo to put on a big spread in celebration. She herself had been too on edge to eat much at their early breakfast over at the nurses' home, and somehow the rest of the day had flown by without her having anything else. She was still full of nervous energy; perhaps it was the sight of her dearest friend finally having her deepest wish come true. Looking at Harry from this angle, you'd never know there was anything different about him; but the big mirror over the fireplace reflected his other side, with the hair swept forward and down but the scars beneath still visible, and the arm on that side at not quite the right angle. Yet he was so very much better than they had ever thought possible and, perhaps more importantly, seemed to be back to his old self, laughing and perfectly comfortable at the centre of the crowd.

The room was warm, and she shrugged out of her smart new jacket, carefully putting it over the back of a chair. Several people had commented on how elegant it looked and she was pleased not to have let Edith down. Everyone said that dressing up boosted morale; all the more important to make sure that they looked the part for the wedding, wartime or not.

'Isn't the best man meant to be looking after the bridesmaid?' Joe appeared beside her, a quizzical grin on his tired face.

'Maybe it should be the other way around,' she said, observing with concern, as she had since he'd first brought Harry to the register office, quite how exhausted he seemed. 'I can see you're not limping any more, but seriously, Joe, how much sleep have you had these past few days?'

Joe shrugged. He too had taken off his uniform jacket and was in his best white shirt, which had started off immaculately starched and pressed by Flo this morning, but now bore a few creases and a smear of jam courtesy of Gillian. 'Not much, if I'm honest. You know I had to get up in the middle of the night to catch the train. Then it seemed unfair to ask Harry to share our old room on his last night as a single man, so I bedded down on the sofa in the parlour. But Ma needed to get everything ready in there this morning and was up before dawn herself. Still, I can always sleep when it's all over.'

'Yes, you'll have your old bedroom to yourself tonight,' Alice said, keen to reassure him.

Joe looked at her. 'What do you mean? I thought Harry and Edith would have it.'

Alice clapped her hand over her mouth. 'Forget I said anything. I assumed you'd have heard.'

'Heard what?'

Alice cocked an ear at a voice drifting through from the hallway. 'That's Mary arriving now. You'll find out any minute.' Then, despite Joe's stern and direct glance, she refused to say anything more until her colleague, who had drawn the short straw and worked all afternoon, emerged into the living room, with Charles behind her.

Edith hurried across to her friend, who gave her a big hug and then presented her with a smart cream envelope. The bride carefully drew out a sheet of heavy paper with an embossed heading, and then gasped. 'Mary! You shouldn't have! That's too much — and after you lent me such beautiful things as well.'

'What does it say?' asked Harry, too far behind her to see.

'It's two nights at the Savoy hotel. I can't believe it. I've only ever looked in through the window,' breathed Edith. Harry looked just as stunned.

'Blame Charles,' beamed Mary. 'He has connections there, don't ask me what.'

Charles looked rather embarrassed as all eyes in the room turned on him. 'That's putting it a bit strongly,' he said. 'Still, might as well make use of such things. Besides, if it wasn't for Harry and Edith, I would never have met Mary. So I do rather feel I owe them something.' He glanced lovingly at Mary, and again Alice was struck by the thought that Mary's fears about him were baseless. He obviously thought the world of her.

'How was that?' asked Clarrie.

Harry laughed, remembering now. 'It was when I won that big fight, just before the war. Edie came to cheer me on, and brought her friends. Afterwards I was approached by Major Jimmy Ingham, who wanted me to think about boxing for the army — and Charles was with him.'

Mary grinned. 'And the rest is history. So don't feel we've done you a favour, it's actually the other way around, and this is the least we can do to thank you. We thought you might fancy a bit of privacy now you're a married couple.'

Harry smiled across at Edith. 'I'm sure we can make the most of that.'

'Harry!' Edith pretended to be annoyed, but was obviously delighted with the extravagant gift. The Banham home was the most welcoming possible, but nobody could claim it provided much privacy.

She carefully put the headed paper back into the envelope, thinking that she would have to pack a bag for the occasion. She hoped she had enough smart clothes; she had assumed she would spend the next few days in her new in-laws' house and wouldn't need to dress up to the nines. She would slip away upstairs as soon as the fuss died down. She realised that it still meant they would be back here to celebrate Christmas, which she didn't want to miss. She had brought over a few of her nicest outfits for Christmas Day, so they would just have to do for the posh hotel. What an idea — to stay at such a place with Harry. A thrill ran through her.

So her thoughts were occupied when the sound of the front door shutting once more reached her. Absently she wondered who it could be; all the nurses who were coming had now arrived, and so had Harry's old school friends. Perhaps it was someone from his old workplace, the hardware shop.

When the latecomer strode into the room she was completely unprepared. Everyone turned to look at the stranger, a short man in army uniform, with dark hair just like Edith's. He fixed his challenging gaze on her as the room fell silent.

'Frankie,' she breathed.

19

The moment seemed to stretch on for ever. Then her brother spoke.

'Very nice, I see.' He kept his voice polite but she could hear the sneer in it. 'No food shortages around here, then.'

Edith gave herself a shake and attempted to play the host. 'This is my brother Frankie,' she announced to everyone. 'Come and have something to eat. Harry will fetch you a drink, won't you, Harry?' She shot a meaningful look at her new husband, who nodded.

'Coming right up,' he said easily, and only Edith caught the note of curious concern.

Frankie allowed himself to be steered to the table, still loaded with all manner of treats, but turned and stared at the man. 'Is that him, then?' he asked Edith, not bothering to keep his voice down. 'He's the unlucky bastard you snared, is he?'

Any idea that her brother had come to give them his good wishes and even those of the rest of her family was firmly dispelled. Edith sighed inwardly. She had known they wouldn't give the wedding their blessing. They had no interest in anything that might make her happy.

They had never understood why she wanted so desperately to be a nurse, and had mocked her while she worked hard to pass her school certificate, which none of the other Gillespies had ever bothered with. Ever since her big sister died she had been driven to help others who were sick, but she had been too young to explain that. They despised her efforts, always claiming she wanted to get above herself. Frankie had come to freeload on the food, that much was obvious as he heaped his plate, and her best course of action would be to minimise the damage and get him out of here as soon as he had finished.

Harry handed his new brother-in-law a pint of beer, which Frankie downed almost in one go. 'I'll fetch another, shall I,' Harry said, more as a statement than a question, and headed into the scullery where Stan had set up a miraculous keg of beer, somehow obtained by the ARP station and brought round as a present. Joe was refilling his own glass.

'That the brother, then?'

'One of them,' Harry said grimly. 'First time I've seen him, or any of her family come to that. I'd have happily kept it that way, and she didn't think any of them would come, but he could spell trouble.'

'You get back in there and enjoy the party — don't let him ruin it for Edie,' Joe urged him. 'I'll keep an eye on things. Here. Take this pint.'

Harry stepped back into the main kitchen, recognising the expression on Frankie's face. It was close to how those ignorant lads had looked at him — a mixture of contempt and disgust. Still, so far their guest had kept a civil tongue in his head.

'Much obliged I'm sure,' Frankie said now,

accepting the drink and gulping down half of it. Then he demolished several greedy mouthfuls of food. 'Any chance of some more of this?' He waved his plate at his sister. Edith leant back a little to avoid anything splashing her beautiful pale blue dress.

'Of course.' She smiled politely, realising he was showing her up and enjoying doing so.

Alice stepped in. 'I'll do it. More corned beef and pickles, is it? It'll give you two more time to talk.' She took the plate, ignoring Frankie's tactless stare.

'Is that your friend? She's a bit of all right, isn't she?' Frankie sank the rest of the bitter and looked around for another refill.

'She's my bridesmaid,' Edith said brusquely. The thought of Alice looking favourably on her brother was as remote as Mars and she didn't see any point in giving him false hope.

Frankie jutted his chin at his sister. 'I'm not good enough for her, is that what you're saying?'

'I said nothing of the kind,' said Edith briskly. She told herself she shouldn't be surprised at his reaction; Frankie had always had the ability to take offence at the tiniest imagined slight.

'Nah, come to think of it she looks a bit on the snooty side for me.' It didn't stop him accepting the refilled plate from Alice, as his gaze wandered around the room and came to rest on Clarrie. 'What about her? You know what they say about girls with red hair.' He leered across the mound of food, his eyes a little more unfocused after the alcohol.

'Drop it, Frankie,' Edith said. 'I know why

you're here and it isn't to wish me well. Eat that and then bugger off.'

'Charming. So you've still got a filthy mouth on you when it suits you.' Frankie didn't bother to pause in his eating as he spoke, and again Edith stepped back to avoid being sprayed with food. 'Bet they don't think you talk like that at your la-di-da nurses' home. Just think of all the things I could tell them about you.'

Edith could have kicked herself — she was getting drawn into the old arguments all over again. She didn't respond to his comment, instead looking away.

'Couldn't you get a proper man, then?' he went on. 'Had to settle for a reject, did yer? Now I come to look at him closely, he ain't got more than one working arm, has he? And all those marks on his face. Messed him up good and proper, they have. Better hope everything else is in full working order, eh?' He raised his eyebrows in a disgusting insinuation. 'Or is he all wonky down there too?'

'Get out, Frankie.' Edith had lost what little patience she had. 'He's more of a man than you'll ever be, that much I do know.'

'Oho, touched a nerve, have I?' He set down his plate and swaggered in front of her, as the conversations around them petered out.

'Just leave,' she said. 'Leave now.'

Frankie laughed unpleasantly. 'Don't like me speaking the truth, is that it? My poor big sister had to go and pick someone who can't do the necessary? Not firing on all cylinders below the belt, is that it?'

Edith winced and noticed Alice doing the same but, before anyone could say anything, Harry was across the room like a flash.

'You heard your sister. You'd better get out.'

Frankie sneered up at his much taller brother-in-law. 'What, you going to make me?'

Harry took no time to consider, but reacted on instinct — throwing a powerful punch with his good arm and connecting with Frankie's nose. Frankie went down like a sack of potatoes.

For a moment nobody said a thing. Edith's hands were over her mouth, her eyes horrified. Alice stared as if she couldn't believe what had just happened.

Then Charles started to clap. 'Well done, Banham. Worthy of your championship bout.' He smiled in admiration. 'No point in talking to some chaps — they'll never catch on. Sorry, Edith. Don't want to ruin your special day, but he got what he deserved.'

Harry staggered with relief, having feared he had indeed ruined the party. Now Edith looked at him with careful approval. 'Are you all right?'

Harry sighed but then straightened his stance. 'Yes, it's him who'll have the sore head tomorrow.'

'And a broken nose,' added Alice, with her professional judgement.

Charles nodded. 'That's as maybe. But I for one am glad you've still got what it takes, Harry, wounds or no wounds.' He spun round to address the sea of faces. 'Some of you might not know this, but Harry here had one of the great secret weapons in the boxing ring. Everyone expected him to deliver his knockout blows with his right hand. Of course some boxers are southpaws, but word soon gets round. The great thing about Harry Banham always was,' and he paused, 'he could hit with either.'

Joe looked across at his brother and then at Charles and grinned at both of them. 'That was it. We never spoke about it — didn't want the local papers to catch on. But it looks like you can still deliver the decisive punch when it counts.' He stepped forward. 'Charles, let's you and me see this gentleman out. No need for the groom to bother himself any further.'

Charles nodded, pitching up his sleeves. But as he did so he turned to Harry. 'I'll make sure Major Ingham hears the good news. Jimmy will want to know, be in no doubt.' Then he and Joe each took one side of Frankie's still unconscious body and lifted him up and then out.

'I'll just go to check that nose.' Alice followed them. Even if Frankie had done his best to spoil his sister's wedding feast, that didn't mean she could let his injuries go untreated.

Edith wasn't sure whether to laugh or cry. How typical of Frankie to turn up and taunt her and, far worse, to say such unforgiveable things to Harry. She didn't blame her new husband for lashing out. To have gone through what he had, only to have some uppity, obnoxious squirt insult him like that. She hoped some of the guests weren't too shocked.

Gazing around, she realised that most of them had taken it in their stride. Of course, they'd been used to Harry in his fighting days, and she knew that not all of his fights had taken place inside the ring. If there had been trouble, people used to call on Harry. Mary looked a little surprised, but that was all.

Flo pressed a glass of shandy into her hand. 'Put it behind you, my love,' she said. 'I'm sorry your brother got thumped, but he asked for it. Now let's all raise a glass to Edith and Harry — and may their marriage be a happy one!'

★　★　★

Even though it was close to midnight and the room had an enormous window, it was still warm. Harry thought of how freezing his barracks had been that first year, and then the many hospitals he'd been in since. Even last night back in his old bedroom, you couldn't have called it anything but slightly chilly. No, this was the height of luxury all right.

The bedside light with its ornate and tasselled shade was still on, and he propped himself on his better arm to turn to gaze at Edith. She had fallen asleep on her side and her dark curls were spread across the crisp white pillow, her pale shoulder rising and falling with each breath. It hardly seemed real, spending the first night of their marriage together in a room such as this.

Not that he would have minded where he spent it, as long as he was with her. Harry had thought for a long time that this would never happen at all, that he wouldn't make it through or, even if he did, she wouldn't want him. He wouldn't have blamed her. He had prepared

207

himself for the worst, in those dark days, weeks, months when he had drifted in and out of consciousness. If she were with him, he would have been happy in a tent. The prospect of having her to stay at his parents' house had seemed about as good as he could possibly have hoped for.

This place was in a completely different league. He'd always known that Major Ingham and Captain Charles were from a very different background, and Mary obviously found such things completely normal, but to have a room like this, and all to themselves . . . you could fit the whole upper floor of Jeeves Street into it. It was madness. Yet Harry loved it, the sense that they were making a new start in such a different place, even if it was only for a couple of nights.

Beside them on the beautifully carved bedside table stood a silver bucket of ice, condensation still dripping down its sides, with the green glass neck of an empty champagne bottle peeping above the top edge. He and Edith had laughed as they'd tried to drink it. They'd only ever had it once before, on that fateful night when he'd won his title and Major Ingham had seen him fight. That night, just as now, Charles had bought the bottle. Edith had sneezed and sneezed, and announced that — though it was a lovely thought — she really preferred shandy.

Then they had set aside their glasses and made the most of this unexpected and luxurious privacy. How different to make love on such a bed, with none of the furtive hurrying that they'd had to cope with before. Edith was more beautiful than ever, even though she had been shy about how skinny she was becoming. He didn't care.

They'd finished the strange-tasting fizz and then, despite herself, Edith had dozed off. Harry was reluctant to put the light out, wanting to prolong the moments that he could drink in the sight of her, for once not rushing around, but happily sleeping after the best evening either of them could remember. He didn't want to lean over and turn off the lamp in case she woke up.

Slowly he moved so that he could lie on his back, one arm behind his head, and stared up in the subtle light to the elaborately carved ceiling above them. It was the absolute opposite to the ceiling back at home, with its telltale lines in the plaster from where someone had trodden too heavily in the attic, and the dent from where he'd let loose his catapult as a boy. He'd tried to blame Joe, but neither of his parents had believed him. Then there was the old mark from where he'd stood on his bed and practised blowing smoke rings. He still couldn't do them.

His mind turned to the events of the afternoon. He'd been in his element, with everyone he loved around him, teasing him, saying he'd have to knuckle down now, while he could see Edith's friends were delighted for her. Then, how swiftly it had all changed when her brother had arrived. He had thought that maybe she was exaggerating when she used to say she didn't get along with her family; it was so unlike his own background. Now he understood why, if Frankie was typical of the Gillespies.

He couldn't imagine Joe or Mattie saying something like that to him. They might bicker at every opportunity, but to deliberately insult your own sister on her wedding day — it was beyond belief. And as for what he'd implied about Harry . . .

Harry winced at the memory. The trouble was, it was too close to his own fears. He had wondered for a long time if he'd ever be able to perform again. Then, when he could sense his old energy returning, he'd worried that Edith would find him repulsive because he looked different.

Tonight had settled some of those concerns. She certainly didn't seem to find him repulsive. She'd been every bit as loving as he'd remembered her, and he had returned to the memory of her many, many times as he lay on his sickbed. She was his comfort, his rock, his joy. He should put aside those old worries and be thankful that he'd met such a woman who wanted to be with him for life. He'd been relieved beyond measure that his physical fitness hadn't deserted him when it counted. It had been on his mind for far too long.

He had to take care of his hand, though. He'd connected with Frankie's nose with great force and had bruised his knuckles, not that he'd admitted to it. He smiled wryly to himself. His brother-in-law was going to have a lovely purple face for Christmas.

But maybe he shouldn't have hit him. That had been in the heat of the moment. Joe wouldn't have done something like that — he'd have talked to the man, told him to leave and held firm until he'd gone. Not that his brother had said so in as many words, but Harry could always tell when Joe didn't approve of what he'd done.

It was because it was too close to what Harry had dreaded. Also, he knew, he just knew, that other men thought the same when they looked at him. In their eyes he was washed-up, a failure by his mid-twenties. His career was over before it had begun, and he looked freakish. Would people judge Edith for sticking by him? He couldn't bear that. Perhaps he shouldn't have married her after all. What if she was humouring him? Or what if he had condemned her to a lifetime of being pointed at, of people whispering behind their backs, speculating about what she saw in him, if she was ripe for the picking?

Horrified at the direction his thoughts had taken, he abruptly turned over.

'Whh . . . aat?' Edith stirred sleepily.

'Nothing. I was just putting the light off.' Damn it, the very thing he'd tried to avoid. She'd had a long day, she needed her sleep.

'Let me look at you again before you do.' Edith gazed up at him, her eyes darker than ever, a smile on her drowsy face. 'I thought so. I'm in bed with you in a swanky hotel room. Who'd have believed it? Harry, look at us! Aren't we lucky?'

Unable to resist he dipped down and took her in his arms. 'I'm the lucky one,' he breathed. 'I can't take it in. You agreed to marry me and here we are.'

211

'And it's Christmas in two days. I can't wait. We'll be with your parents again.'

'Now don't tell me you'd rather be in my old room than here?'

Edith snuggled against him. 'Oh no, don't think I'm ungrateful. This is lovely. But it's not real, is it? It's nice for a change, but that's all.'

'So you won't mind spending Christmas night at Jeeves Street?'

Edith hugged him back. 'Seriously, Harry Banham, I can't think of anywhere I'd rather be. Just as long as you're there too.'

Harry rested his chin on the top of her hair and breathed in that unique mix of shampoo and a sort of spiciness that was always Edie. 'In that case, Mrs Banham, I assure you I will be.'

'Mrs Banham!' Edith giggled in delight.

Later, with the light off at last, Harry settled down to sleep, reassured once more. He had to put that sense of dread behind him. He absolutely must not let those sad old fears take hold.

20

Gladys knew she didn't have to go into the nurses' home on Christmas Day, but she wanted to. Even with all the shortages, it felt so festive in the common room. There was the big bowl of precious tangerines that Edith had so generously shared, the lovely tangy scent from the fruit filling the room. It was such a rarity these days and all the more special for it. Fiona had insisted on buying a proper Christmas tree, which stood to one side of the piano, and everyone had helped make decorations to dress the branches. The piano itself had sprigs of holly arranged across its top, and more holly was tucked around the edges of the picture frames.

Bridget and Ellen had managed to obtain a big bag of pine cones. Some had been set aside as fire starters, but they had carefully painted the rest to make table decorations for the canteen part of the room, adding scraps of ribbon and tinsel to them. Now they sparkled in the dim daylight and Gladys felt her heart beat faster in the joy of the moment. She took a deep breath in.

Outside all was frosty but in here the fire burned brightly in the grate. Gladys hummed happily to herself as she made her way to the kitchen, thinking of the carol concert the night before. It had become a tradition at the Victory Walk home, and she loved it. Mary played the piano, and Gladys could sing her heart out, enjoying the familiar tunes and finally confident that she could read all the words to any verses that she couldn't remember. At first she had been embarrassed when one of the nurses praised her voice, but now she basked in the compliments, realising that her voice actually brought pleasure to others.

It wasn't big-headed to think so. She had done nothing to deserve her fine voice, but she loved the fact that her singing helped the rest of them to join in and have a go. As Mary had pointed out, she herself couldn't sing properly if she was playing at the same time, and somebody had to start the vocal parts. So Gladys was a vital element of the concert. She felt warm inside at the thought. After so many years of not being appreciated, it was wonderful to know she could do something well.

She gasped in surprise when she saw who was in charge of the kitchen that morning: none other than Fiona, the superintendent. 'Come in, come in, no need to go into shock,' she said cheerfully, her hands moving at top speed as she peeled a pile of carrots. 'Cook has her own family to attend to on a day like this.'

'But don't you want to have a day off for once?' Gladys hastily reached for her apron, somewhat nervous at sharing the countertop with Fiona.

'Day off? Why would I want one of those?' Fiona shook her head. 'The devil makes work for idle hands, as they say. Besides, while I know you all love Christmas; where I come from we prefer

Hogmanay. So I told Cook I would step in. I've nearly finished the carrots, so will you tackle the swede?'

'But what about the oven?' Gladys knew that Cook always had everything timed to the last second, and she was worried that nothing would heat up in time.

'All on already,' beamed Fiona, sweeping the carrot tops and peel into the largest bowl. 'Turkey's in, kettle's boiled, pudding is steaming. You'll want these for your compost heap in the victory garden, won't you? Excellent. Now I shall move on to the potatoes. When you've done that, maybe you'll oversee those marrowfat peas, which I put to soak last night after the concert, so they should be good and ready.'

Gladys mentally took a step back from the blast of Fiona's energy. Then she found a sharp knife and set about preparing the pile of swede for roasting.

★ ★ ★

'So will you not be staying with us to eat, my dear?' Fiona's face, flushed red with the steamy heat of the kitchen, was full of concern. She pushed a drooping strand of auburn hair behind her ear.

'No, no, I only came in to help prepare,' said Gladys hurriedly, wiping her hands on her apron before untying its belt. 'I got to get back to my house. Ma can never manage the young ones on her own and I'm not sure my sister will be much help.'

'Ah, yes, I see, I take your point.' Fiona whirled round and found a spare ceramic bowl, one of the few items in the kitchen as yet unused. 'Then you had best take your dinner with you. No, no, I won't hear of any objections. There's far too much here, even allowing for generous portions, and of course some of the nurses won't be eating here today. Edith and Alice will be with the Banhams; Mary has gone to join her fine captain. So there's plenty, and it won't keep, as you well know. Besides,' her eyes twinkled, 'you grew most of it.'

★ ★ ★

By the evening, Gladys was exhausted but content. She'd ended up bringing back the bowl filled with roasted vegetables, topped with a plate full of turkey, and a separate bowl full of peas. She'd somehow managed to balance it all on the short walk from the home to her house. The food had made all the difference to her own family's celebration, which would have been miserably meagre without it. Her mother had half-heartedly cooked a scrawny chicken and boiled some potatoes, but there was scarcely enough to go round all the hungry faces. Thanks to the Victory Walk additions, all six of her siblings were now full and satisfied.

Apart from Evelyn, that was. She stood with her back to the cooker in the small kitchen, her arms folded. 'Couldn't you even get no bread sauce?' she asked.

Gladys paused, her hands in the soap suds in

the sink, halfway through the big pile of washing up. 'Are you having me on?' she demanded. 'We had Bisto, didn't we? I saved that specially for today. I didn't see you bringing anything extra to the dinner table, so don't blame me.'

Evelyn huffed. 'What, am I meant to be grateful for the leftovers from your precious nurses?'

Gladys turned around to face her petulant sister. 'Yes. As a matter of fact, you are.' She went back to the dishes. 'And since you're here you can pick up a tea towel and help clear this lot.' She knew that Evelyn was sulking because she had no pub to escape to this evening. It was the one night of the year the Boatman's was shut, leaving Evelyn pacing about like a caged tiger.

With little alternative, the younger woman picked up a tea towel and began to wipe the plates stacked on the rack, making room for the others that Gladys had washed. With very bad grace she piled the clean, dry ones on the countertop. 'Well, I'm not. Sticks in my craw, taking charity from your holier-than-thou nurses.'

'Still ate it though, didn't you,' Gladys said, not bothering to hide the impatience in her voice.

'It would have looked rude not to. I don't want to set a bad example to the little ones,' Evelyn replied loftily. She clattered down another couple of plates.

'Steady on, we ain't got any of those to spare,' Gladys groaned. Evelyn's help always came at a price. She reached for the kettle to top up the water in the sink, and then set it to boil again so that there would be enough to soak the greasy roasting pans. 'Anyway, what are your plans for the new year? You must have thought about what you're going to do.'

Evelyn spun around. 'What do you mean?'

Gladys looked at her, unsure where the aggressive tone had come from. 'Well, you're going to turn twenty in a few months. That means you'll have to enlist for something. Do you know what yet? You already told me you don't want to join the nursing reserve, but you know I'd help you if you changed your mind.'

Evelyn's expression was one of pure disgust. 'You got to be joking,' she breathed. 'Touching all them strangers, hearing them moan on about where it hurts — not on your nelly.'

'Didn't stop you coming to us for help when you sprained your ankle,' Gladys observed.

'Oh stop going on at me. Nothing I do is right for you, I know that,' Evelyn snapped.

'It's not up to me, I'm just saying what's in store. You'll have to do something,' Gladys pointed out. She scrubbed the saucepan which had been used to boil the potatoes. Her mother had managed to burn the bottom of it. 'You better pick whichever thing you think you're good at.'

Evelyn shrugged and looked away from her sister's penetrating gaze. 'I know what I'm good at. Singing, being on stage. But you don't take me serious,' she complained.

'The government won't take you serious, more like. Unless you plan on joining ENSA.' Gladys gave up on the saucepan and put it to one side to soak. 'You probably left it a bit late for that.'

Evelyn gave her a poisonous look. 'I might not have. The American feller is coming back and Max is going to make sure I sing for him this time. I could get a spot in the chorus, I bet I could.'

Gladys raised her eyebrows. This was pie in the sky, she was sure of it. Even though people joked that ENSA stood for Every Night Something Awful, she didn't think they'd be in a hurry to sign up an amateur singer who'd performed only in one seedy pub.

'What, you don't believe me? Well, he will. He promised me. Max has influence,' Evelyn said grandly. 'You're just jealous. You'll be stuck here doing the same old thing, minding the kids, cleaning for those bleeding nurses and bandaging up some poor fool what got caught in an accident or whatnot. I'll be off travelling the world, helping entertain the troops and doing my bit, just you see. I've had enough, I'm going up to read my magazine.' She flung down the now-sopping tea towel and flounced off, slamming the kitchen door and making the plates still on the rack shake.

Gladys sighed, and hung the dripping towel over the rail beside the oven to let it dry properly. She set the roasting pans to soak and carefully sorted the cutlery back into its drawer. She had no reason to be jealous of her sister — despite the non-stop nature of her work, she loved it and could not imagine swapping it for a life of travelling and uncertainty. Yet she was unsettled, as Max was very obviously still in the picture, and filling her sister's head with impossible dreams. It could lead only to disappointment — or worse.

★ ★ ★

Joe breathed on his hands to warm them and stamped his feet on the steps of the National Gallery. He wasn't sure if the lunchtime concert was his sort of thing, but he was willing to give it a go. Who knew when he would next have the chance to hear music, of any kind, apart from crackly broadcasts over the wireless. Then he spotted Alice and waved.

She waved back, balancing a shopping bag with her other hand. She must have been successful in finding something to buy in the West End, even with the rigours of rationing. He was pleased for her. Secretly he thought she was looking more tired and thinner than when he'd last had leave, not that he would voice such a thought aloud. She deserved a treat, and if her idea of fun was to go to a classical music concert, then who was he to deny her? She'd told him that only Mary from the group of nurses really enjoyed them, and she was with her parents until New Year. Joe had offered to accompany her without hesitation.

She smiled as she came towards him. 'I'm so grateful you're giving up your last day of leave to come to this,' she said. 'Don't worry, it won't be stuffy. All sorts of people come to these things.'

Joe laughed. 'Well, I'm accustomed to all sorts

of people these days. You don't have much chance to get away from each other on a ship. Anyway, I'm not giving up anything. I'm pleased you suggested it.' This was true enough, even though he would never have gone to a classical concert before the war. It was never a hardship to spend a day with Alice. Far from it.

'Good,' she said, grinning. 'Even though we spent Christmas with your family, it felt as if we didn't get five minutes to have a chat between just the two of us.' He could see she was trying to seem cheerful, hiding her regret.

He nodded in agreement. His mother had of course put on the most delicious Christmas dinner, rivalling the wedding feast, with a houseful of eager guests. He wouldn't have changed that for the world, but it had been impossible to have a private conversation. Not that he had anything to hide from his family — but there were some matters that he preferred to talk about with Alice alone. He knew she would understand and he would not have to explain the background. 'There's a lot to catch up on,' he replied. 'Look, we have a little while before it starts, don't we? So tell me your news.'

She picked up on his urgency. 'Do you mean it's easier to speak out here, where nobody will overhear? Sounds as if you have something to tell me. Spill the beans, then.'

He nodded again, knowing she had read his tone. 'Well, sort of. It was little more than a rumour really, but word was going around my base just before I left.'

She raised her eyebrows in anticipation. 'Go on.'

'You know last time I was home we mentioned the German codes?' His gaze swept the area behind her to check there was nobody close, but the crowds were milling beyond the base of the steps in Trafalgar Square and no one could overhear. 'I'll be quick as I can so nobody comes close enough to pick up what I'm saying. Well, it looks as if there might have been a breakthrough. By the backroom boys, that is, nothing to do with me. They say they've cracked the big one.'

Alice's eyes widened, in excitement and admiration. 'Really? Goodness — that would be wonderful.'

'Early days yet, of course,' he cautioned, 'but yes, that would have a huge effect on the safety of all the shipping. Imagine all the convoys crossing the Atlantic getting through without the U-boat risk. It's a big leap forward if it works.'

Alice's face lit up. 'Do you mean all the vital supplies like nylon stockings will make it through? There will be a lot of happy nurses thanking you if you can manage that.'

'I'll make it a priority,' he assured her seriously. 'We'll leave all those GIs and crates of tinned food back in the States and fill our holds with nylons.'

'It will help morale,' she said, equally serious, and then she threw back her head and laughed. 'You men have no idea the effort we go through to overcome the lack of stockings. Dyeing our legs with tea, drawing seams up the back of our legs. And then of course it's freezing cold.'

Joe laughed back at her. 'Some of you, maybe. Don't tell me you do that, Alice.'

She blushed a little, wondering if that meant Joe had been looking at her legs all the while. 'Well, no, actually I don't. But plenty of us do. Edith, for example — she's a dab hand. Come to think of it, so are most of the nurses you know. And I'm sure I could, if the need arose.'

'Oh, absolutely. If the need arose.' He paused, watching as the chilly breeze lifted the stray strands of her dark blonde hair. For once she was wearing it down, not pinned back in its neat bun for work. It suited her. 'Your turn. What's on your mind these days?'

Her face, its blush fading but still rosy from the breeze, took on a genuinely serious look. 'You heard about the discussion in parliament about the Nazi death camps? I mean, I know it's been talked about for a while, but this was a proper announcement. They really are trying to rid the Fatherland of Jews. It doesn't bear thinking about.'

He shut his eyes briefly in sympathy. 'I know, I heard about that too. It doesn't seem possible in this day and age. It's barbaric. No other word for it.'

Alice nodded. 'It's horrible. It's even worse for Belinda. She keeps worrying about her brother falling into their hands somehow — you know he's a pilot, so it could happen. Makes it all feel even more real. She doesn't talk about it much but you can tell.'

'Of course.' Joe looked into the distance. 'If anything it makes me even more determined to see this through, to do everything I can to bring this war to an end and make sure we win. We have to, there's nothing else for it. The alternative is simply impossible.'

'I completely agree.' She looked up into his determined face. While she would have expected nothing less of him, somehow hearing him say it bolstered her courage. He had never failed when called upon to show bravery, and he was one of many thousands of others who felt the same. 'Well, we should look on the bright side. Surely Hitler has made an error trying to attack Russia at the same time as Western Europe. All those men of his are stuck in Stalingrad. That's bound to weaken him. That, on top of the losses in North Africa.'

He brought his gaze down to meet hers. 'Yes, you're right — of course. Might have known you'd be on top of the facts.'

She punched him on the arm. 'Stop teasing me. I just like to keep well informed, you know that. As you do yourself, don't deny it.'

He raised both hands in surrender. 'All right, I admit it. We're both as bad as each other.'

'That's more like it.' She grinned and then glanced at her watch. 'We should start to think about going in. They get very busy, you know, and this is the first concert after the Christmas break.'

He turned to head up the steps with her. 'The only thing is,' he said cautiously, 'that if the Atlantic convoys are safer, then my skills might be needed elsewhere. I don't know where — or even if that's what will happen,' he said quickly, catching her glance. 'It would make sense, that's all. So I'll be prepared for whatever comes next. Don't be surprised if you don't hear from me for a while.'

She halted her ascent of the steps, swallowing hard. 'Of course. I know you'll write when you can. Just let me know in the usual way.'

'I will. You know that.' For a moment their eyes met and that sense of deep connection flowed between them, in a way that happened with nobody else. He put a hand on her arm. 'Come on, we're holding people up. We should go inside now.'

Biting her lip, she nodded. She remembered how her stomach had dropped when he'd told her how his ship had been scuppered and crew members had died. Her admiration for his bravery was mixed with a very real dread for his safety. She wouldn't even contemplate what she might feel like if he failed to come home. Life would be changed for ever. It would be unbearable.

Then she was back to her steady, practical self, pushing away the feelings that must stay hidden. 'We should. You'll enjoy it, see if you don't.' But before they got to the door she took his hand as it rested on her elbow, escorting her along. 'Promise me, Joe — stay safe. If you possibly can — stay safe.'

21

It wasn't as if Peggy had expected that James would arrive on the front doorstep and shower her with gifts. She knew from his regular letters that he would not have much leave over Christmas, and many of the GIs on his base were being invited to spend the festive lunch with local families, to learn more about British customs. He would have to be back at base by late afternoon, which hardly allowed for a trip to London. However, she felt a little let down when 1942 turned into 1943 and still there was no word.

It wasn't until the second week of the new year that a battered-looking brown paper parcel arrived, bearing her name in his handwriting. She took it with delight from the postman, but also with some suspicion. Ever since poisonous Mrs Bellings had handed over the letter she had received in error, Peggy was on the lookout for ominous delays in any correspondence from James. It wasn't as if she directly distrusted the postman; he seemed perfectly friendly, especially now that he'd got the hang of who lived where in their neighbourhood. It was more a question of wondering if anyone was interfering somewhere along the line.

She had never found out who had attacked her

in the alley. She didn't know where to start, as she hadn't seen who it was, hadn't recognised the voice, or noticed any possible witnesses. She had to hope and believe it was a one-off, and whoever it was had said their piece. She'd laughed off the scratches on her face, telling Mrs Cannon that she'd tripped at work and landed on some rough stone. It was close enough to the truth to account for the marks, and they'd soon faded. She'd risked using some of her precious store of makeup to cover them until they vanished completely.

Now she thanked the postman and took the parcel through to the dining table, fetching a sharp paperknife so that she could salvage as much of the packaging as possible. She could hear her landlady singing to herself in the kitchen, mopping the floor.

The postmark showed it had been sent three weeks ago. So he had thought of her and intended this as a Christmas gift. Peggy felt her heart beat a little faster. She wondered if he had received what she had sent him: a smart dark tie, pattered with tiny spots. She wondered if he'd get the reference. It was the closest she could find to the kind worn by the Ink Spots in one of their recent pictures. Even if he didn't make the connection, she thought it was just his style. She'd tried to forget just how much of her pay packet and clothing coupons it had set her back.

Carefully she cut the string, winding it into several loops so that it could be put away in the 'useful bits and pieces' drawer. Then she set about undoing the brown paper. The outside layer would be no good as wrapping, as it was torn in many places. It would do on the fire, so she balled it up and tossed it into the grate. The inner layer she folded and set aside with the string. Within nestled a small cardboard box and an envelope, which she tore open.

It was a card, showing what she took to be an American cabin covered in snow. The gables were edged with glitter. It was breathtakingly pretty, and she ran her finger along the rough line of sparkling silver, amazed that a man should have the delicacy to choose this. She opened the card.

'To Peggy. Season's Greetings and with best wishes for a happy 1943. All my love, James.'

Her face flamed. All his love. Did he mean that? It was just the sort of thing people wrote on cards. He had probably written all of his in exactly the same way; she mustn't think it meant anything too special. All the same . . . he wouldn't say it to just anybody, would he?

The very idea made her fumble as she cautiously opened the box. The scent hit her before she drew back the final delicate paper. It was soap — proper lavender soap, totally unlike the sensible, practical kind she used every day. This was soap to pamper yourself with.

She lifted it to her nose and inhaled. It was how she imagined walking through a field of lavender would be — not that she'd ever come close to doing such a thing. It was high quality, she could tell by the smooth feel of it, and by the little purple flowers printed on the wrapping. It would have been beyond her means before the war; these days it was not only rationed and expensive but almost impossible to find. That made it priceless, to her at any rate.

'What have you got there, dear?' Mrs Cannon asked as she came in. Peggy started, nearly dropping her present. She'd been so caught up in the card's message that she hadn't heard the older woman stop her work in the kitchen.

'A late present from James.' Peggy held out the soap so that her landlady could smell it. 'Isn't it lovely?'

Mrs Cannon bent her head to it and breathed in. At once a smile lit her face. 'Isn't it! That takes me back to when I was younger.' Her eyes grew misty. 'Back to when I first met Mr Cannon. He bought me something like this, maybe not as grand, but that smell . . . ah, it does me good. There's nothing quite like it.'

'We'll share it,' Peggy said impulsively. 'We must.' It struck her that Mrs Cannon hardly ever mentioned her late husband. She knew that he had died long ago, before Peggy had met Pete, and there was very little in the house to show that he had ever lived there. She had wondered if that meant the marriage had been an unhappy one. Now she realised it might be because Mrs Cannon could not bear to be reminded of her loss day in, day out. She understood that all right.

The older woman gave a small chuckle. 'No, no, dear. It's for you. It's obviously very special. That young man must think a lot of you, to have sent such a gift.'

'Maybe.' Peggy felt shy at considering the idea

in front of her mother-in-law. It felt disrespect-ful. 'Well, I shall leave it by the bath, so if you'd like to use it then you can. It would be a waste for it to sit there drying out, after all.'

Mrs Cannon smiled gently. 'If you say so. But we'll both know who it is intended for.' She spotted the folded paper and string. 'I'll pop these in the drawer, shall I?'

Peggy recognised that she was trying to make an excuse not to pursue the discussion, again maybe because the thoughts of her own loss were too painful. She nodded dumbly. What was she doing, she wondered suddenly, letting herself be drawn to a soldier like this? She knew the risks they ran. What if she had to go through another loss, reviving all that she had endured in the aftermath of Pete's death? That she was still enduring . . .

Yet James had sent her this beautiful present. She could feel her blood fizzing with suppressed excitement. He liked her, he really did. This meant more than a casual turn on the dance floor — not that their last turn had felt casual, anything but. Yet she didn't want to presume. She hardly ever saw him. She didn't want to make assumptions, to build unreasonable hopes on what was at best a few hours' acquaintance. Even so, she could not help but wonder what this might lead to.

Mrs Cannon eyed her carefully. 'Peggy,' she said slowly.

'Yes?' Peggy held the soap in her hand, sensing its coolness.

'You do like this young gentleman, then?'

Peggy noticed how the skin around Mrs Cannon's eyes had grown more lined recently, and how papery it was. How hadn't she seen this before? With all her WVS activity, the woman had seemed to have a new lease of life, always out doing something or meeting the other women in the service. Peggy had forgotten how old she must be. She didn't want to add to the burden of her worry. Unthinkingly, her hand went to her face where the scratches had been.

Mrs Cannon nodded, acknowledging the movement. 'It's all right, dear. You don't have to pretend. I know those marks didn't come from an accident at work.'

Peggy gasped. 'But . . . '

Mrs Cannon smiled gently. 'I wasn't born yesterday, you know. People don't like what they don't understand or what they think is different. Promise me one thing, my dear.'

Peggy nodded. 'What?'

Mrs Cannon sighed. 'Be careful,' she said. 'That's all. Promise me you'll be careful.'

★   ★   ★

Alice knocked on the now-familiar front door, which was still in terrible condition. She considered if she should report the landlord, but then thought that the tenants wouldn't thank her for causing trouble. It had taken so long to get the grandmother to trust her; she didn't want to risk it. All the same, she wondered what sort of reception she was in for this time.

'Good, I'm glad it's you, miss. Nurse.' The

231

familiar little girl opened the door, rubbing her hand across her face.

Alice took one look and realised what the trouble was. 'Hello, Pauline. Is your gran in?'

Pauline shook her head. 'She's gone to the shops, miss.'

'What about your mother?' Alice asked, more in hope than expectation.

'No, it's just me brother and me. You said to call you if he was took sick again. It's him *and* me this time.' She scratched at her chin as she spoke.

Alice picked up her Gladstone bag. 'Shall I come in, then?' She stepped inside as Pauline led the way into the living room. It was in no better state than before. Dirty clothes were piled in one corner, dirty plates in the other. The remains of a fire smouldered in the grate, giving little heat on the cold winter's day. On a stool in front of it sat Larry, but the room was so dark that Alice could not make out his face other than in silhouette.

'Remember me, Larry?' she said cheerfully. 'Why don't you come over here by the window so I can see you. Then I can help you. What's wrong, then? Why did you want to see me?'

The little boy twisted away, too shy to speak, let alone come close.

Pauline huffed in exasperation. 'She won't bite, you daft sausage. She wants to make you better. Get over here, do as yer told for once.' Still he didn't move.

'Why don't I take a look at you first then?' Alice suggested, crouching to the girl's level.

'You seem to have a bit of a problem with your face.'

Pauline turned so that her face was illuminated by the dull light coming through the filthy window. 'It's this red stuff, nurse. It bleeding itches, all the time. Driving me round the twist, it is.'

Alice surveyed the rash from several angles, without touching it. 'Tip your head back,' she said, squinting at the girl's skin. 'And to the side once more . . . All right. I know what it is. Is your brother suffering from the same thing?'

'Course he is. Larry, get yerself here so Nurse can look at yer face.'

Reluctantly Larry rose from his woodworm-infested stool and came over, hanging his head. 'You'll have to look up a bit so that I can see you,' Alice said as encouragingly as she could. 'That's it, come right beside the window. Do like your sister did — turn to each side and then lift your chin up . . . yes, I see. Does it make you want to scratch it?'

Larry looked down at his feet in their boots with no laces. 'Yes, miss,' he whispered.

'How long has it been like this?' Alice turned to the girl again.

'Couple of days. Gran said not to bother you cos it was just cold sores but I thought, what with him being so ill before, we was better to ask you. It isn't like the sores what we had before.' Pauline's face twisted with worry. She clearly didn't like going against her grandmother.

Alice immediately sought to reassure her. 'You did the right thing, Pauline. What you've got is far from uncommon, but it's worse if you aren't healthy when you get it. It's a bit more serious than cold sores. We have to keep an eye on Larry. He's still a bit small for his age. Aren't you?' she said kindly.

'It's not his fault, miss,' Pauline said hurriedly. 'They tease him at school something rotten.'

Alice sighed. She strongly suspected malnourishment was to blame for the boy's lack of growth, and also as an underlying factor in catching the rash; children with low immune systems were more susceptible. Lack of hygiene was another contributor. Larry was vulnerable on all fronts. 'No, it's not his fault at all, nor is it yours. Have you been going to school while you've had the rash?'

'Course we have. I don't want him to miss his lessons,' Pauline said staunchly. 'But Miss Phipps said we was to come home early today. She don't want no others going down with it. Will it spread like wildfire, miss?' Her eyes lit up.

'Quite possibly,' said Alice severely. 'You weren't to know, but yes, it's contagious. You don't want all your friends catching it, do you?'

Pauline scuffed her feet. 'Ain't got no real friends since Dottie got evacuated. And like I said, lots of the other boys picks on Larry.'

Alice sighed. 'That's a shame. All the same, we'll get you sorted out. What you have both got is called impetigo. That's a skin infection. It will probably get better by itself if we leave it, but it could take a long time and we don't want you missing all that school.'

'No, I don't want to miss it either,' said

Pauline. 'I like it now I've got Miss Phipps again.'

Alice grinned, knowing that her friend Janet Phipps had a soft spot for Pauline, just as she herself did. 'Exactly. So we should try to speed up the healing process. First of all, have you got any carbolic soap?'

Pauline laughed. 'Soap, miss? No, we don't have any of that. Gran don't hold with it. She says it's a waste of money when you can just wet yer flannel and wash in cold water.'

Alice could guess what the money was spent on. Gran's thirst for gin was unquenchable.

'It so happens I have some in my bag. It's important that you use it. You've got to try to fight off infection and cold water on its own won't do it. Can you warm up the water you wash in?'

'No, miss.' Pauline said it quietly, as if she knew this was wrong, but wasn't in a position to do much about it.

Alice shook her head. 'While you have this rash, you really should. Let's try now. Where's your kettle?'

Now it was Pauline's turn to hang her head. 'Pawnshop, miss.' Alice could hardly hear her.

'So you can't even have a cup of tea?'

'Don't drink tea, miss. Me and Larry has water . . .'

'And I know what Gran's favourite drink is.' Alice sighed. 'What about milk? You should get that on ration.'

Pauline shrugged but clammed up. Alice had a horrible idea that the grandmother sold it or swapped it for more gin. She made a decision.

'Right, you two. It's not far to the nurses' home. You're coming with me. I'll give you some ointment for your rash but there's no point unless you are clean first. Have you got any clean clothes to change into?'

'Not really, miss.' Pauline sounded ashamed. Alice realised that the girl was growing up; that she knew how much worse her home was compared to those of her schoolmates.

'Doesn't matter. I expect we can find you something.' Alice knew that Mary often helped with clothes swaps at the church hall, or they could send round to Miriam or Flo for WVS assistance. How she longed to go to work on this room and make it clean enough for the children to recover. 'Get your coats and scarves — Larry, do you have a scarf? Never mind, we'll get you one.' Now she had made up her mind, Alice wanted them out of the filthy house as fast as possible. Keeping her smile in place, she escorted the children out of the door.

On the short journey to Victory Walk, she reflected that it didn't matter how much she tried with this family: as long as the children lived in that place, they would be sitting targets for all kinds of diseases and infections. The adults simply had no interest in keeping them or the house clean. She would have to do her best and lead by example, and just hope that some of it sank in.

22

Evelyn was in a particularly bad mood, even by her standards. Gladys frowned as her sister flung down her apron and pulled on her woollen cardigan, which Gladys had mended very carefully so that it looked good as new. Evelyn pouted in the mirror in the back kitchen, reaching into her pocket for a stub of bright lipstick. She drew on a cupid's bow, blotted it on a scrap of newspaper and reapplied the slash of scarlet. Angrily she twirled her hair and fastened it with a slide, then tried again when the first attempt didn't satisfy her.

'What's the matter?' Gladys asked. She noticed that her sister's hair was even blonder than usual; she must have redone it earlier in the day.

'What do you care?' snapped Evelyn, her reflection in the mirror glaring across the room. She stabbed the sharp end of the slide into the disobedient curl.

Gladys raised her eyebrows but said nothing. Sometimes that was for the best when Evelyn was like this.

After a few moments she relented. 'It's that Patty. She thinks she's got Max wound around her little finger but she's wrong. He only pays any attention to her to make sure she sings on the nights I'm not there and does it on the cheap. It's me he wants really. If she reckons I'm going to disappear and let her take him off me, she's got another think coming.'

Gladys swallowed hard. 'I didn't realise things had got that far with you and Max.'

'There's a lot of things you don't realise,' said Evelyn.

'So he's not just a friend, then?' Gladys thought that a friend wouldn't dump you on the floor of the first-aid post, but she knew better than to take that approach. Perhaps her sister would confide in her, and that way she could start to help her.

Evelyn laughed harshly. 'Of course he's not just a friend. What would I want with just a friend?'

'You've got to have friends,' Gladys said at once. She could not imagine life without hers. She had never had any while she was growing up, after being forced to leave school to help her mother raise her younger siblings. That had all changed since getting to know the nurses. Now she knew she couldn't be without her female friends.

'Stuff and nonsense. What you need in this business is contacts,' Evelyn said grandly. 'That's what Max always tells me. He's known for his contacts, and he's happy to share them with me.'

Gladys wondered when her sister had become so harsh. What a grim way to look at the world. 'Yes, but — '

'Don't bother.' Evelyn tugged on her coat, picked up her little clutch bag that had replaced the old beaded one and made for the door.

238

'Don't wait up, and don't tell Ma.' She swept out.

Gladys stared at the door as it swung shut, her brow creased with concern. On the one hand, her sister was too old to tell off. She was almost twenty. By that age, Gladys had been effectively in charge of the household for years, as well as working full-time at the Victory Walk home. She'd had no time to go gadding about, off to pubs to meet men. So in one way Evelyn probably had far more experience, certainly of that side of life.

Yet Gladys knew that in many ways Evelyn was still a girl, used to having things done for her, not taking responsibility. Perhaps she had let her get away with too much. After all, Gladys had been only too aware when growing up that her own childhood had been taken from her; she didn't see why two of them should suffer. Also, it wasn't up to her to discipline a sister who was only two years younger than she was. That was a parent's job; but their mother had never shown much inclination to step in, collapsing with bad nerves whenever there were difficulties, and their father had not been seen or heard of for years.

Gladys was rooted to the spot with indecision. Evelyn was annoying, and hurtfully dismissive at times, and yet she couldn't truly wish her to come to any ill. The more she became embroiled with Max, the more certain it seemed that things would end badly. Gladys did not want to interfere and yet it seemed increasingly obvious that she ought to do something, rather than sit back and wait for bad news of some kind.

She was off duty tonight, for a change. The little ones had been fed, washed and the smallest were already in bed. She could say that she was going out to check on the first-aid supplies — her mother had never shown any interest in the details of her work and would be unlikely to question her. Gladys decided to pay her first-ever visit to a pub. She would rather it wasn't the Boatman's, but beggars couldn't be choosers.

★ ★ ★

Gladys was nervous as she approached the building, which huddled against the towpath to the canal. It was only dimly lit by intermittent moonlight and the ever-present searchlights that raked the skies, but even so she could tell that several roof tiles were missing and some of the upstairs windows had been boarded up. Of course, many places were still showing signs of bomb damage, but somehow this seemed more like poor maintenance than a consequence of the Blitz.

She hesitated as she got to the door. Women didn't go into pubs alone, particularly ones like this. What if the men inside misunderstood what she was there for? What if Evelyn saw her? She hadn't thought this through at all but had acted on pure instinct. Truth to tell, she was terrified. But she'd come this far; she couldn't go back now.

Cautiously she pushed open the door and stepped inside. It was noisy and quite crowded, mostly with men around tables and clustered at the bar, but a few women stood here and there. None of them was Evelyn. Gladys looked for the telltale bright blonde hair but there was no sign. At one end of the pub was a small makeshift stage, a piano beside it, and a woman possibly in her late twenties was draped along the lid over the keyboard, flashing her heavily made-up eyes at the barman. Perhaps this was Patty. Gladys was unsure whether to ask her if she'd seen Evelyn, or whether that would make things worse for her sister.

A movement to one side of her made Gladys jump. A young man was coming towards her, his face in shadow until he came closer and caught the light of a lamp, its shade ripped and tipped at a strange angle. 'Hello, remember me?' he said kindly. 'You're that friend of Mary's, aren't you?'

'Y-yes.' Gladys knew she'd seen him before but struggled to recall exactly when and where.

'I met you down your victory garden one time. I was with Billy Reilly. And Kenny, look, he's over there, the one in the glasses.'

She felt a little less nervous as the memory fell into place. 'Oh yes, of course. Sorry, I don't know your name.'

The young man smiled and held out his hand. 'Ronald. Ron for short. I didn't expect you to remember.'

Gladys took his hand and shook it, relieved he had spared her the embarrassment of forgetting who he was. 'It's coming back to me now,' she managed to say. 'Yes, of course, you said you came here sometimes.'

He nodded. 'Can I buy you a drink?'

She started. 'N-no, no thank you. I wasn't going to stay long. I just wanted to see if someone I knew was here.' She was too nervous to drink anything, even if she'd wanted to. She appreciated the offer, though; anyone looking at them would think they had arranged to meet and it was just a normal conversation. 'I won't be stopping for a drink. Don't let me keep you from yours,' she added hastily.

'Don't worry, it can wait.' He frowned. 'Is it your sister you're looking for? Didn't you say she sang here sometimes?'

Gladys gave a small smile despite herself. 'You've got a good memory,' she said, impressed.

Ron chuckled. 'Not really. I'm always forgetting things at work — just ask Billy. But I remember you seemed worried about her and it stuck in my mind.'

Gladys nodded, her smile vanishing as she steeled herself to finish what she'd come for. 'Well, she's younger than me so I have to keep an eye on her,' she explained. 'Is she here tonight? Have you seen her?'

Ron's gaze dropped and he wouldn't meet her eye. He looked as if he was trying to avoid saying something.

Gladys somehow held her nerve and asked again. 'Is she? I can't see her here but was she around earlier?'

Ron twisted his hands together in awkwardness. 'Yes,' he said after a few moments. 'I saw her at the bar a while ago.' He sighed. 'You might as well know the worst. She went out the back with Max — d'you know him?'

'I've seen him in passing,' Gladys said darkly. 'I wouldn't say I know him.'

'Best keep it that way,' Ron said shortly.

Gladys frowned. 'I can't help it. I want to see Evelyn. Just to put my mind at rest, to know she's all right.'

He shrugged, and she noticed how kind his face was, even though it was etched with concern, and maybe with a little sympathy. He obviously didn't like or trust Max. But she couldn't give up now.

'She's your sister, so I know what you mean,' he said. 'Max won't want to be interrupted, though. He's got a proper temper on him. I'd stay well clear if I were you.'

Gladys gasped. Did he mean that the man might hurt Evelyn? Was she just making things worse by turning up here? 'I-I'd still like to see her,' she persisted. 'Can you help me? Please? I won't try to talk to this person if you think it's not a good idea. I don't want to cause no trouble. But I'm worried about her, I can't help it.'

Ron's face winced with unease. 'I don't blame you. All right, come with me, but stay close and don't make a noise. We'll go to the side door and see if we can spot her. If she's on her own you could call out and get her attention. How about that?'

Gladys nodded. 'Yes, let's try that. Thank you, Ron.' She felt very reliant on the good graces of this young man she scarcely knew. Yet if he was a friend of Billy's, he must be all right. Billy was as solid as a rock.

Ron pushed his way through the crowd, easing a space for her to snake through behind him, keeping a close watch in case any of the drunker men made an unwelcome move. Gladys realised they all assumed she was with him. Well, if it meant they left her alone, that suited her fine.

At the far end of the noisy bar was a half-glazed door, its frame covered in once-cream paint, now discoloured by nicotine. Ron carefully turned the handle and stepped out into a storage area, open to the elements on one side, facing a rundown courtyard. Barrels were stacked around, crates of bottles heaped in piles, and broken glass glinted underfoot. Hardly the spot for a pleasant drink on a fine evening. The light spilled out from behind them and Ron hastily pulled the door to.

He held one finger to his lips in an exaggerated fashion so she couldn't fail to get the message. Then they stood still and listened.

A low rumble of a male voice — not shouting in anger but clearly displeased.

Then a higher voice, a woman's, trying to appease him by the sound of it.

Another rumble, ending in a menacing growl.

The woman answering back but not fiercely. A high-pitched laugh.

Then more low noises, less easy to distinguish, before a shaft of moonlight allowed Ron and Gladys to pick out the couple. They were leaning against the brick wall adjoining the neighbouring property, him tall and burly, her slight and with bright pale hair. He was pulling her closer and she was winding her arms around his neck and looking up into his face. They couldn't see her expression. He grabbed at her, reaching behind her and pulling up her skirt.

'Come on,' Ron whispered abruptly. 'Back in the bar, quick. Before they notice we're here.' He pushed Gladys back to the half-glazed door and they fell through into the warmth of the smoke-filled snug.

Gladys could hardly believe what she'd just seen. Maybe she shouldn't have been surprised; Evelyn had said Max was more than a friend. But to do that, right out in the open, and on such a cold night . . . what sort of hold did this man have over her sister?

'You all right?' Ron asked anxiously.

'Y-yes. I think so.' Gladys found she was shivering.

'You sure you don't want a drink?' he asked solicitously. 'You've gone all pale.'

Gladys shook her head. 'No, honestly. I'd best be going. I don't want to stick around and have her see me, not now. But thank you anyway.'

Ron pursed his lips. 'Let me just down the rest of my pint and say good night to Kenny. Then I'll walk you home.'

'Oh really, there's no need . . . '

Ron turned to face her. 'You've seen what sort of place this is. There's every need. I go as far as the main road anyway — that will take you back to the nurses' home, won't it? Is that the direction you'll be headed for? Well, then.' He stepped across to the table in the corner, where Kenny was sitting with two other men with their backs to them. Kenny looked up and smiled as if to tease his friend, but his expression darkened as Ron must have told him not to jump to the wrong conclusion.

Gladys shut her eyes and tried to drive away the image that was now burned on her mind: her sister in the arms of that foul man. How could she? Her little sister.

'Come on.' Ron nudged her elbow. 'Time I was going anyway. I'm on the early shift tomorrow. I've asked Kenny to keep an eye out for when your sister comes back into the bar — he'll make sure she gets home all right.'

'Thank you.' Gladys felt the word was hardly adequate but didn't know what else to say. 'I wish I hadn't seen what we just did. But at least I know the worst now. At least I know.'

23

Spring 1943

Harry gazed around him at the walls covered in shelves and filing cabinets. This would be his new workplace. He'd never seen himself as a pen-pusher but it looked as if this was what he would become. The desk at which he sat was scratched and dull, and his long legs barely fitted underneath it. Already he felt cramped and uncomfortable.

Through the one window he could see khaki-coloured vehicles parked close together. Perhaps he could learn to drive one of them in the future. Meanwhile he was stuck here, booking them in and out, keeping records of their maintenance, watching out for when spare parts needed to be ordered. Not budgeting — that was someone else's job. He had already been told in no uncertain terms the limits of what he was to do, and how frowned upon it would be to encroach on somebody else's territory.

Harry sighed and flexed his arm muscles to ease the tension he could sense was building. He should be glad finally to be doing something useful again, not stuck in hospital any more, now back in active service. He had his special ointment to apply to his remaining scars and wounds, and exercises to do in order to improve his arm movement, but as long as he kept going to regular check-ups he didn't need to be under a doctor's daily care any more.

The trouble was, in his mind he had still not fully adjusted to the idea that this was as active as his service was likely to get. Men he had trained with were off fighting in North Africa or the Far East. Some had not made it through, but at least they had seen plenty of action. In his head he was still a fit young fighter, eager for glory, dealing with physical hardships and discomforts as part of the job.

Harry knew he should be grateful, and if the worst physical discomfort he had to put up with was a bit of cramp in the legs, then he was lucky. He rolled his shoulders to ease the pain in his neck. His injured arm responded with a twinge, but nothing compared to what it used to be like when he moved it. Perhaps those exercises were working and his arm would get back to something like normal, in the end.

He had to keep believing that. After the drama of the wedding, the stay in the grand hotel and the wonderful warmth of a family Christmas, it had been difficult to wave goodbye and come here to his new base, the closest to his old hospital. He and Edith had always known they would not be able to start their married life living in the same place, but it had been tough to leave her there in Dalston after so many nights together. He shut his eyes for a moment, remembering his beautiful, brave wife. He wondered what she was doing right now. Pedalling that cranky old bike along the bomb-damaged terraces, most likely. He grinned in spite of himself at the image, wishing he was there with her.

'Asleep already?' came a sharp voice.

Harry sat up straight and made his expression alert. His immediate boss was a tough woman in her forties, greying hair clipped severely, her army uniform immaculate. He was glad he had made an effort to press his own into sharp creases, but being caught with his eyes shut had probably undone any good impression he had hoped to make.

Before he could answer, she plonked a pile of manila files on his desk. 'Requisition orders,' she said shortly. 'See that they match what's actually been done to the relevant engines. Report any discrepancies to me before lunch. That should keep you awake at least.' Without waiting for a reply she marched out again.

Harry stared at the folders, his heart sinking. This was what he was in for, until the war ended. His dreams of winning a medal for bravery would never come true. Nobody got a Victoria Cross for perfect administration. Reluctantly he drew his pen towards him and opened the topmost file. So be it. This was the hand that fate had dealt him and he just had to get on with it.

* * *

Peggy welcomed the arrival of spring, the first shoots of green on the bare branches of the trees, the sparrows chirping more noisily, the evenings growing lighter. It meant that she could fit in a

249

walk around the park after her regular shift at the factory, and she relished the exercise after being cooped up inside all day. The air was warmer too and she could pack away her heavy winter coat, wondering if she would be able to have a new one next year. It would make a nice change, but this one would last for another cold season, if she was honest, so she folded it carefully and added some dried lavender in muslin pouches to go in the pockets. She hated the smell of mothballs, and some people said this worked just as well.

Now she waited for the knock on the door. Peggy had run into Edith when she was on an early visit that morning and they had decided to go for a walk together after they had both finished work. Peggy had come back to the house first, to change her shoes and try out her latest piece of home-made jewellery, a cleverly cut brooch made from three scraps of plastic and some left-over enamel paint, highlighted with zigzags of nail polish. Peggy was quietly pleased with it. It made her feel smart and modern, even if it was just for a walk with her friend.

As she pinned it to her lapel, there came the sound of the letterbox. Peggy hurried down the stairs but Mrs Cannon got there first and was already smiling at Edith as Peggy reached the hall.

'Come in, dear. Have you got time for a cup of tea?'

Edith looked across at Peggy, already in her jacket. 'That's very kind, but perhaps we'd better go straight out to make the most of the daylight,' she said. 'I'd love to another time, though.'

Mrs Cannon nodded understandingly. 'Of course. You are always welcome, you and the rest of your colleagues. I know how hard you work. Is everything all right?' she added, catching Edith's expression as the shorter woman turned in the weak sunlight coming through the open door.

Edith shrugged. 'Oh, it's probably nothing.' She glanced back over her shoulder as Mrs Cannon pushed the door to behind her, keen to keep the warmth in. 'I'm most likely imagining it.'

'Imagining what?' asked Peggy.

'It was so quick, I might have misunderstood,' Edith said. 'Just across the road there, in one of the houses opposite — I caught sight of someone staring at me as I knocked at your door. A young man, by the looks of him. He didn't look very friendly. But it could have been about anything.'

Peggy frowned. 'Which house exactly?'

Edith pointed in the general direction. 'It had a dark red door.'

Peggy nodded. 'I know the one. Mrs Bellings lives there. But I don't know about a young man. She's on her own. She hasn't got any children, has she?' She turned to Mrs Cannon.

The older woman pursed her lips as she tried to remember. 'There's a daughter, a couple of years older than you, I would say. She got married before the war and moved away. Let me see now . . . Yorkshire, I think it was. Full of airs and graces as I seem to recall, never too keen to come back to visit her mother.'

Peggy couldn't help but think that if Mrs Bellings had been her mother she wouldn't have been in any hurry to come home either.

'Wait, now. She said something the other day.' Mrs Cannon's expression cleared. 'It will be her nephew. She told me her sister's boy had gone into the army and wanted to spend a part of his leave in London. Wants to enjoy the high life up in the West End, I dare say.'

Edith nodded. 'Well, good luck to him. Looks as if he could do with something to cheer him up. Come on, Peggy, let's make the most of the weather.'

'Yes, you go on and do that,' said Mrs Cannon, shutting the door behind them.

* * *

'Listen to that. Is it a blackbird?' Edith came to a halt and looked up into the trees. 'Just up there. Maybe your eyesight is better than mine.'

'I doubt it,' said Peggy, peering up into the branches. 'Isn't your work often detailed and delicate? And you don't wear glasses.'

Edith laughed. 'I'm all right for close-up jobs. I had to take some stitches out earlier. Dr Patcham said I'd be good enough and just to keep a steady hand. As it turned out the patient was more nervous than I was and I spent so long reassuring her to get her to stop shaking, I didn't have time to worry. She didn't like needles. I told her, she'd have been in deep trouble if Dr Patcham hadn't sewn up her arm, as she'd caught it on broken glass.'

'Easy to do,' said Peggy. They'd all had narrow escapes from similar incidents — there were so

252

many smashed windows everywhere.

Edith linked her arm through her friend's and strolled on. 'Hard to believe we're at war on an evening like this,' she sighed.

'Apart from the trenches and sandbags,' Peggy pointed out. 'Oh, and the number of people in uniform.' There were several men in air-force blue and some Wrens on the other side of the stretch of green.

'All right, but you know what I mean.'

'Yes,' Peggy admitted. 'Sorry, I'm just teasing. How about your own man in uniform — have you heard from Harry lately? It must be difficult, getting married then having to be apart directly afterwards.'

'Well, you'd know,' Edith replied.

'Exactly, that's why I asked,' Peggy confessed.

Edith walked a few paces before answering. 'Well, of course we knew that this is what it would be like. There was no chance we could live together, or even be in the same city. He's got a desk job now, so that's something.'

'Bet he hates that,' Peggy said at once. 'He never could sit still at a desk, even when we were at school. Always wanted to be up and doing something, or out playing football. He always used to say that desks were for people like Joe, not him.'

Edith nodded. 'He won't say so in his letters, of course, but I have this horrible feeling you are right. He can't go back to proper active service, though. I wish I could be with him to help but it's not possible. So I write and tell him how much I miss him, and hope for the best. When I get my next leave, I'll go and see him, but that won't be for a while.'

Peggy nodded and smiled wryly. 'It's hell, though, isn't it. Now that you know what you're missing.'

Edith grinned. 'It is. He's everything I hoped for and more, and his injuries haven't changed a thing. I just hope he keeps believing that too.' They followed the curve of the path beneath more trees, with birds singing brightly overhead. 'Anyway, what about you? Are you still writing to that GI?'

Peggy gave a small smile. 'Yes, I am. Do you think that it's bad, too soon after Pete?' Her voice became anxious as she asked the question.

Edith shook her head. 'None of my business. If he makes you happy, then why shouldn't you? Dunkirk was almost three years ago. We're not getting any younger either.'

Peggy gazed up into the trees. 'I know. But even so, James is special. He's not like any old soldier I've been dancing with. He sent me some lovely soap for Christmas, I told you, didn't I.'

'Lucky you,' said Edith, with heartfelt sincerity. 'My hands are red and raw by the end of the week as we always have to wash in carbolic between patients. I'd love something really soft, but it's so hard to find.'

'That's only one reason why he's special,' Peggy went on. 'He sent me a Valentine's card too, and he'd made it himself. Can you imagine a man doing that? He'd drawn a picture of a couple dancing, and she was in a spotty dress and he had a spotty tie. Just like the one I sent

254

him for Christmas. It's our little joke.' She blushed a little, having got carried away with her description, as she hadn't meant to tell anyone. 'You know, like the Ink Spots. It's silly but I don't care.'

Edith giggled. 'You'll have to get yourself a spotty dress then. He must be clever, to be able to draw like that. I wish I could.'

Peggy twirled around. 'He's so kind and understanding. You'll have to meet him the next time he comes to town. I sent him a card too, but I can't draw for toffee. I got it down the market.'

'It's the thought that counts,' Edith assured her. 'So when is his next leave?'

Peggy stopped twirling and grew more serious. 'I don't know. I don't think he does either — I'm sure he'd tell me. It can't come soon enough, if I'm honest.' She blushed again, unsure if she should give away how deeply she was beginning to feel for the young man.

But Edith had picked up on her tone. 'You really like him, don't you?'

Peggy bit her lip. 'Yes,' she said, after a pause. The blackbirds were singing their hearts out in the branches above. 'It's not like when I first started walking out with Pete — that was completely different. We'd known each other at school; we had the same group of friends; we lived a few streets away from one another. This feels like . . . a leap into the unknown. He's from a place I've only ever seen in films; he talks different, he looks different, and yet . . . ' She twisted her hands together. 'It's like I've known him for ever. It doesn't make sense, I realise that.'

Edith nodded sagely. 'Sounds as if you've got it bad, Peggy. Well, good for you. It's not every day that someone like that comes along. You'd better make the most of it.'

Peggy exhaled deeply, even though she hadn't been aware that she'd been holding her breath. 'I'm so glad to hear you say that, Edie. I've been wondering and wondering what to do — whether I'm being daft, or letting him sweet-talk me like some of them do — '

'He doesn't sound like one of those types,' Edith interrupted, knowing how her friend had been treated in the past.

'And he's a soldier, of course. Anything could happen.' Peggy stated the obvious. 'What if I do care for him and what if he feels the same — then he goes and gets killed too?' She came to a halt and faced the nurse. 'I don't think I could survive that twice. It almost killed me too, when Pete died. Well, you know what it's like more than most.'

Edith agreed sombrely. 'Yes, it's the worst feeling ever. All the same,' she took her friend's arm again, 'you can't let that stop you. What if he does come through the fighting? What if you hadn't made the most of what time you could have had? Wouldn't you regret that more?'

Peggy by now was almost in tears, the full realisation of how she felt dawning on her, and the impossibility of it — and the impossibility of saying no. 'What do I do, Edie?' she breathed. 'What do I do?'

Edith shook her head. 'I can't tell you, Peggy. Only you can decide. But, well, I know you, and you've never been shy of taking a risk.' She raised her eyebrows. 'Have you?'

Peggy acknowledged what Edith was saying. Sometimes she'd taken silly risks, with servicemen she'd met when dancing or drinking down the pub, but only because they didn't really matter and she hadn't felt that she mattered much either. Now the stakes were raised. She didn't feel like that silly, desperate young woman any more.

'You're right,' she said. 'It's all about what I'd regret more, isn't it? I don't want to get hurt that badly again, I really don't. But if I didn't try — then I don't want to be an old woman looking back and thinking I was too much of a coward to try again. I think he's worth it, Edie.'

24

'Evelyn, are you going to be much longer?' Gladys stood in the cramped back yard outside her family's small kitchen, waiting by the woodworm-riddled door to the privy they shared with all the other houses backing onto the yard. 'I'm going to be late for the nurses if you don't hurry up.'

There was a coughing noise. Then her sister spoke, her voice weak but full of mockery. 'Oh we can't have that, can we? Can't keep the precious bleeding nurses waiting for a minute or two.'

Gladys moved from foot to foot in irritation. She knew they wouldn't mind if she was five minutes late, but it was a point of pride. She loved it that they all knew they could rely on her. If by chance she was to be late, she would prefer it was for a better reason than her younger sister hogging the privy. She waited for another minute and then rapped on the splintered door. 'Are you all right?'

There came the sound of more coughing, and then another noise — the unpleasant sound of vomiting. Gladys winced. 'Evelyn, what's going on?'

Evelyn cleared her throat. 'There was something wrong with the water down the Boatman's. Everyone said their drinks was tasting funny. Not that I had more than one,' she added hastily.

'Are you sure that's what it is?' Gladys called. 'You haven't gone and caught a bug, have you? I don't want to infect anyone at the nurses' home.'

'That's right, think of them before you think of me — of course they're more important,' Evelyn replied viciously. 'Don't you worry, it ain't no bug. Now bugger off.' She laughed feebly at the attempt at a joke.

Gladys sighed and gave up, going back inside the house on the cool spring morning. In truth the proper bathroom at Victory Walk was much nicer, but she preferred to get straight to her work, not spend her first few minutes doing her ablutions. Well, today would have to be an exception. She grabbed her coat and bag in annoyance and set off on the short journey up the road, along the streets of small terraced houses packed closely together. She was still in good time; it was not long after daybreak and there were few people about. Some were clearly dressed for an early shift at the factories, others were most likely making their way home after a night fire-watching or on antiaircraft duty.

Evelyn had refused to talk about Max when Gladys pressed her for details after the dreadful night in the Boatman's courtyard. Gladys could only hope that her sister would see sense and realise that the older man was using her. Yet Evelyn still seemed convinced that he would help her in her ambitions to go on the stage. For that, she appeared to be willing to put up with his attentions. Gladys shuddered.

Her sister had taken to teasing her that she

didn't know what real life was like. In many ways she was right, as Gladys had hardly left Dalston and until recently had not met many people. Yet her contact with the district nurses and, even more, her evenings on duty at the first-aid post had changed all that. She might still be in Dalston, but the world and all its troubles were coming straight to her.

It was quite possible that there had been a problem with the drinks at the Boatman's. She had seen for herself what the standard of cleanliness was down there. It was also possible that her sister had been lying about how much she'd had. Gladys was willing to bet that Max was happy to lay on a few potent spirits in order to have his way with a more compliant Evelyn. He was just the sort of man who would see that as a good investment.

Or Evelyn might be mistaken and she did have a bug after all. Gladys hoped not. She really did not want to bring infection into the nurses' home. God knew that they faced enough of that in the course of their work.

She pushed open the side door to the home and listened. Cook was up and about, judging by the clattering of pans in the kitchen. She would be preparing the porridge to see the nurses through their morning rounds on the district. 'Won't be long!' Gladys called out, so that her colleague would know help was at hand. She hung up her coat on a hook on the back of the service-room door and put down her bag, dipping into it to retrieve a flannel. She might as well have a good quick wash in the luxury of the proper bathroom on the lower-ground floor of the home. It had hot water on tap — a real treat.

Then there was the other explanation. Gladys caught sight of herself in the little mirror over the sink, which she had polished only yesterday. Her face was drawn with worry. Evelyn might taunt her about her lack of experience, but you couldn't be around nurses for long without knowing why some women were sick in the mornings. ·

Gladys didn't know what she would do if Evelyn was expecting a baby. She doubted very much that Max would be any help if that turned out to be the case. Their small home was packed to the rafters with children as it was. She'd done her time looking after her siblings; she didn't want to be responsible for another one. Would Evelyn be capable of raising a child? Lots of women younger than her were doing so — but they weren't Evelyn, with her head in the clouds, relying on Gladys to make sure all the day-to-day practicalities were dealt with.

People would look down on her and, by association, the whole family. Gladys sighed. Evelyn would be dragging her down again, just as she had begun to pull herself out of poverty, with her Civil Nursing Reserve training. She was well on her way to becoming respectable — it wasn't fair. Surely she deserved her chance at life too?

She met her own eyes in the reflection. No point in worrying about it; she could do nothing to change the situation, and it might turn out to be a bug or too much drink. She had to keep her fingers crossed that the worst was not going to happen. Wringing out her flannel, she opened the door and prepared to begin her working day.

★ ★ ★

Belinda shook her hair free from its navy ribbon and then bound it up again, attempting to corral all the stray tight curls. She and all of her colleagues were vigilant about hygiene, but today it felt more important than ever. She'd come across three cases of gastro-enteritis on her calls already, and it was still only lunchtime.

'Is it just me?' she asked, taking her bowl of mixed vegetable and pearl barley soup to the table where Bridget and Alice were already sitting. 'If I'm not much mistaken, there's a nasty new bug going around. Alice, one of your young friends has gone down with it.'

Alice looked up from where she was spreading her bread with a thin layer of margarine. 'Oh really? Who's that?'

Belinda folded her tall frame onto the old wooden dining chair. 'Poor George. You know, the one I met when the wall collapsed.'

'Janet used to teach him at St Benedict's.' Alice nodded. 'What's wrong with him?'

Belinda reached for a slice of bread from the platter in the middle of the table. 'I was visiting one of his neighbours with a broken leg and decided to drop by on the off-chance, to see how he was doing. I thought he'd probably be at school, but he wasn't — he's got this nasty bug and his mother had kept him at home. He's not in danger; he's more miserable than anything else. He was meant to be playing football with Benny after school but he won't be able to do that for a while.'

Alice frowned. 'That's a shame. He's a good lad underneath all his naughtiness. Did you tell his mother to keep his fluid levels up? Sorry, of course you did.'

'Of course I did.' Belinda pulled a face.

Bridget finished her soup first. 'I was ravenous,' she explained. 'I took on two extra visits this morning, as Ellen wasn't feeling up to all her rounds — don't tell Gwen. I think she might be going down with it too. I'll pop over to the flat to check on her in a minute but then I'll come right back here; I don't want it as well. We've too much to do to get sick.'

Belinda nodded. 'You're telling me. But I could manage an extra visit this afternoon if you like. Mrs Caffrey's been taken into hospital again, so I shan't have to change her dressings. That means I can help, if Ellen's not up to it.'

'Thanks.' Bridget rose, concern for her friend and flatmate etched on her face. 'Not if it makes you late though.'

Belinda shrugged. 'I was only going to the pictures with Geraldine from the ambulance station — nothing important. Don't think twice about it.'

Alice finished her own soup as Bridget rushed off. 'I promised I'd see Janet for a cup of tea after work — I'll check that she knows about George. She doesn't take his class any more but the form teacher might need to know. She ought to be able to tell me if many of the other children have got it.'

'That would be useful,' said Belinda. 'I'm always wary when there's an outbreak like this. Tomorrow I said I'd help Miriam prepare one of her spare rooms for the latest family of refugees from Austria. They won't thank me if the first thing they do is go down with a bug.'

'Goodness, no.' Alice rose as Gladys appeared behind them. 'It's all right, Gladys, I'll take these plates back to the kitchen. Have you had your own lunch yet? Thought not. Why don't you take my place here with Belinda?'

Gladys nodded gratefully, but really she was thinking hard about the conversation she had just overheard. So there was an outbreak of gastro-enteritis going around. She could feel the tension draining from her body in relief. That was all there was to it. Evelyn had picked it up somewhere, maybe from the filthy Boatman's. She had got all het up over nothing. All that was wrong with her silly, infuriating sister was a stomach bug.

* * *

Mattie dug her small trowel into the earth in the window box, which was carefully balanced on the sill of the back kitchen in Jeeves Street. Frowning with concentration so as not to disturb the other plants, she pulled out the biggest one. Triumphantly she held up her bounty.

'Look!' she beamed. 'The first radish of the year. Isn't it a beauty?'

264

Kathleen laughed and applauded. 'It is. Proper ruby red, that is.'

Mattie nodded in appreciation and dug up two others. 'There, one each: for you, me and Ma. We can dip them in a bit of salt and they'll be lovely. I know it's only a little thing, but I do enjoy springtime when the new vegetables start to be ready. I feel I've done something to help.'

Kathleen smiled in acknowledgement. 'You're clever, Mattie. I'd never know what to plant and when. Then you fit so much into this space.' She looked around the area, just too big to be a yard but not really worthy of the title garden, especially with the big mound of the shelter in the middle. Still, Mattie had made use of the earth piled on top of that, and sowed seed for salads. Any old container available had been put to use for potatoes, just beginning to show their first leaves.

Later on there would be tomatoes and cucumbers in the lean-to greenhouse. Mattie had persuaded her father to bring back any reusable glass that wasn't dangerous from bombsites, and to use it to construct the makeshift hothouse. Kathleen wondered whether to ask Billy to do the same, although their space was much smaller and she didn't want Brian to collide with any sharp edges.

She hoisted little Barbara higher onto her shoulder. 'When you're bigger you can have one of Auntie Mattie's radishes too. Would you like that?' She grinned into the little face, which grinned back at her. She was such a good baby, easier than Brian had been — but then, he'd gone hungry for many of his early months. Despite the war, Barbara was being well fed with a balanced diet, and Kathleen gave thanks every day for such a healthy daughter. The only downside was, her arms ached when she carried her for too long. 'Let's find your pram,' she said.

Mattie followed her inside, and washed the radishes at the sink. 'I've been thinking,' she said as she dug out a small plate and the salt.

Kathleen looked up from settling Barbara. 'That sounds serious,' she teased.

Mattie shook her head and her untidy hair swung about her face. 'No, really. I know I help out by growing vegetables as well as looking after the children and doing the housework with Ma, but I wonder if I shouldn't do more.' She trimmed the leaves off the little plants and added them to the compost crock.

'But you work so hard,' Kathleen protested. 'You're never still, Mattie.'

Her friend wiped her hands on her apron. 'All the same. I mean, look at Billy. He works a full shift down the docks and then does an evening as an ARP warden. So does Pa — works eight hours then patrols the streets more nights than not.'

'But when they come home they have a meal waiting for them and a clean house,' Kathleen pointed out.

Mattie shrugged. 'What about Clarrie, then? She does a day in the factory and then goes up on the roof for a night of fire-watching. And then she helps her mother around the house, specially now her sister is away. I think I should do more.'

Kathleen narrowed her eyes at her friend. 'How do you mean? What's brought this on all of a sudden?'

Mattie shook the salt onto the plate and took it to the big wooden table. 'It's not sudden, not really. It's been on my mind for a while,' she confessed.

Kathleen cocked her head. 'Is it something to do with Lennie?' she asked. 'What with him being away so long?'

Mattie hung her head. Sometimes they didn't even mention her husband's name for weeks at a time. They were coming up to the third anniversary of Dunkirk, when he had been taken prisoner. But just because they didn't speak of him as often, that didn't mean she had forgotten him. She missed him every day.

'Sort of,' she said, with the slightest catch in her voice. 'He did his bit and then he got taken out of the fight. I feel I owe it to him to carry on what he started. Does that make sense?'

Kathleen frowned in puzzlement. 'Maybe. I'm not really sure, to be honest.'

Mattie dipped her radish into the salt and took a bite. 'Here, try.' She pushed the plate across to her friend. 'It's like, if he was on the front line fighting, I'd know he was helping to make us all safe. But he can't do that now. He's stuck in that POW camp. So it's up to me.' She took a second bite, nearly finishing the small red globe. 'The children are older now. I'm not feeding them myself any more. Gillian and Brian are both four — not long before they go to school. Alan's two. I could leave him with Ma, just like I do when I

267

go shopping. He wouldn't mind — he'd hardly notice.'

'I'd help,' said Kathleen at once. 'He's used to me as well. If you're serious about this. That way, I'd feel like I was doing my bit to help, even if it isn't much.'

Mattie waited a moment before replying. This idea had been going round and round in her head for weeks, months even, but it was the first time she'd spoken the thoughts aloud. She was still feeling her way to making sense of them. She knew deep down it was her way of carrying on what Lennie had started. She rarely talked about his absence, of how she hadn't imagined their life like this. To complain would do nothing to change matters. So she hid her sorrow, keeping it to herself, until those hours of the night when her children and parents were asleep. Then she could sob into her pillow, worried to distraction about what conditions were like in his camp. Whether he was all right or sick, knowing he would not want to worry her in the few letters he managed to send. Wondering if she would ever see him again.

Doing some form of war work would be a distraction, if nothing else. Yet she also wanted to show him that she was doing her utmost and to make him proud of her when he did return. It was a way of boosting her faith that he would come back to her, to their children — finally to meet Alan, born after his father had been captured at Dunkirk.

'Yes, I am serious about it.' There, she'd said it. 'You know lots of factories have nurseries now, or the WVS will know of council places. Ma could find out.'

'It might not even be for very long,' Kathleen said quickly, now filled with optimism. 'Billy says the tide has turned, that after Monty won in North Africa the Germans are on the run.'

'Maybe.' Mattie didn't want to get her hopes up. 'I don't know about those things. That's Pa's business — or Alice's. I just want to do more. Besides, we aren't out of danger. Look at those explosions recently.'

'But they were anti-aircraft shells, weren't they?' Kathleen grew anxious once more at the memory. They hadn't landed near her new house or on Jeeves Street, but they were still in Hackney, and so close enough to remind them all of how perilous bombs could be.

'Whatever they were, it makes me even more sure I need to join up. I wouldn't go away, I'd have to stay with the children, but maybe a factory like Clarrie and Peggy work in. If they can do it, then so can I.'

Kathleen nodded, impressed at her friend's courage and resolution. She wouldn't want to be separated from her children for one minute longer than she absolutely had to. 'Of course you can,' she assured her.

25

Peggy nervously patted her hair. She always felt it looked a bit dull: not stunning red like Clarrie's, or strikingly dark like Belinda's or Edith's. Mary's chestnut waves were enviable, too, and they all knew that she had more money than most to spend on keeping them that way. Perhaps Peggy's hair was closest in colour to Alice's: dark blonde or light brown, depending on how you looked at it.

But Alice never went out of her way to dress up to look special. She was neat and tidy — elegant, even — but making an impression was not her main aim. Whereas Peggy, particularly at this moment, desperately wanted to look right.

She had wound her hair into rags overnight to give it shape, and brushed it carefully until it shone. She had sewn new buttons onto the seasons-old cotton dress to make it smarter, and pressed it until the edges on her collar and lace cuffs were razor-sharp. Her best home-made brooch was pinned to her jacket's lapel, and the scuffs on her shoes were hidden by a fresh layer of polish, buffed to a bright shine. Truly, she could not have done more.

Perhaps she had no need to be so worried. James had seen her in her dancing best, but also

270

when he'd taken her unawares by turning up at the house that time; he hadn't minded then that she was not all dolled up. But she wanted to be special, to impress him. What if some of the other GIs saw her when she met him near the Red Cross dormitory where he was again staying for his leave? She didn't want to let him down.

It had been so long since she had seen him. They had written, of course, and he had sent her that beautiful soap, which was now all gone, and the drawing for Valentine's Day. People could change, though. She hoped against hope that he hadn't.

If anything, her own feelings had grown more solid since they had last met. He was such a contrast to the men she met in everyday life — the fellow workers at the factory, usually those too old or unsuitable for the Forces, or the dock workers who were exempt from conscription. She liked her men friends well enough, but she'd had the best one of those and now he was gone. The rest did not compare.

James was a gentleman, considerate and caring; he listened to her. He was also, to her eyes, magnetically handsome. She had always preferred men who could dance well, but to combine that talent with looks like his — that just made him irresistible. What if some other girl thought the same — and happened to live conveniently near his East Anglian base? She didn't think he was the cheating type, but she'd been wrong before.

Why were the butterflies going crazy in her

stomach as she approached the place where they'd chosen to meet? They were getting worse, not better. She could hardly walk the final few paces. Her legs had turned to jelly.

Then there he was: handsome as ever and smart in his uniform, his eyes gleaming with pleasure at the sight of her. She ran towards him and suddenly all her worries flew away. He was here and she was in his arms. Nothing else mattered.

★　★　★

'I reckon you been taking dance lessons since I last saw you,' James said towards the end of the evening. 'You're even better than you were. Those steps ain't easy but you never missed a beat.'

Peggy chuckled in appreciation. 'I had the best partner, that's why.'

'We make a good pair, don't we?' James halted suddenly, as if aware of what that might mean. He glanced around the crowds of dancers taking a break from the floor, some clutching cold drinks, some fanning themselves with programmes. It was very warm.

Peggy looked up at him and into his velvet eyes. 'We do, don't we.' She had caught some envious glances as they'd moved together around the dance floor, keeping perfect time. It was reassuring to know that their peers were admiring their performance, but for Peggy it was much more important that James thought she was good — his was the only opinion that really mattered. She hadn't let him down. 'Boy, it's hot in here. How come you aren't melting?'

'I must be getting used to your British weather.' His face creased in amusement.

'Is it warm where you're from?' She realised they hadn't spoken much about his life in America. Again she was struck by how little she knew of it. 'Is it like in the pictures?'

He shrugged. 'Depends which movies you mean. If you're thinking of the plantations of *Gone With the Wind*, it ain't like that — leastways not where I was. We often went to New York City, so I'm used to big places, same as you, except there's no bomb damage, of course.' He smiled again to take the edge off the observation. 'Mighty hot come the summer, all the same.'

Peggy nodded, trying to imagine it. London could get pretty stuffy at the height of August and it was uncomfortable until the sun went down. How would she manage somewhere hotter than that? Then she brought herself up short — she was getting ahead of herself, making an assumption that one day she'd find out.

'Here.' He gave her his programme so she could fan herself, which she accepted gratefully. 'Care for another lemonade?'

Peggy shook her head. 'I'll go pop if I have any more.'

'Another dance, then?'

'Listen — they're finishing up. This is the tune they always play for the last one of the evening.'

'So let's hit the floor one more time.' He took her hand and they squeezed into the crowd, making the most of the final song, slow and sweet.

Peggy swayed in time to the music, loving the sensation of his arms tight around her. 'I wish we didn't have to go,' she murmured.

He nodded, his chin resting on her shoulder. 'But we do,' he said softly.

'I know. I just wish . . . ' She tightened her arms on his body, sensing the taut muscles beneath. 'I wish we could be together more. I don't want to let you go.'

'Nor me, Peggy. Not now I've found you. Will you come out with me tomorrow? I've got one more day of leave.'

Peggy had put her name down for the Saturday early shift, keen to make up for the fact she wasn't fire-watching like many of the others. Quickly she calculated when she would be free. 'We could meet for tea?' she suggested.

His eyes told her he would prefer to stay in her company for far longer, but he nodded. 'Tea, a proper British tea,' he smiled, and then bent to kiss her swiftly before the band played the final notes. They held each other tightly until the last chord faded away and the crowds around them began to disperse, reluctant to let each other go on this night of precious moments together. Time seemed to stand still. The lights were still dimmed and she thought she saw his mouth move, cast a little into shadows by the shifting waves of men and women leaving the floor. Was that really what he was saying? 'I love you too,' she whispered, but did not know if he had heard.

Next morning Peggy wasn't sure if she'd dreamt it. She went through her shift in a daze, hardly noticing when anyone spoke to her. Several colleagues teased her for it, but she didn't react. They taunted her that she must have had such a good night out that she was too hung over to answer, but she smiled vaguely and ignored them. Eventually they gave up.

Clarrie had the day off and so there was no need to explain anything. Peggy mechanically assembled her boxes and stacked sections of piping and rubber seals, forgetting to look for any scraps to be made into jewellery, just wanting the minutes to go by faster. The wireless played music to encourage them to work harder, but she ignored that too, though usually she would sing along with any tune she knew.

She was glad that Mattie had rearranged her interview with the factory. Her friend had asked her if there were any vacancies, as the factory was an easy distance from Jeeves Street and she would know workers there already. Peggy had offered to show her around if she could coincide with her shifts, but Alan had gone down with a late cold and so Mattie hadn't wanted to leave him. Peggy knew that she would have made no sense today and was relieved, even if she felt a little sorry for poor Alan.

It felt like the longest ever shift, but eventually the wireless played the news on the hour and she was free to go. 'Coming down the Duke's Arms?' called one of the men who had such poor eyesight he couldn't join the services. 'Or what about the tea shop down the market?' shouted the woman who'd worked alongside her earlier that morning.

'No, I've got to go somewhere else,' Peggy replied, oblivious to their nudges and speculative glances. She exchanged her tired old overall for her pretty light jacket, tore the protective scarf from her head and delved into her handbag for a hairbrush. Then she found her compact mirror and stub of lipstick and carefully drew on a pink cupid's bow. It wasn't much but it was the best she could do in the circumstances.

She all but ran from the factory gates to the bus stop, willing the service not to be delayed. It was still afternoon and the sun was bright in the late spring sky, illuminating the main road as she squinted to see if there was any sign of transport. She reckoned most folk would be coming the other way at this hour of the day, returning from a trip to the West End. It wasn't yet time for the evening revellers to set out. People around her had either been working or shopping locally, by the looks of them. She was the most dolled-up there.

The bus had a few spaces left and she treated herself to a window seat on the top deck, staring out at the streets as they passed through Hackney to Islington, past Sadler's Wells and into Holborn. She moved closer to the window to make space for an older woman who smelled strongly of cigarettes. She resisted the hints of conversation. She was too excited to think about anyone other than James.

She might have known there would be some delays to the journey. The conductor announced that the bus would have to terminate early, as a road ahead was shut because of a burst water main. People grumbled but nobody made a loud fuss, as it was just the sort of thing you had to expect these days. Peggy followed the other passengers down the curved stairs at the back of the bus and weighed up her options. She could try another route or she could walk through the back streets and cut through. That would be quicker. Besides, she was in her sensible shoes. She set off as fast as she could, hoping James would wait.

There he was, next to the entrance to Lyons Corner House on the Strand. She rushed to meet him, her smile wide. All the doubts of the previous evening had vanished. She wasn't in torment that he had found someone else or didn't want to see her; by the expression on his face, he was as keen to meet up again as she was.

'Am I late?' she gasped.

'No, not really. All right, maybe a little.' He grinned his open grin and she felt the tiredness from her shift vanish. 'Do you want to go in? You Brits like a cup of tea and a scone — is that how you say it? — at this time of day, don't you?'

Peggy cast a glance into the busy tea room, noting the shoppers with their purchases piled around them, or at least those who had been lucky enough to find what they wanted. The hubbub of conversation was audible even from beyond the doors. Tempting as it was, she knew they would have to shout to be heard. 'No,' she said decisively, 'let's walk. Have you ever been along the Embankment?'

James shook his head. 'Can't say as I have.'

Peggy slipped her arm through his and guided him down the narrow streets towards the water. He looked up at the old buildings, their windows taped or boarded up, their grand porches and side entrances sandbagged, but still impressive. 'Wow, this is like walking through history,' he said. 'Look at those arches, all pointed. They must have been there for . . . how many years?' He glanced at Peggy but she laughed it off.

'I don't know. I don't really think about it. Hundreds, maybe. I'm the wrong person to ask — I never took much notice of history at school. It never seemed to have much to do with how we live now.'

He nodded as they walked on. 'I know what you mean. Still, to have this all around you — I guess it's different if you live here all the time, ain't it? You got no reason to come and visit these places.' He sighed, gazing about them. 'Makes it all the more important to keep it this way, make sure the bombs don't do any more damage. You can't replace this sort of thing.'

'I suppose not.' They came out of the narrow street and down to the broad sweep of the Embankment. Peggy pointed towards Hungerford Bridge.

'That got hit a couple of years ago, and the station as well. People were killed. There were some offices on the other side that took a hit too. You never knew which trains would be running back then. It kept us all guessing.'

James nodded solemnly. 'I can't even imagine, Peggy. You must have been very brave. I don't want to think of you in danger like that, it makes my heart sore to think about it.'

Peggy shrugged. 'I wasn't brave, not really. Not like some of my friends. You met Belinda, the very tall one with black hair. She almost got burnt by acid when rescuing a little boy with a broken leg. Or Billy, our ARP warden — he got knocked over by a drunk driver in the blackout. We've had all sorts — it's strange, we sort of got used to it.'

James gave himself a small shake. 'That ain't right; you shouldn't have to get used to stuff like that. It's not normal.'

Peggy gave a small smile. 'I know that now, looking back on it. But at the time you just have to get on with it. You go in to work even if you haven't slept much, cos you know the gas masks have to be made. It's just how it is.'

James turned and took her in his arms. Above them the trees were in full bloom and the new green leaves stirred in the breeze, sending patters of shadows down onto the pavement. 'That's bravery, Peggy,' he said seriously. 'We're being trained to go into battle and half of the guys think it's one big game. I don't think it is — but it'll be action, and if we do it well then we might get praised for being heroes. But you folks, you stayed at home and you kept everything going. The fight couldn't go on without that. You told me your man died, and your baby that never was, and yet you kept on going through all of that. Now that's what I call bravery.'

'Oh, stop.' Peggy felt her eyes fill with tears and couldn't look at him.

'It's true.' He traced the line of her chin and she had to meet his gaze. 'Peggy, you're beautiful, you know that?'

She blushed, her hair blowing in the breeze, not knowing what to say. 'I . . . I . . . '

He stopped her protest by kissing her, and instantly she responded, knowing how well they fitted together, wanting never to let him go. The light sunshine warmed his uniform jacket and his carefully combed hair had the slight tang of Brylcreem, and yet it was a scent like nothing she had ever encountered before. At the same time it seemed deeply familiar, as if she had been waiting for it all her life. She tightened her arms around his waist. 'James . . . ' she sighed, and almost cried with the sudden flood of emotion.

'Peggy, my beautiful Peggy.' He sank his face into her flyaway hair. 'Did you hear what I said to you last night when the band were finishing? It was all so loud, I didn't time it right at all, and I don't know if you caught my meaning or not.'

She turned her face against his shoulder, resting her cheek against his jacket. 'I don't know if I heard it right. Did you hear what I said back to you?' She wondered if she was tempting fate, even by asking. What a fool she would seem if she'd got it wrong.

'Can't say I'm that good at lip reading,' he said, and she could feel his breath warm on her scalp, 'but I could have sworn you said the same thing to me as I said to you.' He held her tighter still. 'I love you, Peggy. That's what I tried to tell you when that band was doing its last number. I love you, because you're beautiful, and brave, and your eyes light up when you laugh, and you can jitterbug as well. What more could I ask for?'

Peggy gave a small hiccup and gasped for air. 'I thought that's what you said. I wasn't sure, I didn't want to assume. But I said I love you too. You make me feel . . . like flying. Like I never thought I'd feel again. Like the bad things are behind me now.'

'That's right, Peggy. Put those bad things away. You can't change them but you got me now,' he said seriously. 'I ain't going to let you go. You can rely on me. I'm going to treat you like you deserve, cos you are one very special woman. I'm a lucky man.'

Peggy blinked hard. 'R-really?' she managed to say, and laughed in happiness. 'Oh James, I thought my mind was playing tricks on me. But we're here, aren't we? We're here together. I don't care what people say. None of that matters, cos I've got you.'

He swept her around, lifting her off her feet. 'Yes you have. Be very sure of it. I've got you safe, Peggy. That's all there is to it.'

For a magical moment there was nothing but the two of them looking into each other's eyes, the light from the trees filtering through the leaves and the glint of the sun on the Thames beyond the river wall. Then a train must have disgorged its passengers at Charing Cross, as a swarm of people swept down the steps from the bridge and began to flow around them. Reluctantly Peggy broke away, stepped back and

281

took his hand. 'Come on, I'll give you another part of my tour. See that down there? That's Cleopatra's Needle . . . ' And she drew him away from the bridge, along the pavement, but walking on air.

26

Edith picked up her sandwich and looked askance at it.

'What's wrong?' asked Harry. He took a bite of his.

She laughed. 'Oh, you know, coming to the country, I thought there might be different bread. But this is the same national wholemeal loaf we're having to get used to back home.'

Harry smiled back, enjoying the fact that she referred to Dalston as 'home'. 'Same rationing all over the place,' he pointed out.

'And at least the filling is better. Fresh eggs!' Edith licked her lips. 'And lots of cheese. I wonder if they have any extra to sell. I could take them back to Victory Walk, and to your family too.' She nibbled delicately at the crust. The dining area of the little inn was brightly furnished with green and white gingham tablecloths and matching curtains, making it cheerful and welcoming. It was a far cry from the honeymoon at the grand hotel, but Edith felt more at home here. Two whole nights away with Harry — she could hardly believe it. 'You were so clever to find this place, Harry. It really is as if we are on holiday.'

He reached for the salt. 'I've never been on a proper holiday,' he said.

'Me neither.' The idea would never have even occurred to Edith's family.

'When the war's over, let's go somewhere. I don't know — Brighton. Southend. Blackpool. Anywhere!'

Edith beamed at the thought, but secretly had no wish to spend longer than necessary away from the safe hubbub of a city. This was different — a short spell away from real life, to enjoy Harry's company. The inn was in a small village, but just a bus ride away from Harry's base, and so she didn't feel too cut off. But for anything longer, she was not sure. 'Brighton would be lovely,' she decided. 'We'll go there when it's all finished. Let's swear to do it.'

'We will.' Harry set down his plate once more. 'How are things at home? Have you seen the family recently?'

Edith nodded. 'Of course. I went round to get all the news just before coming down to see you. Mattie's started work at the factory now, alongside Peggie and Clarrie. She likes it and the children don't mind — they don't really notice as they're with your mother or Kath lots of the time anyway. Kath's talking about working there too once she's stopped feeding Barbara.'

Harry nodded, finishing his sandwich. The waitress came across to clear their plates, casting a look at him as she did so. He flinched.

Edith glanced up sharply. 'What is it?' She gazed into his face, which was suddenly stricken, all his good humour of a moment ago completely gone. She reached for his hand across the table. 'Harry? Tell me.'

He turned away, his mouth twisting. He would not meet her eyes.

'Harry.' Edith was worried now. 'Was it when she came over? She's gone now, back to the kitchen. Come on, you can tell me.'

Harry gave a quiet groan. 'Did you see what she did? She saw my face and stared. She thought I was strange.'

Edith frowned. 'She was only here for a second. There wasn't time.'

'There was. I saw, I could tell. It happens a lot.' He shifted in his seat, his expression stark. 'Everywhere I go, people stare at me. Not so much on the base or in East Grinstead; they're used to it and I'm not the worst. But everywhere else. I'm too odd, I frighten them.' His voice wobbled and he gazed down at the crumbs on the tablecloth. He was shaking.

'Harry!' She grasped his trembling hand more tightly. 'Come on, this isn't like you.'

He pulled his hand away. 'Maybe I'm not like me, not any more. I'm different, Edie, surely you can see that.'

'Not underneath,' she said staunchly. 'That's where it counts, Harry. You know that.'

He groaned again. 'You say that, Edie, but you know me. People I meet for the first time, or who I pass in the street — they haven't got a clue what I'm like underneath or how I was before. I'm just a strange bloke with a scarred face. They turn away, they don't want to know.'

She shook her head, her eyes dark with sympathy, unsure what to say.

'I'll have to get used to it, I know. They warned me, but I had no idea how bad it would be, just little things, day after day.' He paused, sighed, shifted again. 'I thought that once I was out of that hospital bed, up and about again, that would be it, I'd be all right. I mean, I knew my arm would hurt and I couldn't box with it, but I wasn't prepared for how everyone would treat me.'

'You still managed to sock one to Frankie.' Edith smiled determinedly.

'Yeah — sorry about that.'

'No, no, he deserved it. I can't tell you the number of times I wish I could have done the same.' She sat forward in her seat. The little dining room was very quiet, just the faraway sound of dishes being washed behind the closed kitchen door.

'He got to me — I know that's what he wanted, winding me up like that, and winding you up. You'd told me often enough, I can't say I was surprised. It's because he came out and said aloud what everyone else thinks when they look at me.' He clammed up.

Edith picked up her chair and moved it to the other side of the table so that she could put her arm around Harry. She rested her head on his shoulder. 'He's an idiot, Harry. We got to ignore him.'

Harry's body was rigid, resisting her touch. 'All the same, he was right in one way.'

She turned to look up at him, but said nothing, waiting for him to go on.

He swallowed hard, still refusing to meet her gaze. 'I feel less of a man, Edie. It's an awful thing to feel. But I'm not what I was, I'm not a proper man.'

'You were a proper man last night, if I remember rightly,' she said at once.

He gave an involuntary smile at that. 'Well, that's because I was with you. You make things better, Edie. You work some kind of magic, you do.' He relaxed a little. 'If I had you by my side twenty-four hours a day, it would be another thing altogether.'

'I wish I could do that.' She gave him a squeeze. 'I'm here in spirit, you know that, don't you?'

'Of course. And I'm with you, always,' he assured her, stirring slightly.

'Look, why don't we go into the town or something, stretch our legs,' she suggested. 'You said they're used to it there, what with all the pilots having their surgery in that hospital. We could go to the pictures.'

Harry winced again.

'No, don't worry, I'll be with you — ' she began, but he cut across her.

'It's not that. It's what happened to the cinema,' he explained. 'The Jerries got it last week. One plane came over, saw a load of tanks going down the high street, went to bomb them and hit the cinema. Killed about a hundred people, injured twice that. Enough to put you off going to the pictures, that is.'

Edith gulped. 'Yes. Oh, the poor people. So you're under fire down here still — we haven't had much recently, a few explosions back in May . . . that's terrible.' She gathered her thoughts in a hurry. 'Then let's go for a walk somewhere else; it'll be good to get some fresh air.'

Harry nodded and got up. 'Good idea. One of the mechanics at the base stayed here before with his girl, that's how I knew this was a decent place, and he drew me a rough map — says there are some good views near here. Let's do that.'

'Work up an appetite.' Edith grinned, getting to her feet as well.

Quickly she changed her shoes for something sensible and flat, suitable for a country walk. She would do her best to admire the view, even if it was bound to be a bit rural for her taste. It didn't matter as long as she was with Harry. She would not let anything spoil their all-too-rare precious time together.

Yet she could not help but worry about him. It was all very well when she was here to defend him or bolster him against the unthinking glances. She was sure most people weren't hostile, simply curious. He was never anything less than a proper man to her. But if he felt otherwise, she didn't know what she could do about it. She would have to come up with something, though; that much was clear.

★ ★ ★

'Ron! Seems like I ain't seen you for ages.' Billy slapped his mate on the back, sending puffs of particles from his dusty jacket into the still air of the warehouse. It was warm, too warm for the hard physical work of shifting items around the docks.

Ron stood up straight, easing his protesting back muscles. 'Oh, that's a heavy one. Me arms have forgotten what lifting is, being as I took a few days' leave.' He leant against a tall crate. 'Me brother Alfie came home for a week, first time he's done that for ages, so him and me took Ma and Auntie Ida out on the town a bit. Well, Hyde Park. Loved it, they did.'

'Bet they did.' Billy couldn't remember the last time his mother had been well enough to go that far. She had only just managed to help push Barbara in her pram around Butterfield Green. 'So they're all feeling better now, are they?'

Ron nodded. 'Auntie Ida's legs have been on the mend ever since Edie and her mates helped treat her. Ma's not too bad, thanks, considering she's not getting any younger. Alfie, well now, he's got some news.' He grinned at the memory. 'You know when I went to see him when he was first in hospital in Portsmouth after getting shot down, I told you there was a really helpful nurse? Looked a bit like the film star — that Vivien Leigh? Not that he knew that, he couldn't even see her. He just liked the sound of her voice.'

Billy wiped his forehead, where a film of sweat was forming in the heat. 'Yes, I recall you said something like that. I met her when I visited; she did look a bit like her.'

'He's only asked her to marry him. Sly old sod, he's been seeing her on the QT ever since.'

'He never!' Billy laughed, impressed. 'Good for him.'

'I could tell she was a bit sweet on him from the word go, him being a hero and a pilot and all that,' Ron explained. 'Not that nurses can have favourites, but she was kind to him when we didn't know if he'd ever see again or not.'

'But he can see now?' Billy couldn't imagine going blind, especially when you were still in your twenties. He touched wood for luck.

'Yes, he was lucky. He can't fly any more though, his eyesight will never be what it was, but he teaches navigation to air-force recruits. He always was good at school learning, our Alfie. Not like me. Ma said he got all the brains and didn't know where they came from.'

'You don't do so bad yourself, Ron,' Billy said loyally. 'So what did she say, this Vivien? Going to make an honest man of him, is she?'

Ron laughed. 'She's not really Vivien, she's Lizzie. Well, the thing is, if they got married right away, she might have to stop working, so she said yes but they'll have to wait.'

Billy nodded. That was tough but it made a harsh kind of sense. Hospitals needed their nurses these days. You had to make personal sacrifices in such times. 'Alfie all right with that, is he?'

'He'll have to be. Anyway, there's a fair chance he'll be posted up to Scotland somewhere, so even if they were married right away they wouldn't see one another much. You and Kath are the lucky ones, Bill.'

Billy pursed his lips in acknowledgement. 'We are, Ron, and not a day goes by that I don't give thanks for it. I never thought it would happen, that she'd marry me, and I'm happier than I can say.'

'You don't ever hanker for the single life no more then?' Ron's eyes gleamed as he teased his friend.

Billy huffed. 'As if. What would I want that for? Got my lovely Kath, got the nippers. Keep me on my toes, they do. All right, I grant you I'm a bit short on sleep — and don't look at me like that, not for the reasons you're thinking. Barbara might have started teething, that's the reason I got these big purple bags under me eyes. We got to take it in turns carrying her round the room, it's the only way she'll settle.' He sighed as if it was the hardest job in the world, but Ron wasn't fooled for a minute.

'Poor old you. So no trips down the Duke's Arms in the near future.'

'Probably not,' Billy admitted. 'Not that Kath would stop me, she's not like that. But I'm too knackered. And what's that other place you and Kenny went to? You said it was a bit rough but worth it cos it was cheap.'

As if summoned by his name, Kenny came into the warehouse, wiping his glasses as he did so. 'All right, Bill? Ron, so you've decided to join the world of work once more, I see.'

'Very funny.' Ron glared at his mate. 'Leave it out, you'd do the same if your brother came back for a spot of leave. Anyway, Bill, you mean the Boatman's. I ain't been there for a bit, to tell you the truth. I got put off. Some of the clientele weren't to my taste, you could say.'

Kenny rocked back in mock offence. 'What are you saying, Ron? Meaning me, are yer? Charmed, I'm sure.'

Ron shook his head. 'You know very well who I mean.'

Billy watched the exchange carefully, not

291

knowing what they were on about. He sensed the air of usually friendly banter had taken a darker turn.

Kenny pulled a face. 'All right, fair point. It ain't the most salubrious of pubs and I never said that it was. Anyway, you missed the latest. We had a bit of a to-do there earlier on this week.'

'Oh?' Ron clearly wasn't sure if he wanted to be drawn in.

'Yeah, the Old Bill was there. Looking for the landlord's bastard brother, they was.'

Billy caught the sharp look that passed between the two other men.

'What, that Max feller? Why, what's he been and done now?' Ron asked warily.

'Gawd knows,' said Kenny. 'Aside from the usual, wheeling and dealing out the back when he's not banging the singers. They said something about coming on behalf of the military police. He's dodged conscription or something like that. He'll have to keep well away if he's got any sense.'

'I wondered how he managed to avoid the call-up,' Ron replied, frowning. 'What with black-marketeering not being a reserved profession and all that.'

Kenny shrugged. 'But will he keep away though? It's a bit of a honey pot for him. He's got that Patty Walker singing nearly every night, and I don't think he's paying her in hard cash, if you get my drift.'

Ron swallowed hard. 'And that other singer, the younger one — blonde hair, pretty, but not much of a voice?'

'I don't think he's interested in her for her voice,' Kenny said, then clapped his hand over his mouth. 'Sorry, I just remembered. She's the sister of one of the nurses, isn't she? The one who came down the pub that time when she was worried. You got me looking out for her that time. Well, the nurse has got reason to be worried. That blonde kid is still hanging round but not singing as often. I don't know what's going on but something's not right.'

'Nothing's right with that place — it's a dive,' Ron said, cross now that he hadn't followed up on Gladys's concerns. 'Her sister is decent through and through; she don't deserve any grief from that Max. He's a nasty piece of work and no mistake.'

'All right, don't get your knickers in a twist.' Kenny looked as if he wished he'd kept his mouth shut.

Ron held up his hands in apology. 'Not your fault, Ken. I ain't cross with you, it's myself I'm mad with. I knew he was up to no good with her, but I ain't done anything about it. Now you say something else is going on, and he's wanted by the police on top of it. And I've just stood back, forgetting it.'

Billy grew concerned. 'What's it to do with you though, Ron?'

'That sister. Gladys, what works at the nurses' home and does first aid in the evenings.' It was all coming back to him now. 'She don't have anyone else to help her. I don't know if she's even clocked that things have got worse. I'm going to tell her.'

'And then what?' Kenny demanded. 'Ain't none of your business, Ron. Crossing paths with Max will only lead to trouble, you know that as well as I do.'

Ron squared his shoulders. 'That's as maybe. She's a good'un, that Gladys. She shouldn't have to worry about her sister like that. I'm going to warn her, and then if she wants me to help, I will.'

27

Peggy had taken great care with her new outfit. She had never claimed to be gifted with a needle, but she had tried her best, and persuaded first Clarrie and then Mrs Cannon to help her. Now, as she straightened her collar and adjusted her cuffs, she thought it was as good as she could possibly make it.

She had had the idea months ago, when James had sent her his picture of a couple dancing, the woman wearing a spotty dress. Peggy had decided there and then that she would have one just like it.

She knew it was an extravagant use of clothing coupons, but she reckoned it would be worth it, just to see his face. She knew he would recognise it at once and share the delight at what she had done. She wanted to see his eyes light up with appreciation.

At first she had scoured the shops and market stalls, hoping to find a close match. It was a long shot, but she thought if she tried enough places, she might strike it lucky. She didn't mind if the colours weren't the same as in the picture. The main thing was it would be in a spotty fabric.

As the weeks and then months passed by, she began to despair of ever finding the elusive spotted dress. She ranged further afield, using her days off to try to hunt one down. Still success evaded her. There were no dresses with polka dots to be found, not in Dalston, or Islington, or further east, or even in the West End. Peggy had balked at paying central London prices, but had decided to splurge her savings if she found the right thing. Yet even on Oxford Street there was no sign of the magic dress, so she had been unable to surprise James on his last visit to the capital.

They had had a wonderful time together, nevertheless, and as he hadn't known about her plan, he could not be disappointed. He went back to his army base none the wiser. Peggy, however, decided to follow a different plan: she would find the material and make the dress herself.

Clarrie had helped her choose the pattern. Peggy knew she would have to keep it simple, and not include the little flourishes the woman in the drawing wore — flounced sleeves, flared panels in the skirt. That didn't matter. She would do the best she could. Clarrie showed her how to lay out the paper pattern and arrange the fabric flat, how to pin and tack and use tailor's chalk. Peggy concentrated as hard as she could, full of admiration for her clever friend. She was glad she had chosen a fabric with small dots; she could see that bigger ones would need careful matching and she wasn't sure she would have had the patience for that.

When Clarrie had cried off one evening, regretfully admitting she needed to catch up on her sleep as days of working at the factory followed by nights of fire-watching had left her exhausted, Mrs Cannon had stepped in. She had shown Peggy how to sew buttonholes, and Peggy had duly copied her example and slowly finished the task. It had taken hours but finally Mrs Cannon pronounced herself satisfied with the result. 'You don't want to scrimp on the buttonholes,' she explained. 'Too small and you can't do it up, too big and the whole thing comes undone. You can't have that — not if you are doing the jitterbug.'

Peggy had stared at that, not realising the older woman had heard of the dance craze. That had made Mrs Cannon laugh out loud, knowing only too well what was going through the girl's mind. 'Oh yes, in my day we used to go dancing as well, you know,' she had chuckled. 'You young folk didn't invent it.'

Now Peggy blushed a little at the memory. She knew she would never have completed the dress without Mrs Cannon's help. She turned and looked at the side profile, noting how the skirt swung in a flattering way. It was a bright turquoise with the polka dots in contrasting white, and suited her colouring. Truly, even if she said so herself, it was a lovely dress.

James was to call for her before they went out. She had made some savoury scones as well as ginger biscuits, in case he hadn't had time to eat beforehand. The train journey would most likely be delayed in some way and she didn't want him going hungry on her account. She made her way downstairs from her room, to check all was in readiness.

She was too excited to sit still, thrilled at the prospect of seeing him again. Her heart was beating so loudly she thought the neighbours must be able to hear it. She paced around the small, neat kitchen, waiting for the knock on the front door. She poured herself a glass of water, drank half and then realised she didn't want it. Shaking her head, she tipped the rest of it away down the sink. Her hands shook a little.

Peggy knew that she was being silly and that she would simply have to resign herself to waiting, but patience had never been her strong point. She rearranged the plates, then put them back in their original positions. She checked that there were enough tea leaves in the tin, and that the tea cosy was in its usual place in the dresser drawer. She was seized with the urge to stand at the open front door and gaze down the street, but felt that would look bad. Yet now and again she did so. Somehow she had to keep calm and pass the agonising minutes until he turned up.

★　★　★

Evelyn was waiting for Gladys as she rounded the corner after work. Gladys slowed down, wondering what her sister could want. Lately she'd hardly seen her, and she wondered if she was deliberately avoiding her.

Evelyn came to meet her halfway along the street, her face flushed by the summer heat. 'Got a moment, Gladys?' she asked, with a nervous smile.

Gladys frowned. 'Not really. I got to get changed and get the tea on — not unless you've already done it?'

Evelyn looked down at her feet in their pretty highheeled sandals, the sprained ankle a thing of the past. 'Ah, no, sorry.'

'Didn't think so.' Gladys moved to go past her but Evelyn put out a hand. 'Just a minute, Glad. It won't take long.'

Gladys picked up on the anxiety in her sister's voice. She halted and observed Evelyn carefully. She didn't look ill — far from it. Her blonde hair shone and her skin was clear, if a little pink. She'd managed to keep her curves and if anything had put on a bit of weight, which suited her. In fact Gladys thought her sister had never looked better. What was going on?

'All right,' she said reluctantly, knowing that every minute spent out of the house increased her risk of being late for first aid. 'Shall we go inside anyway?'

Evelyn shook her head and her pretty bright curls bounced in the strong sunlight. 'No, let's walk along a bit. No point in worrying Ma.'

Blimey, thought Gladys, when had Evelyn ever concerned herself about what might worry their mother? Still, there was no point in prolonging her distress. 'You'd better tell me what all this is about,' she said.

'I will. Just not here. Turn down this way, and there's that spot where three houses got hit — nobody will overhear us there.' Evelyn led the way along the cracked pavement, balancing skilfully on her narrow heels, with Gladys hurrying to keep up. This must be important for such cloak-and-dagger behaviour. Crossly she stuffed her hands into the side pockets of her serviceable grey skirt.

'Come right back, behind this wall.' Carefully Gladys picked her way across the bombsite, avoiding the smashed brickwork and shattered roof tiles. Anything remotely useful had been taken away as salvage, and what was left was just rubble. Weeds were growing in the oddest places, a cheery buddleia poking out from what must once have been a livingroom doorway. Several butterflies were fluttering around its purple flower spikes.

Evelyn ducked behind the remains of an internal wall, and they stood in the ruins of somebody's back kitchen. It must have been decorated with floral-patterned wallpaper, the scraps of which were now stained with rainwater and scorches from the bomb blast. The edges swayed in the light breeze.

Gladys sighed. Her sister seemed reluctant to start, but time was tight. 'Come on then, Evelyn. Out with it. What's wrong?'

Evelyn shut her eyes for a moment. 'I'm havin' a baby,' she said.

Gladys stared open-mouthed at her. There was silence apart from a couple of bees buzzing around the buddleia. 'But . . . I thought it was a stomach bug,' she said eventually. 'That time you were sick in the privy. Was that . . . have you been hiding it all that time? It was ages ago.'

Evelyn nodded miserably. 'I know you heard me and I told you it was bad drink down the Boatman's. It wasn't really. I thought you'd be on to me like a flash.' Her expression seemed to imply that this was all Gladys's fault for not

300

guessing her secret.

Gladys put a hand out to steady herself against the dirty wall. 'There was a bug going around then. Even the nurses got it. Then when you didn't say nothing else, I thought you was better.' She paused but Evelyn didn't respond. 'Is it Max's? Does he know?'

Evelyn bit her lip. 'Yes, of course it's Max's. What do you think I am? I don't go with any old Tom, Dick or Harry. And no, he doesn't know. He'll kill me. He hates kiddies. He won't want to know.'

'Are you sure? Shouldn't you tell him anyway?'

Evelyn tutted in exasperation. 'He's had to go away for a little while. I need to get this sorted out before he comes back.'

Gladys frowned again, thinking she must have heard wrongly. 'Get it sorted out? What do you mean?'

Evelyn rolled her eyes. 'You know. Get rid of it.'

The bees were still buzzing as Gladys absorbed what her sister had just said. 'You . . . you want me to help you get rid of it? Get rid of your baby?'

Evelyn nodded. 'Yes. That's right. I don't want it and Max definitely won't want it. Like I said, he'll kill me if he finds out. So I got to act now, while he's not here. You must know somebody what can help. All those nurses and doctors you mix with — surely one of them has said something. I can't be the only one in this predicament.'

Gladys gasped. 'I can't ask the nurses something like this. They don't get rid of babies. They save them, and the mothers.' She remembered some of the horror stories she had heard about mothers who'd tried to lose their babies and ended up very sick indeed. 'It's not safe to do something like that, Evelyn. You can't. You might bleed to death.'

'Thanks a bunch,' said Evelyn sourly. 'I didn't want to tell you, to be honest, but you're my only hope. You know the right people, even if you don't think you do. Try, Gladys! Who might have said something, all that time you've been there?'

'No.' Gladys was horrified. The very idea that she might ask the nurses such a thing — what would they think of her? Her reputation would be ruined. They might insist she stopped doing first aid. How could Evelyn assume she would be willing? Even if she had been, she knew enough to realise Evelyn had left it very late. She'd been sick in the spring. She was lucky that her bump wasn't showing.

'But I will help you bring it up.' Gladys felt her heart sink at the promise. She didn't want to have to care for another baby, not after all those years of bringing up her siblings. Yet this would be her niece or nephew. She couldn't abandon this child, no matter how it came to be conceived. Her mind shrank away from the memory of her sister and Max in the pub's back yard.

Evelyn stamped her foot in impatience. 'No, Glad. That's no good. There ain't going to be no baby for you to bring up. I got to take this

302

chance while Max is out of town to get rid of it. He'll just dump me otherwise, and Patty will be right in there as soon as you can say knife. She's been waiting for her chance for ages, seeing if I'll slip up. Well I ain't giving her the satisfaction.' She spoke quickly, urgently. 'If you won't help me then I'll find somebody else.'

'No, Evelyn! It's not safe!' Gladys cried, but her sister had had enough. Even in high-heeled sandals, she could move swiftly, and before Gladys could stop her she was away, hurrying from the bomb site, her head held high.

Gladys slumped against the dirty wall, the news and the oppressive evening heat making her head spin. How could Evelyn imagine that Gladys would help her to put her life in danger? It went against everything she believed in, and everything she had been trained for. Yet, by not helping, she was perhaps pushing her sister to take an even more dangerous route, trusting herself to somebody with no proper medical experience at all.

Grimly she brushed the brick dust from her light summer jacket and old skirt. Time to go home and see to the children. Whether or not they were shortly to be joined by another new family member, they still needed their tea, and it didn't look as if Evelyn would be there to help make it. It was all down to Gladys, yet again.

* * *

Mrs Cannon was not surprised to find the house in darkness when she opened the front door later that evening, but was alarmed when a noise came from the kitchen.

'Who's there?' she called, hoping that she sounded braver than she felt. You heard such stories about burglars, emboldened by the demands of the black market. They could have been watching and knew that she had left at teatime and that Peggy had gone out with her young man after that.

'It's me.' The voice quavered.

'Peggy, why are you sitting in the kitchen in the dark?' Mrs Cannon hurried into the back room, astonished to see the young woman lit by the dim glow from the window. She was sitting slumped over at the small table, utterly dejected. Quickly Mrs Cannon struggled with the blackout blind and then lit the gas lamp.

'Peggy, what's happened?'

Peggy raised her tear-stained face. 'He didn't come,' she said blankly. 'James didn't come.' Automatically she rose and adjusted the blind, knowing her landlady couldn't reach it properly.

'Leave that, dear. We'll think about it in a moment.' Mrs Cannon took off her cardigan and hung it over the back of one of the wooden chairs. 'Have you heard from him — did he send word?'

Peggy shook her head and slumped down again, resting her head in her hands. 'No, not a thing. I've been waiting since you left. I haven't heard from him — not a note, nothing.'

'Let's have a cup of tea.' Mrs Cannon bustled into action. 'Everything feels better after a nice cup of tea.' She set the kettle to boil and reached for the old tea tin with its picture of roses on the side. Pete had bought it for her when he was still at school, and even though it was a bit battered, she could not bring herself to replace it.

Peggy tried to muster some enthusiasm for the idea but her 'yes please' was dull and mechanical.

'He'll have been delayed,' Mrs Cannon predicted. 'You know how these things are nowadays. He probably couldn't find a way to let you know. Don't lose heart, Peggy. He'll have set off in good faith but the trains will have let him down.' She pushed the blue cup across the table.

'Yes, I expect so,' said Peggy slowly. 'That must be it.'

'It will be, dear.' Mrs Cannon spoke reassuringly but cast an anxious glance at the girl. 'Don't go worrying that it's something worse when it probably isn't.'

'No, of course not.' Peggy attempted a smile but did not sound convinced. She pulled the cup towards her but made no move to drink from it.

'You know how fond he is of you,' Mrs Cannon continued. 'That lovely soap he sent, that clever drawing, all the places you've been to since then. He won't have wanted to miss seeing you. Something will have happened to prevent him coming.'

'Yes,' Peggy repeated, but her voice was full of doubt.

Mrs Cannon wrinkled her brow. 'Peggy, you don't seriously imagine he decided not to come? To let you down?'

Peggy turned in her seat so that she did not

have to meet the woman's gaze. 'How do I know?' she said brokenly. 'We hardly ever see each other. He could easily have met somebody else, somebody who lives closer to the base. Or decided he doesn't love me any more. I just don't know.'

'Oh my dear.' Mrs Cannon stretched her arm across the table and patted Peggy's hand in an uncustomary gesture of affection. 'It doesn't seem very likely, does it? That's disappointment talking, that is. Of course you're upset that he hasn't come, but it won't be because he's changed his mind about you. It will be trouble with the trains. Tomorrow you'll get a message or a letter or something, and all will be right again. You'll see.'

Peggy nodded but still did not touch her tea. 'Maybe you're right.' She shifted a little in her seat. 'Don't worry about staying up with me. You must be tired. You've been busy all day — you must be dying for some rest.'

Mrs Cannon nodded. She had spent the morning at a WVS canteen, the afternoon sorting children's garments for a clothes exchange, and then the evening at another WVS meeting. She was well and truly ready for her bed. 'That's very considerate, Peggy. If you don't mind I shall take my tea with me and go upstairs. Don't you sit up late worrying about nothing. A proper night's sleep will work wonders, and then everything will seem better in the morning. I'm sure you'll hear from him then.'

'Goodnight.' Peggy tried to look as if she

believed the reassuring words. She waited until the older woman had gone upstairs and then rose, dully packing away into tins the scones and biscuits that she had made with such hope and love. No point in wasting them. She'd used all the sugar ration and Mrs Cannon might as well savour the benefits, even if James couldn't.

Wearily she emptied her tea cup and dragged herself upstairs. Lying awake, fully alert, as if she still expected him to knock on the door, she went through the endless reasons why he had not appeared. There were so many sensible ones, but she could not shake the fear that he had changed his mind about her. It was no use. She was fully committed now and she knew that if he had gone off her, she would be lost. She had to hope that he was all right, that it was a silly delay, but her fear kept her awake as the moonlight tracked its long patterns across her bedroom ceiling.

28

Ron had reluctantly allowed Kenny to persuade him to visit the Boatman's one more time. It wasn't that he thought he'd enjoy himself, but he wondered if it might be useful. He was apprehensive about speaking to Gladys without proper evidence. Maybe he'd overhear something that would help her warn her sister.

Kenny had been enthusiastic, mainly because the beer was cheap and plentiful, unlike in some of the pubs where drink had grown hard to come by. Ron could guess what that meant — this place was getting supplied via the black market. Well, of course it was. That sounded like Max and his brother all over. Now Kenny waited at the bar, its wooden surfaces and panels stained with drips from the smudged glasses.

Ron felt strangely nervous about speaking to Gladys again. He couldn't put his finger on why, exactly. He knew he wasn't God's gift to women and could be a little awkward, but he wasn't completely wet behind the ears. He could usually strike up a conversation, hold his own. There was something about her that had impressed him. She had obviously been very ill at ease in the pub, and yet it hadn't stopped her doing what she thought was right. He owed it to her to get all the facts, and then he would seek her out.

It was taking Kenny an age to get served. The barman, the landlord, was clearly distracted, running off every time he seemed about to take the drinks order. Ron pulled out his handkerchief and wiped his forehead. It was warm, oppressive even. Perhaps there was going to be a storm. He could do with a nice cold beer.

Finally Kenny returned to the little table with two pints. There were no beermats, but then the table had seen better days. Ron took a sip and the foam made a creamy moustache above his lower lip. Kenny laughed at his friend and pointed. 'Look at you, Father Christmas.'

Ron grinned at the weak joke but his mind was elsewhere. 'What's he doing?' he asked, nodding to the barman, who was yet again disappearing behind the scenes.

'Dunno.' Kenny set his glass down. 'He's been like that all evening. There's some sort of palaver going on but not sure what it is.' He shrugged. 'Maybe it's that Max fellow. Thought I saw him earlier, although I thought he was dodging the coppers. Hope he keeps to that side of the bar — he's enough to put you off your drink.'

'I agree.' Ron had no desire to cross swords with the big man, but he was keen to know, all the same, if Kenny was right.

They fell into a comfortable silence, each alone with his thoughts. It had been a busy day at the docks, and the work had been hot. It was good to sit and sink a beer, even if Ron would rather have been in the Duke's Arms. Kenny was watching his money though.

The quiet mood was interrupted when Evelyn came through the swing door from the street outside, her hair blonder than ever, her figure more obviously curvy than before — even Ron noticed. Kenny raised his eyebrows in appreciation. Ron pulled a face at him. 'Don't even think about it, she's trouble,' he muttered.

'Suit yourself.' Kenny wasn't offended.

She went straight to the bar. 'Where is he?' she called through the archway to the back room. She had on a loose pale blue tunic, gathered above the waist, and Ron observed how she seemed to be standing a little way away from the bar and yet she was leaning on it. She must have put on some weight. Lucky her, to be so well fed when everyone else was having to go without. Unless . . .

Ron didn't have any sisters and neither did his close friends, but something about the girl's stance put him in mind of Kathleen when he'd seen her after she and Billy had announced they were going to have a baby. It wasn't obvious, just the way her centre of gravity had altered. If she hadn't been at the bar like that, he might not have seen, or thought nothing of it. Now he was on full alert. Was this the consequence of what he and Gladys had witnessed that time in the yard?

'Hold your horses,' called the barman, out of Ron's line of sight.

This seemed to infuriate Evelyn. 'Don't you tell me that!' she shouted. 'He's kept me waiting for ages. I know he's back there. I'm coming round.' With that she swung open the wooden flap at the end of the bar, through which the barman would come and go when collecting the glasses, and let it crash down again behind her as

310

she disappeared behind the row of optics to wherever the landlord had gone.

Ron turned to Kenny. 'What's going on?'

'Best to stay out of it,' Kenny advised. 'It'll be a private tiff. None of our business.'

'Yeah, but she's Gladys's sister and he's a bully who's twice her size,' Ron pointed out, getting to his feet.

Kenny frowned up at him. 'What you going to do about it? Come on, sit down, finish your pint, and then it'll be your round.'

Ron suddenly lost the desire to drink from the murky glass. 'You have it. I'll just pop around the back, make sure it's all right. Don't worry, there's a side way through; that Max fellow won't even know I'm there.'

Kenny looked doubtful but pulled the half-finished pint towards him all the same. A beer was a beer.

Feeling as apprehensive as he had all those months ago with Gladys, Ron edged through the side door and into the storage area. It was much hotter now, and still daylight, although that was fading fast, partly due to the gathering grey clouds. The air was thick and humid, and his shirt was sticking to him. Perhaps Kenny was right, this was none of his business. He could pretend he hadn't noticed anything, go back to his friend and pass the time of day over a fresh pint, return home and sleep the sleep of the just. Yet he knew he could not.

Out of nowhere there came a scream and the sound of a door banging open.

'Get out there, don't you go spreading your

filthy lies,' snarled a male voice, and there was a thud as something or someone fell to the floor. Ron craned his neck to see but there were too many stacked barrels in the way to get a clear view.

'It's not a lie!' cried a woman — Evelyn's voice by the sound of it. 'All I need is the money and I can sort it all out. It won't take no time at all then I can be back good as new, do the concert — '

'For fuck's sake there ain't no concert, not any more. Have you not heard a word I said? I got to make myself scarce around here and I don't need your lies. You try to get any money from me and you'll be sorry.' Another thud, and a whimper from Evelyn.

'Don't hurt me,' she begged. 'It's not like that, don't take on so. I wouldn't ask if it wasn't yours.'

'How the hell do I know that? I seen how you look at all the men in here. Could be any one of them what got you up the duff. If it's not just something you cooked up to fleece me.' Feet shuffled and scraped against the stone floor. Evelyn whimpered again.

'Let me go. You're hurting me.'

Max gave a savage gasp. 'You think I'm hurting you? You call that hurt? I'll show you what hurt is, you lying bitch.' He grunted and then Evelyn screamed even more loudly.

Ron twisted around the barrels and had to stop himself groaning in horror as for the first time he got a direct view of the couple. Max was towering over Evelyn, who was lying abjectly on the ground. With another grunt Max swung his leg and his boot connected with her stomach. She tried in vain to shield it with her arms but he pulled at her and landed another kick right in the abdomen. Then another, and yet another. He was beside himself with rage, his eyes almost shut. Evelyn's screams continued and then abruptly halted, but not before Max had landed one final powerful kick into her crossed arms.

Ron had seen enough. He could not stand by and watch Max tormenting the young girl. He edged around the stacks of barrels, squeezing through the gap to reach the back yard.

'There, now you won't spread no more lies.' Max wiped his hands on his dark trousers, once part of a sharp suit but now dusty and smeared with stains. Then he looked up as Ron emerged into view. 'Who the bloody hell are you?'

Ron took in the bulk of the man but reckoned he himself was no pushover. He lifted heavy weights all day every day at work. If it came to it, he would give as good as he got. 'Stay away from her,' he gasped.

Max snorted in contempt but made no move to attack. He seemed to be weighing his options. Ron took a step towards him and at that the big bully of a man showed his true colours and turned and ran, through the door on the other side of the yard. It slammed hard behind him.

Anxiously Ron slowly approached the figure on the ground. The light was very low now but her pale tunic was clear against the dark stone floor. She was very still. He bent to feel for her pulse, trying to think what Gladys or the nurses would do. 'Evelyn, can you hear me?' he asked. 'Evelyn, wake up.' Then he saw the slick of blood, shiny and viscous, spreading around her.

★ ★ ★

It was Gladys's turn to shut the church hall, and so she methodically went around checking that each gas light was properly turned off, that the supplies were packed away, and finally that the big entrance door was locked. It was heavy, but she tugged on it to make doubly sure. She didn't want anyone breaking in and stealing their precious medical equipment; it was far from easy to replace at short notice.

She could see that there had been a heavy rain shower. Earlier on there had been a rumble of thunder, and she had been grateful for it, as it had been unbearably humid up until then. Now the air was fresher and colder. She breathed it in deeply.

'Gladys! Is that you?' A figure was approaching on a bike, water from the many puddles splashing from the wheels. Whoever it was appeared soaked to the skin. She peered at him in uncertainty.

'Who is it?' she called, trying not to be anxious.

'It's me, Ronald. Ron. Billy's mate.' Ron squealed to a halt, more rainwater spraying up and drenching his trousers, but he paid it no heed. 'Gladys, you got to come with me. It's Evelyn, she needs you. She's being taken to the hospital.'

Gladys almost dropped her bag in shock. 'What? What's happened to her?' She couldn't tell him her immediate thought: that her sister had gone to one of the backstreet quacks who claimed to have failsafe ways of getting rid of unwanted pregnancies. If that was the case, then it would be her fault. She should have tried harder to help. Fear gripped her throat.

'I'll tell you as we go,' said Ron. 'Quick, hop on.'

Gladys stared at him, intermittently lit by the arcs of the anti-aircraft beams. 'I . . . what?'

'Hop on. You know. I stand up to pedal, you sit behind me. It'll be the fastest way.'

Gladys shook her head. 'I don't know how.'

Ron was perplexed. 'What, you never done this after school with your friends?'

'No,' said Gladys, reluctant even now to admit that she had had no friends because she had hardly gone to school. Now was not the time for such confessions. It sounded very unsafe, and she'd never had a bike, and besides the roads were soaking wet. Yet how else was she to get to Evelyn? She steeled herself. 'Show me,' she said.

Ron took a deep breath. He'd never come across anyone who hadn't done this before, and these were not ideal conditions in which to begin. Still, it wasn't as if they had much choice. 'Sling your bag here with my jacket,' he said. 'Then you'll be able to balance and have both hands to hold on to me.'

Gladys gulped. 'I have to hold on to you?'

'Well, yes. How else are you going to stay on? I have to have the handlebars to steer with. So you

315

hold on to me around the waist. Sorry I'm sopping wet — there was a cloudburst as I set off.'

Gladys nodded, seeing there was little alternative. 'Yes, I heard it.' She put her bag on his jacket as instructed. 'All right. I'll try.'

'That's the spirit!' said Ron, doing his best to sound encouraging. 'Never mind the rain, eh? It's just a bit of water.' He stood up on the pedals and felt her arms go round him. He wouldn't even think about that, not right now.

'It's just a bit of water,' echoed Gladys, beyond worried now for her sister, but determined to get to the hospital as quickly as possible, no matter what. Slowly and unsteadily, they set off.

* * *

Gladys had never been in the hospital at night before. She had had a few first-aid classes there during the daytime, before she finished her Civil Nursing Reserve training, and so she knew her way around. However, nobody in her family had ever been treated here as they could not afford it. All of her mother's many childbirths had happened at home, usually with Gladys helping out when she was old enough.

Now she tried her best not to be spooked by the shadowy corridors. She was too concerned about Evelyn to think about the state of her jacket and blouse, covered in wet patches from where she had held on to Ron. Somehow they had succeeded in covering the distance to the hospital without falling off the bike. In the back of her mind she had noticed how fit he was, how he had pedalled the weight of both of them as if it were no trouble at all, expertly shifting his balance to counter her clumsy attempts to stay upright. She had never been so close to a man before, and had hardly ever touched one, apart from when performing first aid. Now she had held one around the waist for what felt like a very long time, although the hospital had not been far away.

Ron strode along beside her, making sure she found the right ward. 'I won't get in your way,' he said. 'I just want to know you've found her. Also, if you don't mind, I would like to know how she is, after . . . after what I told you I saw.'

Gladys drew in a sharp breath, horrified all over again at what had befallen Evelyn. From that first moment, when Max had abandoned her at the church hall door, she had known he was a bad type, but never in her wildest imaginings had she thought he would do something like this. While a part of her was relieved that her sister had not tried to get rid of the baby in some filthy back street, she was now consumed with worry about what sort of state Evelyn would be in or, worst of all, if she had even survived the attack.

The ward was busy, and Gladys glanced around to check if there were any familiar faces. The hospital was close enough to her house and Victory Walk for somebody to recognise her, or her sister. She would rather no one knew of Evelyn's condition, for the sake of her sister's reputation. She wondered which ambulance crew had brought her in and whether the ARP had been involved; there would be a good chance that she would either know them or they would know people she worked with. Once he had summoned help, Ron had set off to find Gladys before anyone had arrived, leaving Kenny to wait for whichever service was nearest.

Thank goodness he had remembered her saying that she worked first-aid shifts at that hall. She didn't know how she would have found out otherwise. Ron had said that Evelyn had not been able to talk when he'd left — she was still knocked out. Gladys knew she would be forever grateful to him for rescuing the young woman and then coming to find her, in that awful weather on top of everything else. She shivered at what might have happened had he not been there — Evelyn could have been left to bleed to death on that filthy stone floor.

She could not see her sister in any of the beds as they walked down the centre aisle. A nurse came towards them. 'It's very late. We don't receive visitors at this hour,' she said severely.

Gladys swallowed, a lifetime of obeying the rules telling her that she should turn around and go. However, she stood her ground. 'I was told my sister is in here and her life is in danger. Evelyn. I am a Civil Reserve nurse myself,' she added, and was pleased to see that this piece of information carried some weight.

'I see.' The nurse paused, and then relented. 'It is most irregular but, under the circumstances, you had better come with me now. And you are?' She turned to Ron.

'A family friend,' he said, and Gladys cast him a grateful glance. 'But now you've found her I won't hang around. I got to get back to Ma, she'll be worrying where I am.'

'Yes, you go,' Gladys said, not wanting him to be witness to Evelyn's sorry state but sad to see him leave nonetheless. The ward nurse swept her along to the bed at the end, curtained off.

'Be very quiet now,' the woman said. She reminded Gladys a little of Gwen: old school, stern face, but with an air of complete competence. Her sister would be in good hands here.

The older woman drew back the starchy fabric, which smelt of disinfectant, and Gladys stepped through the gap behind her. There lay Evelyn, her face deathly pale, a big cut on her cheek, and utterly still. Another nurse stood by her pillows, monitoring her pulse. At the foot of the bed stood a doctor, maybe about thirty years of age but with thick glasses perched on the end of his thin nose.

Gladys thought for a moment that she might faint, but then her training took over and she rallied. 'How is she?' she asked quietly, her eyes never leaving her sister's pallid face.

The doctor looked up, and his glasses fell askew. 'Her sister, also a nurse,' the first nurse explained.

Gladys could tell the man was very tired, but he was instantly sympathetic. 'I'm afraid it is not good news,' he began.

'Will she . . . will she . . . ' Gladys could not manage the words to name her worst fear.

He sighed and turned to face her. 'Your sister has lost a lot of blood,' he said in a low voice. 'I expect you can tell by her colour. However, we have succeeding in stemming the blood loss and her temperature and pulse are improving — is that not the case, Nurse Michaels?' He glanced to the young woman at the head of the bed, who nodded briefly. 'And so we may reasonably expect that she will continue to improve. All other factors being well, she should gradually regain consciousness.' He shook his head. 'You knew she was pregnant, I take it?'

'Y-yes.' Gladys saw no point in denying it.

His eyes darkened. 'She obviously sustained severe abdominal injuries during her attack. I am very much afraid to tell you we were unable to save the baby.'

Gladys looked down at the floor, the shiny grey lino, the precise hospital corners of the bed sheet. 'I see,' she said quietly.

'Now you mustn't upset yourself,' the first nurse said, clearly mistaking Gladys's lack of fuller response for grief. 'Maybe it is for the best. To be honest, after tonight, the baby could very well have been extremely damaged, even if it had lived. Perhaps it is better that it and the mother and you yourself were not put through that. As it is, your sister will have known very little about the actual loss. The, er, process. I too am very sorry.'

Gladys felt a lump in her throat. The poor baby. Even if both parents had not wanted it, she would have cared for it somehow. She would have managed. She had just about got used to the idea of a new child in the family, even though it was far from what she had wanted. All the same this would have been Evelyn's own flesh and blood. It was a tragedy, whichever way you looked at it. She realised that the ward nurse was staring at her and she had to say something. 'Thank you for trying,' she croaked, though her tongue stuck to the roof of her mouth.

'We are as confident as we can be that we will at least save your sister,' the stern nurse continued, her voice kindly now. 'You must not fret about her. Now that you have seen her and know what condition she is in, you must be reassured, a member of the medical fraternity like yourself.'

Even in this terrible situation, Gladys's heart sang at those words. A fellow nurse was acknowledging her training and expertise. Even though she did not feel very professional at the moment, she had been recognised. Evelyn might have scoffed at her but it was that very training that had won her admittance to her sister's bedside.

'Yes, I understand,' she breathed.

'Perhaps you should go home and rest now that you have seen her,' the nurse continued. 'Please leave me your address so that we can contact you if we need to — which I do not anticipate,' she added quickly. 'It is purely a formality. Then you may return tomorrow during regular visiting hours. I dare say your sister will be in need of comfort.'

Gladys looked at Evelyn's face. Maybe she had regained a little of the healthy colour she had boasted these past weeks. She did not know how her sister would react to the news. Nodding, she took her bag and turned away, making her way back through the row of beds and back outside to the starlit hospital entrance.

29

'It's kind of you to let me tag along,' Edith said, hurrying after Mary and Charles as they left the cinema. They had all wanted to see *The Life and Death of Colonel Blimp* for weeks. 'Are you sure I haven't been too much of a gooseberry?'

'Nonsense.' Mary waited for her shorter friend to catch up. 'If we thought that, we wouldn't have asked you. I know how much you like Anton Walbrook. Now we'll have time for fish and chips as well. Haven't done that for ages, have you?'

Edith shook her head. 'No, not really. We tried when I was down with Harry that weekend but ended up eating in the inn we were staying at.'

Charles looked interested. 'Yes, what was that like? I'm always keen to hear of places for a little trip to the country. You never know when the occasion might arise.'

Edith privately thought that Charles would find the country inn a little beneath his standards, but to say so would let Harry down. 'It was lovely, a real breath of fresh air,' she grinned. 'Bit too fresh for me, though. Between you and me, I'm more at home in a busy city. It's so quiet in the country — I'm always afraid a big cow will come around the corner or something like that.'

'Ooooh, don't.' Mary shuddered. 'I'd be scared if that happened.'

Charles laughed. 'Mary, how can you be

scared of a cow? I've seen you face down the fiercest old doctors when they didn't treat your patients fast enough. The cows would be scared of you, if only they knew.'

'Stuff and nonsense.' Mary clasped his arm as they joined the queue for the fish and chip shop. The aroma of hot fat and vinegar wafted through the open door and Edith's mouth watered at the prospect.

'How is Harry?' Charles asked, giving Mary's hand a squeeze.

Edith shrugged. 'Oh, not so bad. He's glad to be out of hospital at last, back to doing something useful. Not sure he's cut out for life behind a desk though.'

'No, I should think not,' said Mary.

Charles nodded sagely. 'Obviously I don't know him as well as you, but I must say he never struck me as someone who liked to sit still.'

Edith chuckled. 'You can say that again. He's itching to do something more active. Not that he isn't grateful to be where he is,' she added hurriedly, not wanting to sound as if he was complaining — even though he was. She certainly would not tell them about Harry's deeper worries; she had not mentioned those even to Alice. They inched forward, as several contented customers came out of the shop. One was eating a pickled egg.

'Yes, I'm sure,' said Charles easily, taking his wallet from his uniform pocket. 'No, Edith, put your money away. This is my treat, I insist.'

Edith wondered if she should protest and then decided that Charles might be offended if she argued. Besides, he was not short of a bob or two. 'Thank you,' she said, considering herself lucky to have such friends.

'My pleasure,' Charles said, as two more customers came out and they edged along in the queue. The weather was on the turn; ever since the big thunderstorm, the breeze had been keener. Autumn was on its way. 'It does seem a shame that somebody who knows so much about sport and keep fit is stuck doing — what exactly is he doing, Edith?'

Edith gave a little groan. 'Filling in requisition forms.' She knew that careless talk cost lives but really, that was not giving anything away. 'That kind of thing. It's got to be done, I know, and he'll be very accurate, but it does mean that all those years of training aren't being put to good use.'

Finally they reached the counter and Charles bought them their fish and chips. Edith inhaled with pleasure as the portions were served out.

'Salt and vinegar?' asked the woman behind the counter, her face red from the heat of the frying. 'Pickled egg? Anything else?'

'No, no, this is more than enough,' said Edith, mouth watering even more in anticipation.

Charles helped himself to a plump chip, which glistened invitingly. 'Can't be beaten,' he beamed. 'Helps to keep the spirits up, doesn't it?' He stood back to let the two nurses go past him and other customers to surge forward, then stepped swiftly to catch up with them once more. 'Well, I'm delighted to hear he's back in the world of work once more, but it's a shame that it's not something more appropriate to his particular talents.' He paused as he lifted a couple more chips to his mouth. 'We'll have to see if something can be done about it. Leave it with me, Edith, leave it with me.'

★ ★ ★

Peggy tried not to grow too worried when she heard nothing on the day after James was due to visit. She persuaded herself that he'd almost reached London, there had been some kind of hiccup and he'd had to return on a train which then suffered further delays. That way he would scarcely have had time to write a note or send a telegram. He would know Mrs Cannon had no telephone. It was all perfectly understandable.

So when Clarrie casually asked her how their date had gone, Peggy had simply replied that James had been delayed. Clarrie had been instantly sympathetic and demanded Peggy go to the pictures with her so that she wouldn't sit and dwell on it. They decided on a Tommy Trinder and Peggy almost managed to lose herself in the story and enjoy the show.

However, when the days went by and there was still no word, all her anxieties returned. She could not concentrate on her work and several times had to be reprimanded by her supervisor. 'What ever is the matter with you, Peggy Cannon? You're as bad as some of those new girls who just got conscripted,' the forewoman complained. 'It's not like you.'

'Sorry,' Peggy had said, unwilling to explain. It

would sound too humiliating.

Sometimes she wondered if she was being punished, for the way she had gone off the rails when Pete had first died. Looking back, she felt bad about it. She must have hurt Pete's mother, even if Mrs Cannon didn't know the full extent of her wild behaviour. It couldn't be changed, but she knew plenty of gossiping busybodies who had wished her ill when they saw her getting ready to go out on the town.

She didn't deserve another chance at love. This was Fate showing her the error of her ways. She had dared to dream that she might have a future with James, that someone as handsome and kind and interesting loved her. She had fallen for Fate's trap. Now she was hurting all over again, only this time it was her own fault. She should have known that James was too good to be true.

Mrs Cannon tried to cheer her up. 'What if he's been transferred to another base?' she wondered. 'I expect they don't have much time to pack up and leave. He won't have had a moment to get in touch.'

'Maybe,' said Peggy, stifling the reaction that the James she thought she had known would have moved heaven and earth to get hold of her, even if it was simply a scribbled note. He had to be keeping his distance for a good reason, and the most clear-cut one was that he had had a change of heart. Somehow she would have to learn to bear it. If that was the case then she was never going to risk falling in love again. She felt empty, hollowed out, a dry husk.

Sitting in her room she was tempted to reread all of his letters that she had saved, now kept in a shoebox under her bed. She had decorated the box with scraps of coloured paper, making a pattern of dots and love hearts. Silly girl, she berated herself. Believing that he could ever love her. At least he had never seen that box. How he would be laughing at the memory now, if he had.

It was not one of her fire-watching evenings, so Clarrie, worried about her usually cheerful friend, had gone round to visit her. Now she was perched on the edge of Peggy's bed, trying to talk her into a better frame of mind. 'Let's go through your jewellery collection,' she suggested. 'See what colours you are missing, before we paint any more brooches.'

'What's the point?' Peggy asked sullenly.

Clarrie threw up her hands. 'All right, all right, don't then. See if I care either way. I'm only trying to help.'

Peggy looked away. 'I know,' she said, stricken. 'It's just I can't feel that anything is worth it. Not if he's ditched me. It's all a waste of time.'

Clarrie went and stood by the window. It was almost time to put up the blackout blind. The sunset was fading over towards Islington. Soon it would be dark.

'Do you think something might have happened to him?' she asked slowly. 'Other than his changing his mind about you, that is. I don't want to worry you any more than you already are, but what if he's sick? Or, say, broken his arm and can't write?'

Peggy looked up at her tall friend. 'He'd have

asked one of the other soldiers to let me know, wouldn't he?'

Clarrie shrugged. 'He might have. But what if he doesn't have many friends? Or . . . ' She came to a halt and took a breath. 'I know you don't want to think like this, and don't take it the wrong way, but what if his friends don't want him to be with you? What if they think he should stick to his own kind? You know, what with him being a different colour to you.'

'Oh.' Peggy's hand flew to her mouth. 'You think that could be it? I don't know . . . I realise that some old nosy parkers round here don't approve — her opposite, she's the worst. I just ignore them. They were horrible at first, but I thought they'd given up now they've seen how happy we are and that Mrs Cannon doesn't mind. After all, if she's pleased for us, what right have any of the rest of them got to stick their oar in?'

'Even so.' Clarrie didn't want to push the point, as she could see Peggy was very sensitive about it. 'What if he did break his arm or something like that, and nobody would write to tell you? Or worse, they said they would and then didn't?'

Peggy gasped. 'No. That would be too cruel. So he could be there on his sick bed, thinking I know what's happened to him, but I haven't written back? He must think I don't care! He must think I've changed my mind about him! Oh Clarrie, here I've been thinking he's ditched me and he's been imagining the same! I can't bear it!'

Clarrie came across from the window to put her hands on her friend's shoulders. 'Stop it, Peggy. You're working yourself up into a state again. There's a simple solution, isn't there.'

Peggy had given up making any kind of sense. 'Is there? What is that, then?'

Clarrie gave her an exasperated look. 'Write to him, of course.'

★ ★ ★

Alice repacked her Gladstone bag in the unusually quiet district room. She worked methodically, ensuring all her equipment was clean and complete, but her mind was on the news she had heard on the wireless. The Allies had invaded Italy and General Montgomery was leading the troops. She wondered what it would mean for the soldiers, and whether the navy had been involved. Would Joe end up over there? As ever she could not be entirely certain where he was; by the time she received a letter, he could have been posted elsewhere.

With the change in the weather, the first of the coughs and colds of the season had arrived. Not that she was called out for such minor ailments — but her patients had family members who were sneezing all over the place. She took every opportunity to use each visit to promote general hygiene and the importance of always having a handkerchief to hand. However, some of the children would stare at her as if she was talking another language.

She'd gone as far as handing out good cotton

hankies to some of the families. Pauline had looked at them dubiously but had got the idea once Alice had explained why she'd done it. Her little brother had improved since his accident, but there was no sense in tempting fate; Alice would always think of him as potentially vulnerable to germs that stronger children would simply shake off. At least this might stop him wiping his nose on his sleeve.

Alice looked up as Gladys came into the room, a large cardboard box of bandages under her arm. 'Do you need to stock up on any of these?' she asked, her voice cheerful. But Alice could tell the young woman was worried about something.

'No thanks. I've got all I need now.' Alice indicated her bag. 'I haven't seen you for a while, Gladys. Is everything all right?'

Gladys put down the heavy box and gave a deep sigh. 'I been coming in, but not stopping around to chat. I been busy — my sister was in hospital for a bit.'

'Sorry to hear that, Gladys. Is she better now?'

Gladys wouldn't meet her eyes. 'Sort of.'

It had been a difficult few weeks. Evelyn had slowly regained consciousness, as the young doctor had predicted, but that was just the start. Gladys had visited as often and for as long as she could, but Evelyn had been by turns tearful and rude. When she was told that her baby had died, she had simply said 'good'. Gladys had apologised to the nurses who had overheard, telling them that her sister didn't know what she was saying. However, she knew Evelyn had meant what she said.

Over the next few days the doctor had checked her again and again, and then delivered his next piece of news. There was a strong likelihood that Evelyn would never be able to have a child, after the injuries Max had inflicted on her. Gladys had been horrified; her sister was only twenty. Evelyn had shrugged and said she didn't care and actually it was a relief. 'I don't want no kiddies anyway,' she'd said.

'You don't believe that really,' Gladys had protested.

'Oh yes, I do,' Evelyn had maintained.

Now Evelyn was back home, still bedridden but gradually getting stronger. The doctor had offered to arrange help from the district nursing team, but Evelyn had reacted as if he'd slapped her. 'No thank you. I don't bleeding think so.' Once again Gladys had apologised for her, and assured the kindly but harassed doctor that she herself could oversee the nursing and that their next eldest sister could keep an eye on Evelyn in the hours when Gladys was at work or on evening shift.

Gladys had intended to keep all of this to herself, but when questioned by Alice, with that understanding look on her face, it had all come tumbling out.

'So you see,' she finished, 'I been at home more than usual recently. I won't have her get any sicker for lack of nursing. Our sister Shirley can do some of it, but she don't know how to change a dressing or spot signs of infection. I got to be in charge, and run the house, and see to the other little ones, and make sure Ma's all

332

right, cos she's found out what happened and is all upset. I'm glad to come in here for a bit of a rest, that's the truth.'

Alice raised her eyebrows. 'It can't be much of a rest. You never stop when you're here.'

Gladys chuckled grimly. 'Believe me, it's a doddle compared to home at the moment.'

'Well, if there's anything I can do . . . ' Alice offered. 'What about the victory garden? Can I see to that?'

Gladys gave her first genuine smile of the day. 'Yes. Oh yes, would you? I ain't had a moment. There should still be some greens to pick. We could cover some of those beds to keep them going before the cold really sets in. That would be a weight off my mind, that would.'

Alice nodded. 'Then I'll go over later. The others will pitch in as well.' She looked at the harassed young woman. 'So you said Ronald had helped you? That was good of him, but actually it's just what you'd expect — he's like that. Have you seen him since?'

Gladys wiped a hand across her face. 'I owe him,' she admitted. 'He was so kind and he had no need to put himself out like that. But no. I ain't had a moment. Chance would be a fine thing.'

30

Mrs Cannon pushed open her front door, shivering as she did so. 'Brrr, it's cold in here,' she said, hearing the sound of water boiling in the kettle and so realising Peggy had got in before her. Another afternoon spent at the children's clothing exchange — it was pitiful to see the smallest ones with no warm coats for the coming winter. She had done what she could, matching them with whatever was available in the nearest size, but it never felt enough.

'If you make the tea, I'll light the fire,' Peggy offered, coming through while wiping her hands on a tea towel. Mrs Cannon thought that she had recovered on the surface from her disappointment over her young man, but her eyes were sad, no matter how bright she made her voice.

'That's a good idea, dear. You can bend down so much easier than me.' Mrs Cannon groaned a little as she set down her bulging bag. Every little movement hurt somewhere these days, and the colder it got, the worse her rheumatics became. Not that she would complain. 'I stopped off at the market and got some bargains, as they were shutting up stalls. Plenty of potatoes! I shall make us a Woolton pie.'

'That would be lovely,' said Peggy dutifully, as

she hunted for the matches. If she never saw a Woolton pie again she would be delighted, but she couldn't say that aloud. Carefully she coaxed the flames to spread through the kindling. She didn't want to waste the limited supplies of newspaper.

Mrs Cannon came through with the teapot and cups on a tray, which she set down on a small table near the fire. 'Oh well done, dear. I can never get it to catch as quickly as you can.'

Peggy smiled politely but it did not reach her eyes. She took her cup and sat on the less comfortable of the fireside chairs. It was good to take the weight off her feet; she had stood all through her shift today.

'I saw Mrs Bellings as I was on my way home,' the older woman began. Peggy pulled a face; she was her least-favourite neighbour. 'Yes, she was in a bit of a state. You know that nephew of hers, he came to stay with her a few times?'

'Can't say as I met him properly, but I know who you mean,' said Peggy vaguely. 'Didn't we see him across the road with her once or twice?'

'He was in the army, remember. He had leave in the summer and she took him to a show up the West End; she said they had ever such a nice time. Then he had to join his unit in Italy. Well, it's very sad, he's been killed.'

'Oh.' Peggy didn't know what to say. There was no point in pretending she liked Mrs Bellings or had anything to do with the nephew. All the same, it was yet another untimely death in among all the others. She wouldn't wish the sorrow of bereavement on anybody. 'That's a shame. She must be upset.'

'She is, dear. He was her only nephew and they were very close.' Mrs Cannon took a small sip of tea. 'It's hard when the younger generation dies before you. It's not right. I told her, I knew how she felt.'

Peggy nodded dumbly. The loss of Pete was never far from their thoughts and moments like this brought it all back. All the same, she doubted that any relative of Mrs Bellings could hold a candle to Pete.

'Yes, you'd know that all right,' she murmured.

'I told her, time does help. She'll realise that eventually.' Mrs Cannon turned her face away and surreptitiously wiped her eye with her lace handkerchief. 'It will take a while, of course. Perhaps I'll make her a carrot cake to cheer her up. She might not feel like baking, but starving yourself doesn't get you anywhere.'

Peggy gave a tired grin. 'That's very kind of you. She'll like that.' Privately she thought the spiteful old woman didn't deserve it. But then, Mrs Cannon was probably of a more generous disposition than she herself was, Peggy decided. Bereaved or not, it was hard to forgive the nosy old bag her thoughtless cruelty over James.

★ ★ ★

'I'm going to sneeze, I'm going to sneeze . . . ' Edith frantically rummaged in her bag for a hanky and turned away just in time. 'It's so unfair. I'm going down to see Harry again at the weekend and now I'm developing a cold. I'll be all bunged up and my nose will go red and my eyes will water. He won't want to see me.'

'He will, of course he will.' Alice was bracing as they unloaded their trugs from the victory garden in the big kitchen at the nurses' home. 'Plenty of sage and ginger tea for you. Or anything with vitamin C.'

'If we can get it,' Edith said gloomily, resigning herself to not feeling 100 per cent for her long-awaited break. She had not seen Harry since their weekend away at the country inn.

Belinda joined them, with another trug full of vegetables. 'Look at these,' she said, lifting up a bunch of beetroot. 'Gladys will be delighted — you can cook the roots and use the leaves like greens. Two for the price of one.'

Edith reached across and admired them. 'For no price at all, come to think of it. I got the seeds from Mattie, as she had too many for hers. She has to do them in pots, not in the ground.'

'Bet they work just as well though.' Belinda finished unloading them. 'I hear they have another use too — if you've run out of lipstick, you can make red dye from them.'

'There you go, Edie. You can make yourself beautiful with beetroot when you see Harry.' Alice laughed as she sorted them into baskets before storing them in a dark cupboard.

'Marvellous,' moaned Edith. 'My lips will match my nose.'

Belinda gave a snort. 'That's a nice picture to bear in mind. That's made my day.'

Edith made a face. 'You must have had a

pretty dull day, then.' She blew her nose again.

Belinda leant back against the larder door. 'Not really. I had two new cases this morning — an old man with suspected pneumonia, and a child who's not developing fast enough. I was pretty sure the poor little fellow has rickets. He'll have to be taken to the Infant Welfare Clinic, I can't give him the specialist care he'll need, but I can check that his mother has brought him there. Not sure she believed me, but I did what I could.' She scratched her nose. 'Edie, you've got me worried I've caught your cold now. I must be imagining it. Anyway, I don't have time to be ill. I said I'd help Miriam with her new arrivals. Several refugee families have got out of Belgium — they've started rounding up the Jews there too. It never ends.' Her face darkened.

Alice nodded in sympathy. 'Miriam does a lot behind the scenes, doesn't she?'

Belinda sighed. 'She has to. There are so many in need of help. At first she housed them all herself but now she's on the lookout for any spare accommodation. So if you hear of any . . .'

They all fell silent, knowing that this was unlikely. So many houses had been rendered uninhabitable by the bombing during the Blitz, and there had been little chance to rebuild the damage.

'Of course,' said Alice after a moment. 'I could ask Janet to ask around — the school sometimes gets word. It's only going to get worse, isn't it?'

Belinda shrugged. 'It looks that way. I'm going to muck in if I have any spare time. So don't go giving me your cold, Edie.' She smiled to take the edge off her remark. 'I might try that beetroot dye thing myself. That's if I ever go out dancing again. Meanwhile, I had better read up on the treatment of rickets in case that child doesn't make it as far as the clinic.' She picked up her mud-stained cardigan and left.

Edith prodded a beetroot. 'Do you think it works, Al? The dye thing, I mean?'

'Bound to,' Alice said. 'Look at the state of your fingers from where you've touched the juice. Bright red. Very fetching.'

'Maybe I will try it after all,' Edith mused, rubbing her stained fingers. 'I want to look my best for Harry, cold or no cold.'

Alice gave her an affectionate, exasperated look. 'Edith Banham, will you listen to yourself. You know very well that he wouldn't care if you turned up dressed in a cardboard box. As long as he sees you, he'll be happy.'

* * *

It had been almost a month since Peggy had sent her letter to James, fired by Clarrie's theory of what might have happened. It had seemed completely plausible at the time: James with a broken arm, thinking one of his fellow GIs had informed her, but a victim of a mean trick. Yet there had been no reply and Peggy was forced back to her original conclusion: he really had had second thoughts and ditched her, without even telling her.

The nights were drawing in, and it had been another grey day in a series of grey days. Peggy glared at the sky as she came home from her factory shift, thinking that its colour matched her mood exactly. She hoped that Pete's mother was not back yet as she knew she would be snappy and the woman didn't deserve that. She had just about held on to her temper during the shift but it had been a supreme effort. Everyone apart from Clarrie was an idiot.

Pushing open the door she almost tripped on an envelope that was sticking out from the edge of the doormat. She swore under her breath. Whatever it was, it could not possibly be of any interest. She almost left it where it was.

Then she picked it up and let out a muffled shriek.

It was his handwriting. She would know it anywhere. She had teased him that they must learn everything differently in the States as it looked unlike any script she had seen before. She rushed into the kitchen and took it to the window for better light. Her heart was beating hard in her chest, in a mixture of excitement and dread. Perhaps this was it: confirmation that he wanted nothing more to do with her. At least she would know, though. It was the uncertainty that was so draining. Cautiously she slipped her finger along the edge and tore it open.

Half of her wanted to read it and half of her didn't. The seconds stretched into a minute and then she took a deep breath before unfolding the sheets of writing paper.

My dearest Peggy,
You will rightly be wondering what on

340

God's earth has happened to me. To tell you the truth I am not sure. It has been one strange time, but I was mighty glad to get your letter. You got it in one about my arm. I couldn't write for a long time because it got broken — among other things.

Peggy, you have to believe me that I tried to meet you that day. I set off extra early and had almost got to your door. I was one street away, I guess, when this young British soldier came up to me. He said he knew who I was. I couldn't say the same for him but I didn't want to be rude in case he was a friend of yours. I stopped to listen — big mistake.

I won't tell you what he said exactly, but he was no gentleman. Said he knew you better than I did, that you were stringing me along for a joke and that you were secretly engaged to him. I laughed in his face and then he said he had something that would prove it. Like a fool I followed him, down the side of one of those houses — I forget what you call those little alleys.

He had an accomplice there and I have to say they'd planned it all good. They beat me black and blue till I was out cold. I kind of remember they poured something down my throat but there was nothing I could do about it.

Next thing I know I'm waking up in the hospital on our base here. Somehow I'd been sent back to the right place, I guess my papers were still on me. They thought I was drunk to start with. My right arm was in plaster, my ribs were broken, so was my nose, two of my teeth were gone and for a while my head was so swelled up I could hardly see. I couldn't think straight neither. The doctor told me I was talking nonsense most of the time. I knew I had to get a-hold of you but there was no way of doing it.

Lying there for week after week, not being able to do a damn thing, my mind took to wondering whether the man was right. Peggy, I am so sorry for doubting you. It was just that I hated being there and it made me think badly of everyone, so I was ready to believe the worst. Then I got your letter and saw that he had told me a pack of lies. Whether he was jealous of me or was one of those that think the likes of you and me shouldn't be together, I don't know. He was a short little guy, sandy hair, eyes a bit close together, front teeth like a rabbit's. If he'd been on his own he would never have beaten me in a fight, but the scrawny little coward knew that and got a friend to help him.

I could have asked the doctor to send you word, I guess, but by then I wanted to write to you myself. It's taken all this time to be able to hold a pen straight again. I'm going to be AOK, they tell me, now that I'm on the mend. I want to beg your forgiveness in person as soon as I can get leave. In the meantime, my darling Peggy, know that you are in my thoughts every minute of the day and I meant everything I said to you the last time we met. You are the most beautiful girl in the world and I am the luckiest man because I met you. We can't let these ugly people stand in our way. We are meant to be together.

All my love,
James

Peggy reached for the tall wooden stool and sank down on it, her head spinning. He'd been lying there in pain all that time. Some bastard had tricked him with vile lies about her and then they had done that to him, deliberately, and tried to make out he was drunk to discredit him on top of everything else. Her poor, poor James. She had the urge to leave everything and run to his side. But he was on a military base; they wouldn't allow her to visit him. It wasn't as if she was family. A sob rose in her throat.

The description rang a bell, though. A scrawny little coward with buck teeth, but who knew her well enough to work out when she was doing what. She'd made it easy that day — staring out of the window, going to the door, for all the world to see she was eagerly waiting for someone. She might as well have put out a flag.

Mrs Bellings's nephew would have seen it all. Disgusting man. She just knew it was him. All that family had the same prejudiced views, and he had a nasty streak to boot. He'd stared at Edith when she came round, and she didn't spook easily. Perhaps it had even been him who had waylaid her that time. It sounded like his method. He was big and brave when it came to attacking a woman smaller than him, but had to get help for a man his own size. She was glad he was dead.

That was a terrible thing to admit. She'd thought the same, years ago, when she'd heard about the heroic death of the man who had raped her when she thought they were having a fun date. Everyone said he was a saviour of the country — but she'd known his other side. Here was another man who had died in the cause of freedom but had done despicable deeds. She couldn't regret his death.

However, she would not say that to James. She would write to him at once and reassure him, now that she knew he still loved her. Her heart sang even as she wept for the pain he had gone through on her account. He still loved her. She was back in the land of the living, with everything to hope for. She just had to wait a little longer.

31

Flo surveyed the row of glass jars in all shapes and sizes lined up on the big table. 'You're sure you've sterilised them properly?'

Mattie sighed. 'Of course, Ma. Boiling hot water. I'd never live it down if our pickles gave someone food poisoning. Edie would have my guts for garters.'

Flo nodded, and prepared to begin the tricky process of transferring the pickles into the jars. All the surplus vegetables were being preserved, so as not to waste anything. Besides, Flo had plans to use the pickles to barter for food that they had not been able to grow. Her WVS colleagues would happily swap what they did not strictly need for a few jars of her home-made preserves, which glistened ruby red thanks to all the beetroot.

'You hold the funnel and I'll ladle it in,' Mattie suggested. 'No, Gillian, you stay back out of the way. You don't want this to splash on you. It'll make pink marks on your clothes and I'll have a terrible job getting them out.'

Gillian looked up in interest, but was distracted by a knock on the door. 'That'll be Edie and Alice,' Flo said. 'You go and let them in, Gillian. We've got our hands full here.' She didn't want to stop now that they had begun the delicate job.

Mattie sighed with relief as her daughter did

as she was asked without arguing. It was high time Gillian started school; she was becoming too much to handle. Both she and Brian would begin after Christmas when the new term started, but that meant there were still almost two months to go. Mattie adored her daughter but simply could not answer all her questions any longer.

Edith brandished a basket as she came into the kitchen. 'I've brought all I could find,' she said, setting it down. 'Gladys had some extra string in case she needed it in the victory garden, but she says you can have it if she can have some pickles for the home. And look, they had dates for sale at the market. God knows how they got them, so they'll be useful, won't they?'

Flo was delighted. 'We'll set them aside for the Christmas pudding. I'm collecting whatever dried fruit I can, and if we have to change the recipe a bit, then I'm sure nobody will mind. I do like to start baking well in advance of the big day.'

Alice followed her friend into the kitchen. 'How can I help?' she asked.

Flo nodded towards a pile of small squares of material. 'See those? I can't reach them or I'll drop the funnel. If you could lay them out, then we can tie one over each lid with some of the string. Makes it look a bit more special. Gillian can show you how, I expect.' She widened her eyes to Alice in a signal to involve the little girl but at a safe distance from the pickle mixture.

'Oh, of course.' Alice took her meaning immediately. 'So, Gillian, I'll just roll up my sleeves and then you can tell me what you want me to do.'

'All right.' Gillian watched her, as if checking she was doing it correctly. 'You start over here. I'll put out the squares and you cut the string. They won't let me use scissors,' she added.

'Just as well,' said Mattie firmly, as she brought another ladle to the jars. 'The longer we keep you away from sharp objects the better, my girl.'

Flo shook the funnel. 'Have you heard from Harry since last week?' she asked. 'He wrote to say what a good time you'd had on your visit, but we've had nothing since.'

'Only a quick note to say he hoped I'd got back without too many delays,' said Edith. She still had said nothing to the family about Harry's worries. She had tried to cheer him up, but a stay of two nights could make little impression on the gloom that he could not seem to shift. Her joy at seeing him had been tempered with concern. She had to hope that Charles would make good on his promise to come up with something, but nothing had happened yet.

'And did you?' Flo enquired kindly.

'Yes, for once. I was pretty relieved — I'd had a bit of a cold and didn't fancy standing all the way,' Edith confessed.

'Are you better now?' Flo asked. 'Here am I asking you to come over here when you aren't well — sit down, take the weight off your feet.'

'No, no, I'm all right,' Edith protested, anxious not to cause a fuss. If truth were told, she still felt more tired than she ought to be, but perhaps that was down to the ongoing worry about Harry. It was enough to drain you of all energy, but she couldn't afford to slow down when on her shifts. Therefore it seemed to hit her doubly hard on her days off.

'We heard from Joe last week too,' Mattie said, scraping the ladle around the bottom of the pot. 'There, that's the last dollop. Yes, he said he was busy and doing well, but didn't give away very much otherwise.'

'Well, he can't, of course,' Flo pointed out, setting down the funnel on the countertop. 'He's got to be careful in case his letters fall into the wrong hands.' She wiped the spatters of vinegar from her fingers. 'Unless you know anything else, Alice?'

Alice looked up from cutting her string into small lengths, intently supervised by Gillian. 'Well, he hasn't said anything directly,' she admitted. 'I did wonder about one piece of news though. He said that some of the people on the base were talking about putting on a play and that it might be *Julius Caesar*.'

Flo, Mattie and Edith looked blankly at her.

'That doesn't sound like much fun,' Edith said. 'Doesn't everyone get killed at the end, or something like that?'

'I should think they ought to choose a play to cheer everyone up,' Flo said staunchly. 'That's what I'd want, not a boring one.'

Alice smiled. 'Perhaps it's his way of hinting that they might be going to Italy. *Julius Caesar* is set in Rome. I don't think they'd really put that on; it's all a bit grim. He's just trying to warn us that he might be posted over there — or that's my guess, anyway.'

'Really?' Flo gave Alice a quizzical glance.

Alice nodded. 'That's how he lets me know where he is if he can't tell me outright. We've done it that way for years. He usually chooses a book title, but perhaps he realised I wouldn't recognise any Italian ones.'

Mattie took the big pot over to the tap in the back kitchen and filled it with water. 'Well, if you don't, then I'm sure nobody else would,' she said, returning to the table. 'I bet he wouldn't either. He might be good at sums and suchlike, but I've never seen him try to read Italian. The news from over there is good, though, isn't it? Perhaps it wouldn't be so bad if he got sent there.'

Flo nodded reassuringly but all the same her eyes went to Alice.

'I think so,' she said carefully, 'but maybe it's not as easy as they thought it would be. We shouldn't expect it to be over very soon.' She didn't want to puncture their optimism, but some government voices had given the impression that it would be a straight — forward and easy invasion, and it was turning out to be much trickier.

It was at times like this that she missed Joe. All the people in this room were very dear to her and yet she couldn't discuss the news with them like she did with him. He could judge the way the detailed facts were presented and weigh up whether a story was true or if bad news was being kept from them. It made her in turn think harder. Not that it would change the course of what was happening, but she liked to be properly informed, insofar as she could be. She felt safer for it, even if the news was bad.

She wondered whether to raise what Winston Churchill had spoken of a few days ago. Alice, like the rest of them, was relieved that the terrors of the Blitz had receded and they could get on with everyday life, without the immediate danger of bombing, the threat of losing house and home, of all normal routines being disrupted. Though she would never forget what they had gone through, she hoped that was all in the past. The sheer relief at being able to sleep properly in her own bed, night after night, was immense. Nobody could function well on so little sleep over a long period of time.

Yet Churchill had raised the prospect of returning to that nightmare. 'We cannot exclude the possibility of new forms of attack on this island,' he had said. There had been no exact details, but Alice presumed he would not say such a thing unless he had solid intelligence that something was in the pipeline. Should she mention it now?

If Joe had been there she would have waited until they were alone. He might have more inside information; even if he did not, he would have a wide perspective. He could allay her fears like nobody else. But he would not give her false comfort; if the East End was liable to come under fire once more, he would see it as his duty to prepare her, so she was not taken unawares. She valued his advice more than anybody's. He made her feel that she was as in control as it was possible to be — however little that was.

But he was not here. He might be halfway to Italy by now. Or he could have been posted somewhere else entirely, and she would have to wait for his next veiled hint, disguised as a book title, to find out where. Then again, he might still be at his base in Plymouth, sailing from there out into the Atlantic. She sent up a heartfelt prayer that, wherever he was, he would be safe.

'Penny for 'em!' Edith laughed at her and gave her a little dig in the ribs. 'You were drifting off there, Alice. Look, Gillian needs more string cutting. We can't finish the pickle jars without it, so look lively.'

'Of course. Sorry.' Alice jolted herself out of her reverie. Gillian was watching her closely and there was no sense in worrying the little girl, who was becoming alarmingly good at picking up on any undercurrents in the adults' conversation. Maybe she had inherited her Uncle Joe's lively mind.

'I was saying that we should start to plan who brings what for Christmas,' Mattie said. 'Edie reckons that your victory garden will have plenty of Brussels sprouts. Shall I put you down for those? You will come here for Christmas, won't you? Unless you were going back to your parents, of course.'

'Oh, er, yes, I'd love to.' Alice hadn't thought that far ahead, but knew that travel to Liverpool would be impractical over the holiday season and she would be better off saving her leave for a week in the springtime. 'We should have sprouts to spare. We've planted lots, and there's only so many the nurses can eat. Edith and I can do that, and carrots as well.'

'Good, I'll make a list.' Mattie was getting more like Flo every day, taking great pleasure in sorting out the fine details in advance so that everyone would have a celebration to remember.

Alice cut her last piece of string and Gillian carefully wound it around the top of the final jar, fixing the bright red and white gingham square in place before Edith neatly tied the ends in a knot, which the little girl's fingers still couldn't manage to do. The sight caught at Alice's heart. She couldn't bring herself to raise the subject of the prime minister's speech. There would be no point; it would worry them for nothing. She could not break the air of contentment.

Yet she longed for Joe to be here, to test out her concerns, and if she was honest, just for the joy of his presence. She wanted to see him, listen to that dear voice, feel that sense of connection that she had with nobody else. It was more important than she cared to say. Perhaps he would make it home for Christmas. All she could do was hope.

★ ★ ★

'Ah, Mary, just the person I wanted to see.' Fiona appeared around the corner of the stairs as Mary descended to the main hallway. 'I'm sure you can spare me a moment.'

Mary nodded at the superintendent, knowing

she had little choice in the matter.

'It's almost that time of year again,' said Fiona cheerfully. 'Will you be able to play the piano for our carol concert? You do it so well. The other nurses and our guests always appreciate it.'

Mary smiled, relieved that it wasn't a telling-off for missing curfew. Charles had brought her back late a couple of times recently, thanks to the diversions that were now the norm; a water pipe had burst and the road had been shut off, and then a bus had broken down and blocked the high road. 'Yes, of course,' she agreed warmly. 'I enjoy it. I wouldn't miss it for the world.'

'Excellent. Oh, and one more idea.'

Mary set down her Gladstone bag, packed and ready for her morning rounds, and waited.

'Gladys has had a difficult time this autumn,' Fiona went on. 'Shall we offer her a solo? She sings so beautifully and hardly ever has a chance to show us. I think she would like to. A few years back I wouldn't have dreamed of suggesting it, but she's come on in leaps and bounds.'

Mary paused to consider. 'What about 'Once in Royal David's City'? She could do the opening verse and then we all join in after.'

Fiona beamed. 'That's the very thing. Not too much to frighten her off. If she were to feel inclined to do even more, then we could take her up on that too . . . '

Mary saw where the superintendent's thoughts were headed. 'I'll sound her out, shall I?'

'If you would be so kind, then yes. I must

detain you no further, Mary. I can see you are itching to get going,' Fiona observed.

Mary winced. 'Itching is right. My first visit is a suspected case of scabies.'

Fiona raised her eyebrows. 'Well, impress upon them not to share towels — easy to say, I know, and we must hope they have the luxury of extra ones. Do your best, that's all.'

'I'll try,' said Mary, as positively as she could. She knew the family had little money for anything spare. The very thought of it made her want to scratch her scalp, but she knew she would have to lead by example and not fall into that trap.

As she took her bike from the rack, she looked to see who else had yet to leave. Edith's bike was still there but there was no sign of the nurse herself. Mary wondered if Charles had managed to bring about what he'd confided to her he had in mind for Harry. It was not her news to tell, but she couldn't help wishing that she could see Edith's face when she heard. She was sure her friend would be delighted.

Then again, Edith had seemed under the weather recently. She had never fully recovered from the nasty cold, even though that was many weeks ago. She wasn't ill exactly, but she was not her usual lively self. Perhaps this news would be exactly what she needed. Mary was terrible at keeping secrets, and had the overwhelming urge to blurt it out every time she saw her friend, but she knew she absolutely must not do so, in case something had gone amiss behind the scenes and it did not come to pass. Gritting her teeth, she wheeled the bike out through the gate and swung herself into the saddle, wondering how long it would be before Edith's face lit up.

32

December 1943

Evelyn sat at the rickety table, half-heartedly stirring the bowl of barley stew that her sister Shirley had set in front of her. Shirley was shooing the four younger children up to bed, to cram into the room they shared upstairs. Their mother had retired to her own bed already, complaining yet again of a headache and bad nerves.

Gladys took all this in as she returned from work. The feeble fire in the grate was doing its best to warm the cluttered living room. Evelyn glanced across at her.

'What's happened?' she asked, catching the expression on her older sister's face.

Gladys set down her bag and unwrapped her woollen scarf from her neck. She didn't know how Evelyn would react to her news but thought she might as well come straight out with it. 'It's the annual carol concert,' she said. 'They want me to sing solo.'

'You?' Evelyn's head shot up as if she'd been stung. 'They asked you?'

'Yes.' Gladys stood her ground. 'Mary wanted me specially. She's the best musician there and she can't play the piano and sing properly at the same time, so she wants me to do it.'

'And will you?'

Gladys nodded. 'I told her I would.'

Evelyn scraped her spoon across the bottom of her bowl with a horrible scratching noise. Then she slumped over it, with a sigh of defeat. 'So you're the singer in the family,' she muttered.

Gladys came to sit beside her, perching on a three-legged stool that she'd once tried to smarten up with some leftover cream paint. 'Not really,' she said. 'Only for the carols. I don't want to do any more than that.'

Evelyn pushed the unfinished stew away from her. 'I was kidding myself, wasn't I,' she said sombrely. 'You can tell me 'I told you so' if you want to. I was never going to be a singer. That Max was just stringing me along.'

Gladys didn't know how to reply. 'Maybe,' she said cautiously.

'Oh, you don't have to pussyfoot around.' Evelyn was more animated now. 'I been thinking a lot now I got all this time on my hands. He was only interested in one thing and it wasn't my singing.'

Gladys met her eye. 'Probably.'

'He'll have scarpered off to his cousin in Norfolk what he used to talk about. Always said if things got too hot for him round here he'd take off to where nobody could find him.' She shook her head, her hair now showing roots in its real shade of mid-brown. 'That's him all over. First sign of trouble and he scarpers. About the only thing he can be relied on to do.'

Gladys shrugged in sympathy.

'Well, it got me wondering.' Evelyn clasped her hands in front of her. 'I fancy getting away as well. I'm no use to you here, I'm just another mouth to feed. I'm no good with the kids and Shirley's a better cook than I am anyway.'

Gladys thought it better not to comment.

'I've decided. I'm getting out of London too. I'm going to join the Land Army.'

'Blimey,' said Gladys before she could stop herself. 'Are you sure?'

Evelyn nodded, and there was a trace of her old determination on her face. 'I know you think I won't last five minutes but, like you said, I got to do something. I quite fancy it to tell you the truth. Tomorrow I'm going to go and sign up for it. Don't try and stop me.'

Gladys swallowed hard, taking this in. Perhaps it was the best solution all round. 'I won't try and stop you. I promise.' It could be the making of her sister, she realised, if she could only stick it out. It had taken a tragedy to push her in that direction, but she could yet surprise them all.

'Good,' said Evelyn, her eyes flashing now with resolve. 'My mind is set on it. I'm going to do it first thing in the morning.'

★　★　★

'Pass me her bib, will you, Billy?' Kathleen prepared to spoon mashed carrot and potatoes into Barbara's hungry mouth. She didn't want her daughter to begin to grizzle during the carol concert. A good feed before they left was the best way to avoid that problem.

Kathleen loved the carol concert and was always filled with warm anticipation when asked to come along. It had become a tradition, a way of starting the festive season, even better because the children were welcome. When Brian was younger she had worried that the nurses were just saying that to be kind, but now she knew they meant it. All the same, there was no sense in taking Barbara along without feeding her first. If she began to cry in earnest, it would try anyone's patience.

Billy found the bib and then checked his watch. 'I hope I done the right thing, asking Ron. He's a bit low at the moment. Ever since Kenny started walking out with that girl he met, he's been on his lonesome.'

Kathleen put down her spoon and looked fondly at her husband. 'Of course you did. We can't have someone feeling lonely at Christmas. I know he's got his ma and auntie, but they don't get out much. When are we going to meet this girl of Kenny's, then?'

'Don't get your hopes up, I'm not sure how long it'll last,' Billy predicted. 'It's cruel to say it, but I reckon she's just passing the time till she can snare some bloke in uniform. Still, he's having fun while it lasts, so we can't begrudge him that.'

Kathleen nodded and returned to her task. She still had to pinch herself sometimes, to believe this was real. The room glowed with light and warmth from the fire, making the tinsel she'd pinned up sparkle. Billy had brought back a little tree after work one night and she and Brian had made decorations for it. They had carefully cut strips of paper and painted them

— all sorts of paper, saved from envelopes, notices, newspaper, whatever they could find. Then they had made them into chains. They had had some left over and decided to loop them through the banisters. She could not have been happier if she had been given the finest decorations from Harrods. The love that had gone into her home-made versions was beyond price.

There was a knock and Ron came in before either of them could open the door. 'Too cold out there to wait,' he explained, rubbing his hands and heading straight for the fire. 'Oh, this is nice, this is. You got it looking lovely, Kath. Warms the cockles of me heart, it does.'

'You silly sausage,' protested Kathleen, but her cheeks glowed pink at the praise. 'Right, my girl, let's get your winter coat on now you're full up. You ready, Billy? Brian, where are your gloves? Well, you'd better find them or you'll get cold hands like Ron here.'

'Yep, you don't want that,' grinned Ron. 'Oh, wait a minute. I forgot. Mine were in my trouser pockets all the time. How daft am I?'

'Daft as a brush!' Brian shouted in delight, chuckling wildly, as Billy passed him his small duffel coat and stripy knitted scarf. Kathleen watched with amusement, deeply thankful that her boy had turned out so well. Instead of taking after his actual father, he seemed to be closer to Billy's sunny nature, and enjoyed meeting his friends. She had held a long-unspoken fear that he might be nervous of grown men after witnessing Ray's violence, but perhaps he had been too young to absorb it. Now he was showing Ron the way out, keen to get to the music. Kathleen carefully bundled Barbara into her pram, and knew that she was blessed. What she had might not look like much to some; yet to have a home, friends, family and a loving husband were, to her, riches beyond measure.

★ ★ ★

Gladys stood still as the final chords from the piano faded away, and then ducked her head in a little bow before returning to her seat in the front row. She had done it. The clapping was for her. At first she had thought that nerves would get the better of her but she had concentrated on her breathing, just like Mary had told her to, and her voice had come out steady and strong. Mary had persuaded her to sing not only the opening verse of 'Once in Royal David's City', but also the whole of 'O Holy Night'. 'I love that one,' Mary had explained, 'but it's no good for everyone to join in. It works best as a solo. Then I can play all those lovely chords and the notes over the top as you sing — do say you'll try it, Gladys.'

Gladys had surprised even herself by how well that tune suited her voice. Mary had helped her to practise and encouraged her to hold the long high notes, until she was confident enough to sing it in front of the whole gathering. Now that she was back in her chair she found she was shaking, all those strong feelings returning in a rush, but this time she recognised it was excitement. She could do it.

She really could sing. 'Well done,' Fiona murmured from the row behind. Beside her, Alice patted her arm. Gladys shut her eyes and wished this moment could go on for ever. It was possibly the best of her life.

Then everyone got to their feet to join in the last carol. Mary played the opening bars of 'O Come, All Ye Faithful' and Gladys prepared to sing again, this time with less force and certainly less trepidation. She didn't need to look at the words; she had learnt them by heart for the very first carol concert at the start of the war. Alice was singing along, and on her other side Edith was making an effort, although not much sound was coming out.

Behind her, Fiona was putting all her considerable energy into the chorus, her Scottish accent still strong. Gwen was much more controlled, missing out the high notes, as if she wouldn't attempt anything she wasn't sure she could succeed at. From further back came some male voices: that would be Billy, and Stan had a fine bass voice. Gladys had seen Brian and Gillian take their seats together and they could be heard trying to remember the chorus, mixing the words with la-la-las when they failed to recall the detail but evidently didn't want to stop singing. Gladys smiled. She was glad they were allowed to participate and not shushed, as she had been when young. This evening was as much for them as for the grown-ups.

Mary tried to prolong the final chord as long as she could, but eventually it came to an end and the concert was over. Gladys was besieged by people coming up to her to congratulate and thank her, many of whom she did not know. The common room was packed, as the event grew in popularity every year. Nurses asked their friends and colleagues; there was Dr Patcham, his eyes glinting merrily as he held out his hand to shake hers. There was Brendan, the ARP warden, making his swift excuses as he was due back on duty. Janet, the teacher from St Benedict's, was making her way over to Alice. Gladys gave a gentle sigh.

This evening brought everyone together in a way that sometimes only music could. She had been a key part of it. A wonderful sense of belonging flooded through her, buoying her up. Yes, they were in the middle of a terrible war and they had every reason to be fearful and sad. Yet on this, one of the darkest days of the year, they had come to this place and sung. While such things were possible, there would always be hope. It filled her with confidence that nobody here could be kept down for long.

'Gladys?' A male voice interrupted her train of thought, and she turned around to come face to face with someone she had not seen in the rows before her.

'Oh.' For a moment she was dumbstruck. 'Ron. I didn't notice you come in.'

Ron shuffled a little awkwardly. 'I came with Billy and Kath and the kids. I was at the back. I didn't want to block anyone's view,' he said, embarrassed. 'I never knew you could sing like that. You were really good. Honest.'

'Thank you.' All at once Gladys was

tongue-tied. She could tell her face was flaming red, and not only because the crowds of people had made the common room unusually hot. 'I . . . I didn't either. Mary taught me. If it hadn't been for her . . . ' She trailed off, uncomfortable at so much attention and yet not wanting to run away.

'I know you're busy and everyone wants to talk to you tonight,' he said hurriedly, 'but, if you got any free time, and don't worry if not, but I was just wondering . . . Gladys, would you like to come out with me, for a drink, or a cuppa, or something?'

Gladys gasped, completely taken by surprise. No man had ever shown any interest in her. Was this a joke? But no, Ron wasn't like that. He was kind, and helpful — and she remembered how strong his muscles had felt as she held on to him that dreadful night on the bike. 'Yes,' she said decisively, amazing herself at her sudden daring. 'As long as it ain't the Boatman's.'

Ron grinned and held her gaze. 'No, I promise, anywhere but the Boatman's.'

Gladys smiled up at him. 'Then yes.' Before she could say anything else, one of the church hall committee touched her arm and started to congratulate her effusively, and Ron had merged back into the crowd. Gladys nodded politely to the woman, who had always seemed too grand to approach before, but her mind was whirling. Ron had asked her out. He liked her — from his expression she could tell this was no joke. He liked her a lot. The best evening of her life had just got even better.

Harry spiked another completed requisition form onto the pile, trying not to shiver as he did so. The hut in which he worked was freezing. Some of the civilian staff, mostly women, wore fingerless mittens, but he couldn't bring himself to do so. That would seem like an admission of defeat. He'd never been one to feel the cold before; but then again he'd never had to sit at a desk for an entire working day before, let alone at one in an unheated hut with a tin roof.

At least he had a warm layer on underneath his jacket. The thought made him smile, as Edith had sent it to him: a long-sleeved, thick cotton collarless shirt that she had found in a shop near Limehouse. Apparently all the men on the docks wore them during the winter. She'd written to say it wasn't from the black market, but Harry wouldn't have cared by that point. He liked the idea of being in the same gear as Billy and Ron and their mates.

'Something amusing you, Banham?' The hatchet-faced supervisor was on his case again. 'Care to share it?'

She really did have it in for him, Harry thought. 'No, just remembering Ma's roast dinner,' he said solemnly, looking down at his desk again before anyone else in the office caught his eye and made him laugh out loud.

'Very well.' She didn't look convinced but she could hardly prove it otherwise.

Silence fell as they all diligently filled in more forms, filed them, passed them along to the appropriate pile. Harry wondered if it really was the cold or whether he was actually dying of boredom. He knew he should be grateful that he was alive at all, when so many with him at Dunkirk had not made it safely home, but it was hard to be grateful all day every day.

A messenger boy went past his desk, barely old enough to have left school. He handed something to the supervisor and almost ran out again, terrified by her glare. Harry felt sorry for him. This was probably his first job and he most likely had had little choice about what he did. Who in their right mind would have volunteered to deal with the supervisor? She was reading the message now, her brow contorting into a deep frown. 'Carry on,' she said, rising abruptly and making for the door at the back of the hut, which led to the captain's office. 'Sanders, you are in charge for the time being.'

'Yes, ma'am,' said the young woman in the corner, smiling sycophantically.

Harry reflected that she had joined their team more recently than him and he might well take that as an insult, but she obviously welcomed the responsibility. The supervisor clearly rewarded those who agreed with whatever she told them and caused no trouble. He avoided the young woman's stare and turned once more to the task of deciphering which vehicles had flat tyres and who had been driving them at the time.

His mind wandered again to Edith, and this time he bit on the inside of his mouth to stop the automatic smile from breaking through. He didn't know how he would have coped in these last months without her. Her letters reminded him that she was always thinking of him, even if they were hours apart. She always sounded so cheerful, assuring him that they would be together again soon and this dreary interlude would pass. He tried to imagine what she would be doing at the moment. Cycling around Dalston, or in a patient's home, or maybe making a quick visit to the market.

He had applied for leave at Christmas, hoping to celebrate their first anniversary in the sanctuary of his parents' house, but he had had to do so via his supervisor, who had bluntly told him that he did not stand much of a chance. Harry had nodded and not revealed his disappointment. He had, after all, been at home for the previous festive season, which was more than many could say. He should not be surprised if he was turned down.

Yet nobody would be using the army vehicles for their regular day-to-day purposes over the Christmas period itself, and so there was no real need for an office full of clerical staff to be stuck here at the ready in case more tyres had to be ordered. They could just as easily order extra in readiness, and all go home. It came down to the spiteful attitude of the supervisor. He tried not to take it personally, but he strongly suspected that this was exactly what was behind it. If she could make his life more difficult, then she would.

Five minutes passed, and then ten. Harry was beginning to think she had disappeared for the morning.

After a quarter of an hour, she returned, her face like thunder. Harry registered this with some alarm. Somebody was for it, that was certain. A look like that could not bode well.

'Banham,' she barked, with no preamble. 'You are to come with me to the captain's office, immediately. Look sharp.'

All eyes in the room turned towards him. The young woman who had been temporarily in charge raised her eyebrows and all but smirked in mock sympathy.

With as much dignity as he could muster, Harry rose. He could not think what he might have done to deserve this, but his heart was in his boots as he wound his way through the assortment of battered desks. He might as well kiss goodbye to Christmas at home.

33

Peggy pulled her scarf up over her nose and breathed out, trying to warm the lower half of her face. Liverpool Street Station was no place to be standing around for ages, and yet there was nowhere else she could possibly be. James had got two days' leave and she was not going to waste a second of it. The moment he stepped off his train, she would be there to greet him.

The trains were delayed, of course. She had already waited for an hour. She had worn her one new piece of winter clothing, her astrakhan-trimmed ankle boots, which had good thick soles on them, but even so she could hardly feel her feet. She had thought about putting on her best pair of woollen stockings, but they were darned. Even though she was fairly sure nobody would see, she herself would know. Then Clarrie had come good, lending her a pair of nylons.

'Wherever did you get them?' Peggy had asked, her eyes wide with wonder. They were like gold dust.

'Don't ask,' Clarrie had said darkly.

There had been no choice but to wear her old coat, as Peggy had not had enough points to buy a replacement; it had been more important to buy the boots, as her previous pair were beyond mending. She hoped that the bright scarf and smart footwear would distract from the coat's worn elbows and shabby bobbled fabric.

She was far from the only one there craning her neck to see if there was any change to the arrivals, or any unexpected movement. Plenty of people of all ages crowded the concourse, some in uniform, all with the same air of expectation. Many carried bags or boxes of gifts. Christmas was only a few days away now.

She hugged her handbag more closely to her, conscious of the pushing and shoving in which a pickpocket could have a field day. She had no intention of letting one make off with the contents of her bag; she had put lots of thought into her gift for James and nobody was going to deny her the sight of his face when he opened the little box.

An older woman, shorter than her, tapped her on the shoulder. 'Excuse me, but can you tell me when the next Cambridge train is due in?'

Peggy turned around to face her. 'Sorry, I don't know,' she said.

'Only my husband is travelling from there, you see.' The woman was obviously worried. 'He's coming home for Christmas. He hasn't managed to do that since the war began. I do hope he gets here.'

'I'm sure he will,' Peggy said hurriedly. 'The trains all seem to be getting through, they're just late.' She felt sorry for the woman in her obvious anxiety, but also a little resentful; James would have to return before Christmas itself. And wasn't Cambridge just up the line? It was no distance at all, in comparison to his journey.

Then she told herself not to be mean. All those years without spending Christmas together must have been hard for them. The woman was dressed in what would have been smart clothes, had they not so clearly been worn many times. Before the war, their paths might never have crossed; she looked like the type who might have gone to the first-class lounge. Now the pair of them were in the same boat, struggling to see above the throng.

A gap in the crowd opened up and there was his train pulling in. 'Excuse me, I must go,' Peggy said, pointing. The woman nodded in understanding. Peggy ducked and wove her way through to the end of the platform, determined to find the best position before any of the passengers went past. Men in khaki hoisted kitbags on their shoulders; groups of young women in WAAF attire linked arms as they strode along, faces rosy with the cold. A few Land Girls laughed and pointed at friends further down the platform. There was a holiday atmosphere but Peggy shut it out, eyes focused in concentration.

There were so many men in GI uniform. What if she missed him? After all he had gone through since they last saw one another, that would be unbearable. Her heart beat faster. It must not happen. She had to look more carefully.

After another agonising minute that felt like an hour, there he was. A little cry broke from her throat and she broke into a run, dodging soldiers, Land Girls and civilians, her coat falling open as she did so.

'Peggy!' He set down his bag and threw his arms around her, swinging her into the air. 'You came all the way to meet me! And look at you — you've found a beautiful dress.'

'I made it.' Peggy laughed into his ear, taking in the unique smell of him, of spice and soap and whatever it was that made him so special to her. 'It's really for summer, but I had to wear it.'

'It's how I always imagine you,' he said. 'It's the one from my picture, isn't it?'

'As close as I could get it.' She squeezed him tightly and only let go when he reluctantly set her down, so that they could walk back to the concourse and out of the busy, bustling station. It was noisy with passengers, railway staff and porters, and impossible to hold a conversation, but it didn't matter. Their connection went deeper than that.

Peggy was aware that they were attracting stares as they walked along holding hands but she didn't care. They had weathered worse than hostile glances. Besides, some of the looks cast their way might have been of envy. She counted herself lucky beyond measure to have such a handsome man at her side. Let the rest of them think what they liked.

'You're not too cold, are you?' she asked anxiously, as their breath puffed visibly in the air.

He chuckled. 'You got to be kidding me. Back on the base, the wind sweeps in straight from Russia. I've never known cold like it. They don't believe in heating our quarters or the mess. This is the lap of luxury.'

She giggled and clutched his upper arm to pull herself in closer. 'No it isn't. It's mayhem. Shall we go somewhere quieter?'

They stepped out of the station entrance and out onto Bishopsgate.

He looked around. 'I came this way last time. Let's break that cycle and find somewhere for a drink, if that's what you'd like.'

Peggy nodded. 'We can come back here to get a bus, but let's get you warmed up first. There's a pub around the corner — at least it was there the last time I looked, you never can tell. I went there once or twice with Pete. If you don't mind that . . . sorry, it's the first place that I thought of.'

James shook his head. 'I don't mind. I'm glad you can say his name. We can't go our whole lives not talking about him, not when he was your man for so long.'

Peggy nodded. 'Exactly.' But her heart sang at his words. Did he mean that they would be spending their whole lives together? It seemed like a big step. Perhaps it was just his turn of phrase. She guided him around the corner into an old side street, the buildings tall and the pavements narrow, so that there was hardly any light in the dull early afternoon. On the far corner stood the pub. It was nothing fancy, and smaller than the Duke's Arms, but she was relieved to see as she pushed open the door that it still had an air of welcome. James held the door as she walked in, and manoeuvred his bag behind her.

A few faces looked up but there were no hostile glances. She exhaled a breath she hadn't known she had been holding. Despite her earlier confidence, she didn't want him to begin his leave in an angry atmosphere. 'What can I get you?' he asked. 'A shandy? Something stronger? I don't mind telling you, I'm having a whisky. I'd have a coffee but you Brits don't know how to make it.'

'That's because tea is better,' Peggy countered at once. 'I don't see what the fuss is all about. But since you're asking, I'll have a port and lemon.' She knew it was early in the day for such a thing — but if she couldn't celebrate James's safe arrival, then when could she?

Settling into one of the comfortable faded benches by a window that faced on to the narrow street, she felt happy and safe for the first time in months. She gazed at James as he brought the glass to his mouth, revelling in how right this seemed. It had been months since they had seen each other, and all manner of doubts had come between them meanwhile, but now he was here, it was as if they had never been apart. It was a combination of total contentment and tingling excitement. She could breathe freely again. He was here; he was hers.

Then she remembered. 'I got you something. It's not special or anything, I just wanted you to have it to open as we won't be together for Christmas.' She reached into her bag and drew out the little box. She had wrapped it in tissue left over from an old perfume bottle. It was a deep green that reminded her of ivy leaves.

'Shall I open it now, then?'

'Go on. Well, you could take it back with you, but I want to see your face when you see what I found for you.'

374

He flashed her a big grin and then carefully pulled back the delicate paper. Slowly he opened the box, and then laughed in delight. 'Hey, you're getting good at finding these things. Where did you get this?' Inside was a shiny tiepin, plated silver but decorated with tiny polka dots.

'Searched high and low, of course.' Peggy smiled back, happy that he liked it and appreciated the effort that had gone into it. It had been only slightly less difficult than making the dress.

Now he undid the outside pocket of his bag and rummaged inside. A moment later he produced another little gift box, flatter, and wrapped in a stripy paper bag. 'Sorry, it was all I could find,' he said. 'You got more talent for those sorts of things, I can see that.' His rich brown eyes gazed into hers and she felt a delicious warm sensation.

For a moment she wondered if it was a ring. No, it was too soon. He saw her hesitation and motioned for her to carry on.

Inside the flat box was not a ring but a delicate bracelet, glinting in the low light of the pub gas lamps. It had tiny blue stones set against gold bars, held together with slim chains. She had never seen anything quite like it. 'It's . . . it's beautiful,' she said, at a loss for words to convey just how much she liked it.

'Say, the blue goes with your frock. How about that.'

'It even fits,' she said, looping it around her wrist. 'How did you know what size?'

He looked a little sheepish. 'I remembered when we were dancing, I could just fit my thumb and first finger around your wrist. I done it specially but you never noticed. Then I said to the woman in the jewellery store, it's about this big. See, there are extra pieces in the box if you need to get it altered.'

Peggy shook her head. 'It's perfect as it is.'

He nodded. 'I'm glad.' Then he paused, looking into her eyes with intent. 'I saw how you looked before when I opened my big mouth — maybe I shouldn't have said 'the rest of our lives'. It just came out.'

'Oh.' She hadn't realised that he had noticed such a fleeting glance. What did he mean?

'See . . . ' He wrapped his hands around the heavy whisky glass. 'That's maybe a crazy thing to say. What with us being in the middle of a war and all. If times were different . . . but then you and I would never have met.' He paused again as if to gather his thoughts. 'I can't promise you anything, Peggy, cos we could be sent off to fight at any time. Just like you can't promise me, working like you do in that factory, bombs falling on you for months on end. Just let's say if we make it through — '

'*When* we make it through,' she interrupted at once.

'Then we'll be together. Here, or in the States, or somewhere the other side of the world — makes no difference. If I can be with you, that is. You don't have to answer now. It's a lot to ask. We both know there are folks out there who want to keep us apart. You don't have to agree, now you got an idea of what the stakes are.' He reached out and held her hand.

Peggy felt her eyes fill with tears and blinked them away. 'I don't have to wait to give you my answer,' she said. The little bracelet chains tinkled softly. 'The more they try to keep us apart, the more I want us to stay together. They can't stop us loving each other. My answer is yes.'

34

Edith didn't know whether to admire the last patient of the day or to be cross with him. Geoffrey Harrison was in his early sixties and she could tell that he was not the sort to think of himself as old. He had immediately told her that he had been a captain in the Great War and had seen action in France, and had no intention of letting a mere illness stop him from going about his daily business.

'I'm in the Home Guard, you know,' he wheezed, propped up on pillows in his big wooden bed. 'They can't manage without me for long. I'm the only one who can lead the drill properly.'

'Well, they might have to,' Edith said briskly. 'You'll do nobody any good by making yourself even sicker.'

'Oh you young women, you have no idea of what it's like,' Captain Harrison began, but Edith held up her hand.

'Don't upset yourself, Captain. You have to save your breath. See now, you've made yourself cough.'

The man tried to respond but could not. Edith shook her head. He had to rest or his pneumonia would get the better of him; it was as simple as that. She could see from his over-bright eyes that he was running a fever, and when she took his temperature it was seriously elevated.

'One hundred and three,' she said, shaking the thermometer. 'No wonder you don't feel well.'

'It's just a chill,' he croaked. 'I got caught in a rain shower. That's all.'

'It's pneumonia, and you have to take it seriously,' Edith told him. There was no point in beating about the bush. 'Dr Patcham has prescribed these red tablets, and you must keep up your fluid intake. Otherwise you must rest. The infection doesn't care what work you usually do.' She refrained from mentioning that people referred to it as 'old man's friend', as it had a habit of killing elderly men. She knew the statistics. Once you were over sixty you had a 20 per cent chance of dying, and the mortality rate doubled if you were over seventy. Even with the newest drugs, it was a potentially lethal illness.

Captain Harrison coughed loudly and cleared his throat. 'Churchill had it earlier in the year, didn't he? He kept going.'

Edith began to prepare a bed bath for him. 'As a matter of fact, he couldn't,' she said. All the nurses had followed the medical bulletins concerning the prime minister's illness with great interest. 'He was so bad he had to cancel lunch with the king. So if he could slow down for a while, then so can you.'

Her patient huffed and harrumphed but in the end had to give in. Edith was relieved. There was no point in fighting pneumonia; rest was the best treatment. She carefully sponged him down, being as reassuring as possible, knowing that he would be embarrassed. She worked as quickly as she could while being thorough. 'There, that will

379

make you feel better,' she said, rearranging his bedclothes before tidying away her equipment into its mackintosh sheeting and back into her big bag.

'Thank you, nurse.' He looked a little shamefaced now. 'Will you be working over Christmas? Shall I see you then?'

Edith smiled. 'No, today is my last day. One of the other nurses will look after you for a couple of days.' Belinda had volunteered to cover the holiday itself, as she did not celebrate Christmas and wanted to save her days off. 'I'd rather have the free time when my brother is back,' she had explained.

'Will you be having roast turkey with your family?' the man asked, more friendly now that he had been made comfortable.

'I'll be with my husband's family,' Edith replied, making sure she had all her bits and pieces before taking her leave. She swiftly scanned the room, which was respectable rather than extravagant, but much better appointed than many of the homes she visited. 'I'll open your window a little, and will tell your wife to close it later. There, how is that? Yes, my husband has unexpectedly got leave after all, and so it will be quite a celebration.' She gave him a wide smile.

'Have a very Merry Christmas, nurse,' Captain Harrison managed to say before coughing once more.

'I'll see you after Boxing Day, and make sure that you rest in between,' she instructed. 'I shall check with my colleague, so you won't get away with anything.'

'Yes, nurse,' he said meekly, but his eyes flashed with humour.

Back outside in the small but extremely neat front garden, Edith fastened her bag to her bike and put on her gloves. She could hardly believe that Harry had managed to get leave for the second year in a row. He had written a few days ago to say there was virtually no chance because his grim supervisor had been worse than ever of late, and yet yesterday, on their first wedding anniversary, word had come that he would be back in time for the big dinner at Jeeves Street.

She shivered with a little thrill at the thought of having him home again. Even though she was dog-tired, she tingled with excitement. Her stomach did a small flip at the idea of him holding her tight, keeping her warm on the cold December night. She would do her very best to buoy up his worryingly fragile confidence and make him see how brave he was. She hummed as she cycled along the potholed road, the light dimming in the late afternoon. Her handsome Harry was coming home.

★   ★   ★

Gladys was appearing out of the side entrance to the Victory Walk house as Edith pushed her bike up to the rack. 'Merry Christmas, Edith,' she said, coming over, her breath puffing in tiny clouds in the cold air. 'I'll wish you it now as I won't be here tomorrow.'

'Neither will I,' said Edith, shoving her gloves into her cloak pockets. 'Merry Christmas to you too. Are you cooking for your family?'

Gladys laughed, her usually plain face transformed. 'No, can you believe it, our Evelyn's doing it — or most of it anyway. She's turned over a new leaf now she's better at last. Says it's her last chance to do something for all of us before she goes away in the New Year.'

'Oh, where's she off to?' Edith was surprised.

'She's going to be a Land Girl,' Gladys told her. 'I know, you could have knocked me down with a feather as well. After spending the last year swearing she'd do no such thing, she's got to report for duty the first week of January.'

Edith raised her eyebrows. 'It could be exactly what she needs. But hang on, won't that mean lots more work for you at home?'

Gladys knotted her woollen chequered scarf around her neck. 'Since Evelyn's been ill our Shirley has been a big help,' she said. 'She can do most of it. She's older than I was when I started looking after the little ones. She likes it, which is more than Evelyn ever did. So I can carry on working for you nurses and doing first aid in the evenings. Might even have a bit more spare time.'

Edith grinned wickedly. 'And do you have any plans for spending that spare time?'

'I might have,' said Gladys archly. Then she had to share her news. 'I'm going to walk out with Ron. He's ever so nice. He took me to a café down by Victoria Park for tea and cake, treated me ever so well. He's so funny, and kind. Doesn't mean I won't stay late here when I have to, though.'

'No, no, I didn't think that for one moment,' Edith assured her. 'I'm glad for you, honest. He's a good man, Gladys — you deserve a bit of luck, after all you've done for everyone else.'

Gladys blushed but nodded. 'I do, don't I?' Her eyes sparkled. 'Well, have a lovely time tomorrow. Enjoy those Brussels sprouts.'

'We will.' Edith waved as her friend headed home, treading carefully as the pavements were already icing up.

Gladys and Ron, she thought. He would be so good for her, making up for all the disappointments she had suffered over the years. He wouldn't take advantage of her, or let her down. He was as reliable as could be. She wondered if Alice or the Banhams knew.

The warmth of the corridor hit her as she hurried inside. First she would unpack her Gladstone bag and make sure everything was sterilised, ready for her rounds in two days' time. Then she would go up to her room and find her smartest clothes for tomorrow. She wanted to look her best for Harry. She hoped her face did not betray how exhausted she felt these days. She wanted to dazzle him when she gave him her news. If that didn't make him feel like a man again, she didn't know what would.

★ ★ ★

The news would have to wait, Edith realised, as she and Alice arrived to find the Banham household in cheerful chaos on Christmas morning. The two nurses had made the short walk to Jeeves Street as early as they could, but Harry had beaten them to it and was now being treated like the guest of honour.

Alice set down the vegetables that they had brought from the victory garden, ready to be prepared in the back kitchen, as Edith ran to Harry and hugged him. He pulled her down onto his lap and there was no chance to talk in private. The house had been decorated with greenery and brightly painted paper chains, which Gillian had insisted on making after seeing what Brian and Kathleen had done. A fire was blazing in the grate, while the delicious smell of roasting turkey was beginning to fill the room. Flo and Mattie bustled around the kitchen counter, peeling and chopping, while Stan offered to make tea for everybody.

Edith struggled to rise and join in the preparations, but Flo told her to stay put. 'We've enough hands here,' she pointed out. 'You two enjoy each other's company, and if we need you then we'll say.' Edith half-hoped this would mean they could snatch a few moments alone in the parlour, but Harry wanted to stay in the limelight, surrounded by his family.

'I got here so early because Charles arranged a lift,' he said, shifting a little to balance her weight more evenly, and she noticed how much more easily he moved his bad arm now.

'Charles? What's he got to do with you getting home from your barracks?' she asked, confused.

'Ah, well, I have news,' he said, grinning broadly. 'I shan't say more till everyone's here — Billy and Kath and the kids are coming over later. Just you wait.'

'I've got some news too,' she murmured, but it was lost in a crash as Mattie dropped a saucepan while trying to lift it down from a tall shelf. Stan hurried over, protesting that she should have asked him in the first place, and the moment was gone.

'So no Joe this year?' she said instead, once she could hear herself speak again.

'No.' Harry's face fell a little. 'It would have been too much to hope for, that we could both have got leave two years in a row. He's sent a card, but he doesn't say where from.'

'I don't think Alice knows for certain either.' Edith frowned. 'So what happened — I thought you said you wouldn't be able to get back? Your supervisor was on the warpath, that's what you wrote.'

'She was and all.' Harry's expression was rueful. 'She made my life hell, always picking on the smallest things and favouring anyone who sucked up to her. I couldn't do anything right. Then she went and called me into the captain's office in front of everybody. I thought she'd come up with some reason to court martial me, or something, her face was so angry. All the rest were staring and nudging each other. I felt such a fool.'

'And what happened?' Edith demanded.

Harry tapped his nose. 'Aha, that's my news,' he said, laughing at her annoyance. 'Don't worry, all in good time. Meanwhile, have a coconut biscuit with your tea — Mattie made them special.' He took one from a nearby plate and bit in.

Edith shook her head. 'No thanks. I'll save myself for dinner.'

'That'll be ages,' Harry predicted, but Edith stood firm. There was something about the cloying sugary scent that put her right off. She'd had some dry toast before leaving Victory Walk; she could wait.

★ ★ ★

Flo always had a rush of contented satisfaction after she set the turkey on the table and Stan stood up to carve it. She watched him now, with a little smile on her face. Despite his years, he was still a good-looking man. If truth were told, he was going quite grey these days, especially around the temples; first the trauma of almost losing Harry, then the rigours of the Blitz and then the daily trials of his ARP duties had seen to that. She knew that she didn't hear the half of what he witnessed on those shifts. He never complained, though. He was her rock, and she felt even closer to him now than when she'd married him, all those years ago.

Glancing around the table, she knew she had more reasons to feel content. There were Billy and Kathleen, together at last and with their young family. Mattie had Alan on her lap, offering him a roast potato. He was growing into a lovely little boy; what a shame his father wasn't there to see it. Flo wrested her thoughts away from going down that track. There was Alice, who found it so hard to get back all the way to Liverpool to be with her parents; Flo prided herself that the serious young nurse could call Jeeves Street her second home. A real pity that Joe wasn't back, to bring a smile to her face; Flo could tell that he managed that better than anybody.

Then there was Harry, joking and smiling, biding his time before breaking his news. She was curious as to what it might be but, in all honesty, as long as he was safe, she didn't mind. All she cared about was that he was alive and happy. She would never forget the horror of nearly losing one of her children. He might be a strapping young man and married for a whole year, but to her he would forever be her little boy. She could feel tears at the back of her eyes as she experienced once more that overwhelming sense of love for him, but blinked them away. This was a time to celebrate.

Edith pushed a carrot around her plate. 'So, go on then, Harry. What's the big secret?' She flashed him a grin in challenge.

Harry set down his knife and fork, having cleared his plate. 'That was the best yet, Ma. And that's saying something. All right, I get the feeling I'm expected to tell you what the fuss is about now. Edith, you wanted to know why Charles of all people had arranged my lift home.'

'I did, yes.' She fixed him with her gaze, willing him on.

'It's because he's going to be . . . not quite my boss, but sort of. He's had a word with Jimmy, Major Ingham, you know, the former boxing champion who got me to join the army in the first place. He needs an instructor on his base. I don't have to be able to hit like I used to — '

'Well, we all know you can, cos we saw it when you walloped Frankie,' Billy cut in, at which moment Kathleen tugged on his arm to restrain him.

' . . . but I have to show the new recruits how to do it. It'll get them fit and toughen them up while they learn discipline too.' Harry was warming to his subject. 'He got in touch with the captain on my old base and he put it all through. My supervisor was furious. Said it shouldn't be allowed and she wanted me punished for insubordination.' He shrugged. 'That's when I thought I couldn't come home for Christmas. She didn't stand a chance, though, being up against two captains and a major. She was outranked, good and proper. So I don't go back to my old unit at all — it's straight off to the new posting after Boxing Day.' He turned to Edith. 'I'm sorry, Edie, it's further away. But I couldn't say no.'

Edith ignored all the gasps around the table, gazing at him and registering how enthusiastic he sounded, more than she'd seen for many months. This new posting could be the salvation of him. She couldn't complain about the distance; she hardly saw him anyway, even though he was relatively close as the crow flew. 'It doesn't matter,' she said. 'As long as you're happy, Harry. I know you hated that desk job. You were wasted there. This will be much more up your street. I wish it was in London but that's just too bad. I'll come and see you wherever you are, you know that.' A lump formed in her throat. If she continued to be so tired, it would be difficult, but she couldn't say that now.

Alice grinned. 'So that's what Mary's been hinting at. She's been like the cat that got the cream these past few days, but wouldn't tell me why. Just wait till I see her.'

Stan nodded and went over to slap his son on the back. 'Congratulations, Harry. You'll be back doing what you love. That makes me prouder than ever of you.'

Harry's eyes grew bright. 'Thanks,' he choked out. Stan was a man of few words and so that short speech carried great weight. 'I never really thought about what it meant to be a coach in the days when I was training, but I know now, looking back, that if it hadn't have been for a couple of them who spotted me in my teens, then my life would have been completely different. I owe them a lot. This will be my way of paying them back.'

Flo nodded gravely. 'I'm proud to hear you say that, Harry. You've made my Christmas. It's the best present you could have given me.' The tears were back and this time she let one fall before pretending to sniff with cold and wipe it away.

'Talking of presents . . . ' Mattie stood up. 'The kids won't wait much longer. Shall we take a break before the pudding and go over to the tree now? I don't think I can eat another mouthful, or not for a while anyway.'

'Good idea.' Alice rose and began to clear away the plates, while Kathleen tackled the leftover roast vegetables, piling them into smaller dishes to save for later.

Edith took a stack of plates from Alice and brought them to the sink in the back kitchen. She had a gift wrapped up for Harry, a beautiful new strap for his watch. She knew the old one was wearing thin, partly because he had a habit of playing with it when he was anxious. With luck the new one would not be subject to such treatment. As for her main present to him — yet again, that would have to wait.

★ ★ ★

Harry stretched out on his old bed, with his arms above his head. His feet pressed against the footboard. 'You can't beat Ma's Christmas dinner,' he sighed. 'I used to think about it, when I was stuck in hospital for all those months. I'd say to myself, when I get out of here I'm going to ask her to cook me a roast.'

Edith raised herself up on one elbow and looked down at him. With her free hand she pulled her cherryred cardigan around her. They had all been sitting in the parlour downstairs, which was warm from the big fire, and now she was chilly. Her shivers were partly from the news she had to break to him.

'You all right?' he asked suddenly, noticing her expression. 'Here am I going on about myself and not checking how you are. I'm sorry. You've enjoyed yourself today, haven't you?'

'Of course,' Edith said immediately. 'It's been lovely — especially your present.' She touched the little locket which hung at her throat, glinting

390

in the light of the old Tilley lamp. 'You weren't going on about yourself at all. It's exciting, your new posting. I won't worry about you so much now, if Major Jimmy's in charge. You've had a bad time this year, I know. Things will get better now, you'll see.'

Harry pulled her closer to him and held her close to his chest. 'I don't know what I'd have done without you, Edie. You make everything seem right when I talk to you. I said some bad things, didn't I? Like about not being a proper man. I want to be a proper man for you, Edie.'

She giggled. 'We'd better wait for everyone else to be asleep, then — the walls are a bit on the thin side.'

He chuckled. 'And after that last helping of pudding . . . '

'Know what you mean.' She took his hand and put it on her stomach. 'Feel that?'

He laughed again and then caught the brightness of her gaze. His eyes flickered to the shelf opposite, and the framed photo there: Joe, Mattie and him when they were younger. He and Mattie looked as if they didn't have a care in the world; Joe was more serious, even then. They had had very few photographs taken in those days, and that one was special.

It dawned on him what she meant. 'Are you saying . . . this isn't all Christmas pudding?'

Edith gave a small smile. 'Well, some of it is, obviously.'

'But you didn't eat much, did you. Not like normally.' He remembered seeing her push the food around, not like her at all.

'I'm a bit off my food at the moment,' she admitted.

'And that's because . . . ?' He waited for her to confirm it.

She grinned more broadly. 'You've guessed, haven't you? You're going to be a father, Harry. I'm having a baby. So I reckon that makes you a proper man and no mistake.'

She waited for his reaction, and for once he was at a loss for words. His face said it all, though. It was a combination of surprise and wonder. 'A baby,' he said at last. Then he sat up straight. 'Oh my God. Are you feeling well, Edie? You should have said before, I'd have looked after you all day. Are you tired? Do you need anything?'

'Only you, silly.' She reached out and stroked his arm. 'I couldn't have said anything before. I've only now found out myself. I wondered why I was so tired, and like you saw, not eating like I normally do, and I went and talked to Dr Patcham. So it's true.'

'Shouldn't you stop working?'

'No,' she said at once. 'Not till I have to. Not till I'm too big to ride a bike. They need me, Harry. I can't just stop, and I don't want to.'

'But all those sick people . . . '

She shook her head. 'We nurses know how best to stop infection spreading. We're trained from day one. You're as likely to catch something queueing up for rations — more so, probably. So don't you worry about me.'

He swallowed hard. 'A baby. Our baby. Our own family.' His face lit up at the idea. 'I hope it's a little girl who looks just like you.'

'Or a boy, then you can teach him to box.'

'I don't mind really. As long as he or she is healthy and safe. Oh, Edie. I love you so much. I can't wait.'

She laughed and pressed her face against his chest. 'You'll have to. He or she won't be here until the summer. It's very early days. We shouldn't tell too many people, just in case.'

She could feel him nodding. 'All right. But I can't not tell Ma and Pa. Then they'll want Mattie to know.'

Edith nodded back. 'Yes, they'll have to know. We can't keep that to ourselves for all of tomorrow, and your mother will have noticed me not eating much, I'm sure.' She paused, not wanting to think of anything going wrong. 'I'm strong and fit — we shouldn't worry. Meanwhile I'll tell Alice. She's bound to notice too, if she hasn't already. She knows what signs to look for, after all.'

'Oh, you nurses.' He put his arms around her again and squeezed, but carefully now. 'There's no hiding anything from you, is there?'

'I should hope not,' she said, and snuggled against him, listening to the sounds of the household settling down after their Christmas, and waiting for the rest of them to be asleep.

35

Alice and Edith sat side by side on Alice's bed in the small attic room, watching as the late afternoon sunset lit up the rooftops over Dalston. Soon it would be time to draw the curtains and fix the blackout blinds. From outside in the corridor they could hear somebody singing 'In the meadow we can build a snowman'. — Mary, probably.

'Do you think it will snow?' Edith asked.

'I don't think so. It's been overcast, but not with snow clouds.' She struggled to form the words, still trying to take in what her best friend had just told her.

Edith was having a baby. She knew that this was what Edith wanted, and that she would be a wonderful mother. Harry would take to being a father like a duck to water; you only had to look at how he behaved with Mattie and Kathleen's children to realise that. He would be in his element; they both would. This child, whether a boy or girl, would be lucky indeed, and would also have the unconditional love of the wider family. Riches could not buy that.

Even so, Alice felt a pang of regret. She had known when Edith married that things would have to change, and yet for months everything had stayed the same. They had gone on their rounds, compared notes in the evenings, cheered each other up or commiserated when needed.

There was nothing quite like talking over a case with Edith. There wasn't anything wrong with the other nurses, but because they had trained together for so long, she didn't have to explain as much. Edith would immediately know what she meant and how to help if there was a problem. So much that happened between them simply went without saying.

Alice had never had a sister; she was an only child. Edith had had an older sister whom she had adored, but Teresa had died while Edith was still young, and she had never quite got over it. Somehow this brought them closer together still; they were more like sisters than friends, Alice realised. They told each other nearly everything, secure in the knowledge that the other one would not back away, no matter what was said. She could not remember ever seriously falling out. They were very different in background and character but it had never mattered.

Now everything between them would alter. Edith's focus would be quite rightly on the baby, and her love of nursing would have to move aside. Alice felt a moment of panic. How would she cope without Edith here beside her? She had never done this job without the steadfast, ongoing support of her best friend, closest confidante, and the nurse whom she would trust above all others in a crisis.

'You all right, Al?' Edith turned sideways to regard her friend. 'Did I take you by surprise there?'

Alice gave herself a shake. 'Maybe. But not really,' she said slowly. 'Now I come to think of it, you've been a bit pale these last few weeks. I thought it was that cold you caught refusing to go away. I was going to ask if you needed to take a tonic or something like that. And we haven't sat together for lunch for ages — you've been skipping it, haven't you?'

Edith shrugged and then grinned. 'I had to. The smell of food made me queasy. I'm all right with dry toast or anything like that, but those stews . . . ugggh. It was safer to stay away and then quickly make a snack in the service room. I didn't want to say until I was sure, though.'

'Quite right.' Alice couldn't quite meet her eyes.

Edith cocked her head to one side. 'You don't mind, do you? You're happy for me?'

Alice nodded. 'Of course I am. No, I really am.' She took a breath. 'I'll miss you though. That's the shock, knowing that you won't be here.'

'Oh, Al, Don't be silly. I won't be going very far.' Edith gave her friend a heartfelt look. 'I'm going to go to live at Jeeves Street, when the time comes to leave here. But I'm going to nurse right up to the last moment. I love nursing, you know that.'

'I do.' Alice's face relaxed a little. 'It's what makes us what we are, isn't it? And it changes us, being nurses. We have to deal with situations that many people don't realise exist. We can't go into a flap or just guess at what to do. Our patients rely on us. It's important.'

'Exactly.' Edith nodded vigorously. 'None of that will change, Al. We'll still be the same people. It's just — well, there'll be another one to think of.'

'Maybe she'll be a nurse.'

'Maybe she will. Boy or girl, you'll be godmother, won't you?'

Alice's face finally softened. 'Of course. Anything you ask, Edith.'

Edith shifted along the bed a little and hugged her friend. 'I know,' she said.

Other titles published by Ulverscroft:

WARTIME FOR THE DISTRICT NURSES

Annie Groves

Alice Lake and her friend Edith have had everything thrown at them in their first year as district nurses in London's East End. From babies born out of wedlock to battered wives, they've had plenty to keep them occupied. As rationing takes hold and Hitler's bombers train their sights on London, Edith tries to battle on bravely while bearing her own heartache, but there's no escaping the reality of being at war, or the new terror of the bombing raids. The girls find themselves caught up in the terrible aftermath, their nursing skills desperately needed by the shaken locals on their rounds. With the men away fighting for king and country, it's up to the nurses to keep up the spirit of the Blitz, and everyone is counting on them . . .

THE DISTRICT NURSES
OF VICTORY WALK

Annie Groves

Alice Lake has arrived in London from Liverpool to start her training as a district nurse, but her journey has been far from easy. Her parents think that she should settle down and get married, but she has already had her heart broken once and isn't about to make the same mistake again. Alice and her best friend Edith are based in the East End, but before they've even got their smart new uniforms on, war breaks out and Hitler's bombs are raining down on London. Alice must learn to keep calm and carry on as she tends to London's sick and injured, all the time facing her own heartache and misfortune while keeping up the spirit of the blitz . . .